Space Girl Yearning

*Our heroine gets the space adventure she yearns for,
and then some!*

by Songstress Selena M
as told to **Mike Van Horn**
with lyrics from her hit songs

Book 3 of the trilogy. This continues Selena's story from
Aliens Crashed in My Back Yard
and **My Spaceship Calls Out to Me.**

What Readers Say About "Aliens Crashed in My Back Yard"

"A wonderful story. I am not much of a fan of contemporary science fiction, but I like the way you write. You have revived my adolescent fascination with science fiction." Thomas Heaven

"This story doesn't fit the typical sci fi mold of far future, evil aliens, dystopian Earth. It's a story of self-discovery, with an alien and some advanced technology."

"Your writing has the voice of a good storyteller sitting with friends reminiscing about events in real life." Terry Lynn Tuttle

"Great story! Kept me coming back to find out what was going to happen next. A good mixture of science, action, and philosophizing. It reminds me a bit of Asimov's writing--maybe because the voice is straightforward, without poetic flourishes. I'm looking forward to the next book." William, Arkansas.

"Too much sci fi focuses on hard-to-imagine technology. But nothing in your stories requires a high understanding of technology or astronomy. And the lyrics are great—girl with an attitude." Justin Boote, Barcelona

"I love the narrative voice – down-to-earth (no pun intended), strong, and funny. And how could I pass by the title?" Sue Weems

"I love the parts where the alien sings along with the narrator. Very touching." Ann, Paris.

"Your characters' personalities and voices are strong and clear, even the little alien who doesn't say a word in English. I connect with the alien, Breadbox. Her singing, her tone, her innocent questions and guilt. I find myself thinking it does not matter what she looks like." MC D'Alton, Australia.

"I love your story, your characters, the narrative, the tone, and the whole kit-and-kaboodle. What an enjoyable read. What a commanding writer you are." Trula, Arizona.

"You have a wonderful way with words and tell a great story. With your insight I might just think you've had some meetings with 'special Aliens.'" Milton, San Diego.

Dedicated with love to my wife B.J.,
fellow traveler through life
and cosmic tall tales

Gratitude to the 4-F Society and Becoming Writer—my two critique groups, other writers who—annoyingly—don't think every word I write is perfect, but who have greatly improved my prose.

To Karen Gault Skelly who transcribed many of my weird chapters after I tromped around the hills dictating them on my iPhone.

To Kyle Kosup who did my author website and helped me get this published.

To Troy Lush who composed the music for my lyrics; to singer Mari Mack who became the voice of Selena; and to Christopher Krotky who produced the music.

To my brother William who produced my books.

And finally to graphic designer Shane Colclough who produced beautiful covers and turned my scribbles into likenesses of my characters.

Table of Contents

The Story So Far

Book 1. **Aliens Crashed in My Back Yard**
"When Impossibility calls your name, my friend, you better listen up."

> A jaded pop singer rediscovers her passion for music when an alien musician crash lands on the hill behind her house; then the government snatches the alien vessel and launches a hunt for them both.

When an alien spaceship crashes on the hill behind the home of pop star Selena M, up along the Northern California coastline, she decides to nurse the surviving alien—a very non-human creature—back to health, and help her go home.

The government thinks otherwise. Whose spaceship is it, anyway? Does it belong to Selena, on whose property it crashed? Or to the Feds, who crave the technology? And what about the poor alien?

The alien, whom she nicknames Breadbox, communicates via singing. She had fled her home world because she didn't want to sing the music mandated by the Elders. Selena has become disenchanted with her own singing. But Selena and Breadbox stimulate each other to sing their most meaningful songs, and to recapture the soul of their singing.

Selena is devastated when Breadbox dies; then the government forcibly removes the spaceship and hides it in the desert.

Selena discovers that the robotic cylinder that belonged to Breadbox has many unexpected powers. For one, it is guiding the spaceship to repair itself. Selena sees that she could take it back from the government and fly off into space. This crazy idea grows on her. She could at least return the vessel with the remains of Breadbox to the home world.

Why does Selena even want to keep the spaceship? Would she give up her singing career for this?

At the end of Book 1, Selena makes the spaceship take off from the desert and go into orbit around the Moon.

Book 2. **My Spaceship Calls Out to Me**
"Stay on Earth and sing, or gallivant into space?"

My space ship calls out to me
Come fly me home
I'm yours, you're my skipper
Just call and I'll come

Aliens on distant worlds urge Selena to come sing on their worlds because she is a rare True Singer. She wants to be true to her music on Earth, but she says, "I have a spaceship—I might as well use it." The government says she hijacked it from them, and they're chasing it to the Moon to recover it.

"If I have a spaceship, I might as well fly off to the stars," says Selena. "Or at least take a trip to the Moon." Her friends think she is nuts, and tell her to let the government have it back. The government spooks, who call her a ditzy chick, come after her to regain control of the vessel and its invaluable technology.

Selena is continually pulled in two directions. She says, "My calling is to sing on Earth." But she keeps getting tempted into other adventures in space:

– Should she return the spaceship and Breadbox's remains to her home world? But Breadbox's clan mother says no, they don't want them.

– Should she just fly off to the Moon? But *Star Choice* is configured for Breadbox's race, not humans.

– She can't do it by herself. But then an astronaut, an astronomer, and a space travel entrepreneur join forces with her. She and two other women form the crew and call themselves the Three Spaceketeers.

– The robotic cylinder, that she calls Wanda the Magic Wand, keeps showing Selena how to overcome barriers to deep space travel. But also warns Selena not to do it.

– The Galactic Librarian, whom Wanda introduces to Selena, entices her to fly to the Galactic Confederation to represent Earth—and be a singer there! "I could have it all—singing and space travel!" But it could be a trap.

Even as Wanda makes upgrades to *Star Choice*, the alien ship is pursued to the Moon by lunar vessels from China, Russia, and the US. It's a cat and mouse game, with *Star Choice* trying to keep one step ahead.

The Three Spaceketeers find a way to outfit *Star Choice* and rendezvous with it on Earth. But circumstances keep Amelie and Dana from making the connection, so can Selena take the journey by herself, departing from the flank of Mauna Loa in Hawaii?

Space Girl Yearning

A glossary of names and places is at the back.

1. Fly Me to the Moon

*S*tar *Choice* landed on Mauna Loa shortly before dawn under Wanda's guidance, right near where I was standing. The sliver of Moon in the east gave scant illumination. Three stubby landing supports extended, and the hundred-ton vessel landed light as a dirigible, silent except for the crunch of lava gravel. The port opened with a sigh, the step folded down, and soft light poured out. I turned and waved at Mike McCreary, hoping he could see me against the open port. Yes! He flashed his headlights. Could be my last greeting with a fellow human!

I turned and stepped inside—as easy as getting on the bus. The air was sweeter and moister than the dry mountain air.

The port closed with a soft but solid sound, and my ears popped slightly. Light from the wall panels was just strong enough for me to find my way to the captain's seat. Before I sat, I looked around, enthralled.

Only then did it hit me. I was slammed by a flood of emotions that took my breath away. Like coming out on stage at my first big concert in the Hollywood Bowl with the dazzling lights and the crowd wildly cheering. I was ecstatic and terrified! All our dreams and discussions and sketches had come to life inside this beautiful spaceship—including the two empty seats meant for my missing Spaceketeers, alas. I burst out crying from sadness and aloneness. I was about to fly off to the Moon by myself in an untested vessel. My knees wobbled from terror. I turned toward the now-closed port. Was it too late to get out and cancel the trip?

"Get ahold of yourself, woman!" I yelled the way Clay would do. I took a deep breath, then another. Inhale, exhale. Phew. Got my heart rate back down to jackhammer mode.

Okay, back to business. I stowed my gear in an enclosure back near my bed, noting the cartons of uninstalled fixtures in the rear.

I settled into my custom-outfitted space seat and closed the restraints across my lap and chest. The view space popped into existence right in front of me, and Wanda's soft voice emanated from it. "Welcome to *Star Choice*, my controlling oki."

I could now see everything in front of the vessel in 3-D, as if I was looking through a large porthole window. Better, actually, because the view space accentuated the light.

"All systems are functioning properly," Wanda announced with what to me sounded like a touch of pride, "and we are ready to depart as soon as you request."

"Let's go to the Moon, Wanda!" I shouted, and instantly felt a slight push back into my seat. The antigravity—or grav—canceled most of the feeling of acceleration, because we leapt off the ground as if shot out of a cannon. By the time I looked, we were already ten thousand feet above the ground, according to the view space readout and my view of Mauna Kea receding. The rate of acceleration was unbelievable; in a few seconds the sun burst over the black horizon like a skyrocket, and then its brilliance was surrounded by the blackness of space and a riot of stars.

I was merely a passenger. I had discussed our flight plan with Wanda, my magical metallic companion, and now she was at the helm, even though she was safely ensconced back in California. When I placed the remote she created for me—that Clay took to Tinian—into the slot in the instrument console, she became the brains for the spaceship. Or perhaps better to say, it became her body.

Even with the grav limiting the G-force of acceleration, I felt the irresistible push down into my seat. It signified the vast power at my command. I could hear unsecured cartons of fixtures sliding toward the rear.

The acceleration continued. We were moving so rapidly that I could see the arc of the Moon increase in size and move against the background of stars as we raced toward it. I asked Wanda to show the aft view, and saw the blue and green and white Earth receding.

Seeing the Earth, it hit me again. The most amazing feeling I've ever had in my life. My tears were flowing so hard I could barely see. I started singing, to keep from crying. *Also sprach Zarathustra* from *2001: A Space Odyssey*. I yelled it out full voice, waving my arms to conduct the imaginary orchestra.

There was California off to the left side, on the leading edge of the continent, just coming into daylight. "Wanda, can we see my house?" The view space zoomed in, making my stomach feel like it does during the Big Drop on the roller coaster.

"This is the maximum zoom," Wanda informed me. I could clearly see Bodega Bay and the Farallones, as well as the Golden Gate, but I could not make out my house through the morning fog. Then we were past it.

"Wanda, let's see Andromeda." The view faded, then re-emerged with Andromeda galaxy spread across the screen in all its glory. Here at last was something so distant it wasn't changing in size as I watched it. It was so large! What before I had seen in the sky as Andromeda was only the bright central core. Against the blackness of space, its feathery arms spread out eight to ten times farther.

"Wanda, can we spot the home world of Breadbox?" The view space zoomed in on a dark portion of the sky, as stars moved out of the field of vision. The view kept boring into the darkness, moving past myriad unnamed stars, until, at the limit of magnification, just one speck remained in the center. A small yellow dot, the same color as the sun. I strained in vain to spot a tiny blue-green world nearby. "Breadbox, my best friend, this trip is for you." I burst into tears all over again thinking of my departed friend in whose vessel I was flying.

Back to the moon view. Wow, I could feel that we were already decelerating after less than an hour! Since we were coming in on the dark side, the Moon went from sliver of light to black disk against the stars, and then eclipsed the sun. In a moment the sun emerged on the other side, and then I directed the view space toward the Moon's surface, rushing toward us. In less than a minute, a chime sounded and Wanda informed me that we were in an elliptical orbit around the Moon that would take us quite near the surface. Less than two hours for the entire trip!

I was orbiting the Moon! *I was orbiting the Moon!* On my very first foray into space. I wanted to tell all my friends. No, I wanted my friends to be here. All of them. This wasn't supposed to be a one-woman trip!

"Wanda, can we call up my Spaceketeers? And Doc and Clay? And Jonn and Noel? And what's for breakfast?"

I sang out the refrain from my just-recorded song, with Wanda humming harmony, just as she had during the last jam session with Breadbox:

> *Just call and I'll come to you*
> *And we'll fly away soon.*
> *Across the wide heavens*
> *Far past the Moon.*
>
> *Just call and I'll come to you*
> *The whole galaxy's our home*
> *On any world anywhere*
> *Just call and I'll come."*
>
> *My space ship calls out to me*
> *Come fly me home*
> *I'm yours, you're my skipper.*
> *Just call and I'll come.*

My face was glued to the view space for an orbit or more before I remembered that others would be eager to learn that I had survived.

But I had to get control of myself first. My heart was pounding and I was trembling so hard I could hardly hold on to things. Excitement or terror? Well, both. Okay, take some deep breaths.

Whew! Who first? Mission Control, of course. Dana and Amelie. "Okay, Spaceketeers! Let's see if these comm stones work from the Moon." I called out their code names to activate the stones. "Hmmm! Danger!

Hmmm, Canuck! Can you hear me? The bird is about to land. We've done it! I'm here!"

Nothing happened. What was wrong? I looked into the view space at the sea of lonely gray rocks in all directions.

Then both came on at once, talking at the same time, from different cities.

"Whoopee! Danger here, Mission Control. All systems A-OK?"

"Canuck here. We've been waiting to hear from you."

Hearing their familiar voices, I just broke down again. "Oh, my friends, I am so scared. I'm so alone. You should be here with me. And I feel guilty that it's me instead of Amelie—a real astronaut."

"Now enough of that," Amelie responded. "Take it easy. Don't let these emotions get in the way of enjoying this miraculous moment."

"Yes, you're right, you're right. This is miraculous. I am so sorry I didn't contact you earlier. The flight just swept me up! I haven't taken my eyes off the view space." I gushed the words out. "And yes, everything went fine. I am so sorry you are not here with me. This is something that should be shared."

Dana said, "I can't see anything because I'm not where Wanda is hidden—but soon will be."

Amelie said, "I'm just leaving Toronto-Pearson, flying to SFO. Sans spacesuit—still not ready."

"As soon as Amelie gets here," Dana said, "we'll retrieve Wanda from her hiding place. Then we can activate the view bubble and see you and what you see."

I had to bring this to a close. "We're about to land, *Star Choice* tells me. I don't even recall the name of the location. Jonn and Amelie chose the site and translated it for Wanda. Remember, I'm really only a passenger. You guys chose well. Looks like the terrain is smooth and level: no craters, no boulders, no cliffs. Since we wanted to land on the sunny side, and I took off when the Moon's dark side was toward Earth, we've landed part way around on the side that faces away from it. So the landing site won't be visible from Earth. I'll call you back when I get set up."

Dana replied, "We'll contact you as soon as we get together with Wanda and activate the view bubble."

I was again alone in my vessel as *Star Choice* settled gently onto the surface of the Moon.

*   *   *

Silence. Utter stillness. Through the view space, I saw only gray moonscape and black sky. This was the Moon. I had made it!

All of a sudden, exhaustion hit me. I'd been running on adrenaline for how long now? Just a few hours ago I'd been on Mauna Loa. A few hours before that I'd done a concert, and then learned that *Star Choice* was under attack and we'd have to move up the trip. And that I'd have to go alone.

4

Before that I'd been up half the night after doing my Waikiki concert, then flying to the Big Island. How long had it been since I'd slept? I was so tired I could hardly rouse from my seat.

And I was alone. All alone on the Moon. I missed my fellow Spaceketeers so much. This was supposed to be a magnificent adventure for the three of us—a girls' road trip! But I was on my own.

I broke down sobbing. I curled up in my fancy captain's seat and bawled. I cried myself to sleep.

I woke up—how many hours later?—cramped and cold. I looked around. I was still on the Moon. Nothing at all had changed outside, but I felt much better. Time to get up and explore.

First, I'd better quickly figure out how to make that toilet work!

2. Moonwalk

Here's what everybody said to me afterward: "Moon walk by yourself? No connection to the ship, no backup? You are abso-friggin-lutely crazy, woman!"

My defense: "It was so beautiful!"

Wanda was not thrilled that I insisted on doing a moonwalk, but I pulled rank. She tried to talk me out of it, naturally. "It's too dangerous. Your suit may have a small undetected leak. Your helmet may not seal properly. You may have trouble walking on the surface. You are unfamiliar with your boots. You can see everything using the view space. We can take readings using the external instruments." I wasn't having any of this. Why would I fly all the way to the moon, then just sit inside looking out at it?

Wanda had built herself into *Star Choice*, handling the vessel's operations and systems, but also the monitors for interior and external observation. So even though Wanda the Magic Wand was hidden back on Earth, when I spoke to Wanda here, she answered. And she constantly kept watch over me. Like a nanny. She watched and commented on every move I made, via the network of tiny view cameras. Annoying but wise, because she pointed out several mistakes I was making.

Even though I had practiced putting on my space suit many times back home, it wasn't the same here with the Moon's lower gravity. I guess I could have asked Wanda to keep the gravity in *Star Choice* set at Earth strength, but I thought that was cheating.

The trip from Earth to Moon had taken only two hours, but it took me an hour to put on my space suit and boots. Reminded me of the first time I went skiing—all the trouble I had getting my boots on. This time I had no handsome hunky ski instructor to help me.

The equipment pack didn't feel right on my back. The oxygen tasted funny. I had trouble getting my helmet to seat properly. The inside of the faceplate was all steamed up by my huffing and puffing. By the time I was done, I was exhausted. I was shaking and chilled and sweating. "Being an astronaut is a young man's game," I said to myself. "But we women are tough."

Finally I was zipped up. I climbed into the coffin-sized air lock at the flat stern, where the escape module would normally be connected. Very claustrophobic, but that way it loses minimal air when opened. The pump sucked out most of the air with a tiny hum that faded as the air disappeared, making my suit puff out a bit. Wanda opened the airlock door, and the remaining air escaped soundlessly, forming a momentary mist of tiny ice crystals. I stood there in the vacuum of the infinite universe. Apparently no leaks in my suit or helmet, if I can trust my instruments. I inched my way down the steps and onto the surface of the moon.

Awesome!

Awesome!

Awesome!

So much more than watching it through the view bubble—or on TV. The entire universe right there, seemingly within reach of my outstretched hand. So clear and immediate in every direction. I felt like a person whose vision is restored after eye surgery. I immediately regretted that we'd landed where I couldn't see the Earth.

Wanda said to me, "You neglected to attach your space suit to the tether…" But I was already several steps away from *Star Choice*. I walked in a little circle, so I could look back at the ship. Even though it's as big as a commuter jet, it looked so tiny and vulnerable against the empty expanse of the Moon.

I looked down and saw my footprints. I could easily kick up a little dust, which immediately settled rather than making a cloud. Even though I understood this, it surprised me that dust fell as fast as a brick. I quickly discovered that hopping was easier than walking in this low gravity.

I stopped to take a look upward. Magnificent! Where's Earth? Oh yeah, it's not visible from here.

I tripped over a rock. Wasn't watching where I was going. I went flying headlong, falling to the Moon's surface, getting dust on my hands and knees. Dust bounced up and stuck to my faceplate, partially obscuring my vision. No hankie to wipe it off with.

I just lay there for a moment waiting to die, figuring something must have broken or sprung a leak. But no, I was still breathing. I was sure glad I had used the toilet before suiting up, because otherwise . . .

The low Moon gravity made it easy for me to push myself back up onto my feet, but I had trouble regaining my balance. I kept hopping around till I could get my feet planted solidly beneath me.

I immediately got the shakes. I was sweating and cold. Trembling so hard I could hardly function. What if I had smacked my helmet on the ground and it had sprung a leak? That would be it. My freeze-dried corpse would be a permanent addition to the Moon. Someday somebody would find my remains and say, "What an idiot!"

I stood there panting, fogging up my faceplate from the inside, so I truly couldn't see anything. My heart was beating so fast, I could hear it.

I just stood there a few minutes till my heart stopped pounding. The suit's dehumidifier cleared my faceplate—inside anyway—so I could see around me. I was maybe ten feet from *Star Choice 's* open port.

If my face plate broke, somebody would find my freeze dried
corpse and say, "What an idiot."

I had a momentary 2001-style fear that Wanda might not let me back
in, due to my terminal stupidity. "Open the pod bay door, Hal." "Sorry,
Dave, I can't do that." But Wanda had left the hatch ajar and the light on
inside the airlock.

But she wasn't silent. Have you ever been scolded by a robot? "This is
how the former crew crashed, by ignoring or overriding my precautions."

I was contrite. I apologized humbly. Did I promise never to do it
again? No. "I want to go out again when the Earth rises, so I can see it
come up over the horizon."

How do robots go "Tut tut"? Wanda asked reasonably, "If you perish,
then who is the controlling oki?"

Yes, I had ignored this question entirely. But I didn't want to think
about it just then. "Just keep me safe! I'll do exactly what you instruct."

"Watch your world via the view screen. I can enlarge it for you."

I'd seen it on TV many times. "I want nothing between Earth and my
eyes except my face plate."

Wanda did not argue with me, as she probably should have. When I
asserted something, she complied. But she pointed out a serious flaw in
my thinking.

"Since your planet's satellite, called Moon, is tidally locked on its
planet, the same side is always facing your world. From our perspective,
that means your world will never rise here where we are located. For you
to see it, we must travel part way around Moon. For you to get the illusion
of it rising, we must be moving toward it. You will have to be inside and
watch it on the view screen."

Well duh, I already knew that. Even so I muttered, "What a bummer," wanting an exception to the laws of astronomy. Maybe I could be strapped to the hull as we flew. "Wanda, let's travel just far enough to see Earth above the local horizon."

*   *   *

Wanda sealed up the ship, we rose some distance, and began moving slowly across the surface. I watched intently through the view screen, as if I could will the Earth to appear. Wanda slowed down the vessel just as the disk of the Earth began to show above the edge of the Moon. No glow in the sky, as precedes moonrise. And the disk of Earth kept growing, till it got four times larger across than the Moon as seen from Earth. It looked huge and so close, more like a globe sitting on the Moon a few miles off. It wasn't quite a "full earth," but close enough. And this meant it was dusk on our part of the Moon, with growing shadows pointing toward Earth.

"All right, Wanda, let's land here, so I can look at it directly." She obeyed me, like a good robot should.

"I will align the port with the Earth, and you can stand just outside the port, attached by winch."

"Wench on a winch," I quipped. Funniest stand up comic on the entire Moon. I carefully put my helmet back on, wiped clean of moon dust.

As I was doing that, I noticed a faint whiff of gunpowder. Very interesting. That's the smell of moondust, I remember reading. I looked at these tiny granules and got a shiver. This wasn't just bothersome grit. Moondust is stardust. This is what everything is made of. Including me.

Yes, I'd heard this many times in song lyrics and poems and sermons. I could hear Joni Mitchell singing in my mind right then. But rubbing this grit between my fingers brought it home to me. I felt my direct connection to exploding supernovas billions of years ago. I am stardust.

I inched down the steps, carefully attached the cable to my suit, and took a few tiny steps away from the ship. As I slowly turned, Earth's orb hit me like a spotlight. We're used to the bright full Moon on a dark night, but the full Earth is four times as wide and much brighter. Its image in the black sky dwarfed *Star Choice*. I stood there mesmerized, like a deer caught in headlights.

It was hard to tell what part of Earth I was looking at. I saw mostly water and cloud cover. Landmasses were obscured enough that they were hard to recognize. And what I saw looked grey or tan, not green. But still, the most beautiful object in the heavens. Home. My home world. The repository of all my history, my family and friends, my music. Everybody's history and family and music. I had never before loved it so much.

I pivoted to my left, in a series of small hops. I was standing in the shadow of *Star Choice*, so the glare of the sun didn't blind me. The stars were so thick and close looking. One very bright one, planet not star, must be Jupiter. I had viewed it many times from my deck back home. I strained to see if I could spot its larger moons here where I wasn't looking through an atmosphere, but I couldn't see them with the naked eye. Well, not quite naked.

"Wanda, can *Star Choice* take a picture of me when I'm standing outside on the surface, with the Earth in the background?"

"What does 'take a picture' mean?"

"Record my visual image so that I can show it to others."

"Yes, I have recorded all your activity outside *Star Choice*."

"Including my fall?" I asked, dreading the answer.

"Yes. Shall I transmit those visuals to Earth?"

3. How to Open a Bottle of Wine on the Moon

Inside, after I calmed down and wriggled out of my space suit, I had Wanda set the artificial gravity and air pressure to Earth levels. Wanda asked through my comm stone, "Do you want to contact friends on Earth?

"I want to get something to eat first. Wanda, what's for breakfast? Eggs? Bacon? Mimosa?"

Wanda responded in classic Wanda-speak, "Your food items are packed in the compartment marked 'Food.'"

I found the compartment, and pulled out a big cardboard carton that had been packed by Doc and Clay before they left for Tinian. I opened it eagerly, then felt deflated, then pissed off. It was camping food: packaged mac and cheese, packaged crackers, peanut butter, packaged soup, packaged juice concentrate. So much for eggs and bacon. But there was enough for three Spaceketeers. I opened some cheese and crackers and a carton of lemonade and sat in my captain's chair. I noticed how easy it was to spread cracker crumbs all over the place. How do I clean these up? Did Wanda create a little robot to go around and vacuum things up? I'm sure she didn't. I'd better be careful with my detritus.

Okay, it was time to interrupt my gourmet feast and call the others. Jonn and Noel first. "Hummm. Spaceman! Starman! Are you taking calls from me?"

Jonn came on. "You made it! Congratulations! Did I choose a good landing spot?"

"Yes. Thank you! You chose well. All systems nominal, as the real astronauts say." I did not mention my tumble.

"Noel is not reachable," he told me. "He's about to make a speech. He didn't want to chance his comm stone squawking in the middle of it, so he hid it in his suitcase. We need to ask Wanda if there is a way to cut these things off, to mute them."

I told him that Amelie and Dana were getting together and retrieving Wanda, so we could communicate visually.

Jonn did his hum of thinking for a few seconds. "Selena, let me make a suggestion. If you will allow me, trust me, to take Wanda to my lab, I will figure out how to interface TV with it. I know you've entrusted it to Dana; she can come and be your watchdog. It will be safe: the government is not going to invade my facility."

"Let's do it," I responded instantly. I had come to thoroughly trust and depend on my Mr. Buck.

I asked him with a mixture of hope and fear, "Jonn, what are you hearing from the rest of the world?"

"Everyone on Earth, it seems, is in an utter tizzy," he replied. "Russians and Chinese are hurling accusations and threats. Our government is convinced I'm behind this. I've had to tune out completely so I could get some work done."

"Well, I'm glad you're taking calls from *me* at least. Things never change, do they?" I shook my head in bemusement. "Jonn, I'll get back to you when Amelie and Dana have Wanda. You can work something out with them."

"Um hmm," he muttered.

"Over and out," I said, but he was already gone.

"Let's call Clay and Doc," I said to nobody. "Hmmm, Teach. Hmmm, Doc!"

Doc came right on. "Selena! You're still alive! Wow, that was a fast trip to the moon."

"You guys did great preparation! Everything went flawlessly. The captain's chair works great. And I must compliment you on your menu selection," I said with only a touch of sarcasm.

"Sorry about that. There at the end, we were a bit rushed with the Chinese Navy bearing down on us. We couldn't wait for the good stuff that was being flown in at the last minute."

"No prob. I was hoping to improve on the way I eat at home." I was munching away on my cheese and crackers.

"Doc, where's Clay? Why didn't he answer the comm stone?"

He was silent for half a minute. "He's in a medical facility here on Tinian. I think we overworked him. He left his comm stone with me to make sure it didn't get lost or taken."

"What?" I sat upright, almost dropping my crackers, and grabbed the comm stone to make sure I was hearing correctly. "That's terrible! What is going on?"

"Don't know yet. I will stick here with him till we know."

"Please tell him I landed safely. And Doc," I wanted to grab him by the lapels. "Have him get back to me as soon as he can. Please."

"Yes, ma'am. I sure will."

*   *   *

Clay's situation worried me. He must be in pretty bad shape to need a hospital. The fact that Doc didn't know what was up gnawed at my gut. But there wasn't much I could do, and I trusted Doc to take care of him. Think positive!

I was still hungry, so I scrounged in the food carton again for something that would assuage my appetite. "Is there anything decent to eat?" Lo and behold, in amongst the camping food, I found a bottle of wine. I was thrilled. One of my favorite Malbecs—with a nice note from Clay rubber-banded around it, saying, "Don't drink this all at one time!"

But something was missing. I ransacked every box of supplies they'd packed for me. No dang corkscrew. "Clay, what kind of cruel trick is this?" I shouted. "Okay, so how am I going to open this bottle?" Alone on the Moon, I was quickly getting into the habit of talking to myself. I looked all around for suitable tools—screwdriver, whatever. It wasn't like a beer bottle, where you could pop the top off on the edge of a table. I should have brought my Swiss army knife with its goofy little corkscrew.

"Come on brain, think. Aha, here's an idea." I'll put on my space suit again for another short moonwalk, I thought. I'll put the wine bottle in this big can and carry it outside with me. It should freeze instantly, breaking the bottle. Then I bring it back in, let it thaw out. The can will hold the wine. I can filter out the glass shards with a coffee filter. Would that work? Maybe it would just evaporate instead.

"Okay, I'm stumped. I'm going to get on the horn and ask my buds." Using my comm stone, I called Jonn again—he's the techno whiz. "Mmmm, Spaceman, Spaceman. Urgent situation!"

Jonn came on quickly and his voice boomed from the pebble on my chest. He asked with only a touch of panic, "What's the problem? What happened?"

"I have no corkscrew to open my wine bottle."

"For chrissakes, woman. I was just about to alert the NASA rescue ship." I knew he was pulling my leg.

"This *is* serious."

"Okay, here's what you do." He hummed for a few seconds. "Take your saber. You do have a saber, don't you? Hold the bottle tightly with one hand, then swing the saber smartly across the neck of the bottle, neatly slicing it off just below the cork. But be careful with your aim; you don't want to cut your hand off."

"I have no saber, not even a light saber, and I know there's no rescue ship. Some help you are."

"Okay, okay. So use your moon machete. Or any metal bar with an edge. But you know, letting little fragments of glass fall into the inner workings of a spaceship doesn't sound wise to me."

"I have big plastic trash bags. I could do the neck slicing inside the bag."

"Here's another thought. Do you have a hypodermic needle? Insert it through the cork; use it to pump air into the bottle. Maybe that will push the cork out."

"No, no needle, I'm afraid." I responded.

"Then perhaps sobriety is the only answer," he said, soberly.

"I'm not giving up that easy."

13

"I can see the headline now," he chuckled, "'First crisis for Earthwoman on moon—can't open wine.' Talk about First World problems. All right, I have to get back to work."

I ended up using a variation of my first idea. I didn't need to go outside. I removed the foil from the bottle top, stood the bottle in the big can and placed it in the air lock. Closed the inside, and slowly pumped air from the lock, then released the residual air to the outside. I could watch it in the view bubble via the small video camera in the lock. When the airlock was about 80% empty, I could see the cork slowly pushing up. Before I could reverse the process and fill the lock with air, the cork popped and wine spurted out like a shaken champagne bottle, instantly freezing. I guess that was because of gases dissolved in the wine. Anyway, I equalized the air pressure and recovered my mostly full bottle of wine, nicely chilled.

I was so proud of myself, and the wine was the best I've ever had. Even if it was in a plastic cup.

4. Moon Gab

"Okay, I'm on the Moon. Now what?" I said to nobody. It wasn't like I had a plan—or any scientific experiments to keep me busy. My goal had been to travel to the moon, and I had accomplished that.

So far, I had scarcely looked beyond the captain's chair and the airlock. Oh, and the food box. I now took my time to explore *Star Choice*, finding things, setting up my bed, figuring out how the food prep and bathing worked. With miniscule amounts of water, I saw. Crammed against the back wall were the cartons containing the fixtures that Clay and Doc hadn't had time to install before the rushed departure. I guess it was now up to me to set up all that stuff.

It was miraculous being inside this sturdy vessel, capable of traveling to the Moon, that had started out as sketches by three women in a noisy restaurant.

I inventoried my backpack. "Did I really come to the Moon with no clean underwear?" Well, astronauts were renowned for returning stinky.

I sat in my captain's chair and gazed into the view space. As I wondered how I was going to make this fancy communications systems work, Wanda's voice burst out from it at high volume, startling me. "My controlling oki! Are you willing to accept contact from people on your world?"

"Yes, indeed!" Oh, goodie. I was ready to talk with my friends, whom I was already starting to miss. "Who wants to talk with me?"

"Your close associates, that you call Spaceketeers. Plus Jonn Buck, who taught Wanda how to convert your world's coordinates into terms I could use for navigation."

"All three together?"

"Yes."

"Then put them on!"

Amelie, Dana and Jonn appeared in the view space right before my eyes. It was startling how real they looked—as if they were sitting across the kitchen table. Of course I had viewed Kateh in the view bubble, but these were humans, and this new view space had much greater resolution than the smaller bubble that sprang from Wanda's forehead.

"This is great! Just like you guys are here," I exclaimed, pushing down a pang of homesickness. It took me a minute to get my throat working. Of

15

course I had no tissues. I covered my face for a moment and wiped my nose on my sleeve.

"Yes. We can see you and the inside of *Star Choice* ," said Amelie with glee. "She's a beautiful baby!"

"Looks big and empty," Dana added.

I nodded. "Yeah, because you're not here," I said, stifling yet another sob. "That's where you two are supposed to be stationed. Your beds are stacked up in the rear. Where are you guys now?"

"They came down to my HQ," Jonn said, "and we're in the inner sanctum, where nobody dares intrude. Dana brought Wanda so we could peer into the magical view bubble and connect with the view space on *Star Choice.*"

"Well, Queen of the Spaceketeers," said Amelie, "You've definitely earned your name—Selena, Moon woman."

"And what's more," said Dana, "I'm going to name my kid Selena Moonwalker."

"Wow! So it's going to be a girl!"

Dana patted her midriff, which so far showed no bulge. "It has to be a girl, and she has to grow up to be a STEM Babe."

"And how is Russell with this news?"

"Russell?" Dana paused and sighed. "Pfeh, that jerk. Russell is history—even before he's history." But I saw a tear escape and run down her cheek.

"Oops. I'm so sorry to hear that," I commiserated. I am so good at asking inopportune questions. "Well, enough of that. What else is happening?"

"Let's talk tech," said Amelie, sliding past sentiment. "Jonn?"

"We just wanted to test out this system." Jonn said, "I'm dying to work out how this technology operates, and how it bypasses the light speed lag of three seconds. Selena, Wanda won't communicate with my engineer unless you authorize it. Your robot is very loyal to you. The best way, I suspect, is to have Rogers, my engineer, talk with Wanda, as Amelie and I did in order to figure out how to give Wanda the Moon coordinates that got you there. Together they could figure out how to channel video from other sources into this system through Wanda. You could then watch TV or interact with others who can input video streams."

"Wow, absolutely! Wanda, would you work with Rogers the engineer and Jonn Buck to connect outside sources of video to your system, so I can view and hear them here on *Star Choice*? And make it two way, so they can see and hear me also."

"Yes, my controlling oki, Wanda will work with them to do that."

Dana asked, "What have you done on the Moon so far?"

"You mean besides sitting here talking with folks back on Earth? And figuring out how to open a wine bottle without a corkscrew?" I toasted them with the cup of red wine I had in my cup holder. (Yes, of course my captain's chair had a cup holder.)

"So far I've only almost died once. During my moonwalk," I admitted.

"You took a moon walk by yourself?" Amelie asked incredulously. Jonn's humming almost became a growl. He leaned forward and looked at me intently. Dana grabbed her face with her hands and said, "Oh my god!"

"Yes, I tripped over a rock and did a face plant. It was easy enough to get back on my feet, and lucky for me Wanda let me back in despite my stupidity. But from now on I'm staying connected to the winch during my walks."

"How many are you planning to take?" Amelie probed me.

"Why take *any* more?" Jonn asked, with just a tiny edge to his normally calm voice.

"I'm on the moon. To get the full experience of being on the moon, I can't just sit inside and watch it on TV, even using this nifty view bubble."

"Wanda, can't you keep her inside?" Amelie asked wryly. "Talk some sense into her?"

"Talk sense into a human oki," Wanda responded. "An interesting concept. That would be a useful capability. She is my controlling oki. I do as she directs."

Growls and grunts of disapproval all around. But hey, it was my moon trip. Once again I wondered at the near sarcasm from Wanda. Was her personality developing to mirror mine?

"Okay, change of subject," I said. "What are we hearing from the world about this escapade?"

"Let me assure you: we don't have radio silence, to say the least," Dana said excitedly. "Your adventure is being covered incessantly on every news and social media channel. As *Star Choice* rose from Hawaii it was spotted and tracked by the military all the way up to the moon. This is making some people very angry and embarrassed."

Amelie added, "So there are questions like 'How did you let her slip through your fingers again?' At the other end is, 'Why are we not coming to an accommodation with this woman? What does she want?' But most are saying, 'Wow this is just totally awesome!'"

Dana said, "They know that your spaceship is on the Moon and they strongly suspect that you are in it, but they don't know that for sure. Could you, or Wanda, provide us with an image of you on the moon's surface, like from your moonwalk?"

"Sure. Wanda, can you provide them with an image to share with others?"

Dana went on. "Your buddy Dr. Hu has been trying to call you, but I haven't put him through without your say-so."

"Thank you for that," I said. "All in good time."

Jonn added, "Various parties have broadcast blustery threats. But they're impotent. All the orbiters had already been withdrawn after *Star*

Choice departed earlier. The American lunar lander never touched down. According to my sources, nobody's prepared to quickly send follow-up missions to the moon."

Dana said, "I've been screening your phone calls since you've left me with your cell phone, but I had to stop; there were too many. We could transfer them through, but you'd be inundated."

"Maybe we should decide who I *want* to talk with, and then I will initiate the calls."

"Well, start with your buddy Eddy Backwater!" Dana counted off with her fingers. "And your agent has been trying to reach you. Morty. And Hu of course."

"What about Clay? I haven't been able to reach Clay yet!" The cold ball of fear re-appeared in my gut.

Dana responded, "I don't know! He was with Doc."

I was quite worried. Why would Clay be incommunicado, even if he *was* in the hospital? Did Doc still have his comm stone? But then *he* would respond to my calls to Clay. I had to find out! Doc would know.

After we finished talking, I tried to hum up Doc, but he wasn't responding. Now what?

* * *

Once again I learned that I must give Wanda very careful instructions. As I requested, she shared a video of my moonwalk—complete with my face-first tumble. This went instantly viral, with millions of views. How many times have *you* seen it repeated, dear reader? Way too many of my claims to fame only go to reinforce my "ditzy chick" label.

But one thing she did well. Wanda and Jonn had worked out a way for me to receive calls from people I had pre-approved, so poor Dana didn't have to screen them all.

"My controlling oki, are you willing to be contacted by your co-singer Eddy Backwater, both of whose names have the same meaning?"

"Yes, indeed, put him through."

"Selena?" His voice issued from the view space. But no video, which indicated he was calling from his cell phone. I wondered if Wanda could arrange to connect with the video function of phones. Not that I needed to see Eddy's scruffy self, or show him mine.

"Eddy, Eddy Backwater, you of all people, calling me here," feigning surprise.

"Wow! Moonlady! You've done it. I am impressed from the bottom of my black little heart."

"Why, thank you."

"I've got something to ask you. I got you a gig, remember? At Slick Slim's? Now you have to get me one. Tit for tat. So, let's do a duet. You there on the moon, me here on good old solid Earth."

I tried to laugh him off. "Eddy, this is a crazy, self serving idea."

"Well, that's me, but it doesn't make it a bad idea. I hear you've got Gibb with you. You choose the music. Could be any of your songs."

"Eddy, give me time to consider it. I'll seriously consider it. Let me get back to you. I don't know what the heck I will be doing here yet. Or for how long." Wow, did he ever have a way of getting to me. I found it very difficult to say no to him. I wasn't sure I wanted to. But I didn't want to be finagled into it, either. Arrgh!

"You know, Selena, there's something else I want to say. Maybe what's most important is for you to be true to yourself and your own singing rather than go traipsing off to the stars."

"I hear you, Eddy. I'm not giving up my singing. I'm a singer. No star trips in the near future. Thank you for reminding me. Talk to you soon." I shook my head. Had I agreed to a concert or not?

Almost immediately, Wanda, my new social secretary, announced that my agent Morty wanted to talk with me. Might as well get this over with.

His voice burst out of the view space. "Selena, what the hell!? What have you done? I'll tell you one thing girl, you come out of this alive, this'll be the best career move you ever made. I confess; I've taken your name in vain. I've been telling people I could reach you."

"What people?" I asked with trepidation.

"We're not talking about Club Xanadu anymore. How about Madison Square Garden? The Houston Astrodome? Albert Hall. New Delhi. Sydney Opera House. That's just the concerts! The interviews! Interview requests, they want to get you on the air. CNN wants to hold a call-in show, with you answering questions from the Moon, if we can rig up a communication link.

"Say, how is this working now?" he went on. "I just called your cell and here I am talking with you on the Moon. I didn't know reception was *that* good. Well, anyway, you could talk to everybody on Earth. Everybody who can get CNN. You'd have a bigger audience than God! Would that sell some music, or what?"

"Morty, slow down." The prospect of being interviewed by CNN from *Star Choice* here on the Moon scared the bejeebers out of me. But if not now, when?

"I should have done this a long time ago!" I said. "I just need to lay it all out there, don't I? After all, I am a singer, and a singer is a storyteller. Okay, let's talk details. And money. I have to finance all this stuff. You have any idea how much I've already spent on this caper? Morty, whatever figure they suggest, multiply it by ten."

"That's my girl. That's the way to talk. Finally you're wising up."

Omigawd what was I committing to?

"I'll get back to you with details. Don't go anywhere." He clicked off.

Why did I agree with this crazy interview idea? I wondered. That's not my style. He just runs roughshod over my sensibilities. Poor me, bitching about a guy trying to make me lots of money. But Eddy's concert idea sounded better. Oh lordy, Morty will be Fed Ex-ing a contract to the Moon for me to sign.

I barely had time to take a potty break on the toilet I was still learning to use, when Wanda announced another caller. "Are you willing to speak with Dr. Edwin Hu, astrophysicist? He said he is your favorite nemesis."

"Oh sure, put him through." I had been putting him off, but I might as well get him crossed off my list.

"Selena, this is your favorite nemesis, Dr. Hu, call me Ed. Call me an idiot. So I have to admit here, I'm glad you got your vessel back—your *Star Choice* —and took off for the moon. Happened just in time, others were coming for it and so here's some of the . . . you know . . . the shit has hit the fan with this. Several groups are so upset about this thing existing that they were coming to destroy it. Even talk of taking it out with a missile, from somewhere that I'm not at liberty to tell. In fact I'm not even sure I know. Truth is I don't even know. They wouldn't tell me either but . . ." He sounded so strange. Had he been drinking? "What our guys decided to do—if they could get ahold of it—was to take a blowtorch to it and cut it up into pieces so that it could be distributed around, hidden in various places, so the baddies couldn't destroy it or take it away from us."

He was blathering on, not his usual professorial self. Drunk. Yes, totally snockered, for sure. I could almost smell the Black Label through the view space. Ah, interesting idea! I wondered, could Wanda add the capability of smell to the view space, along with sight and hearing?

"So, thank you, Dr. Idiot, my nemesis. Why are you telling me all this?"

"Well, s-s-so," he stuttered. "You and I have one thing in common. We both want to take a ride in this spaceship. I know, you're already riding in it, but I want a ride too."

"Um hmm. You know, I have no reason to trust anything you say."

"Yeah, thas right, you don't. So don't trust me. But just hear me out. I have left their employ amidst all kinds of threats, blady blah, but I am rooting for you to succeed on this venture and if you do, then maybe someday, as you said, you will need an astrophysicist."

I laughed. "Ed, what am I going to do with you? We'll see. But don't hold your breath."

"Thas good enough. Thanks. I 'preciate it. Bye."

Call me an idiot, too, but I couldn't help but kind of like this guy. Kind of.

*   *   *

Not much later, Wanda announced yet another caller. But still no Clay. Or Doc.

"Hello Selena, this is Noel. Jonn told me to just call your cell number to reach you. Amazing."

"Good to hear from you." I brought him up to date on my adventure, then asked, "How did your speech go?"

"Funny you should ask. There I was in New York, at Columbia University, preparing to give my standard talk about the possibility of intelligent life elsewhere in the universe. I put on my glasses, looked down at my notes, but I couldn't see anything. My opening joke fell flat, and then I just stuttered and stammered. I was saved by a young woman way in the back who stood up and yelled out, 'Professor Reisen, surely you are aware of the unfolding story of this woman who has acquired a spaceship from aliens on another world and is now communicating with Earth. What does this say about the rarity of alien intelligence? What impact does this have on your talk?'

"I looked at her and took a deep breath. I got tears in my eyes and had to wipe them away with my pocket square. 'Blows my talk right out of the sky, doesn't it? Thank you for asking. Yes, I'm familiar with this event.' I ripped up my notes and threw them out toward the audience. 'Since my prepared talk is history, let's just do Q and A. We're all learning together today.'

"I answered their questions as best I could without betraying your confidences. But I realized that this was the end of my profession as I had known it. I was shifting from teacher to student. And not just me, but scientists all over the world. All our sure knowledge and pat explanations are about to be tossed onto the ash heap of scientific curiosities."

"Noel, I am so sorry to do this to you."

"Oh no. You're not doing it. You're caught up in it just as I am. My tears were not exactly tears of joy. More like exhilaration. I'm excited. And I'm terrified."

"Excitement and terror. Exactly what I'm feeling here on the moon."

"Selena, my friend, we are on the cusp of an exciting new era. I look forward to exploring it with you. Right now, I'm at the airport and nearing the front of a TSA line, and I have to put all my electronics in a basket. I wonder what kind of security will be needed for this new time we'll be entering. Talk to you soon."

"Have a good flight," I said, as Noel signed off.

"Wanda, are others waiting to talk with me? Clay in particular?"

"Many are. Not your friend Clay. No others on your approved list."

"Okay. Still no Clay, eh? Let the rest of them wait."

End of Day 1 on the moon—at least by the clock and by how tired I felt. Less than twenty-four hours since I took off from Mauna Loa. But since Moon days are twenty-eight Earth days long, the shadows moved very slowly.

I called via comm stone and said goodnight to the Spaceketeers. "We miss you!" Amelie crooned to me. "Sleep tight. Don't let the moon bugs bite," sang Dana, who can't sing.

I sure have some excellent friends. "But where is Clay?" I asked myself. "I still haven't heard from him!"

I couldn't sleep well, despite being so tired. This was like jet lag after flying half way around the world. I wished I'd brought some sort of sleeping pill. Fitful sleep, tossing and turning, dreaming of Clay, watching the hours creep by.

5. The Missing Person

Morning, Day 2. Getting my thoughts in order. Who's not there? A familiar pit hit my gut. "Where's Clay? What has happened to Clay? I've got to call Doc again."

"Doc, Doc," I yelled into the view space. "Wanda, can you summon Doc to talk with me?"

Doc came on via his comm stone, so I could only hear his voice. I heard a roar. "Selena, I may have to yell. I'm headed to Thailand. This aircraft is very noisy. I know why you're calling. I have news. Clay is being airlifted back to the US to a hospital there. This was arranged by your friend Jonn Buck. Can you contact him?"

"Yes, of course." My heart dropped. "What happened to him? Why didn't Jonn mention this to me?" I yelled, feeling panic. I was dumbstruck. I had that "this can't be happening" reaction.

"It's just unfolding," Doc yelled over the roar of his aircraft. "They did what they could on Tinian. That clinic is pretty good. They actually flew in a specialist. From Taiwan, I think. Clay's got cancer. Pretty bad I guess. He must have let it go for a while. They wouldn't take me with him. So I decided to go on to Thailand as I had planned. I took his comm stone to make sure it didn't disappear. You still on the Moon?"

"Yes I am. Maybe stuck here forever." My best friend is dying of cancer and I'm stuck on the Moon, and can't go home. I was feeling helpless and frantic.

"See, this is why Clay didn't want to tell you. He didn't want to ruin your trip."

"What an idiot! What are friends for?" I couldn't hold back the tears. I felt a vast pit inside. I felt angry with Clay for not taking care of his health. I felt anger at myself for missing all the warning signs I'd kind of noticed—his painful grimaces, grabbing his side. "Thanks for taking care of him, Doc, and sticking with him. I'll call Jonn." I felt as bad as if I had cancer.

I couldn't get through to Jonn right away, but when he finally got back to me, he told me Clay was in the Stanford Medical Center getting the best possible care. He'd let me know blah blah blah. I was frantic with fear and not knowing.

Finally, Clay called me from his hospital room phone, since he didn't have his comm stone.

"Clay, I've been trying to reach you. What's going on?"

His voice boomed in through the view space, sounding a bit raspy. "Listen, my friend, don't waste time worrying about me. I'm going to be fine. I'm getting the best care possible. Your buddy, Jonn Buck, put me up at the Stanford cancer hospital, under one of the foremost cancer docs in the world. I tried to resist. I told him there was no way I could afford this. I'd have no way to pay him back. He says, 'This one's on me. Let's get you well.' Pretty amazing—me, in the care of the big hard-headed business mogul. I'm sure he's doing it for you. He's got a real soft spot for you."

Then he went into a weak coughing fit. He sounded horrible. "Hey, there are three nurses here signaling me to get off the phone. With smiles, of course. Taking me off for more tests, most likely."

I hardly got to say a word. I finished with, "You've got my love, you big lunk. Get better, and don't harass your nurses." I don't even know if he heard me. That was it.

6. Terror of the Vasty Void

What a way to start my second day, with a frightening talk with Clay. Seemed like I'd spent most of Day 1 talking on the phone.

Yawn! I could go right to sleep again. I announced to Wanda in the view space, "I want to be alone." I wanted to take a moonwalk in the dark. I just had to stand outside again before hitting the sack, despite the effort of putting on my space suit.

I took only a single step onto the lunar soil, with the winch cable firmly attached. I stood silently in utter darkness, except for the stars. People often say it's a riot of stars; it was a quiet riot. As my eyes got accustomed to the dark, I could see the ground faintly, and the outline of my surroundings by starlight.

I held on to the handle of the airlock, even though I was also tethered. The stars looked so close. Seemed like I could reach up and grab them. The next instant they were infinitely far away, and I was in danger of falling toward them forever. I grabbed the airlock handle even tighter.

As I looked up at the brilliant pinpoints, I realized I could travel to those stars. I had the needed tools with me right in this spaceship. This sent a thrill up my spine, and a chill. Excitement and terror, as Noel had said. Space is vast and lonely. I was right in it. Just a thin faceplate between my eyes and the void that extends forever.

I was beginning to feel unmoored. Not unmoored internally, exactly. Just feeling strange. Like a boat drifting out to sea. The farther it drifts, the harder to find its way back. Perhaps it will discover new continents, but maybe it will just keep drifting. A strange feeling came over me, and I found myself turning this chain of thought into a song. The rhythm and rhyming weren't that great, but I could clean it up later. I wished I had Gibb, but he wouldn't play well in a vacuum, so I just sang softly to myself, trying to keep from fogging up my faceplate.

> *I am unmoored*
> *I am adrift on the vastness of space.*
> *Like a boat, lines cast free from the shore*
> *slowly drifting out to sea,*
> *no rudder, no compass, no map*

across the vasty void
Forever to infinity.

The farther I drift 'cross the vasty void
the harder it will be for me
to find my way back from the endless sea
to safe harbor, to home, to thee.
I may discover new worlds out there
Or I might just drift, across the vast nowhere
Forever to infinity.

I am excited, ah th' adventure,
the dreams of magnificence in the sky.
I am terrified, for I shall surely die.
I am lonely, for home and love left far behind.
Across the vasty void I fly
Going where? Nowhere at all. No reason why.
Forever to infinity.

Tears streamed down my face, making a blur of the magnificence of the stars. Then the inside of my faceplate did fog up. I just stood there on the Moon sobbing and whimpering. It took several minutes of yoga breathing to get myself back to normal. Whatever normal is for me.

After I clambered back inside and changed out of my space suit, I rustled through the supply cartons again, hoping to find another bottle of wine. No luck. Phooey. Aha! I'd almost forgotten: I'd brought my flask of Jack Daniels. I dug it out of my backpack, had a tiny sip right out of the flask, and it put me right to sleep.

But I dreamed. Not a nice one. I was standing outside on the surface of the Moon, holding Gibb, trying to play and sing. But I was not wearing my space suit or helmet. In the vacuum, no sound emerged from my lips or my guitar. I couldn't sing. I couldn't catch my breath. It was escaping and so was my spirit. I could see no stars; only pitch black. I felt myself slipping away.

I woke up chilled and shivering, staring into the utter dark and silence. "Wanda? Wanda? Are you here?" I whispered.

"I am with you, my controlling oki," she said in a comforting voice, almost like my mother's after I'd had a childhood nightmare. "What can I do for you?"

Previously I had asked Wanda to turn off the artificial gravity, so I could acclimate to the Moon's lesser pull. "Wanda, would you please turn the gravity back on to Earth level?"

"Yes. I will increase it slowly. Can you feel it?"

The familiar weight gradually came back to me. The weight of my world. "Thank you, my unsleeping tubular friend."

In the morning—that is, when I got out of bed and asked Wanda to turn the lights up—I felt much better. Nuked my coffee in the microwave and sipped it slowly with my hands wrapped around the mug. I somehow expected to look out the window and see the flowers and hear the birds chirping. But *Star Choice* has no windows; when I summoned the view space, I was still on the Moon, with grays and blacks and pinpricks of stars right down to the horizon.

Was it too soon to go home? Was I exiled? Would I ever be allowed to return to Earth without the government taking all my toys? I quickly banished that thought from my mind.

7. Moonwalk at Apollo 11

With the help of Jonn and Wanda figuring the coordinates, I landed *Star Choice* at the Apollo 11 site. I wanted a video with me standing next to the American flag planted there, with Earth in the background. But when we touched down near this hallowed site, I saw that the flag had fallen over and the ground was littered by miscellaneous items left behind—trash. And Earth was high in the sky, thus difficult to include in a landscape shot. I decided to check in with Jonn.

"Hmmm, Spaceman" I called out to my comm stone, "Are you still taking calls from me?"

Jonn responded right away. "I'm sitting next to the phone night and day, awaiting your call," his voice boomed from the view space. I'd have to ask Wanda where the volume control is.

"Jonn, I'm at the Apollo 11 touchdown spot. What I see is the base of the lander that was left behind, a good bit of litter, but no American flag."

"Ah yes, that has been noted from lunar orbit. The flag was knocked over by the exhaust of the lunar module as it took off."

"So then, it's laying on the ground. Here's my thinking. What if I would stand the flag back upright? What if I could bring back a few of the things lying on the surface? Maybe the NASA scientists would like to study the effects of the Moon environment on these things for half a century."

"Fascinating idea." I heard his hum of thinking. "Heat and cold, ultraviolet radiation, micrometeorite impacts. Let me talk with my contacts at NASA, and see what they say. Many people think this site should be a historical monument and that things should not be disturbed, not even the trash."

"I can understand that," I said. "But there are no bones here that should be left in peace. I would be a good anthropologist and photograph where everything is so that after they were studied back on Earth, we could return them to exactly the same spot. Actually, Wanda does the picture taking, via video."

"Already you're planning your next Moon trip?" he asked in a chiding tone.

"That might be the one that you take," I replied.

"How would you retrieve these items and bring them back?" he asked.

I thought for a minute. "Jonn, I did not plan this out. I guess I would take another moonwalk, pick them up, put 'em in one of my plastic trash bags, and bring them back that way. Plenty of room in *Star Choice* to store things."

"Let me check with NASA," he said.

"Jonn, I suspect it's better to beg for forgiveness than to ask for permission. And besides, if they find out later I'm bringing Apollo 11 artifacts when I return to Earth, they're less likely to try to blast me out of the sky as I land."

I could hear his trademark chortle. "You do what you're gonna do, woman. Don't kill yourself."

My moonwalk skills were already improving. I had much less trouble putting on my spacesuit, boots and helmet and navigating through the coffin-sized airlock. Even before stepping outside onto the Moon's surface, I attached the winch cable to my suit, so that if nothing else I could be dragged bodily back to the ship by Wanda.

"One small step for a woman, one huge leap for womankind," I announced to the universe as I stepped outside.

I brought an empty trash bag and a short aluminum rod I had liberated from the foot of my bed. I bent the end of the rod by closing the inner airlock door on it, then pushing it into an L shape.

I crow-hopped out to the first piece I wanted to retrieve—a glove. I discovered that I could not open the plastic bag. Back on Earth, I would blow gently into it—not possible here. It was stuck together, perhaps by static electricity. But Jonn had urged me to bring anything back in a plastic bag to minimize contamination with the air inside .

So, I went back in through the airlock, removed my gloves and helmet, pulled the bag open a tad, and blew into it.

I should mention that I had Wanda turn off the artificial gravity. I could scarcely move inside the ship wearing my space suit when it was held at Earth gravity.

I made sure some air was inside the bag, just enough to keep the sides from sticking together; then I re-entered the airlock. As air was released from the lock, the bag inflated like a balloon. It might have exploded if the air hadn't leaked out. When the airlock opened to the outside, the air from the bag escaped. Tiny ice crystals formed from the interior humidity that rushed away in all directions.

However, not all the air escaped. The bag retained enough air to keep the sides from sticking together, so I was able to walk over to these items, pick them up with my bent aluminum rod and maneuver them into the trash bag. I retrieved the glove, a boot, a camera, and a couple of small baggies with what must have been half-century old freeze-dried human waste—aka poop and vomit.

When I returned to the airlock and filled it with air, the bag collapsed around its contents. They were vacuum-sealed.

When I bragged to Jonn how clever I was, he pointed out that blowing into the plastic bag with my germ-laden breath defeated the purpose of avoiding contamination. And warned me that the waste bags, when brought inside, may thaw out, and not smell so good. Oh well.

I wanted to see if I could set the American flag upright. I had trouble finding it, and when I did, I was shocked. Its stand was intact, lying on its side. But the flag was barely visible—just a faint trace of stars and stripes in the moon dust. It had been pulverized by the extreme elements and by micrometeorites. As I looked at it, I got all choked up. This was my nation's flag, planted here on the Moon. It made me proud to be an American. And a human.

Wanda had faithfully videoed everything I did outside, but how could she get a shot of the flag? We hadn't built a portable camera for me to carry around, and I had been assured that my iPhone with its camera would instantly freeze if exposed to the Moon's frigid vacuum. Plus, I hadn't brought a selfie stick.

No problem. When we departed, I could have Wanda hover over the flag and get a shot of it. No, that's no good! I wanted to be in the shot.

"Wanda, could you raise *Star Choice* off the surface three times my height, move slowly above me, then capture an image of me with the remains of this flag in the dust?" I had to think carefully, because Wanda does things exactly as I ask her. "After the shot, land back exactly where you are now."

Star Choice slowly rose from the surface, moved above me, and hovered. Without me even asking, Wanda gave some slack to the winch cable so I wouldn't be dangling above the ground. I had twin panic attacks. One, that this hundred-ton vessel looming above would set down and crush me, and two, that it would take off and leave me behind.

"Wanda, please don't get any ideas about taking off and leaving me here."

"My controlling oki," she spoke to me softly in my helmet, "I will not leave you behind on this airless world to die of cold and no oxygen. Then I would have no controlling oki."

"Thank you." Her statement verged on sarcasm. Was she developing a sense of humor? That would be scary, especially since it sounded like mine. But that would account for her sending video to Earth social media of me tripping on the surface, after she had warned me not to go outside.

I smiled up toward *Star Choice*, gave a thumbs up, then a peace sign, as best I could with these unwieldy gloves. I'm sure nobody could see my smile or tell who I was through my faceplate. We should have stenciled our names on our space suits, I belatedly thought.

I hoped that the shot of me standing by the remains of the flag would go viral, but no, it was the video of me picking up trash, holding a bag in one hand and the bent stick in the other, like folks picking up litter in the park. A mix of "how dare she" outrage and delight.

When I finally went back inside *Star Choice* and removed my spacesuit, I was exhausted. I had been outside no more than 30 minutes, but this had taken everything out of me. I poured a thimble full of JD from my flask, and collapsed into the captain's chair. Note to self: Next trip, bring a larger flask. And wine with twist off caps.

Later I learned that NASA was appalled when it learned I had disturbed these artifacts. But when I brought them back, they eagerly took possession of them to study.

8. I've Made Up My Mind, I Think

I stayed at the Apollo 11 site for a time, just to hang out and look outside via the viewspace. "Wanda, let me watch the moonscape, the Earth, the starry sky." I wish I'd had my captain's seat built like a recliner, so I could lean back and put my feet up.

I was sitting about where Breadbox would have been in her vessel, seeing the same things that she saw. This must be similar to her first glimpse of Earth. Perhaps she felt the same awe at its majesty.

As I have done many times lately, I talked with my best friend. "Breadbox, what is my next move?" She didn't answer directly, of course, being dead and buried on Earth.

I sat there in the utter silence of the Moon. Besides the soft whisper of air circulating, I could hear nothing but my own breathing and heartbeat, proof that I was a living being. I said to Breadbox, "The Moon is the farthest that my people have ventured so far. I could go onward—go to the stars. What do you think?" I had decidedly mixed feelings about this. Excitement and trepidations. The realization that I could indeed do it, but with the certainty that it would be crazy to do so.

One of Breadbox's melodies floated into my mind. We were singing together—my alto, her organ-chord voice, and Gibb. I heard it as clear as if she were there on the Moon singing with me. I then sang a verse from "Rocket Girl."

> Hey, hi, watch me kiss the sky
> As I long for Earth, watch me cry.
> When I'm far from home,
> when I've crossed all space,
> where I know no-one, no familiar face.
> When I kiss the sky,
> and leap the Moon,
> I wonder why. With a tear in my eye,
> will I see you soon?

I could just about see her there with me, moving her eyestalks in time with my singing.

"Breadbox, my best friend, you gave me back a part of my life that

I had thrown away. I wasn't writing much music. I was living as a near recluse up on the coast. I wasn't performing unless Morty really twisted my arm, and then only half-heartedly. I had bought into my own sad story that singing was just a way to earn money."

She was there beside me, I could swear. I reached out to touch her. "When you and I sang together, we urged each other on. You and I helped each other rediscover the soul of our singing. I owe it to you to nurture and sustain that in my life." With her arm tentacles, she gave the sign of affirmation.

I shut my eyes and looked at her there beside me. "It's true, I have this marvelous spaceship. Yes it was yours, and should have taken you home. But now that Wanda has fixed it all up again, it calls out to me to go far into space—maybe even to the stars."

I looked at her guiltily, and she gave the sign of confusion. "But is this my '*Star Choice*?' Do I want to be the rocket girl I sing about and gallivant around the stars? Or do I want to be a composer and singer—living the soul of my singing? And singing your legacy also, since you never got to go sing with me on Earth?"

She gave the sign of encompassing.

"It was your choice to explore the cosmos." Her arm tentacles and eyestalks drooped downward. "If you hadn't done that, you and I would never have met, and my music may never have flowered. In honor of that, I must make the choice that is true to myself." She looked at me expectantly.

"Exploring the cosmos is also very appealing to me. But my choice is to express my authentic voice in my music. I can't do that if I'm traveling alone through the cosmos. So I've got to go back.

"I'm a singer, not a space farer."

It came to me. I stood up, looked at Breadbox, and announced it to the cosmos. "I'm a singer. I'm a singer and performer and composer. That's what I do. That's what I'm best at." I shook my fist for emphasis. "Despite my reclusive nature, I enjoy interacting with the audience. I wouldn't be happy cooped up alone in a tin can, jaunting around the galaxy. Not even if I had a few close friends with me." I stuck my chin out.

"There, that's settled." I sat back down and took a deep breath, looking in the view space at Earth—my home.

Yes. Clarity. A feeling of deep satisfaction, as if all my soul's tumblers clicked into place together. Finally. I looked around; Breadbox was gone, nowhere to be seen.

Even so, there was another piece. "Now, how do I return to Earth without giving up *Star Choice*, and especially Wanda, who is my robot sidekick? I have to come to some accommodation with Hu and his government hard asses who want the dang thing for themselves." I needed a plan that would give them what they wanted, and let me have what I want.

So, it was time to turn my attention to getting back to Earth. The world where I belonged.

9. Cosmos Reconnected

I didn't want to be a sitting duck on the Moon, in case the various governments trying to catch me found a way to do so. Especially on the side that faces Earth. So I asked Wanda to have *Star Choice* take off again and go into orbit.

After we regained orbit and I did update calls with my crew back home, I got a call that sent a chill up my spine.

Wanda spoke up from the view space and said, "Selena, my controlling oki, the Galactic Librarian sent a message that it wants to connect with you."

"What? How is this possible?" I was shocked, dumbfounded, thunderstruck, astonished! All of the above. This was the last being I expected to hear from again. Why? Because it was impossible, or so I had been assured by Wanda. We had been permanently disconnected by the Confederation when our feckless Agency had messed around with the clone of Wanda.

I thought back to the time several months ago when it seemed Wanda had been killed. Hu and his Agency goons had stolen the clone created by Wanda. While fiddling around with it, they had inadvertently connected with security officials on the home world of Breadbox, a thousand light years distant. The so-called Device Captain of the Galactic Confederation had sent a signal that zapped the clone and nearly zapped Wanda. And it had severed our connection with the Confederation, so I could no longer communicate with the Librarian or with Kateh, the clan mother of Breadbox. Presumably Earth had been forever cut off from the galactic civilization, just when we were discovering that it was there.

But now, here came a request for connection from a being I already felt ambivalent about. This scared the bejeebers out of me. "If the Librarian can contact me after we've supposedly been forever disconnected, then who else can?" As Jonn had pointed out, this could provide a channel for hostile aliens to interfere with Earth, maybe even figure out how to get here. And it would be my fault.

And yet, I was excited and tempted by the opportunity to once again explore the Library. What better thing to do while circling the Moon? Soon enough I'd have to return to Earth—assuming they ever let me go back—and focus on my singing. I may have to give all this up—even Wanda. I felt a deep surge of sadness.

I was suspicious and scared, but enticed. Maybe I should just refuse. "Go away, never call me again," I could say. But no . . .

"Okay, Wanda, let the Librarian connect." I saw no point in refusing. It already knew I was reachable.

Wanda was able to immediately connect me with the Librarian. Did it sit there awaiting my call? Or were there a hundred identical gizmos or beings called Librarian that all do the same thing—and know everything about me?

The Librarian's triangular frosted Christmas tree shape appeared in the view space, with its light on top and its slit of a mouth and eyes. It was much larger than in the old view bubble. More intimidating, one might say. I had no idea how large or small this alien being was, or even if it was a real thing.

"May I have permission to communicate by speaking, my oki acquaintance from a distant star system?" it asked me.

I nodded and grunted yes, in a decidedly unenthusiastic greeting.

"I am pleased to make contact with you once again." it said.

"Are you O-Bloy?" I asked, pointedly ignoring pleasantries.

"I am called O-Bloy," it responded. What did that mean? Well, I am called Selena, and it's not my real name either.

"It has been a sizable measure of time since we communicated," said the Librarian, mixing English and Fedi words. What should we call that—"Fenglish?" Wanda's translation smoothed it out so I could understand.

"How is this possible?" I asked. "We were shut down by authorities from your Confederation."

"I found a way to re-establish contact," it said without explaining how. "I'm delighted to discover that you are reachable."

"Why? Why do you wish to communicate?" I was feeling very grudging and ungenerous, remembering what the disconnect had done to Wanda.

"I wish to continue our conversation," it said simply.

I took awhile to respond, thinking it over. I recalled all the pushy questions it had asked about Earth—questions I had delayed answering. But there was another part. "Will I again be able to explore the Library freely?" I asked hesitantly. Did you ever break up with an old boyfriend, then ask, hey, can I still listen to some of your music? That's how I felt.

"Yes, without limitation, I assure you. As much as you wish."

My attitude immediately improved. Exploring the Galactic Library had engrossed me before the shut down. I had missed that late night activity very much.

The Librarian said, "You must recall that whatever search you conduct, and whatever conversations you and I have, are secure, and will not be divulged to others." I sure hoped that was true. I knew that lawyers and accountants are supposed to keep their clients' secrets. But librarians?

I could see the Librarian looking around. The bulb on its top was slowly pulsating, brighter and dimmer, which I'd never noticed before. It emitted a high-pitched hum, like a distant vacuum cleaner.

"I observe that you or your people have constructed a more capable viewing facility," it said, referring to the view space, and continuing to look behind me. "Your image is larger, steadier, we can see more in the background behind you, your surroundings." The pulsating speeded up to almost strobe light frequency. "I surmise that you are inside a space traveling vehicle. One that is not of a Confederation design. Thus your people are capable of creating such vehicles." Another pause as it looked around more. "I surmise that you or your people, in order to create the viewing facility, which is of Confederation design, were able to repair the personal multi-function device," it said, referring to Wanda. "That is surprising."

I nodded, acknowledging the obvious, but said nothing of the clone.

"This is quite exciting," said the Librarian with no emotion. "Your people, who have had no prior experience with such devices, have rebuilt and improved technologies of the Galactic Confederation."

"Yes, I suppose that is so," I reluctantly conceded. As I thought about that statement, it was amazing to hear the Librarian admit this.

"Are you and your space traveling vessel traversing to a different star system?" it asked, in a soft, friendly voice. The kind of voice meant to entice me to divulge more info than I wanted to.

"No, I am not. I am not traveling to any stars." But I didn't want to admit that I was merely orbiting the nearest moon to my world. Where's the adventure in that? So I said no more.

I was feeling very uncomfortable with this line of questioning. I did not trust this so-called Librarian, but I sure wanted access to the Library. "What do you want to know from me?"

"Information about your world, your world race."

The price for re-establishing contact was for me to keep sharing about Earth—the thing that made me feel so paranoid. I responded, "Let's talk about song and music." Maybe I could steer conversations along safe topics. "That will be for the next time we connect." Then I signed off.

I had to tell my friends about this re-established cosmic contact. I asked Wanda to see who she could rouse. But nobody responded. My buds were all ignoring me? I glanced at my clock, tuned to California time. 3:22 am. All right, I won't wake them up. Maybe I should get some sleep also. But I was too jazzed to sleep. So I watched the stars through the view space, waiting for Earth to appear around the edge of the Moon.

I decided to resume my exploration of the Galactic Library by getting information about the Confed authorities. With a tingle of excitement yet a tinge of foreboding I asked Wanda to request from the Library information on the Device Captain.

Here's the part that stuck in my mind. According to Wanda's

translation, the Device Captain of the Galactic Confederation " . . . will use all possible measures to prevent unauthorized entities from using the personal multi-purpose device, to recover any such device that falls into the hands of unauthorized entities, and to exact appropriate punishment to deter such future actions on the part of others." That was me they were talking about. Yikes.

Was I really beyond their reach? I wondered. Could I somehow expose Earth to all this?

10. What Really Happened

"My dear Type 1 oki friend, companion of my departed and sorely missed clan daughter, I am so glad to make contact with you again. You have been unreachable. I feared something had happened to you."

Not long after talking with the Librarian, Wanda informed me that Kateh wished to connect. This had to be more than coincidence that two distant aliens contacted me one after the other. But I was glad to talk with her once again. I sat in front of the view space and composed myself, wiping the snarl and grumpiness from my face, ready to talk with a cross-cosmos friend.

She paused and looked around behind me, as the Librarian had done. "Oh, I see you have made changes. The shape of the domicile you are in is similar to a space vessel. Is that possible?" All this came before I even said howdy. Wow, I had no privacy at all. I should hang a sheet up behind me. Or perhaps just ask Wanda to turn out the lights. Not that I had any secrets from Kateh.

I smiled and twirled my two index fingers in the greeting sign Breadbox used to do with two tentacles. "Kateh, clan mother of my best friend Nala, I am pleased to talk with you again. The Librarian said it had found a way to re-establish contact once more, but didn't tell me how it did so."

"Ah, I am so sorry," she replied through Wanda. "I can explain this unfortunate occurrence. I have learned what happened. I knew it was the one you call Mr. Rooster who had done that."

"Tell me how it happened," I said. "And how did you know I had been reconnected?"

"I asked my device to notify me should contact once again become possible, and it has done so. Our Device Captain extended our punishment when it terminated the connection of your personal device. I was distraught that I would forever lose contact with the sole friend of my clan daughter Nala. In secret, I queried the Library how I might re-establish contact with you. I was surprised to learn that the credential had been erased but the channel still existed."

She went on, and Wanda translated. "Through a clan cousin, Furu-la, a young female who is familiar with the ways of the Confederation communication systems, I requested a new credential. The Librarian has apparently honored my request. "

I found it fascinating that Kateh, even though distraught over increased punishment, still went behind the backs of the Elders to regain the forbidden contact. She was one spunky alien!

"How did it happen to be shut down in the first place?" I asked.

"The Librarian contacted our Elders inquiring about a voyage to a forbidden world. It asked how one of our vessels had traveled outside the Confederation to your world. This knowledge was supposed to be hidden from the Confed authorities by our Elders, because it was so shameful. Our Device Captain was very angry at this query."

"What?" This took me aback. "I am sorry to say, it was I who revealed that to the Librarian. But it told me that our conversations were confidential." Wow, that blabbermouth could not be trusted at all!

"Our world's Device Captain, the one you call Mr. Rooster, denied that any such thing had occurred. He did not want to confess this transgression to the Confederation superiors. He insisted there was no authorized incursion from our world into any proscribed world. That's all he would say. That seemed to be the end of it.

"But later a strange thing happened," she continued. "A user of the device—apparently not you—requested to connect with our Elders. The Device Captain was immediately notified. Since a channel had been opened originating on your world, he was able to take control of the device and commanded it to cease operation. Then he requested the Confederation authorities to terminate your connection."

"Sounds like I brought this on myself."

"You must currently have use of the personal device bequeathed to you by clan daughter Nala," she said. "I am curious how your device continues to function after the Device Captain commanded it to cease operation."

"Yes, my personal device, that I have named Wanda, was able to restore her entire function. It is very important to me to retain her use." Dare I explain the creation of a duplicate? "The last time you and I communicated, you instructed the device to heed my commands only. So it did not automatically do what Mr. Rooster instructed, and I countermanded those orders. It asked me and I said 'Do not shut yourself down.'" I said that with a smile, remembering this.

"The Librarian assured me that no-one can detect my conversations with it. But my inquiry to the Library informs me that the Librarian must reveal any communication to a formal request from the Security Authority or the Device Captain, either of which can impel notification. The Device Captain could again order my device to cease operation."

"Is the device there with you?" Kateh asked.

"Not physically. She is hidden on the surface of my world. Yet she inhabits this spaceship as if it were her body." I wondered whether those on Kateh's world used their devices as a remote controller. She didn't seem to question this.

"Yes, the space for viewing is a manifestation of it," she said. "I will address it directly."

I heard Kateh speak directly to Wanda using the beedle boop language of machines. Our computer experts use "machine language," but I never heard of any of them speaking it directly to computers the way I would speak French.

Next she addressed me in a voice of authority that was so unlike her usual mild tone. Her skin went a dark burgundy color as she spoke. "My friend, I once again spoke directly to your device, called Wanda. I, Kateh, as the sole oki from Sfofong—the world of its making—who has not disavowed it, I once again assert in the strongest language that you, Selena true singer, are the sole controlling oki of this device, and that no being from any world can request or order its action without your permission. I urge you to honor that responsibility and maintain control of this device. It is very powerful and should not fall under the control of untrustworthy beings."

I could not agree more. I felt embarrassed, chagrined, like the time as a teenager I did something to disappoint my favorite teacher at school.

Tears came to my eyes at the trust she bestowed on me. This being, the clan mother of my former best friend, this strange alien from a thousand lightyears away, conferred control on me of this unknowably powerful device. "I vow to take this responsibility with utmost care for as long as I may live," I replied softly. With my index fingers, I waved the sign for certainty that I had learned from Breadbox.

"Your device is now safe from the Device Captain or any other authority, from my worlds or yours."

I said nothing about the clone. We looked at each other in the view space in silence for a minute.

"Kateh, my dear friend, now that this matter is settled, I would like to ask you what else is happening with your punishment from the Elders."

"Ah, yes," she said, with a voice that sank toward despair. I immediately regretted bringing up that subject. "I do wish to discuss this with you. Things have changed. But I have a request of you. You may refuse."

"What is it? I'll do whatever I can for you."

"Would you be willing to connect via this view device with the other clan mothers who are being punished along with me? And to talk with them?"

"Talk with them? About what?"

"We are struggling with the consequences of the sanctions placed against us by our Elders. Conversations among the clan mothers go in circles."

"What could I do for them?" I asked.

"Because you are a Type 1, a Talki, and so distant from us, yet you became a trusted friend of a clan daughter, I believe we can talk about certain things in your presence that we cannot even discuss among ourselves. You have a way of hearing and explaining that could be helpful."

Omigawd, what would I be letting myself in for? It sounded like a group therapy session. With me, of all people, leading. The weird alien with only two legs, which made me a "Type 1" in Confederation parlance. And that I communicate mainly by talking, not singing, so I was a Talki, not a Singi like them.

This request was startling and unsettling. I had my own troubles. I didn't have the bandwidth to talk with a bunch of distant alien biddies who were being punished for the transgressions of their children.

It's funny: people on Earth are always hoping for some wise alien to show up and help us solve all our problems. And now these beings that are obviously much more advanced than humans are begging me to help solve theirs.

Yet Kateh and I had a bond from our mutual loss—her clan daughter was my best alien friend. I did not want to say no to her.

"Kateh, I am willing to talk with you and the other clan mothers. But this is not a good time."

"Yes, I understand. I wanted to obtain your permission before I approach them. Now I will do so, then recontact you."

How do you set an appointment with somebody across the cosmos? What calendar should we use? Since Wanda knew both our ways of tracking time, we could ask her to arrange the time.

I was willing; I was honored; yet full of trepidation. The kind of smart-ass things I say, I could probably get them in more trouble.

After Kateh signed off, I just sat there looking into the darkened view space. What was I getting myself into? These aliens all had some agenda for me. I could stop it: all I had to do was tell Wanda not to accept their requests for contact. Cut myself off, the way we had been cut off by the Device Captain. But that was so not like me.

Wanda informed me that she was *already* bonded to me, so that the Device Captain couldn't interfere. Kateh's instructions added nothing additional. But they mattered to me.

Even so, Kateh's story about the Librarian revealing to the Device Captain and Security Authority what I had told it in confidence angered me. How could I ever again agree to share information with it?

Two intense contacts in a row! I needed a rest. For now I just wanted to enjoy the peace and solitude. I picked up Gibb, sat again with my feet up, and hummed and strummed a few Breadbox tunes. Ah, the peace and solitude of space! Fat chance.

11. First Ever Concert From Space, Live From the Moon!

"Attention, my controlling oki," Wanda's voice broke into my guitar-strumming reverie from the view space. I was annoyed; it was like the phone ringing when you're making love.

"Yes? What is it?" I snapped.

"There is a requested contact by one of your approved people," she said smoothly. "It is Eddy Backwater, he of two names that mean the same."

Oh lordy, of all people, he was the one I least wanted to talk with. I should just turn him down.

"Okay, put him through," I grumbled. "Connect him. Link him up. However I should say it."

I was surprised to see his image pop into the viewspace, not just hear his voice. Surprised him, too.

"Hey, Sel . . . Wow! Looks like you're in the catbird seat there, girl! Your very own spaceship, I am impressed. Jealous of all the attention you're getting, but impressed. And I see you're already holding your guitar, ready for our little duet from the stars."

"Huh? What are you talking about?"

"Remember? You agreed to do this little concert with me—you in space, me here safe of Earth. Your two ladies set this up for me." Had I told them to do this? I didn't remember approving that. I guess I kinda remembered.

"You ready? They're ready for us." He looked off to the side, searching for something. "Yes, she's ready!" he shouted to somebody.

"Oh shit, is it today?"

"Sorry to rush you, Sel, but we're on the air." He turned around so his back was to me and shifted so that I saw the TV camera positioned to catch both of us, including me swearing. What about my hair? My make up? I was a mess. I quickly switched from a scowl to my performance smile.

Eddy played emcee. "Good evening, folks, or good morning, depending on where the heck you are on this great planet of ours. This is a first—a bit of a concert from outer space, with my friend Selena M, who as you know is on the Moon just now." He turned to me. "Hey, Sel, wave hi to everybody!"

Seeing I was on camera, I choked back the string of expletives I was about to let loose. I gave my best showtime smile and waved. "Hello

43

world," I said.

"Selena and I go way back. We have a love/hate relationship. I love her; she hates me." That was my line; he stole it from me.

"Folks, seeing her now, you might think she's sitting in a sound stage in Culver City, California, but I know you've seen the hilarious videos of her out walking around on the Moon. Right now, we're going to try doing a couple of songs together even though we're a million miles apart."

He turned to me, "What should we do first, my dear?"

This unfolded so fast, I didn't have a chance to get nervous. I had done TV before, of course, but I missed the audience. Even though I still get a bit of stage fright after all these years, and looking at the people in the front rows can make me forget my lines, a live audience energizes me. It's a lot easier to belt out songs when people are applauding.

Okay, let's make the best of it, I thought. I had just re-committed to being a singer. So let's sing.

"Greetings, all my friends and fans. It is breathtaking looking at our beautiful world Earth from space. I'm actually orbiting high above the Moon. I'll do some numbers with a space theme. Let's start off with one I did in Hawaii for a bunch of astronomers." I played "Let Me Lead You Astray," and Eddy rhythmed in on the refrain. I was surprised he knew my pieces so well; he must have been practicing. I followed up with "Rocket Girl" and then "My Spaceship Calls Out to Me." Then Eddy did a couple of his numbers.

I must confess: it went much better than I expected for an unrehearsed gig, and I got into it. Eddy and I actually play pretty well together. An hour passed quickly, with only a few commercial breaks.

"Sorry folks, that's all the time we have just now," Eddy announced. "Hopefully there will be more. And Selena, just FYI, we had over fourteen thousand tweets requesting "Cotton Candy Lovin'.'" You still got it, girl." Cheers and whistles came through the view space. I've never turned down a request for an encore.

"Okay, I'll do it! Folks, here's 'Cotton Candy Lovin'!" Afterward, I could hear the applause, like distant surf, that went on for some time. Where was the live audience? Sounded like a lot of people. I listened till the end, lapping it up.

After it was all over, I called Eddy back through the view space. "Yes, whassup?"

"I want to thank you for setting this up. I forgot how much I enjoy doing concerts like this. Singing to people. You done good."

"The pleasure is all mine, my dear." He paused for a moment, then added, "Selena, you should get back to Earth and be a singer, not traipse off to the stars. You hear me?"

"I hear you. You're right. That's what I need to do." This was the most kinship I'd ever felt for him. Maybe being alone in space had made me soft.

As I reviewed this show later, I grimaced. The production quality was terrible. Essentially a TV shot of a TV shot. But the sound was pretty good. If I planned to do concerts from space, Wanda would have to put together a better set up.

The response from Earth was overwhelming, in the news and social media. I was moved. And excited. Later I learned that I had my all time best day of music downloads. A few of these events, I could recoup my cost of this whole moondoggle. Ka-ching went the strings of my heart! Eddy told me he earned enough from this one event to put his daughter through the college of her choice.

Ah, the material benefits of my renewed commitment to singing on Earth!

This glow lasted about half an hour—until my next contact.

12. Pushy Alien

"Tell me about song and music on your world," the Librarian asked me as soon as it contacted me again, parroting what I'd said I was willing to talk about. I was so angry at this smooth talking whatever it is. I was ready to say, "No more contact!"

Ah the irony. Just a short while ago we had bemoaned the cut off of contact with the cosmic society. Not just me, but Jonn and Noel and the Spaceketeers, who were eager to explore the Library to learn the secrets of this advanced civilization. And now in my pique I was again ready to cut it off. I asked it once again to explain what had happened.

"Your connection credential was terminated," explained the Librarian. "It wasn't the Library that disconnected you; it was the authorities that control devices."

"But won't these authorities just shut us down again once they find out?"

"You now have a new code. They won't know it, unless you contact them."

Or unless you let it slip again, I thought. "Why are you doing this?" I asked in my interrogator voice.

"I wish to learn about you and your people, as I have said previously."

I shook my head. "But my mind is made up. I'm focusing on my singing, not traveling through space." I turned partly away from the view space, as if to dismiss the request.

"Yet you *are* traveling in space," it pointed out patiently.

It can't take no for an answer. I glowered into the view space and resumed my harangue. "Why did you reveal to authorities what I told you in confidence?" I yelled. Talking with this emotionless entity made me so angry.

"My role is to acquire information. I merely needed to confirm what you told me," it explained without emotion or apology.

"But because you did that, they made an attack on my world. They cut off my connection. What the hey, it sounds like you'll share anything you learn about my world with people—nasty aliens—who can use that information against us. So I don't want to reveal significant information to you." I've been more polite to ex-boyfriends.

It was silent. The topknot ball blinked furiously. Was I about to be cut off again? The Librarian spoke softly to me. "As you wish." It sounded almost contrite.

More silence. "Does that mean I cannot explore the Library on my own?" I asked, fearful of the answer.

"Explore it as you wish. I will not interfere in any way." We regarded each other. "I have enjoyed our communications, my unfamiliar oki contactee."

Then we disconnected. I immediately felt the sadness and loneliness of breaking up with a friend. But clearly, this decision was in keeping with my commitment to focus on my singing—assuming I could ever return to Earth.

*   *   *

As the Librarian was about to sign off, up popped a little face in the foreground of the view space. It spoke with Wanda's voice. Was this her avatar? I'd never seen it before. Had she just created this or herself? Why now? Looked like a little Polynesian god carved out of green jade. Or like the stir stick of a Hawaiian drink. Was this how she visualized her own face?

Wanda told me that Morty wanted to talk. I nodded okay, and his voice boomed out of the space in front of me as soon as the Librarian signed off.

"Selena, sorry to interrupt your important work there. Just had to check with you. I'm about to finalize an interview with CNN, and I want to make sure you will still be floating in space."

"Morty, I'm circling the Moon."

"Moon, space, it's all the same, as long as you haven't landed back on Earth yet. They want an interview with a space traveler."

"When?"

"Next day or week or so."

"I don't know how long I will be staying here. I'm hoping to come home soon. Better make it quick, and let me know ASAP."

"Will do. Will do. Hey, I caught your concert with that country singer. You two weren't half bad, I must admit. Even though you went around me on that one."

"Sorry, Morty. You'll get your cut. Might be enough for you to retire on."

"I've been checking on your music download sales. Speaking of retiring, you're raking it in."

"I'm not retiring; I'm just getting started, Morty. I've got a lot of singing to do. That's one thing I've gotten clear on up here."

"I'm glad to hear it, sweetie. Listen, gotta go. I'll get back to you *mach schnell*."

13. Stuck in Space

Icouldn't get a break! Dr. Hu was calling me yet again. He called by phone, so I only heard his voice, rattling out of the view space. His voice boomed out a belch before I could even say hello. I missed the days when people could only message me, so I could ignore them. Yes, I took the call, but I just sat there waiting for him to say something.

He hiccupped. Must have been drunk again. Or still. "The government guys are determined to bring you back. They got so angry when you did that concert. I, by the way, enjoyed it. I like those songs. I'd already heard them. Did I tell you I got a bootleg copy from my buddy who was at your sing-along in Hawaii? But the Agency, they were angered by the space concert because it rubbed their noses in the fact that you had single-handedly taken their spaceship, and advertised it to the entire world."

"Oh lordy. What's with these guys?" I said with an exasperated scowl, trying to convey as much disapproval as possible. Not that it would do any good.

"You're stuck up there in space. They're not giving up on you. They can't get you right now. But they'll wait you out, till you run out of food. You have to come back to Earth someday, unless you can eat moon dust; then they'll grab you." He snickered and hung up.

He sounded just like the nasty little boy who pulled girls' pigtails in third grade. Just another threatening, blustery call from him; not even worth getting upset about. But I did anyway.

"Grrrr! [Expletive deleted]!" I swore loudly to the cosmos. From joy and ecstasy to fear and loathing in five short minutes. Jonn had said there's no way they can come get me, but this made it seem even less likely that I'd be going home any time soon. Well, it was nothing I didn't know. I took a deep breath. I needed some of Hu's yoga breathing.

Back home I'd go climb my hill to work out all the pissed offness. On the Moon I could suit up and go for another moonwalk. But here, I had nowhere to go. No, I just went back into the sleeping area where beds should have been and did some jumping jacks. And screamed as loud as I could. "AAAaaarrrrgghh!"

Phew! That felt better.

Wanda was alarmed. "My controlling oki, what has occurred? Are you injured?"

"No, I'm fine. Just experiencing some strong emotion. Anger."

"Could you please describe these emotional states so that I can better understand the human experience?" she asked me.

How could I describe anger when I'm angry, I wondered. I did my best.

She must have gotten it to some degree, because she said, "Perhaps with vigorous movement and loud self-expression you can metabolize the substances that contribute to these negative physiological states."

"You nailed it, my friend. I just need to burn out the anger. Thanks for looking out for me." Huff, puff, jump, jump. Grumble, grumble. I ran in place as if I was on the treadmill from hell.

14. Temptation

Before I could even rustle up a snack from my meager larder, Wanda announced another contact. "The Librarian has a message for you," announced Wanda. "Delivered to me. Would you like me to repeat it to you?"

Uh oh. Was this spurned Librarian going to become a cosmic stalker? "Well, sure, why not?"

"The Librarian wants to offer you something. A gift. A recompense."

"What gift might this be," I asked with sarcasm. This Librarian would try anything to get in my good graces again.

"A boon, it says."

"Boon? What's a boon?"

"It would like to explain."

Here's where I should have said, "No way. Bug off, you sneaky alien creature." But my curiosity always gets me. "All right. Let's give it two minutes. Then cut in and tell me I have another call. Okay?"

The Librarian appeared in my view space, topknot ball flashing, eyes squinting and blinking. "We are pleased to discover that you have recovered from the unfortunate disconnection caused by us."

"Thank you. I have recovered." I sat there stony-faced with my arms crossed. Forgiven but not forgotten.

"I am not contacting you to ask any questions. As recompense for this error on our part, we would like to offer you a boon."

"A boon?" I wondered how Wanda had come up with that word to translate what the Librarian was offering. Did it mean a reward? Recompense? Or a bribe?

"Since you are a singer of songs of some repute on your world . . ." This had to be pure flattery. It had no idea of my repute, regardless of what I believed about myself. " . . . you may wish to view other performers from the worlds of the Confederation who come to a special place to sing the songs of their world. It is called the Songstone."

The viewspace shifted from the Librarian to a panorama on a different world. It was dusk. It looked like an ancient stone amphitheatre. I saw a jumble of huge shaped stones, as if the Greek Parthenon plus Stonehenge had collapsed into a pile of rubble. I put my face right up close to the view space to see the dim tableau better.

"This is the Songstone on our leading world called Everbright, where people from all Oki world races come to sing," droned the Librarian in its documentary voice. "Others always await so that the singing never stops.

The Librarian communicated with Wanda with the beedle boop language instructing how to establish an ongoing connection to observe this scene.

If this was Everbright, so named because the lights were always shining, why was the light at this place so dim? A mournful droning sound echoed off the stones. Then a moaning whooshing noise—like wind in the trees on Halloween. Was this singing? For my first glimpse of an alien world—one I supposedly wanted to travel to—this was not promising.

At the base of the jumbled megaliths in a circle of smaller stones was a small bonfire. Behind, barely illuminated by the flames, was a being I could not quite make out, droning a strange sad melody punctuated by what sounded like hiccups. It stood in a clear flat area I guess you'd call a stage that looked out over semicircles of rough stone benches that ascended up a slope. An amphitheatre with performers but no audience. Our viewpoint was from the top of the amphitheatre.

"Wanda, what size is that being on stage that is singing? How tall compared to me?"

She was silent for a moment. "I have just located information on this worldrace from the Library. If standing erect next to you, its head would be below the level of your shoulder.

It looked like White Rabbit in Alice in Wonderland, if the white rabbit were a large, scruffy grey rat.

If that thing was four feet tall, then some of those stones must have been twenty or thirty feet high. This was indeed a huge ruin.

The Songstone attracted a bizarre diversity of alien singers.

51

"Wanda, if this monument is so important to this powerful galactic civilization, why has it been allowed to collapse into ruin?"

"This structure is older than the Confederation—more than forty thousand of your world's years. It was already collapsed when the Confederation was born. The oki races that formed the Confederation decided to keep it as it had been, rather than restore it. It signifies the ultimate ruin of even the most substantial and powerful things. So as world races sing at the Songstone to keep their stories alive, they are reminded that in the end, all disintegrates. Two contradictory messages kept in balance."

That was a fascinating philosophical observation, I thought! I flashed on the song Breadbox had sung:

> *The universe is cold and uncaring*
> *Life is a nothingful scum*
> *We life, we always seek meaning,*
> *Where no meaning can ever be found.*
> *So let us sing our story*
> *To build our short lives around.*

Now there was an image of a tiny being in dark surroundings, poor lighting, a whiny voice— kind of a monotone chant, not particularly impressive.

The Librarian spoke over the display of the Songstone. "I offer you full access to view the Songstone with no unwanted interference from me."

I was hardly listening to the Librarian. A new singer had emerged from the shadows at the rear of the stage. A tall willowy being, all white, that looked like a will o' the wisp. It sang in a high, tremulous voice, yet quite melodious—an enchanting song.

The tempo picked up and the being leapt into a swirling dance like a dervish that swooped back and forth across the performance area. In and out of the tall megaliths. Leaping then crouching. Its voice swooped with it, from high soprano to deepest alto. Arms flailing. White skirts swirling and spiraling from different levels. If human, the skirts would be swirling from knees, hips, shoulders, and head. I feared it would swirl too close to the fire and catch alight.

The voice, the singing, was in complete synchrony with the dance, as if they were all parts of the same communication. I recalled how Breadbox always spoke lovingly of the songdance, where there was no separation between the two halves. I was immediately drawn into it. Oh, I wanted that song! I wanted that dance! I wondered if Wanda had recorded it. Could Wanda translate the lyrics for me?

I was entranced by the Songstone and the singer. I didn't notice that the Librarian had departed. I forgot that I was zipping around the Moon in a small cylinder, and my government was issuing daily threats at me.

I forgot that I had nothing to eat but meager reserves of packaged camp food. I even forgot about my missing friend Clay. I was there with the swirling singer.

15. They're Shooting At Me

My Songstone reverie was rudely broken by news from Jonn. When he called, I thought it would be with an update on Clay. "Selena, I'm just hearing that two—and possibly three—nations are planning to launch more rockets toward the Moon to come after you. I don't yet know what they think they're doing. They're no longer using YouSpace because they think I'm on your side. Well, it's true. I am on your side. I'll keep you informed."

"Jonn, when can I come home?" I asked plaintively.

He sighed. "Sorry to say, I'm having very little luck with the government . . ."

He was quiet for a few maddening seconds. "Noel and I have been trying to put together a team of heavy hitters that would give us more clout and visibility with key senators. We get interest—everybody's interested in this vessel and its technology—but they are reluctant to jump on board."

"I know. It's run by a ditzy chick who stole it from the rightful authorities, right?"

"They don't put it quite that bluntly, but, yeah."

"If I came back to Earth and handed it over to the government, then these experts would get on board?" I sensed a possible way of getting out from under this burden. But no . . .

"Yes, they would, without question. But—and here's the big but— the government shows no interest in doing something like that. If they retrieve it, they will haul it off to some secret inaccessible spot—probably in pieces—and study it on their own. They don't even want to include NASA. I'm hearing this from right near the top." Then he was gone without a word about Clay.

I was just starting to work up a snit about this when Wanda said smoothly, "My controlling oki, I detect chemical powered rockets emerging from the large orbiting vessel from your world that is in a similar orbit. These rockets are apparently targeting *Star Choice*. They are smaller than the previous ones, but accelerating much faster. I must take evasive action, so please make sure you are protected in your seat from any sudden acceleration of *Star Choice*."

A stab of fear hit me as I leapt into my seat and fumbled with the harness. Not a moment too soon! I immediately felt the pull of acceleration as *Star Choice* made a move one way then the other that its artificial gravity could not fully counteract. I could hear the heavy cartons in back shifting back and forth. If *Star Choice* decelerated suddenly, they'd all slide forward, probably crushing me.

I watched in the view space as Wanda zoomed in on a pinpoint of light moving rapidly toward us. It seemed to swerve; I guess that was us swerving out of its way. Then a flash of light that filled the view space.

"It detonated," announced Wanda in a calm voice. "I detect fragments and gases and radiation. But not close enough to affect us. *Star Choice* has kept you safe, my controlling oki."

The flash of light was instantly replaced by the dark of space once again.

"I detect other rocket launches," Wanda announced. "I'm confident I can evade them." I wish I shared her confidence. I had this realization that I could be here one moment, then blown to atoms the next, and I'd never know. I would just be gone. I viewed this with curiosity, as if I was thinking about some distant stranger.

I never saw any of the other missiles. I sat trembling, clinging to the arms of my seat. Plus I felt a surge of motion sickness from the swerves of *Star Choice*. Despite my efforts to hold it in, I vomited, and it went all over myself, since I was belted into my seat. The artificial gravity at least assured it got on me rather than floating around the cabin. But what a mess! I was sweating and woozy, scared and angry. "Are Hu and his bastards firing missiles at me? My own government?"

Wanda was apparently keeping watch on me. She was contrite, "I am so sorry to cause you this physical discomfort. If they fire more rockets at us, I can use the defenses of *Star Choice* to push them aside a small amount, as we did when on the surface of the Moon, and to move in the opposite direction in a less drastic maneuver, thus causing you less distress. I am also changing trajectory to place *Star Choice* in a higher orbit beyond the reach of these weapons."

"Thank you my friend," I said to Wanda while panting. "Thank you for getting us through safely."

Jonn called again. His visage appeared in the view space. "I've just learned that the Chinese are firing missiles at you, intending to destroy *Star Choice*."

"Yes, Jonn, we already know. They missed, so far. But you say it's the Chinese? Why?"

"Here's what I'm hearing . . . wait, what happened to you? You look terrible!"

I recounted the missile events to him, including my upchuck.

"Oh lordy, oh lordy, closer than we thought. Look, here's what you do. Their range is limited. Tell Wanda to take *Star Choice* to a higher orbit."

"Yes, she's ahead of you on that. Already done."

"Their maneuverability is quite limited. Or you could even come back and orbit Earth. In a high orbit you are untouchable. It would take them a year to program a vessel to approach you there.

Again he looked around the cabin. "I'm sorry about the mess. And you don't have very good laundry service there either," he said with a smile that looked like a grimace.

"That joke fell flat, Jonn Buck. I have no clean clothes."

"It's my fault. I should have told you earlier to get farther away from that orbiter. I had no idea it was carrying missiles it could fire at you."

"Why, Jonn, why? Why do the Chinese want to take me out?"

He was silent. "Here's what I'm hearing. They view this as an uncontrollable disruptive situation. Because you are American, they figure you will eventually come to some accommodation with the American government."

"Yeah, don't we wish?" I said with maximum sarcasm.

"The U.S. will then have access to these alien technologies that'll give us a massive advantage militarily. Further, you yourself have said that you want these technologies to be shared with all the peoples of the world. But pointedly *not* with the governments. That's the last thing many governments want, certainly including China's. But they're the only ones that can do anything about this currently. Not that others wouldn't want to blast you out of space if they could."

"Oh my, oh my," I said, feeling chagrined. "So, with my good intentions, I've brought this on myself."

"My sources in China don't support the view that your vessel should be destroyed, but they assure me it's the view at the top. From their leaders' perspective, *Star Choice* is better off obliterated. So we've got to work to keep you safe. And I'm sorry to say, our own government is waffling on this matter. But at least they're not shooting at you."

Wanda had *Star Choice* climb to a much higher Moon orbit. So instead of the Moon being this huge body I was orbiting just above, it was a medium-sized ball out there in space, slowly rotating beneath me. I did my best to clean the vomit off my outfit, the captain's seat, and the floor, and scraped it all into the garbage disposal—the opening into which all waste is fed to be recycled by the maker machine.

I thought about Hu's threat of waiting till I ran out of food. In principle the maker machine could produce edible and nutritious food for me made from this waste—not unlike the sustenance provided for Breadbox through her feeding tube. But the very thought of it made me gag and shiver. I'd have to be really hungry! But it could happen.

I glanced back at the view space, which showed how high we were above the Moon. I caught a breathtaking view of the Moon and Earth. They were somewhat aligned, with the sun off to my left, so I was seeing the lighted semicircle of each. The Moon appeared several times larger than Earth, since I was closer to it. But what struck me was how much brighter the Earth is than the Moon. When we see the full Moon in a clear sky, it seems very bright. But Earth, with its reflective clouds and oceans, is much brighter. What a magnificent view! "Wanda, make sure we capture this view so we can share it with people back home."

Could I afford the water it would take to clean my clothing? It wasn't like I had a lot of extra outfits to change into. "Ah, perhaps I'll try the flowered frock this morning." As if. Maybe I'll just have to stink for a while.

16. The Maker Machine

I needed to cool down, relax, and play some music. Forget about the smell of vomit. I looked around for Gibb. He wasn't where I'd left him. Oh no, there he was, way back by the rear airlock, on the floor, upside down. I rushed back there. When we were attacked, in my hurry to buckle myself in, I had forgotten to secure Gibb. The evasive maneuvers had tossed him around.

Gingerly, I picked him up. I could tell right away his neck was cracked. Two tuning pegs were bent. One string was broken.

I sat there in disbelief. How could I have done something so stupid and careless? I was always so careful with him. He'd never been damaged like this. This could be the death of him, like a horse with a broken leg.

Now I was in a fix. Food supplies dwindling, I smelled like a dive bar at the end of Saturday night, and now my song companion was broken and unusable.

I cried. I put my face in my hands and sobbed. I was royally screwed. What option did I have but to surrender to the authorities? Call Hu and wave a white flag?

"What kind of a future do I have as a musician, if I can't take care of my instruments?" I wailed.

"Wanda, are there any tools on *Star Choice* that I could use to repair Gibb? Any glue?" I knew there were none; we hadn't designed them or brought them aboard.

"Only one," Wanda replied. "Perhaps you could use the device you call the maker machine that is used to repair problems with *Star Choice*."

That's something I would never have thought of. "Could that work, Wanda? How would we do that?"

"My controlling oki, I suggest you bring your stringed music device to the work station where the maker machine can easily access it." I did this. First I loosened the strings to take the stress off the neck.

The maker machine is a contraption that looks like a metallic octopus with eight gooseneck tubes emerging from the ceiling. At the end of each tube is an oval ball about the size of the float inside a toilet tank. One of the oval balls descended from the ceiling on its tube, and hung down just far enough for me to smack my head into it. I moved it so it hovered just above Gibb on the table.

58

Small threads or tendrils extended from the ball. "With your hand, slowly guide the ball to the place that is damaged," Wanda instructed. "Guide the filaments to the damaged spot, and hold the broken pieces together as they should be oriented, if you can."

These filaments felt alive. They felt like very thin prehensile threads, about the diameter of thin spaghetti. It was like guiding tiny fingers. It was spooky—alien spooky. Nothing about Breadbox ever gave me this feeling. The filaments wrapped firmly around the broken neck and held it in place. It was like a spider wrapping a fly in its web. Gave me the shivers.

"Now guide other filaments to the bent metal parts." I guided some to the bent shaft of a tuning peg, and they wrapped around it, caressing it, feeling it. I guided others to an intact one, and they felt it. Wanda said, "I will tell the device which is the broken part, and which is the model to restore it to." Tendrils surrounded both broken knobs and an unbroken one.

"What about the fine cord," Wanda asked me, referring to the broken guitar string.

"I need to be able to reconnect them as on the unbroken part. I can do that after these pieces are fixed."

"Do you want the maker device to recreate the same material? Or use a functionally similar material that is stronger?"

"I want it to look the same, and function the same, and produce sound the same."

"I inform you now, time is required for the repair." I watched this slow process while holding the neck together. I expected something like

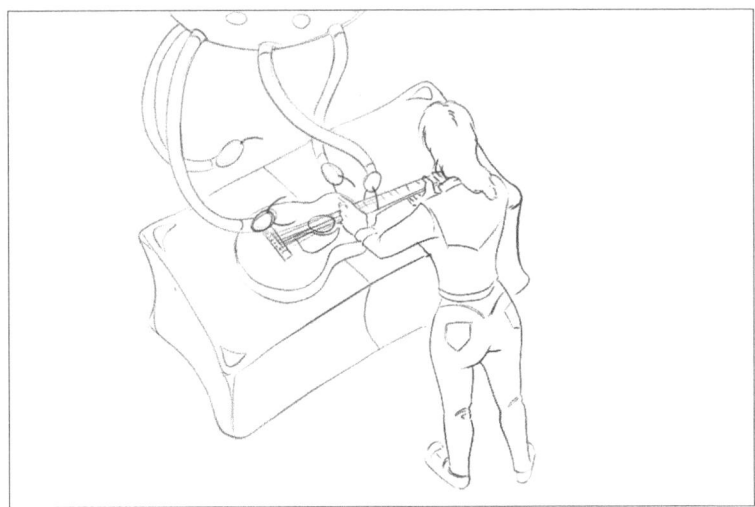

The maker machine repaired Gibb as good as new.

epoxy glue between the two pieces. But instead, it regrew the material. I could see fibers spreading, penetrating, knitting together the two pieces. Initially, the mend was a different, darker color, but gradually the original color returned. Soon I could not tell where the break had been.

As this was happening, the bent pegs, wrapped in other filaments, were straightened. The metal appeared very shiny, like liquid mercury, then gradually straightened up. This took about a minute.

I then held the two ends of the broken string together, and other filaments spiraled around it. I couldn't even see the string beneath them, but a minute later the filaments unwound, leaving an unbroken string.

How strong would these repairs be, I wondered. A guitar is a high-tension device. I carefully rewound the strings on the pegs, looking for any sign of repairs coming undone, but saw none. I then tuned Gibb and played a song. "Gibb, you are a reborn guitar!" I played a thank you song to the maker machine.

"This is magical!" I said to Wanda. "Thank you so much for restoring my second-most important instrument. After you."

I had a thought. "Wanda, imagine if I had a broken bone. Could it regrow and repair my bone?"

"Ah, a hypothetical. Yes, my controlling oki. This device is often used for such purposes on the worlds of the Confederation."

"Even though my arm bone is inside my body?"

"Yes, it can operate across a short distance. The closer the filaments are to the object to be repaired, the faster they work, and the less energy is required." While we were talking, it found a weakness in a different string, and repaired that.

"What else can it do?"

"I want to inform you that it detected impurities in the objects it worked on, and removed them, thus strengthening them."

"It can remove impurities? Impurities, hmm? I sure have some impurities. In my clothing. This vomit," I said with a wrinkled nose.

"Yes, that can be removed. It can easily detect the original material and the improper additions. You should remove your items of apparel, and put them on the workstation."

I stripped—even my undies—and placed everything on the table, grunge side up.

"These are organic and synthetic fibers. The device can easily detect which materials are supposed to be there and which are superfluous." I watched the device's fingers work over my filthy clothing.

"The device also detects worn and broken fibers, which it will restore to original condition if you wish."

"Absolutely! Please do. Wow! They'll be better than new."

I ran around inside *Star Choice* in the buff, dancing and singing. I did a dance around the view space with the images of the Moon and Earth inside and the stars beyond, hooting and trilling. Kind of like a witch around a cauldron. Was this a new part of me emerging?

What would happen if someone called me on the view space and saw me like this? I told Wanda not to accept any calls. But wait. *Star Choice* has eyes and cameras everywhere. Wanda was probably videoing me as I ran around buck naked. I pleaded with Wanda not to share any video she was storing with anybody, period. She promised. Could I trust her?

Then I had a wonderful idea. "Wanda, could you turn off the gravity for a short while?" I had this crazy urge to float around the cabin with no clothes on. Why the heck not?

"In principle, yes, but it may not be advisable. This vessel is not designed with hand holds and restraints needed for zero gravity. If you moved suddenly, you could push yourself across the interior and injure yourself on the other side."

"I've got to try it. This is a once in a lifetime chance. And who knows how long my life may be? Turn the gravity off, and I'll just stand still, and drift off the floor a bit."

Why does Wanda always do what I instruct? As soon as the gravity went to zero, I could feel it. A marvelous floating sensation. I wiggled my toes, and this small movement pushed me off the floor at an infinitesimal speed. But once above the floor even a few inches, I had no control. I slowly rotated upside down. I waved my arms, trying to swim in the air. A touch of panic!

"No no, just calm down," I yelled at myself. I stopped thrashing and just floated, turning in slow-motion cartwheels. What a wonderful feeling this was! Like floating in water, but without the water. Parts of me that I always worried about sagging just didn't sag at all! Ladies, you know exactly what I mean. I could move my limbs in any direction with no resistance. I wondered what it would be like to sleep this way.

I was half way to the ceiling with my head pointed at the floor when I felt some disorientation, and with that a touch of motion sickness. Oh no, not more vomiting, please! And then I had to go to the bathroom. I could create one hell of a mess this way!

"Wanda, I'm ready to come down. Turn the gravity on very slowly, so I can drift back to the floor safely." I came down hands first, able to grab the edge of the table, and twisted myself back into normal orientation with feet on the floor.

I roared with laughter. That was wonderful! What an experience! I was giggling with joy for minutes. I decided that next time I'd string up some ropes to hang on to.

My clothing was clean. Cleaner than new, probably. Before I put things back on, I took a thorough sponge bath myself, so I was worthy of my clean clothes. I realized afterward I should have climbed up on the table and had the tendrils work over my skin to clean it. That could be slightly bizarre. But I'd get clean. And all my blemishes repaired! Could it remove wrinkles? Hmmm. I'd have to think about that.

I couldn't wait to tell all my buds about the maker machine repairing Gibb and cleaning my clothes. I decided that cavorting in the nude would remain my secret—for now anyway. "We seem to be safe at this higher orbit." I told them. I felt much better. The floating experience had been like going to a spa. It completely wiped away my tensions and anxiety.

I watched the Songstone and sang and played my rejuvenated Gibb along with the distant alien singers. I almost forgot that I was still stuck here in orbit around the Moon with a diminishing food supply.

17. O My Princess

Icouldn't stay away from the Songstone, even though most performers were forgettable. But then one grabbed my attention. The strangest being of all was performing. A solo singer, tall, with a long skinny neck, a round flat face with large wide-spaced eyes. Kind of like a Raggedy Ann doll. From its head sprang tendrils or twisted hair—like snakes from Medusa's head. From its chin hung fibers that looked like moss. It was clothed in a spreading gown of mottled purple. Several swaying limbs—arms?—were covered with the same material. I could not tell whether this was clothing or costume or part of the being itself.

It sang in a clear, high alto. The melody was enchanting. "This melody could go right to the top of the charts on Earth," I said to myself. Wanda translated from whatever language it was singing, but I would have preferred subtitles.

> *…and then . . . oh what shall befall us now?*
> *My princess, my beloved princess.*
> *She took the rusted iron bar*
> *From the cage that had imprisoned her*
> *Held hostage against the return of the Three Voyagers.*
> *She sharpened it to jagged death*
> *Using the terrible steaming acid.*
> *When the meganaut called Burnehkadur came to her*
> *He in his disgusting magnificence*
> *To take her as his mate*
> *To bear his accursed spawn.*
> *She, my princess,*
> *She thrust the jagged rusty iron bar deep into his core.*
> *She watched, retching, but with a slight smile*
> *As he staggered back and fell*
> *Gurgling out his life.*
> *She pulled free the bar. Once more*
> *She thrust it into his eye*
> *Deep into his mind and twisted it.*
> *He was no more.*
> *But what then for her?*

Oh my princess. She sat hunched on the cold stone
And awaited her fate.
They came over the wall for her,
And through the ponderous gates.
Swords drawn . . .

I was dismayed when Wanda's avatar interrupted the performance; notifying me I had an incoming contact. This time from Kateh. "Wanda, wait till this performance is over, please!"

But the singer had stopped. It kind of curtsied and sank into a sitting position on the stone floor, face downward. Almost like the Wicked Witch of the West dissolving into a puddle of water. Omigawd I wanted to know the rest of this story! What happened to the princess?

I sighed. Of course I was happy to talk with Kateh, but . . .

"I have put off going to my male phase," Kateh said to me after brief greetings. She was kneeling on all her tentacle feet. Her skin was mottled grey, very little color. Her eyestalks drooped. She didn't quite look at me. I was alarmed at her state.

"What? What are you saying?"

"I am so sorry to tell you of my poor fortune. I must confide in somebody, and you are the only one."

"Please, you may tell me. I will listen. Do not worry. Tell me again. I did not understand what you said."

"I have put off going to my male phase."

"You can do that? What does this mean?" I had to think back to Breadbox's explanation of the four phases of sexuality the Fofonoloy went through: juvenile, female, male, and elder. The females raised the young, then after transitioning to male, fathered young.

"Yes, for a time. I can continue eating the female food, which retards emerging maleness. But if I do this for too long, I lose both maleness and femaleness."

"That sounds terrible. But why?"

"My work as a clan mother is not finished. I want to support my Clan Haw mothers. I can only do that as female."

"I see." I didn't see at all.

She turned even paler and turned her eyestalks downward, not looking toward me. She said so softly I could hardly hear her, "I fear being given a terrible male assignment."

"Huh?" Becoming male didn't sound that terrible to me.

"In times past, there were also clan fathers. Males and females raised our young together. But males and females together are a powerful team—adventurous, creative, hard for the Elders to control. Mothers alone can be bullied, controlled—especially when we don't hang together."

Yes, I remembered the crew of Breadbox—a young male and two young females. Willing to challenge the deepest taboo of their world and take an illegal adventure to unknown worlds. "But Kateh, as a male, won't you become a clan father?"

"When the Elders gained control of our society, they separated males and females, and made males superfluous, except for carefully selected ones to father the young. And those being groomed to become Elders. Those are given 'elder food.'

"We see males. They live among us. But not as mates. They are given low-quality male food. They are like neuter phase, neither male nor female.

"The Elders assign the roles that males must take. Ones they do not approve of are given roles that lead to great discomfort, low status, and short life.

"There are roles so unfortunate that the males allow themselves to be killed rather than be subjected to them. And I am in disfavor."

"That is terrible! What can I do for you?"

She was silent. I could see her quivering. "Perhaps nothing more than keep alive the memory of our shared loved one, Nala."

"This I will do forever," I promised. I was at a loss. And to think, all I had to put up with were rockets being fired at me.

We remained silent for a while, before she spoke again. "The clan mothers will not view you."

I waited, questions dangling. What could I say? A bunch of aliens like Kateh were unwilling to look at me in the view space. I hadn't been thrilled at the prospect anyway.

She explained, "If the clan mothers of Haw present a strong front and sing our case forcefully, and draw in mothers of other clans, the Elders may be swayed. They may reverse our punishment and allow us to go on to honorable roles as males. And perhaps father the next generation.

"Yet the mothers are afraid. Because my fate is their fate also—they may not be allowed to procreate as males. The clan of Haw may be greatly diminished in status and numbers if so many clan mothers suffer this fate. They rightfully fear this.

"The way around this fate is to bravely join our voices to sing the glory of the voyage of our young that perished on your world. But now the voices and songs of the mothers are scattered and weak. It is my hope that your voice, your strong voice, the voice of a Type 1 who is also a True Singer will reawaken their bravery."

Ah, finally I understood her aim. It seemed preposterous that I could have such an effect, but at least I understood what she wanted.

"But why do you think I could help?"

"You are a Talki, you speak plainly and directly. We are Singi; we communicate indirectly. We are bullied and we easily acquiesce. Yet the Elders are weak, and will give way if we present a strong unified presence."

I nodded. They needed a pep talk. Could tough Coach Selena get them all fired up to confront the bullies? "Perhaps there are one or two that are brave enough to look at me, and I could play some music for them to ease their fear," I suggested. These beings were calmed by music the way I am calmed by food. I jumped out of my seat and retrieved Gibb from the rear, and without even tuning him, played part of Song For Home that was based on the music of Breadbox. I improvised a few lines on the spot, and sang them softly to Kateh, using the melody of Breadbox.

> *May we never forget.*
> *The bonds of true oki*
> *must span the broad sky*
> *linking kindred spirits*
> *in the oneness of heart.*
> *Our most valuable gift.*
>
> *This is the message*
> *We must convey.*
> *We must sing it together,*
> *We must sing it today.*
> *We must sing it together,*
> *We must sing it each day.*
>
> *Who but us can sing this?*
> *None but us can sing this.*
> *The power of our souls shining through.*
> *From the fog to the sun shining through.*
> *The song of Clan Haw shining through.*
> *The voice of Clan Haw singing true.*

On the second run through, she sang along with me. By the third and fourth time through it she was adding her own riffs. I could see color returning to her skin patches. Her eyestalks perked back up to vertical. "Yes, perhaps you are right," she said. "I shall try one more time." She stood upright and bowed to me, her fore tentacles crossed in thanks.

"All we want is to have our sins forgiven," she added. "But we also want to restore our old ways of living.

"Thank you, my friend, Selena True Singer." She signaled goodbye and faded from view, voicing the melody.

If only I could get my audiences at home energized that easily.

On the one hand, her culture was so different, I could not begin to fathom it. On the other hand, it was just like helping a friend at home. It was disheartening—but in a weird way reassuring—to see that this alien race, so far advanced in technology, got tangled up by the same problems we humans have.

18. Medical Emergency

I decided I'd better call and check on Clay again, but he didn't answer his phone for a while. When he did, he sounded far away. Since he was on the hospital room phone, I couldn't see him; only hear him.

"You've always been my best buddy, Selena," he croaked. He sounded terrible. "I admire what you've done with your music and I'm astounded by this latest escapade of yours. It's been a pleasure being your neighbor and friend."

"Clay, you're talking like it's all over," I squawked.

"I'm calling to say goodbye," he replied, even though I had called him. "Your buddy Jonn Buck had me see his oncologist. The doc told me this cancer is pretty far advanced. 'This has been hurting you for a while, hasn't it?' I told him it only hurts when I laugh. Ha ha. He said the options were limited at this stage. I told him, I choose to die at home, and I'll soon be taken there.

"It's my own damn fault." He sounded like he was stifling a sob, and then he coughed. "I've ignored the symptoms for fear of what I'd find out. Now that my fears are confirmed, it's too late."

"Clay, if you hadn't stuck with me, I would never have done this. You've got to beat this so that when I get back there you and I can go down to Locals Only and wow those suckers. I can't do it without my bosom buddy."

"I'm afraid it's too late. I left it too long." He had a coughing fit, and then said, "The nurse is here to do something. Let's talk again. Later." He hung up.

I was in shock. "Wanda, we let Breadbox die," I wailed. "I cannot lose another friend." I completely broke down. "What can we do for Clay?"

"My controlling oki, I sense your distress. What would you like me to do in this matter?"

"What can be done? I don't know. Could you use your advanced health care power to save Clay? You told me you could help preserve well-being of crew members."

"In principle, yes. But I am not familiar with human bodies and diseases. I could possibly discover this from the Library. Also, not at a distance. I cannot make such a bodily correction quickly without the devices built into *Star Choice*."

"Then I'm going home to get him," I asserted rashly. "We'll get Clay up here on *Star Choice*."

I called him back at the hospital. I wish he'd had his comm stone with him. "Clay, don't give up. Hold on. Wanda may be able to reverse this disease."

He mumbled a reply. "This stuff they give me to ease the pain makes me feel dopey."

I then used the comm stone network to alert Amelie and Dana of the situation. Amelie went into a tizzy, so unlike her. She had her own crisis. "Crikey, we've got to hide Wanda better. These government people are poking all around. Wanda is building instruments so we can do video without her. She's also building a second view space at Jonn's lab."

These sounded like great ideas. But did I authorize Wanda to build these things? I couldn't remember. Was I the controlling oki, or not? I'd been gone only a short while, leaving Wanda on Earth with Dana and Jonn, and everything was seemingly spinning out of control.

Amelie went on. "They interrogated Mike McCreary at Mauna Kea about the evening he drove you up the mountain. He couldn't deny it. He told them he heard you talking on a walkie-talkie, then he drove you up Mauna Loa and dropped you off. In the dark he could hardly see any spaceship. He didn't tell them anything they didn't already know."

I thanked her for letting me know. I hardly had the bandwidth to pay attention to the latest shenanigans of government spooks.

Who to talk with next? Jonn seemed most likely. I got him out of some important meeting by shouting into my comm stone. "I have to come home to get Clay onto *Star Choice*."

"Hold on a minute. Let me get some privacy." I heard a door slam, then, "Okay."

"Jonn, I've got to get Clay into *Star Choice* so he can get treatment to save his life. I've got to chance a return to Earth." I was crying, nearly screaming. "We've got to save him!"

"Selena, calm down a bit. I'm familiar with his situation. What can be done on *Star Choice*?"

I pulled myself together enough to answer. "Instruments on this vessel can extract materials from the surroundings. Wanda says it could learn how to extract key stuff from the malfunctioning mass so that it can no longer grow. Once it's gone, hopefully it will be replaced with healthy tissue by the body's healing processes."

"That sounds suitably miraculous," Jonn said. "But extract what stuff? I better ask my oncologist. And also, even if this is possible, how does Clay get onto *Star Choice*?

"What if we just swoosh in and grab him?" I asked plaintively.

"Heh heh heh. You, the cosmic fugitive, the notorious spaceship hijacker, are going to brave the defenses of the US Air Force?"

"Yes, something like that, I guess. But where could we land to pick him up?"

"Stanford Med Center has a heliport." He did his hum of thinking for several heartbeats. "But you would need to come down out of space very rapidly, make a pickup, then depart rapidly back into high orbit. How fast can *Star Choice* move through the atmosphere without sustaining heat damage?"

I asked Wanda, "How fast can *Star Choice* fly through the atmosphere and land? We need to pick Clay up very quickly and evade those who would try to stop us."

She replied, "*Star Choice* can use its push force to move air aside as we pass through, thus reducing heat build up from air friction by more than 90%. Moving through atmosphere rapidly takes more energy, but we can do that. So we can fly as fast as we need to."

I relayed this to Jonn.

"Okay. Just hold on. I need to make a couple of calls. Let me see what I can put together." He clicked off. What I loved about Jonn is how this hard-headed captain of industry was willing to jump on board with my half-baked schemes—and make them happen.

"Wanda, if we can do this, what preparations do we need on *Star Choice*?" I yelled into the viewspace.

"I will instruct *Star Choice* to deploy the maker machine that you have used, which is also the matter extractor. How will your friend be arrayed? Horizontal?"

"Yes. I believe he would be on a gurney similar to the one that Breadbox used."

"Perhaps that gurney should be secured to the worktable that the maker machine previously used."

Jonn called back. "It's a go. On this end we need at least twelve to eighteen hours time. We can have Clay ready at the helipad. I'm sending my oncologist—with only a small amount of arm twisting—plus his chief nurse. Can you accommodate two medical personnel plus Clay? Can you assure their safety?"

"I think so," I whimpered. Assure their safety? Hell, I couldn't keep myself safe. "If we can get beyond the reach of missiles. I think we've got that figured out." I thought for a minute. "They'd better bring some food. I only have dry camp food."

"They will bring everything they need." He rumbled for a minute. "Okay, here's what you need to do. You are currently in a high lunar orbit. You need to depart that orbit when *Star Choice* is on the backside of the Moon and start a trajectory that will insert you into an Earth orbit. We should bring you in over the mid Pacific Ocean, then begin a rapid descent toward the coast of California coming in from the southwest. Decelerate, but don't hit the thick lower atmosphere until you're almost here, then descend steeply. Have Wanda calculate when *Star Choice* will be ready to begin that descent and tell me. Give me as much lead-time as you can." He clicked off.

I looked back at the large cartons containing beds and seats and room dividers for the Spaceketeers that had been stuffed into the crew area during the hurried departure from Tinian. Plus the tools to install them. Hopefully I could figure out how to set them up and attach them to the floor. Fortunately the toilet, shower, and cooking area had been completed and well tested by me.

I spent the next few hours unpacking fixtures and trying to install them in place according to instructions that I had helped write. I know, women shouldn't have to rely on men for such tasks, but I sure could've used Clay's help. He'd always done these things for me.

Or Doc, of course! I roused him on the comm stone from some beach in Thailand deep into mai tais, explained what we were up to, and asked him to walk me through the steps to attach the beds and chairs to the floor. "You just pound the pointed pegs into the floor with a mallet," he explained, quickly sobering up. "The floor kind of opens up to receive them, then grows around them." This was a much easier method than the one we had described in the instructions.

Fascinating! This was the same process the vessel had relied on to repair itself—fibrous metal that behaves like wood. He told me that if I needed to move them, just pry the pegs up a bit with this other tool, and the floor would release them. This dang ship is alive! I just hoped it didn't feel pain when I pounded nails into it.

I could do this! It was easier than assembling mail order furniture. But still, it was hard getting everything into just the right position. I worked up a real sweat.

As I assembled beds and chairs, *Star Choice* opened a slot in the ceiling and the maker machine again deployed all eight of its balls on tubes over the worktable.

In the midst of this construction crunch, Amelie called again via comm stone. "They raided Dana's place, trying to get Wanda. Fortunately Wanda was at Jonn's lab, making small devices for us, and earphones for you. But I wanted to let you know; we're sending Wanda to you with Clay. We will no longer require her to stay in touch with you via video. She built a miniature view bubble into the comm stone for each of us."

"That was fast. I hope she can operate on Clay just as fast."

I was flattening the last cartons when Jonn called. "Ready when you are. When your trajectory comes up on California, get ready to take a steep dive." Yikes! I hurried to get the two extra seats completely nailed down. Then I threw the tools into my storage locker.

"We're ready," I said. "What are we going to do?"

"Ask Wanda to follow my instructions," he ordered.

"Okay. Wanda? Can you do what Jonn says?"

"Yes, my controlling oki."

Jonn called out "Mmm, Wanda," and we had a three-way comm stone hookup. "Wanda, bring *Star Choice* down forty miles south southwest of the Golden Gate Bridge. Offshore about ten miles to minimize the onshore impact of sonic boom. As you near the surface, turn eastward. Cruise at an altitude of 1,000 feet. Come to the precise coordinates I will give you at a fast but subsonic speed. As you come onshore, gain altitude if necessary to maintain ground clearance of 500 feet. Watch out for small slow-moving aircraft and large birds. I will upload an image of the landing site.

"A door will be open. Touch down on the white cross with your aft hatch facing that door, and about thirty feet from it. Open the hatch and be ready to receive a gurney—a wheeled cart—with a person on it, plus two other people. Plus supplies. Selena will greet them. As soon as they are aboard and secure, take off vertically and accelerate back to your high Earth orbit, where Selena will again give you directions. Got it?"

"Yes, Jonn Buck."

"Thank you, Wanda," Jonn said. This conversation was fascinating. Jonn was talking with Wanda as if she were here with me, when she was actually in his lab, at least physically. But her "mind" was here on *Star Choice* with me, perhaps living in the view space. It was hard getting used to a being that could be in two places at once.

My thought quickly went to Gibb, who had suffered in the previous actions. I ran back and strapped him to the storage cabinet. Oh, and what about all the flattened cartons I had just emptied? I could just see them flying all over the interior with *Star Choice* 's rapid changes in direction. I looked around frantically. Only one place to cram them—in the rear airlock. I opened its interior hatch and slid the cartons in there edgewise, then slammed shut the hatch. When we landed, they'd be the first thing unloaded.

"My controlling oki, if we will change direction rapidly, you should be securely attached to your seat, in case the change in momentum is greater than the grav can compensate for."

"Selena," Jonn yelled, "let's stay connected via comm stone throughout, okay?"

"Yes, sir!" When he spoke in that voice, I felt like I should salute. "Thank you, sir."

Jonn gave the signal to start the descent, and *Star Choice* plunged toward Earth like falling down an elevator shaft. Thank goodness for the artificial gravity! Even so, my heart was in my throat and I was afraid my stomach would follow. I noticed a few unused fasteners floating around the cabin. This was eerily similar to the vessel's ill-fated first approach to Earth, which ended in the crash that began this whole adventure.

We plunged dizzily downward, but pulled up just before smacking into the Pacific Ocean. I confess I closed my eyes there at the end. We covered the horizontal distance to Stanford in less than two minutes. *Star Choice* swerved toward the helipad and arrived just as a double door swung open. Jonn stood to the side waving us in. We turned to arrive stern first and landed right on the big white X.

Wanda announced, "*Star Choice* will retain partial lift because we do not know the support capacity of this landing surface." Good. I sure hadn't thought of that.

I exhaled. How long had I been holding my breath?

19. Zip Zip!

Needless to say, you cannot swoop down on San Francisco from outer space without being spotted by radar and scrambling a few F-16's. Thus this transcript—another of the ones I obtained from an unnamed source after this whole adventure was over:

[*Transcript: Phone con between Gen. Dickson and Col. Bird.*]

— General Dickson, Nessie failed to come back around the Moon.

— If it's orbiting the Moon, it has to be regular.

— It's several hours late.

— Damn, it must have landed again—on the backside.

— Whoa! It just came out of nowhere, from an unexpected direction, plunged straight down toward Earth, and landed south of San Francisco. Yes, at Stanford University. The radar shows a steep trajectory from outside the atmosphere—From the southwest. I admit it took us by surprise because whatever comes down must first go up. And we of course had picked up no launch signals.

— Yes, Colonel, it's those unknowns that get us every time. Where did it go?

— Satcon shows it landed on the roof helipad of the Stanford Medical Center.

— I guess that means air to surface missiles are not our first choice. Why did it land there, do you suppose?

— Major Payne just contacted the hospital brass. They referred him to Jonn Buck.

— Jonn Buck? Of YouSpace? How does he fit into this? I thought he was busy launching our lunar orbiters.

— We are just about to connect with him.

— Kick him up to me, Colonel, right now.

— Yes sir!

* * *

(*Back to the Stanford Med Center heliport.*) As I watched from the viewspace inside *Star Choice*, a gurney emerged from the double doors of the Med Center, pushed by two people in lab coats. Another was pushing a cart loaded with stuff—suitcases, boxes, and equipment bags. Then yet another dolly with oxygen tanks. And, thank goodness, sleeping bags—which I hadn't even thought of.

I ran back toward the big aft hatch, yelling at Wanda to open it. I pushed all the flattened cartons out onto the asphalt, then jumped down onto the landing pad to see if I could help. My first steps back on good old Earth. I said to myself softly, "Another giant step for womankind—getting back in one piece."

Even with the scissors lift, it took all of us to lift the gurney and the carts up into *Star Choice*. Poor Clay was unconscious and barely recognizable, with drip I/V feed and oxygen mask. Two medics with white coats, backpacks and doctor's cases climbed in through the open side hatch.

Finally, one more cart containing boxes. Two guys tossed them onto the scissors lift and up they came. What was this? I wondered. I pulled back the lid of one of the boxes. Food! And not just dry packaged stuff. Did I see a wine bottle? Oh boy. And a corkscrew attached with a rubber band. Yes!

"What about water?" Jonn asked. "Should we fill up your tank?" Good idea. I hadn't thought of that.

"Wanda, how do we refill our water supply? How much do we need?"

"Fresh unrecycled water is at 7 parts out of 10." Sounded like I hadn't been using much. "I will open the internal water port."

But how to fill it? With a garden hose, of course. There it was, coiled over the spigot right next to the doorway.

One of the men dragged the hose over. I clambered up into the hatch, and he handed it up to me. Wanda displayed in the view space where to stick it. "Turn it on full blast!" I yelled.

"Jonn, come over here!" I handed him a large trash bag. "This is my collection from the Apollo 11 site." His eyes just about popped out. It's the most surprised I'd ever seen him look. I tried to hide my smirk.

Then he had a surprise for me. "Selena, I want to hand this directly to you." He held up a blue medium-sized duffel bag and put it just inside the hatch. "Clean clothes—packed by Amelie and Dana—plus a special toy for you." I slid it farther inside and was surprised how heavy it was. Wow! It had to be Wanda!

"Oh, thank you Jonn!"

He grinned. "Now you never need to come back. Except to return your passengers. Wait. One last thing." He handed me a paper bag with the top twisted around the neck of a bottle. I could tell by the shape it was Jack Daniels. "Now git, before the Air Force arrives."

"Double thank you, sir! You know how to make a space girl happy." I leaned down and gave him a big hug.

I stood up, turned around, and attended to my new passengers. "Come aboard. Introductions in a minute," I yelled over the confusion.

At long last I was able to insert Wanda into the slot on the control panel where she belonged. This was symbolic, because the way *Star Choice* had been rebuilt, Wanda no longer needed to be physically present. Unless, of course, we planned to use a jumpsite to fly to other stars.

"Wanda, as we ascend, what direction will be down? I need to know how to secure things."

"*Star Choice* will retain its horizontal orientation, so that any excess acceleration that the grav can't handle will be perceived as a downward push, not toward the rear of the vessel. This will take more energy pushing air out of the way, but we will soon be above the atmosphere."

"Folks, let's get Clay's gurney secured to this worktable back here. The table has straps made of this weird material that we can wrap around the gurney legs and then fasten it to itself. Be careful not to bang your heads into those things hanging from the ceiling, like I did. Then let's push all these other boxes back between the beds, which will keep them from sliding around.

"This vessel has artificial gravity, called grav, set at 1G. But to evade any possible pursuit, we may accelerate faster than the grav can compensate. So you need to be secured into your seats."

I ran back to the hatch, dragging the water hose, and gave Jonn a thumbs up. My earlier hysterics were gone. He waved and smiled. I said, "Wanda, shut the hatch and let's go."

"Everybody secure? Good. Seat backs and tray tables in the full upright position, please." Bad time for a dumb joke. "See this big bluish sphere you can see into? It's called a view space. When we communicate with the ground, people's faces will appear here, and their voices. We can also watch what's happening outside in it. It should be a breathtaking sight." I stopped to take a breath. "Hi, I'm Selena Morisot." We were already accelerating rapidly straight up.

"Oh, we know you," said the doc. "You're the most famous spaceship hijacker in the world. I'm Herb Kleinschnitt and this is Mary O'Malley, my chief nurse. Call me Herb. No doctor stuff. We're with the Stanford Health Center and Oncology clinic. I say, this view is magnificent!"

We shook hands while hanging on to our chair arms. "I'm glad I've never needed to make your acquaintance," I said with a grin.

The view out the viewspace as we accelerated back into space was indeed breathtaking. My new passengers were enthralled. "Can it be true," Herb asked, "that you have a 3-D TV view of the outside? That would indeed be miraculous!"

"Yes, one of many miracles." It was already old hat to me. "Hope we can create some more while you're here."

Jonn and I were still connected via comm stone. Through the stone, I heard his cell phone ring. "Buck here."

Another voice. Jonn's cell must have been on speaker. "Jonn Buck, this is General Dickson. Colonel Bird says you are involved with the UFO that just landed at Stanford. And now it's taking off again. What the hell is going on there?"

"Good day, General. I urge you to take no precipitous action. My oncologist, Dr. Herbert Kleinschnitt, and his head nurse have accompanied a very sick patient onto this vessel. It will ascend into high Earth orbit where the doctor will work with the instruments on board to treat the man's cancer. They will then be brought back to Stanford."

"General," came a new voice through the phone, "the UFO took off again, just before our interceptors arrived. Radar shows very rapid acceleration. It's already above the atmosphere."

Jonn cleared his throat to get attention, and spoke into his cell phone. "General Dickson, I think this episode illustrates two important lessons for us. One, there is no way in holy hell that we are ever going to be able to corral this alien vessel against its will. Two, the capabilities on display, should they be successful, are earthshaking in their impact on Earth and its citizens. Thus, the discussion about blowing this vessel out of space or the squabbles with the Russians and Chinese are ludicrous!

"As you well know, General," he went on, "other nations of the world are not going to sit by and allow the United States to claim all these technologies for itself. Thus, our plan to set up a foundation to shepherd the fruits of technology available from this vessel—perhaps under the auspices of the United Nations—needs to be approved forthwith. Do you hear me on this?"

"Yes Mr. Buck, loud and clear. I will be briefing the President immediately after our conversation. One question. What assurance do you have that despite the positive benefits, this vessel or its creators pose no threat to the United States or to the people of Earth?"

"I'm confident that this is the case," said Jonn. "It would be difficult to explain quickly, and the best person to explain it is Ms. Morisot, who is currently attending to the care of the cancer patient. But I suspect that by later today we can arrange a hookup where she can talk directly with you or even the President. However, regardless of anything else, there is no immediate threat. There are no alien spaceships rushing toward Earth, except the one that was just here."

"All right Mr. Buck, I'll accept that for now, since you are our expert on this. Let us stay in touch. Over and out."

"Goodbye, General."

"Oh, Mr. Buck, one more thing. Are you planning to take a ride in this consarned thing?"

"If I had the opportunity to travel into space on this vessel, I would indeed be tempted, sir. On this trip though, I willingly gave up my spot to my oncologist and his nurse.

"Sir, I'd like to say one more thing. The approach has been somewhat unorthodox, but I think you must grant that I have accomplished my mission for you of getting this alien vessel back to Earth."

"Yes, for all of about five minutes," said the general with his normal sarcasm. "That thing makes our F-16s look like Piper Cubs."

Jonn said, "It's high time for you and me to work out a way for it to set down smoothly at SFO to a hero's welcome. And return my medical crew and hopefully a recovering patient. And Ms. Morisot."

"We'll see," answered the general. "We'll soon get back to you on that one. I doubt we'll force your cancer doc into permanent exile in space."

I explained to my guests how the comm stones work, so they could understand the conversation emerging from my chest.

"Out of curiosity, where are we going?" asked the doc. "Back to the Moon?"

"No need," I replied. "Just an Earth orbit high enough that we are beyond reach and interference. I must ask you, how did Jonn Buck entice or coerce you to volunteer for a mission like this?"

The doctor had a glow on his face like a kid with a new pony. "If half of what Mr. Buck says is true, I wouldn't miss this for anything! Carrot and stick, he said. Either be in on it or be left behind as this technology makes our life work redundant." His nurse nodded her head vigorously in agreement. She was smiling, but I noticed her grip was tight and her knuckles white. Like she was waiting for the roller coaster to plunge over the edge.

The doctor said, "I have long been a volunteer for Doctors Without Borders, but this is the most amazing assignment I have ever had. Way beyond borders!"

20. ICU in Orbit

Within a few minutes *Star Choice* was leveling out into orbit, and we turned our attention to Clay. "What is Clay's prognosis and how long does he have?" I asked. I could hardly bring myself to glance at him, he looked so bad.

"He is stable but we need to do whatever you have planned as soon as we can," said the doc. "What is our next step here to get started?"

"That thing hanging down from the ceiling is the instrument we will use. I call it the maker machine or the matter extractor, depending on what we're using it for. It is meant to repair things by extracting tiny bits of matter from one place and depositing it somewhere else. Like molecules and atoms, even." I described the guitar repair and the vomit removal. I told them how *Star Choice* had repaired itself after it crashed, and how, following our design, it had remodeled its interior to make it suitable for humans.

"This ship repaired itself, twice, and it is confident it can repair human bodies as well. This is the first time operating on a human. But it is a common practice on the alien worlds. Alien races also have cancer, I've been told."

Suppressed incredulity. I guess that's how I would describe the looks on their faces. "Has any such operation been done before?" Herb asked.

"Not on humans," I admitted. "I would have no confidence in it, except that I've seen this vessel do so many amazing things."

"We wouldn't be here if there were any other option," the doctor said.

"Once we get it going, I'll do my best to explain the magic to you. It has a template of a human body—taken from me—kind of like an MRI I guess. I will instruct it to accept your guidance if it has questions."

"And first I have to tell you about Wanda." I pointed at Wanda in her receptacle. "She is the voice of the vessel, and its brains. You can talk with her pretty much as you do with me, and she'll let you know if she doesn't understand. Wanda, this is Herb and Mary."

"Hello, Wanda." he said.

"Hello, Herb, medical expert."

"And this is Mary." I said.

"Hello, Mary, other medical expert."

"Hello, Wanda. I have never spoken to a space ship before," Mary said as if speaking to a small child.

"I will use my persona that I have created for Selena, my controlling oki."

Herb looked at me, "What is a controlling oki?"

"In theory, it means she obeys me and does what I tell her. Sometimes she knows better than I do."

"Sadly, this is true of all our technology, isn't it?" he said. "All right, let's get to work here. What do we do? Are we more than observers?"

"Wanda, can you move the matter extractor into place above the gurney?" The arms of the metallic octopus extended downward toward Clay.

Four of the oval balls on flexible tubes moved down from the ceiling into position above Clay. Then long filaments extended from them, getting close to Clay's skin, but not quite touching. Each tendril ended in something that looked like a tiny glass droplet.

"Wanda, can you tell us what is happening?" I asked. "How does it know what to remove?" I asked, worried that all the high tech would pass me by.

Wanda explained, "The extractor understands cancer. Oki races of many worlds have cancer. The device seeks a component of the cancer cells that, when removed, will render the cancer not functional. Cancer cells differ from normal cells; the membrane's surface is negatively charged. This helps identify them. This process is called biological error correction."

Jonn's voice emanated from the view space, startling me. I guess he'd been listening all along. He explained. "I asked Herb what substance we could extract from cancer cells that would kill them. One single thing that all cells contain. He showed me a large protein molecule with potassium atoms near the core. Remove the potassium, it can't function. It dies. So we could just remove the potassium, right?

"But the body is full of potassium atoms. Can't pull it all out. So we have to remove a large enough piece of a protein so that it is something found only in cancer cells, yet small enough so that it is common to all cancer cells. Herb gave me a schematic of the molecule he recommended, and I have uploaded it using the same method we used to communicate components to Wanda for your *Star Choice* upgrade."

Jonn went on, "The challenge is communicating this to Wanda so that the extractor knows what it is looking for. I asked Wanda how to do this. We had to give her basic chemistry lessons—starting with the periodic table of elements and atomic numbers. Wanda had to go to the alien's library to get the equivalents. Fortunately chemical elements are the same everywhere. She—see, even I'm calling it a 'she' now—only had to understand the upper rows of the table up to iron. This molecule is mainly carbon, hydrogen, nitrogen, oxygen, plus a bit of calcium, potassium and sulfur.

"As an aside, I'm certain it will stir Noel's juices to see how similar some of the alien proteins and amino acids are to the ones on Earth."

"Okay, all this makes sense," I said, almost truthfully. "I can kind of follow it. But I've never understood how Wanda or *Star Choice* can make substances move from one place to another without passing through the stuff in between, whether it's the human body, or rock on the Moon, or metal on a wrecked spaceship."

"Yes, this is the alien magic," said Jonn. "I had to get into this with Wanda in order to build the extra view space on Earth. The beads on this device will extract molecules from the cancerous tissue, even though they're separated by several inches. The tiny particles just pop through a few inches of space—from inside the body to the glass beads—without passing through the intervening space. Wanda explained it's like a miniature version of the star jump."

We waited for a few minutes while Wanda did whatever it was she needed to do. Then Jonn continued.

"Now Wanda and the extractor see what must be removed. Herb has the MRI of the cancer's spread. He will guide the extractor to the proper locations on Clay's skin and tell how deep. The extractor will focus on that area, and remove only the target substance."

Herb said, "I also have a portable ultrasound wand I can use to image the cancer. We must also make sure we don't create poisons in the body, but leave behind bits that it can clean up by normal metabolic processes. Once these critical molecules are removed from the cancer tissues, the cancer cannot reproduce; it will die and be gradually removed from the body by its own healing processes."

"We'll do the spreading cancerous filaments first," said Herb. "If we see that they are stopped, then if we need to, we can return Clay to the Med Center to have the large central tumor removed."

"How long will this take?" I asked. "Days? Hours?"

Herb shrugged. "We have no idea; this is a question for your instrument. We don't know how your instrument works."

"Wanda, can you tell us how long this will take?"

"We must answer your question by experiment," Wanda explained. "It will be slow because I am being very cautious in my instructions to the device. We are not familiar with the bodies of your kind, even though you are similar in many respects to other races. Furthermore, when we have done similar procedures on oki with such malignancies, their disease has not been so advanced."

Wanda asked, "My controlling oki, do I have your permission to communicate freely with your medical experts regarding the ongoing procedure?"

"You most certainly do, and do whatever Herb and Mary ask you. Our goal is to save the life and restore the health of my friend Clay."

Herb consulted images on his large iPad, then he and Mary guided the extractor balls to places on Clay's skin that he marked with a soft marker. The glass beads on the ends of the filaments caressed Clay's skin.

I sat next to Clay, holding his hand, continually on the verge of crying. Clay had been sedated, but he came out of it, opened his eyes, groaned and looked at me. He was startled by the contraption dangling from the ceiling above him. "How did I get here?" he asked. "Where am I? I must have died and gone to heaven!"

"I hope not, sir," I said with a smile, "because that would mean I'm dead also."

He grimaced, "Oh, it hurts." He breathed like somebody trying to avoid moving a painful body part. "They keep giving me sedatives to reduce the pain. I would rather bear it and be here with you."

"We can reduce his pain without putting him out," Mary said.

The hours passed. The extractor moved above Clay's body almost imperceptibly. It was hard to tell if anything was happening. Wanda occasionally told us that the extractor had finished the removal of substances from a tumor in some part of the body, and was moving to the next one. Good news!

During these hours, I made the beds, cleaned all my crap out of the bathroom, and then assembled what would pass for dinner. Keeping busy helped push down the deep anxiety I felt.

In our high orbit, days were about twelve hours long. That was the time it took us to go around the Earth. But we paid little attention to that. Even the most magnificent views become ho hum after awhile. When I got tired, I went to the crew area and napped and so did the medical people. They wanted to stay with him the whole time, but there's only so long you can do that. When they gained more confidence that Wanda was making progress and something was happening, and that no more information was needed from them immediately, they also rested.

I took my turn sitting with Clay, talking with him, keeping him company. I prepared food, such as it was, using my humble rations— much upgraded by the new stuff given me at Stanford.

I gave progress reports to everybody back on Earth, and listened to the latest teeth gnashing by the Agency. How could they stay so pissed for so long?

By Day 2, progress was evident. Clay's eyes were once again bright blue. When he smiled, I figured he was ripe for ribbing. "Clay, for your food, I'm having the doctor make a hole in your side so that we can shove in the feeding tube of Breadbox."

His laugh had a hint of wheeze. "Oh, that's great! Just make sure that I get some bacon and chocolate in there—and some Malbec."

This gave me a chance to chide him over giving me a bottle of Malbec with no corkscrew, and to brag about how I managed to open it, even so. "Alas, there's none left."

I didn't view the Songstone while the docs were with me. I had installed a folding divider for the sleeping area, but there was no sound privacy. I wished I had a virtual reality headset with a built in view bubble. I asked Wanda if she could create one for me. I described it with numerous hand gestures.

"Yes, in principle. If specifications exist in the Library. I shall seek them. View bubbles are complex. They take time and special materials."

A short time later Wanda reported on her search. "I find no such specifications in the Galactic Library."

That's strange, I thought. Does this mean I have thought of some gadget that doesn't exist in the entire Galactic Confederation? What an interesting thought: that we humans—primitive by galactic standards— could invent new things based on their technology. Or maybe a headset like that would be way old fashioned to them. Or perhaps they had funny shaped heads that couldn't hold headsets.

I asked Wanda a question that had been poking up in the back of my mind. "Could this maker machine do biological error correction on me?"

Wanda replied, "Yes, it could find and correct errors in your cell structure that could otherwise shorten your life. So you would likely live longer. This is a common practice among Oki world races." Then she added, "It is better to do this before you have a serious malfunction."

That idea sent a thrill of emotion coursing through my body. Very enticing, yet scary. I remember saying once that if I could be immortal, I'd want to be thirty-five forever. Well, I was already past that. Could this error correction roll back the clock?

*   *   *

I asked Wanda, "Why didn't Breadbox use this process to preserve her life?"

She replied, "She could have, even though the vessel was greatly damaged. But she did not request to use me in this way."

"Why not?"

Wanda said, "Hypothetical. Perhaps she did not have a sense of how to use me in this manner."

I shook my head. "I suspect that she did not want to extend her own life in ways that her dead crewmates could not do."

Everybody called to talk with Clay to raise his spirits—using either comm stones or their miniature view space gizmos. To use the view space we had to stop the process and wheel Clay's gurney forward to where it was, so comm stones were preferable.

"Spaceketeers, are you ready to come into space?" I asked Amelie and Dana if they wanted to hop aboard when I dropped off Clay and the docs. At first they were excited, but they demurred.

Dana said, "Yeah, I still can't endanger my baby. However, we can get you a new care package with some better stuff in it and we will have that available when you drop Clay off at Stanford."

"Oh yes, please do that."

Amelie said, "I still don't have a functioning space suit."

"Amelie, if one of those missiles hits us, having no space suit will be the least of your worries."

"Thanks, that makes me feel a lot more confident."

"Why are you even going back into space," Amelie asked me, with just a touch of attitude.

"Two reasons," I said. "First, the agreement that will safeguard my rights has not been finalized. I don't want to risk having *Star Choice* taken from me again. Second, I want to do another concert from space. See if we can get better production quality.

"And . . . I haven't yet taken a trip to the stars."

Gasps all around.

"Hee hee. Just kidding."

21. Clay is Recovering

L ights were out astern. I heard gentle snoring. Not sure who it was. I decided to take this opportunity to watch the Songstone some more, so I slid the divider closed and settled down by the view space with my new earphones on. I wished I could see more of the white wraith I had viewed earlier, but alas another group was on stage. This time, two trios, standing apart facing each other. They sang alternating lines, one side pleading, the other jeering and cynical.

> May the Gods sitting atop the snowy ridge,
> > *May they freeze their preposterous posteriors.*
> Arrayed in their jewels and finery,
> > *Tacky and tawdry and frayed and fake.*
> May they judge me fairly, may they believe me.
> > *They care not a whit for you.*
> I did not intend the ill that befell their favored.
> > *They set the two of you against each other for the sport of it.*

Next they went at each other with what I hoped was a mock battle, using sticks the size of swords to smack at each other. Then with a growl and a roar, they ran off into the darkness. Their confrontational style surprised me, but it was hysterical.

As the next group moved onto the stage I felt a hand on my shoulder and almost jumped out of my seat. I turned; it was Clay. I pulled off my earphones. "Clay, should you be up?" I looked up at him; he looked so much better. His face was calm, no hint of pain.

"Probably not. I was just lying there, looking up at the ceiling. Boring. They disconnect the gizmo during sleep periods so I can get comfortable. Say, those are some weird creatures you are watching. Can they see you?"

"No, fortunately. This is more like watching YouTube." I asked Wanda to shut it off for now, and turn the view to Earth below so Clay could see it.

"Clay, I am so glad you're here and alive, and recovering. Here, sit down." I grabbed his hand and guided him into the seat next to me.

"Me too, my friend, me too. I had given it up. No idea your alien magic could do something like this." He held onto my hand. "You know, I never wanted to go into space. But this isn't all that bad. Our world down there is breathtaking, isn't it?" We just sat and watched the world flow past for a while in the view space, like watching out the windshield of a small plane.

But I had to get something off my chest. "Clay, you're an idiot, and you really hurt my feelings, by not telling me what was going on with you."

"I know. I'm a fool. I was ashamed. I didn't want to admit it to myself, let alone you. I was terrified. I put on the big strong manly façade to cover it all. I figured that if I just died, I'd get away without admitting my stupidity to anyone."

"No no, it doesn't work that way. Everybody would know how stupid you were."

I stood up, went over to him and gave him a hug. A gentle hug, but a big sincere hug. Then I punched him on the shoulder. "That's for sending me a bottle of wine with no corkscrew." We laughed.

"If something happened to you, who was I going to talk with over Malbec? And I want to let you know, I have a lot I need to talk over with you."

I swiveled my seat so I could reach over and hold his hand again. We just sat there, enjoying being alive.

22. CNN Interview

In the midst of Clay's treatment, my agent Morty got back to me and said, "Are you ready for your CNN interview?" No, I had totally forgotten about it. But why not?

They had obviously worked with Jonn to get the TV show linked to the view space. I was amazed at the quality of it. The interviewers and I could see each other, and the audience could apparently see both of us.

The interviewers were Brett and Lisa—two of my favorite talking heads. Unlike some of my prior media interviews, they treated me with respect. After all, how could they not? No one could deny I had an alien spaceship and I was orbiting high above Earth. They put me at ease and I ended up telling the whole story.

I explained the original crash and my relationship with Breadbox, up to her death. I glossed over the actions of the government, but bragged about how I had recovered the spaceship. I regaled them with what I had done on the Moon. I explained what my desire was for the spaceship, and why I thought there wouldn't be any aliens coming. I tried to explain the likely implications of this anti-cancer procedure we were performing.

I mentioned Breadbox's home world, Sfofong, but I cleverly avoided saying anything about the galactic civilization, the Library, or the Songstone. Or Wanda and the amulet.

A couple of times I paused, concerned I was saying too much. But once I get talking, I don't want to stop.

They moderated a call-in Q and A from people anywhere in the world, via phone, Skype, Twitter, whatever. Wonderful questions. In case you missed this interview—of course the whole thing is on YouTube—here are a few of the questions to give you a flavor:

"Are there ETs with you now?"

"Is it really magical?"

"How did you learn to fly that thing?"

"What does the space ship smell like? Can you shower up there?"

"What's the food like?"

"Do you talk to yourself because you're so lonely?"

"Do you live in zero gravity so you can do flips around the space ship?"

"What do you do with the hours and hours of down time?"

"Are you ever scared?"

"Are you writing a song about this?"

"Does being in space make it hard to tune your guitar?"

And my favorite, "Will you marry me, Space Girl?"

This went on for far more than an hour, and I could have kept going. I loved being the center of attention. But I told them I had limited time to talk with them now because we were, in essence, in a hospital room and I was a caregiver for a good friend of mine while he was getting medical treatment by this magical technology.

I turned to see that Herb had edged up behind me to watch. He asked if he could say something. He signaled for Mary to come stand beside him. He introduced both of them, then made a statement.

"We've been on this spaceship from a distant world, using an instrument it contains to treat a cancer that was so advanced that the man had asked to go home to die. In just a few days here, it appears that the cancer has been neutralized.

"This is a concrete example of applying advanced alien technologies to benefit humankind. One man this time. Imagine multiplying this a million times over. A billion times.

"As an oncologist, I see clearly that this medical technology could revolutionize cancer treatment on Earth, once it became widespread. And also the treatment of many other diseases.

"We could gather exemplar pathogens of serious diseases. For example, malaria. Bring them to the lab, figure out how to counteract them using this technology, then make that process available to all people. Within a generation, we could wipe out all serious diseases in the world.

"Would this be worthwhile? You bet it would. I've heard all kinds of arguments against this: It would cost too much. It would mainly benefit wealthy people. It would mainly benefit people in developed nations. It would be disruptive of the current health care industry. If people live longer, it could cause a population explosion.

"These are good problems to have.

"Think of the next generation. Think of the people who won't die young of cancer. Think of all the children who won't die of ebola or dengue or malaria.

"But there are people who are so antagonistic to this effort that it is not safe for us to conduct this medical experiment on Earth; we have to fly into space beyond the reach of those who would stop us. I urge you, people of Earth, to talk with your leaders, and get them on board with this effort.

"I want to give a shout out to Selena Morisot and Jonn Buck for the risks they've taken to make this happen. I am honored to be a part of it. Thank you." He stepped aside.

I was wiping away tears as I faced the audience. "What could I possibly add to that? Thank you, Herb. Thank you Mary. And thank all of you out there for watching. Selena M in high Earth orbit signing off for now."

Herb and Mary and Wanda reviewed the progress, then Herb announced that enough of the cancerous tissue had been neutralized so that the natural healing processes of Clay's body could take over. "Wanda told me that your maker machine's tendrils were finding nothing more to remove. They've gone over his entire body multiple times. I've confirmed this with my ultrasound wand, which is clearly less sensitive."

He and Mary began cleaning the instruments they had brought. "This process sounds a bit like the practice of using maggots to eat away rotting flesh around wounds. And even though that had a yuck factor, in its time it was an effective treatment."

"Wanda, what is being done with the substances being removed from Clay?" I asked.

"It is being contained. It can be made available to the doctor, should he wish, but there is nothing of value because it has been broken down to its basic chemicals and molecules."

"Okay," I said. "The time has come for us to plan our return. I'll get in touch with Jonn."

If there had been any doubt, this episode truly did make up my mind for me. I saw how selfish it would be for me to dash off to distant worlds and withhold such beneficial technologies from humankind.

23. Sneaking Home

"We may be able to get you back down in time to catch the Stanford–Cal game," I announced optimistically to Herb and Mary, who were sitting with me watching the Earth roll past in the view space while Clay snored peacefully behind us. They were arguing over features on the ground below. It's a lot harder to point out countries and rivers and things when there are no boundary lines showing on a map, and key parts are obscured by clouds.

The easy return was not to be. Jonn's face popped into the view space, blocking out the Indian Ocean, with an unwelcome message. "I don't know what various parties are going to do. I do not believe the U.S. will interfere with the return of your passengers. But what about when you depart again? I can't risk your lives with a return to Stanford."

"Well, I can't keep them up here in orbit," I countered. A glance at Herb and Mary proved they agreed with me.

"I have a suggestion," Jonn asserted. "I'm in Singapore talking with some highly placed people about opening a plant here to manufacture components for Flashcar. They want me to do that. They are also eager to have access to technologies on *Star Choice*. They know I'm up to my eyeballs in your project. So when I broached the subject of letting *Star Choice* land there temporarily to offload your passengers, they said they could make available an aircraft carrier. I'm sure *Star Choice* can land on it and take off again without incident. It will happen very quickly. No one will expect that. And Singapore will defend against any intruders."

"An aircraft carrier? That's pretty amazing!"

"Let me say that Singapore is willing to host the *Star Choice* Foundation! Its high tech sector is one of the top in the world. Obviously, landing there will be less convenient for the doctors than landing back at Stanford, but a lot more secure."

I asked Herb to come up front to the view space so Jonn could explain the whole thing to him. I apologized to him for all we were putting both of them through. He shook his head. "Doctors Without Borders has taken me to many combat zones where I've been shot at. And you're the only one who ever shared your whisky with me."

Jonn was still in the view space. "Tell me what supplies you need to restock your larder so I can have that ready for you. Overhearing what

Herb just said, I'm guessing you've already finished off that Jack Daniels I gave you."

Following Jonn's instructions, *Star Choice* veered out of its orbit in the plane of the ecliptic. We belted in securely and swiveled the seats so that our backs would be toward the deceleration and turning. We knew we would not be able to evade radar tracking while in space. Once again, *Star Choice* dropped toward Earth over the southern Indian Ocean, a region of minimal instantaneous tracking. We flew northeastward at sub-orbital speed, passing west of Australia at an altitude that used the curve of the Earth to shield us from distant radars. In the pre-dawn darkness, we descended rapidly while passing above Sumatra. By the time they figured out where we were going, hopefully we would have landed and taken off again.

Just as we were landing, the Singapore state department notified all other nations that it had invited an unorthodox vessel to dock briefly, and that it would forcefully repel any attempted interruption. (They had previously informed Indonesia of our inbound path.) Any interference would be deemed an act of war against Singapore. Jonn had assured me that nobody wanted to take on the Singaporean military. Its navy, air force, and marines were top quality, to protect this small island nation surrounded by much larger ones. I felt so sad that my own nation was unwilling to make a similar declaration, thus necessitating this landing half way around the world.

The Singaporean carrier was moored in the harbor, surrounded by other ships. Jonn was there to greet us on the deck. I spotted him as we zipped in, using his comm stone as a homing device. He stood near a large white X. The carrier was surrounded by several missile frigates with missile batteries aimed and at the ready. On the deck near where we landed was a large medivac helicopter.

The sea was calm; there was no pitch to the deck. We landed soft and smooth, just a few yards from where Jonn was standing. Men in white uniforms rushed from an open doorway pushing a gurney and two powered flat carts. Other men in camo gear and berets ringed us, machine guns pointing at the sky. Not sure what they could do against an incoming missile but it sure looked impressive. Brought tears to my eyes. At least some powerful people here on Earth were on our side.

Wanda opened the aft hatch and warm humid air flooded in. I didn't realize how stinky it was inside until I smelled fresh sea air. Clay wanted to walk out but Herb prevailed on him to sit on the gurney with its back tilted up. I grabbed him and gave him a hug and kiss that just about pulled him off the gurney. He looked 100% better than when we had loaded him on.

"Herb. Mary. I am so grateful to you for the sacrifice you've made." I gave both of them a huge hug as well.

Herb looked at me over the top of his glasses. "My friend, I would not have missed this for anything. This will change the way medicine is done on our world, for cancer and many other things. I am honored to be a part of it. I am your vocal advocate from now on. You are doing the right thing, and I am with you." He took both my hands in his. "Anybody who would go through this risk, this hazard, for a friend, is . . . I have trouble finding the words. You are amazing. Be safe. Be safe until this government craziness passes and sanity again prevails. I will help Jonn in whatever way I can to bring this about."

Jonn came over as the others were disembarking. He grabbed my hand, then gave me a big hug. It's the most emotion I'd ever seen him express. "How are you doing, Moon Lady?"

"I'm doing fine. What an experience! Wish I was staying here."

"I'm sure sorry we aren't yet ready for you to stay on solid ground. I'm sorry I can't hop in there with you to keep you company back into space. If this event hadn't unfolded so rapidly, Amelie would be here. As it is, I put together a bundle of clean clothes for you, following her instructions."

"You went shopping for underwear for me?"

"Oh no. Oh no. I wouldn't dare take on such a responsibility. I delegated this to a young Singaporean woman who's about your size, and had Amelie coach her during the shopping trip."

I handed him my garbage bag of dirty laundry. But I kept the outfit that had been sanitized by the matter extractor.

He shook his head. "If I were less scrupulous, I could sell all these grungy items for enough to recoup much of my costs. 'Worn by the lady in space!' Just kidding."

"Your imagination is way too weird." I punched him in the shoulder.

I gave him a kiss. "I can't tell you how much I appreciate all you've gone through to take care of this for Clay."

He had to play down his part with a 'twas nothing response. "I was already here in Singapore. They are courting me to build some components here, so I had some leverage with them."

I sighed and looked around at my beautiful world. For the moment, all was well, and I felt at peace. The pre-sunrise colors in the east were magnificent. Behind me, a rain squall. As the sun rose above the horizon, it created a rainbow in the gray clouds. No, a double rainbow! That had to be a sign of good luck.

Ha! Good luck with that.

24. Back Into Orbit, Alas

*S*tar *Choice* took off from the Singaporean aircraft carrier, angled up into the sky, and headed east above the equator across the South Pacific back toward high Earth orbit. It was miraculous and magnificent, but I was barely paying attention.

Half an hour into my flight, I rousted Jonn out of a meeting with Singaporean bigwigs. "Jonn," I pleaded like a kid, "I'm ready to come home. I'm tired of this. I've had my space jaunt. Make something happen. Hu said they plan to just wait me out. Now I have a lot of food, but I have no desire to keep orbiting for weeks or months. I told Amelie I wanted to do another concert from space, but my heart's not in this just now."

"Yes, I hear you. There's movement on the ground, believe it or not. Two things: Singapore is seriously negotiating with us to sponsor a foundation to oversee the technology of *Star Choice*. I'm in a meeting with them right now. Nearby nations—Australia, Indonesia, Malaysia, the Philippines—are on board with this. They'll do nothing to oppose it. They want some of the gravy.

"Secondly, your CNN interview, with Herb Kleinschnitt's brief statement at the end, has had a positive impact in many parts of the world. Especially in the US. Public sentiment is turning. People see a popular singer and a respected doctor talking to them from space, and it's not an alien UFO any more. They ask, why is our government harassing these people?"

"So, how long do you think?"

"A Senate committee says it wants to bring in Noel and me to brief them. That's the best sign yet."

"Make it happen, sir," I implored. "Make it happen. You know where to find me."

My spirits rose as *Star Choice* rose into space. I sat watching the Earth turn beneath us in the view space. What a gorgeous world! I opened Jonn's gift of Jack and poured a tiny amount into a cup. No idea how long I'd have to make this last. Mmm, so tasty, even though I would have preferred it on the rocks. Could Wanda make ice cubes? Then I retrieved Gibb, sat cross-legged in my captain's chair, and sang to myself.

Just then I received a contact from Kateh. "Oh no," I muttered, "She's assembled the clan mothers who are now waiting to connect so I can solve

92

their problems."

"Kateh, clan mother of my dear departed best friend Nala, whom I called Breadbox. I am so pleased to hear from you. Do you bring news about the plight of the clan mothers?"

"Selena, best friend and caregiver of my sorely missed clan daughter, I have enjoyed our past conversations."

"As have I. What shall we discuss now? Are your clan mothers with you?"

"No, not at this time." Her momentary silence spoke volumes of frustration.

"Since I have been unsuccessful inducing them to talk with you, may I take this opportunity to tell you a bit of our history? It may help you understand why I wish to engage you with them."

I looked at her with a bemused smile. A history lesson? But I said, "Please do. I would love to hear that."

"We Fofonoloy were once renowned explorers of star systems. But we trod on the worlds of others, and were forced back to our own world. We were a proud race, on top of the Confederation hierarchy, but we were too pushy for beings with Type 2 bodies that don't stand upright.

She spoke like a college professor giving a lecture. Should I be taking notes? "Many world races felt we were encroaching where we were unwanted. The leaders of the Confederation confronted us, asked us to curtail our explorations and stay closer to home.

"The Confederation is dominated by Type 1 races like your kind. We were defeated, beaten back, forced to give up our joyful lives of exploration and interchange. Our elders were intimidated, afraid we would be banished from the Confederation."

This was fascinating, but I wondered if this would relate to why the clan mothers didn't want to talk with me.

"This led our Elders to ban exploration and innovation, except for trivial things. A new culture emerged—timid, controlled by conservative Elders.

"We became more Talki, less Singi. Singing became constrained, channeled into certain types of expression. The Elders told us what to sing. That is why Nala fled; she was unwilling to be limited in her singing."

"Yes," I replied. "She told me all about that."

She continued. "Our world is so beautiful, but we are forbidden from enjoying most of it. We are limited to enclaves. The rest is reserved for others—semi oki and lower beings.

"We were made to be ashamed of our own body type, our own spirits, our own surroundings, our own dreams and desires, our own accomplishments.

"That is what we have become. Sad to say, most of our kind seem content."

She began speaking with more fervor, which Wanda captured well.

"We cower before the Type 1s, yet we despise them. We know our technology and tools are superior to those of the leading worlds of the Confederation, yet the Type 1 races lord over us, tell us what we can and cannot do. We are held in check by those we consider our inferiors."

This echoed much of what Breadbox had told me, back under the oak tree near her crashed vessel. It rekindled feelings and memories I thought I'd safely tucked away.

How could an advanced star faring race regress like that, I wondered? Could this happen to Earth?

And what could I do about it? "My people are Type 1 Talkis, the kind your people despise. So how could I possibly help your clan mothers?"

"They need to listen to a clear Talki voice like yours," she replied, but I couldn't see it.

"I will try—if they will talk with me."

I shook my head as she signed off.

*　　*　　*

I was looking down on the west coast of Africa when Hu called once again. "You may have waited too long. I'm on your side, but I can't control what these people do."

"What are they doing now?" I asked.

"It's what they won't do. The Agency won't interfere with the Chinese effort to kill the so-called UFO. That's you. When you landed at Singapore, you should have stayed landed. I hate to say it, but this may be the last time we talk. I do like your music." He just stayed silent for a while. I could hear him breathing. Then he hung up.

He was so irritating. What were the Chinese up to, I wondered? I went back to serenading myself till I dozed off.

25. Running For My Life

Jonn called while I was sleeping. I was dopey. "I have bad news. China has put a platform into orbit from which it can fire rockets. So make sure you take *Star Choice* into a very high orbit, perhaps a quarter of the way to the Moon. I know you have shielding to protect you from Van Allen belt radiation, but I don't know how effective it is. No reason to take chances. So you should get beyond it.

"I will be orbiting in the middle of nowhere, won't I?" I said as I instructed Wanda how much higher to take us.

"Yes, I'm afraid so." A long pause. "Selena, I want to tell you something else."

He said this in the tone of voice you use to tell your long-time lover you're breaking up. I was afraid he was going to say, "I'm fed up with your crazy alien spaceship adventure. I've got to focus on my real work." I kind of squinched up, waiting for it. But instead . . .

"I have told General Dickson that YouSpace is resigning from their project, effective immediately, because they won't guarantee the safety of your vessel—and you."

"What?" I gasped.

"They gave me some mumbo jumbo about *Star Choice* not being property of the United States, and having no treaty with whomever the rightful owner is, so by international law they cannot agree to defend you."

Tears of relief just burst forth. I couldn't control myself. I cried like a baby.

"I think that is bullbleep and . . . what is the matter with you?"

"I thought you were bailing on me. I am so sorry to be the cause of you losing this lucrative contract."

"Now listen, my friend. You caused nothing. This is on them." I could see that Jonn was not good at dealing with a crying female. He stuttered and bumbled and made no sense at all. Until he said softly, "I am on your team, lady."

This caused me to cry all the harder. Until I just burst out laughing. "What a crazy situation this is, Jonn. I would have folded long ago if not for you."

*   *   *

I remember visiting family in the Midwest long ago. My uncle came in to where we kids were playing and announced, "There's a tornado heading this way. We'd better take cover in the storm room." We all huddled in this closet with just one dim light bulb and a noisy ventilation fan; then we waited and waited, expecting destruction at any moment. That's what I felt like in this situation. Waiting for destruction. It never happened back then; would I be so lucky this time?

Wanda broke into my reverie and said softly, "There's a rocket heading toward us from near your world, but it is not close. I can evade it. It is not a chemical rocket, and is moving slowly. I find it curious. I can see a sequence of rockets being fired from a vessel in orbit at the top of the thick atmosphere. These rockets start with rapid acceleration, then that engine is replaced by a different type of engine. Lesser thrust. Different radiation signature."

I watched as Wanda zoomed in on rockets going in different directions, none directly toward us. Then Jonn's face popped into the view space. I said to him, "Jonn, I asked Wanda to put your face in a corner of the view space, so I can keep watch on whoever is shooting at me."

"That's fine. You know what my mug looks like. We'll do the same on our end. Selena, I want to ask your permission to bring a colleague into this conversation. Rogers, one of my consulting engineers. Formerly of NASA and military spacecraft testing. He can advise us on getting you through this threat safely."

"Yes, I remember Rogers. By all means, bring him on. Hello! Selena here. Is it Roger or Rogers?"

"Rogers is my family name. So obviously my nickname is Buck."

"Ah yes, Buck Rogers. Do you have a little robot sidekick?"

"That would be Twiki. I wish I did. Jonn says you really do have a robot sidekick."

"Yes. That's Wanda. Not as cute as Twiki. But she's the brain of this spaceship. Wanda, I want to include Mr. Buck Rogers in our conversation."

"Yes, my controlling oki."

"Selena," Jonn said, "Rogers pays close attention to the space programs of other nations, including the Chinese. He has some insight into the current situation."

"I can describe what is happening, but not why," Rogers said. "The Chinese have launched two platforms into low Earth orbit, scarcely above the atmosphere. From these platforms, they are launching two-stage rockets with a high-thrust initial stage to get close to Earth escape velocity, then a main stage that is an ion drive. That's surprising. They have repurposed these from their Mars mission. Must have been a hurry-hurry effort. Ion drives have low but continuous thrust. I would only use one for an expected long pursuit.

Jonn grunted agreement. "They have launched a number of these rockets. All are moving slowly into higher orbits, even as you do the same.

They may be able to attain the altitude of *Star Choice*. But they can't catch you. If they fire missiles, you should be able to stay far enough removed to evade them."

"I'm tracking something via satellite feed that doesn't appear in your view space," Rogers said. "Be careful of one in a much higher orbit. They launched it separately from a site in far western China. As if to sneak above you while you're fixated on all these lower ones. It may have multiple missiles in an external bracket."

"Selena, make sure you are secured," Jonn warned, "because *Star Choice* may have to take evasive maneuvers. I sure wish *Star Choice* had some offensive weapons."

"Me too!" I said, making a hand gesture of shooting a pistol. "I guess *Star Choice* could have created some when it was on the Moon. I never expected we'd have to defend ourselves in a dog fight."

"I'm researching this on my laptop," Rogers said. "These ion drives could chase *Star Choice* all the way to the Moon. Or beyond."

I watched with growing alarm as the rockets spread out in a pattern, but always moving in our direction. It reminded me of a pack of wolves stalking a bear.

"The large one at top altitude is a weapon platform, firing a spray of missiles," Jonn announced, "each starting in one direction then veering toward *Star Choice*. Wanda, can you evade these?"

Unlike the others, whose voices emanated from the image of their faces in the view space, Wanda's seemed to come from the entire space. "Yes we can evade them, but if this continues, our energy reserves will grow low."

"Wow, that was unexpected!" Jonn shouted. "A laser burst from a rocket at a lower altitude."

Rogers replied, "Ground telescope indicates it has a mounted laser cannon that can be swiveled to aim."

Wanda confirmed. "Not quite on target. Strength reduced by distance. Some of its energy absorbed by radiation shield. *Star Choice* will accelerate farther upstream. We are taking a weaving trajectory based on random changes."

"Another laser bolt," Jonn yelled, sounding surprised. "From the top altitude weapon platform."

"We are hit by the energy beam!" Wanda exclaimed. After a short pause, she said, "Indirect. But damage." She sounded analytical, the way I would tell you I just had a mosquito bite. But the effects were immediate. The lights dimmed and the grav diminished, which made me feel like I was falling. Just for a second or two. She spoke to me in a voice that came from her body, not the view space, so it had a completely different tone. Soft, muted. Sounded anguished to my ear. "My controlling oki, I am injured. *Star Choice* was hit in the left side propulsion bar. Propulsion is reduced. I will endeavor to retain all interior comforts for you." I had never heard Wanda sound like this. I couldn't respond; my teeth were chattering.

Another laser flash. I could see it in the view space, but off target. The weapon platform had us in its sights. I was a sitting duck. There was no escape—I was about to die. I was too terrified to do anything.

"Take collision trajectory!" Rogers yelled frantically. "Selena, tell *Star Choice* to change course and fly directly toward the top vessel."

"Wanda, do what he says," I squeaked, hardly able to speak.

"Yes, my controlling oki."

"Wanda, use your strong remaining propulsion to take a sharp trajectory toward that weapon platform, so you can use your push force against it that you told me about. Nudge it aside and any missiles they fire at you. This should be easier to do if you're heading directly toward them."

Wanda responded, "Yes Rogers. Maximum push force will be deployed as we approach the top vessel." I watched stars rotate across the view space as we changed course. I was slammed into my seat by G force greater than my grav could compensate for.

I finally spotted the platform that had fired lasers at us. The view space zoomed in on a dark, ungainly contraption, bristling with cylinders that must be missiles.

Then a yellow circle appeared around it. "Our push system is tracking it," Wanda said. Wanda extended our push force straight ahead—a slender cone of energy like a knight's jousting pole, designed to push space debris aside.

I saw several cylinders detach from the platform and flash away in our direction. I awaited impact and death, but they moved past us on both sides. Then flashes of detonation. No whoosh or bang, but I did hear some thumps. "Pieces of debris from the explosion hit *Star Choice*," Wanda announced, "but no damage."

Even as it fired missiles at us, the platform was pushed aside with enough force to break it into fragments. A second later we flashed through its debris field. Then the view space was empty. Wanda said, "Yes. Push force deflected the vessel, causing it to break apart."

Safe for now! I wondered briefly if there'd been a human crew.

"Whoopee! We got one!" Rogers exulted, watching from the safety of Earth. I felt less enthused. I was drenched in sweat and my heart rate must have been 200.

"My friend," Jonn said, "We are all holding our breath for you. We recognize that this is life and death for you, even as it feels like a video game to us. Let us get you out of this peril."

Rogers was apologetic. "So sorry to take this lightly. Jonn is right, I was way out of line."

"Apology accepted, Mr. Rogers" I nodded my head and tried to calm my heart. "It was your idea that let us escape its attack. You demonstrated that *Star Choice* does have an offensive weapon. I wish we had one in our tail."

"I doubt the push beam would work against a laser beam," said Jonn. "Let's not put it to the test."

As we watched, the lower vessels fired laser bursts, but they were apparently too distant from us, Wanda said. "Only a spreading wave of strong energy. Temporarily we are out of range."

Rogers explained, "Once they fire it takes them a while to recharge before they can fire again. You are far enough from them that the light speed lag will make it very difficult for them to target you if you make small random unpredictable trajectory shifts. Even if they miss you by a couple of arc seconds."

I had no idea what direction we were travelling, except that Earth kept getting smaller behind us.

I wondered if we had lost them. Jonn observed, "We are fast, but they are slow and steady. We are the hare, they're the tortoises, and the hare is injured. They may be able to chase us all the way to Mars."

Wanda confirmed this by announcing, "My controlling oki, my energy reserves are dwindling. To recharge them, I need a time without drain on the system."

I responded, "I thought *Star Choice* had unlimited energy. I thought you recharged from the space behind space."

Wanda replied, "Maximum reserves are quite high, yes. We can recharge as you describe, yes. But it takes substantial time. Not instantaneous. We cannot perform this function while being pursued. I am sorry, my controlling oki. So many demands on my reserves in recent time periods. I will enumerate. The rapid descent and ascent through heavy atmosphere required much energy to push air away. Matter extractor and maker machine require much energy. All the recent evasive maneuvers. And now we must compensate for injury to propulsion."

The view space displayed the various missiles changing direction to pursue our new direction. "These pursuit missiles are a lot more powerful than we anticipated," Jonn observed. "We didn't know China had such weapons."

Rogers replied, "Well at least we've forced them to reveal the direction of their weapon development."

Jonn grunted. "This will be of little value if we lose *Star Choice* and Selena."

"Continued evasive maneuvers will serve in the short time, but each shift allows them to overtake us a fraction, and draws down energy reserves rapidly," Wanda informed us.

"How do they track us?" I asked. "By radar?"

Rogers responded, "I have learned through covert sources that they can track ultraviolet emissions from the propulsion of *Star Choice* when it is accelerating or changing course. So if you're taking evasive action, you're easier to track. But if you don't evade, they can more easily draw a bead on you. I suspect they would then simultaneously fire lasers from several rockets, which may overwhelm your defenses."

Each such pronouncement seemed to spell doom to me. It was just a matter of time till they got me. "*Star Choice* will eventually be overtaken, so we must take some effective evasive action soon."

"Is there a way to lose them?" Jonn asked. "Could *Star Choice* put on a burst of speed, then cease accelerating so she couldn't be tracked by ultraviolet?"

"You'd have to obscure the initial acceleration, or they'd know your new trajectory," replied Rogers.

"Even if that worked, it would only be temporary," I countered. "They would eventually spot us again. I've got to be going somewhere. But where can I go? I'm still a sitting duck, awaiting death."

26. So Many Ways to Flash Out of Existence

At this point Amelie and Dana and then Noel all joined in the call via their comm stones with the newly added tiny view bubble each had. Fascinating to see all their images arrayed in the view space as if they were together in one location. We had to bring them up to date. "I'm still alive, but just barely."

Jonn summed up. "*Star Choice* has learned to evade the missiles, but Wanda must be vigilant and use a lot of her energy and attention, and also move into more distant orbits or trajectories. She's hampered by the damaged propulsion. Wanda and *Star Choice* both need to recharge and that takes some time. It must drift in space without acceleration, or else land."

Now I had an astrophysicist, an astronaut, the head of a rocket company, a space weapons expert—plus one college student—all trying to figure out how to save me. With a brain trust like this, I should feel pretty good you'd think.

But no. I whined, "I don't want to just drift in deep space, waiting to get fried by a laser."

"Where could we go that they can't follow?" Amelie asked.

"Could we get back to Earth?" Dana asked. "Land in a place where no one dares attack?"

Jonn pointed out, "The closer you come to Earth; the less space must be defended by the Chinese. It's like flying down a funnel. Plus, *Star Choice* is low on juice. It may be difficult to make a rapid plunge through the atmosphere. I kick myself for not foreseeing this when *Star Choice* was safe in Singapore."

"Maybe you should go to Mars," Amelie suggested.

Wanda broke in. "Mars currently orbits on the opposite side of the Sun from Earth. Very distant and higher up in the Sun's gravity well. Travelling to that world would take a lot of power."

"And be easy to follow," said Jonn. "Either fast, requiring a lot of power you don't have, or slow, and be vulnerable to your pursuers."

An idea had been poking up from the bottom layers of my mind, and despite my best efforts to shove it back down, I blurted it out. "We could go through the star jump. Nobody could follow us there."

Total silence.

"That's crazy!" yelled Amelie. "You can't be safe in our solar system, so you want to jump to a whole different star system?"

Wanda said matter-of-factly, "Jumping to a different star system requires less energy than traveling to Mars."

"Go to the stars, not to Mars," said Dana with an attempt at lightness.

I countered my own idea. "It is crazy. We might not be able to get back. The propulsion system may not be able to get us back here. I may be marooned there."

"Agreed. It's crazy," said Amelie. "Next idea?"

No other idea was immediately forthcoming, so I said, "Well, while we're trying to think of other alternatives, Amelie and Noel, you should figure out where *Star Choice* could jump to if no other option appears."

Jonn had been quiet. "Selena, is this even possible?" Everybody went silent, awaiting my answer.

I sighed. "I have Wanda now. I have the jump codes. I have *Star Choice*. I say yes, it's possible. Wanda, is it possible?"

"Yes, my controlling oki, it is possible. It may not be advisable."

I nodded emphatically and waved my fist. "I tell you, it's not advisable! I don't want to do this!" I looked at everybody in the view space. "We'll jump somewhere and I'll never be able to get back. Or the jump won't work—it's untested since it was rebuilt. Or the propulsion system won't be able to power us back here. I am scared, people! Scared to the depth of my soul." Then I paused a moment and took a breath. "But it may better than getting blown to smithereens. If we don't do something, I'm dead anyway."

No one said anything. This was on me. It was my life that hung in the balance, and they all knew it. "Wanda, can we get back? Please tell me."

She responded, "Yes, we can return, if we have sufficient time, and if I can recharge, and if I can repair the propulsion system." That was a lot of ifs.

"Wait a minute," Rogers broke in. "What does this mean—go through the star jump? I have no idea what you all are talking about."

Jonn gave a shot at explaining this. "Alien vessels like this one travel from star to star, not by using some kind of warp speed, but by tunneling from one star to another without passing through the intervening space. They use terminals that have been positioned in orbit around various stars."

"This is way beyond my pay grade," Rogers said, shaking his head in disbelief. "Where are these terminals?"

I didn't know the answer to this, nor did Jonn or Amelie. I asked, "Wanda, where is the jump terminal for our world?"

"At the leading gravity balance point between your world and your sun."

"Ah," Noel exclaimed. "Lagrange point! Makes perfect sense. I wondered how they could stay in place over eons of time. The leading point is L4, which is one sixth of the way around the sun in the same orbit as the Earth."

"One sixth?" Jonn asked with incredulity. "Well, that would be the same as the distance to the sun—about 93 million miles. How long would it take *Star Choice* to travel that far?"

"Time required for travel depends on our velocity relative to it," Wanda said, stating the obvious.

"And being able to outpace the rockets behind me," I pointed out. "If they get close, I never get there. Or anywhere."

"Okay, this is just half the equation," Noel said. "Where would you go, and how would you get there?

I had always resisted revealing my amulet to people, for whatever reason I had forgotten. Time to let that go. "Jonn, your view space can mirror ours on *Star Choice*, right? A crystal that I have contains a map of all the jump codes. Watch this."

I unfastened the thin chain around my neck, removed the amulet and inserted it into a slot on the console beside Wanda. A 3-D star map of the Milky Way appeared in the view space. "Do you see this star map also?"

"Oh, yes! Magnificent!" Everybody oohed and ahhed.

"Where have you been hiding this?" Jonn asked.

"I wear it around my neck on the same chain as my comm stone. Hiding in plain sight."

Those I could see in the view space had their mouths agape looking at the majesty of this 3D map of our galaxy.

"But this must show billions of stars," Amelie noted, going immediately to the practicality of it. "What good does this do us?"

"Wanda, in the view space, zoom in on Earth's star, called Sun," I said, "and show neighboring stars, out to maybe fifty lightyears." The image spread as our view zoomed inward past millions of stars. I wasn't sure what the initial perspective had been. Seemed like it had been from outside our galaxy, which was totally impossible. Maybe not for whoever created this, though. Finally, one insignificant star showed in the center of the view space, with other stars spread out around it. "There's our sun, folks.

I could hear Noel giggling. "This is more than I ever hoped to see!" he said with a young boy's glee. "Look at this! I can recognize other stars. See the brighter one close to the Sun?" He pointed with a pencil. "That's Sirius. And see right next to the Sun? That's the Alpha Centauri group," he said, waving the pencil. "This must be Betelgeuse. And Vega there. I only recognize the big ones. Oh my, I could dive into this all day and night."

I explained a key point. "I'm remembering something that Breadbox, my alien friend, told me long ago when she was first telling me about this crystal. This map doesn't show every star—only the ones with jump codes. Plus some large, bright signpost stars. She told me there are innumerable red and brown dwarfs that don't show, because nobody ever cared about them. Likewise not all the double or triple star systems that lack planets anybody ever wanted to travel to. Also black holes and other unappealing destinations."

"Wanda, reveal the codes," I requested. Next to each star appeared a small squiggly tag. "These are the codes that *Star Choice* reads to activate the jump to a particular star system from our jump site. It's actually a small piece of music."

"How did you find out all this?" Jonn asked.

"I've had Wanda as a tutor. And lots of time on my hands floating around in space."

It took a moment for this to sink in. They were looking at this like seeing the Rosetta Stone for the first time.

"Okay, I see the concept. So, where should we jump to?" Jonn asked.

"This is a Jonn, Amelie, and Noel question," I replied.

Noel jumped in. "I presume we prefer a star system nearby in cosmic terms, not half way across the galaxy." I was pleased that these guys were saying "we" even though it was just me up here. It indicated they saw themselves as key members of the team. I was always a bit insecure about that. "We would also prefer a somewhat earthlike world that has water and hopefully oxygen—in case these needed to be replenished."

"Why nearby?" Dana asked.

"We want to send Selena to a world about which we have some astronomical data. That means close. If we had more time we could get the big gun telescopes to gather more data on the best candidates, so Selena is more likely to jump to a hospitable planet."

"Why does it even matter what kind of world she jumps to?" Rogers asked. "She's not planning on landing anyway."

"Because. Two reasons," Amelie said. "Selena might need water. Drinkable water. Not ice or steam. Also, well, psychological reasons. It would be very depressing to orbit some bleak, cold, dark world. Or a gas giant. Even temporarily."

"And what if, by some strange chance, Selena can't return right away? She would need some possibility of life support," Dana added.

"Selena, didn't you say that all the worlds on this jump network were of interest to beings like us? That sounds like earthlike planets to me," Amelie said.

Noel wagged his pencil like a professor. "Way too many 'earthlike' exo-planets have turned out to be not very earthlike at all. We can't assume that."

They were all busily talking with each other. "Listen, everybody, while you are working on this, I want to talk to my oldest friend, Clay. I'm going toward the back where I have privacy and I'll use the comm stone."

Let them decide my fate. I trusted them more than anybody else. If I could get out of this, they'd be the ones to figure out how.

I unbuckled from my seat, grabbed the comm stone, and left the view space, which was serving as the party line connection for these various people—and as their video display. I walked to the rear and sat on the maker machine worktable. I spoke softly into my comm stone. "Mmm, Teach. You there?"

It took him only a few seconds to answer. It sounded like his 2 am voice. Where was he? Must still be in Singapore. "Yeah, I'm here for you, Selena. I'm worried about you."

"Clay, I'm sorry I woke you up."

"No prob. I had to get up for my talking rock anyway." A really old joke, but I giggled even so. "Hold on a sec," he said. "Now that I'm awake, I've got to take a pee."

He was back in a minute. I dove right in. "I feel my death approaching, Clay. I'm about to take a step and I cannot see how it can work for me. They always said I'm a ditzy chick and in way over my head. Right now I really feel that way." I explained the crazy chase through space, the damage to *Star Choice*, and the plan to jump to a different star.

"Selena . . . Look, woman . . . I don't know what to say. I have no wisdom, no wise words on this. What I know is this: The magic of *Star Choice* and Wanda saved my life, brought me back from the almost dead. Can Wanda save you now? Let's ask her."

"Wanda, can you talk with me while you're working with those others?"

"Yes, my controlling oki," she said through my comm stone, so Clay could hear her also.

"If we have to jump to a different star system, are you sure you can you get us back here safely?" I'd already asked her this more than once, but I needed reassurance big time.

"Wanda will do all that can be done to protect the life of Selena, my controlling oki. And to save the amulet. It is also important to save. Jumping from one system to another is a common occurrence among vessels of the Galactic Confederation. *Star Choice* is one of the most capable vessels. Wanda is confident of this, as long as we have the opportunity to recharge energy reserves."

"So we have to jump somewhere, cruise for awhile, then jump back?"

"Yes."

"Okay, let's do it. Or die trying," I said with resignation.

"That's not funny," said Clay.

"Well, it's the damn truth. Thank you, Clay, my best buddy." I wanted more than anything else to hug him and let him squeeze me.

"As much as I don't want to go back into space, I wish I were there with you. Take care."

"Thank you, my friend. I'd rather go boogie with you down at Locos Only. I'm going back up front with the others." I didn't even remember to ask him how he was doing.

When I returned to the command section of *Star Choice*, the brain trust assembled in the view space was ready for me.

"Here's our plan," explained Noel. "Astronomers have identified a few earthlike worlds around sunlike stars out to about a hundred lightyears. We will correlate these stars with the starmap projected in the view space, and make sure they have jump codes. We'll make sure Wanda notes those jump codes, plus of course the one for our solar system. We're choosing two or three, since we don't have enough reliable data on exoplanets. Here are a few candidates. We've detected water vapor in the spectra-analysis of this one," he said, pointing at a pinprick of light with his pencil. "If the first one isn't suitable, you can jump to another one. Does that make sense? Does it meet with your approval?"

"Yes and yes," I nodded. "I'm on board. I mean literally."

"Okay then, let's talk details."

We had to figure this out while *Star Choice* was still being pursued by the laser-firing rockets. They weren't close now, but they could catch up.

"If *Star Choice* were at full power, you could accelerate and leave them in space dust. But you're limited," Jonn said.

"Right now we're ahead of them," Amelie added, "but we have to keep making tiny evasive maneuvers, which slows us down and uses lots of power that we can't spare."

"Their laser blasts have spread enough that all *Star Choice* experiences is a slight heat surge," Rogers said. "What do you think, Amelie?"

"Heat build up can be very dangerous in space," Amelie said. "What does *Star Choice* do with the heat?"

"I'll ask Wanda."

"My radiation shield can easily transmute small amounts of infrared radiation into a usable form. But not a large direct charge like the one that injured us."

"God, they just keep firing," Dana said. "They fire a barrage, then pause to recharge, then fire again."

"Too bad you can't release a cloud of particles behind you that would absorb or deflect the energy from the lasers," Rogers said.

"That's interesting," I said. "Maybe we could do that. Water plus metal particles stored in the maker machine as potential raw material. I could set them in containers in the rear air lock, then open the lock. Air escaping would push them out and they'd spread into a cloud that would stay behind us for a good while."

"I like that! If they fire lasers into that cloud, it will just light up the cloud," Amelie said.

"As long as they are behind you," Rogers said. "They'll soon learn they should spread out more."

"If you're going to change course toward the jump site, you don't want them following you there," Amelie said. "So you've got to lose them. We don't yet have a plan for this."

"I have an idea . . ." said Noel, with a hint of conspiracy.

27. Possum

"Ladies and gentlemen," said the news anchor, "it is with heavy heart that I announce the likely death of singer Selena Morisot, who has fired the imaginations of everybody on Earth by flying an alien spaceship into orbit and then conducting interviews and music concerts from space. Her vessel, which she dubbed *Star Choice*, has apparently been severely damaged by laser weapons fired by rockets launched from China, and is no longer space worthy. All signals and communications from the vessel have ceased.

"This information comes to us from an unnamed source within the federal government that must remain anonymous because he or she is not authorized to release it.

"I switch you now to Dr. Max Burns, a consulting engineer at NASA, and an expert on lasers. Dr. Burns?"

"Thank you, Rick. The last communication from Ms. Morisot informed us that there was an intolerable build up of heat within the vessel and that instruments were beginning to fail. We surmise that the pursuers trained several laser weapons on the vessel at one time. The cumulative effect overwhelmed the vessel's systems. We spotted a cloud of particles indicating an explosion aboard the vessel. No messages since that moment."

"Thank you, Dr. Burns. No government authorities will speak to us on the record at this time. We will keep you apprised of developments. Now back to your regular newscast."

*   *   *

Dear readers, hopefully this didn't alarm you too much. It shows how we got the missiles off our tail and made our getaway. We arranged for "leaks" from "authoritative sources" that we—I—had been killed. It gives me the shivers to even think about this broadcast again.

Did it work? Yes, well enough. I'm still here telling my story. Our sources said the Chinese rockets had lost the target and were going into maintenance orbits. Word was that they were quietly happy that they had destroyed us, but feared the backlash—including from their own public. So they were not admitting anything.

Noel's idea had been to time a quick change of trajectory to coincide with the release of a cloud of stuff out our tail—just as an octopus eludes pursuit. We ejected many gallons of wastewater that contained small particles of metal (from the stash of raw materials *Star Choice* holds) out the rear hatch. It immediately froze and dispersed as a cloud of ice crystals containing flecks of metal. Good radar reflectivity. All radar eyes must have focused on this cloud, so from their perspective, *Star Choice* just vanished. The cloud's spread obscured our course change. Also contained flecks of other stuff. You know what "wastewater" is! I hoped they flew right through it.

I don't know what I was feeling so joyful about. I still had the impossible star jump ahead of me. Even if we made it, I'd be farther away from home than ever. Great possibility for disaster, very small chance of survival.

28. Nowhere Fast

We put on a burst of acceleration on a trajectory toward the jump site. So we were headed "sideways" along Earth's orbit. Either we'd make the jump or we'd just cruise aimlessly around the solar system.

"How long will it take us to get to the jump site now?" I asked.

"Length of time similar to four of your days," Wanda replied. "If *Star Choice* had full power, we could accelerate continuously and arrive there in just part of a day. We must conserve power to use for the jump, and we also want to remain unseen by those vessels that have pursued us. I shall begin my energy recharge process."

That's fine, but what would I do for four days drifting alone in space? Days of boredom alone in space. Much preferable to stark terror, I must say. My team members promised to take turns holding virtual hands with me to keep me company.

We had some interesting conversations.

"So if we're on a trajectory and not under power, they cannot track us?" I asked Rogers.

"You show only visual wavelengths, or infrared," he replied, "but a dull grey vessel in deep space is pretty invisible. Unless it's spotted moving against stars. That's called occultation. Highly unlikely. And if some observatory did spot you, they're unlikely to report that to the Chinese."

"Remind me again what these jump sites are?" Rogers asked. But I'm sure he wasn't the only one who was unclear on this notion.

Jonn was best at giving succinct explanations. "They are small objects orbiting at a Lagrange point that when activated will open a hole in space that a spaceship can pass through and emerge at another site orbiting a distant star.

"Each site has a code built into it. We use the code of the site we approach plus the code of the site we wish to jump to. Linking the codes creates a momentary hole in space where in essence these two jump sites merge into one. The vessel passes near one site and emerges near the other one as if there's no space between them."

"What powers these jump sites?" Amelie asked.

"Wanda told me they are inert until activated by an approaching vessel," I said, proud of my growing expertise. "We alert them as we are approaching, then use a burst of energy to activate them both as we pass by. We indicate the size of our vessel—and the size of the needed hole—by the strength of the energy burst. The vessel must pass within a certain distance of the jump site."

I glanced around at the faces in the view space to make sure they were still with me. "The faster we approach, the more energy it takes, the greater the risk of hitting a boulder, and the greater the chance that we miss the site. Slower is safer but takes longer. On this trip, slow is a benefit."

"I'm concerned about a jump terminal situation at a Lagrange point," Amelie said. "Those are magnets for space junk. How does a vessel avoid collision?

Noel opined, "Even when such space junk is thick, it's pretty thin."

I explained. "Wanda told me that *Star Choice* extends our cone of push force ahead of it to nudge any particles or pebbles out of the way. If it's too large to nudge, we dodge. But you saw what we did to that spaceship trying to fire missiles at us."

*   *   *

Here is one memorable conversation that took place a day into my cruise that I recall vividly. Rogers the engineer was back at the view space with Jonn, who had apparently briefed him on many of the details of my alien interactions.

"Wait a minute. Wait a minute." Rogers was all fired up. "Okay, so there were aliens here recently. The evidence is, you have their spaceship, and you're in it. But then, there's this network of star jump sites you're telling us about. And there's one here especially for Earth. That means there have been aliens here before."

"Yes, obviously."

"When was this?" he pushed.

"Don't know exactly," I admitted. I'd never asked myself this question. "This jump site could have been put here millions of years ago."

"Put here a million years ago," Rogers repeated. "But then we could have been visited by aliens any number of times since then, right?"

"I don't know. How would I know? The aliens who came here seemed to think this had been done long ago—by a long extinct civilization."

"But we don't know that, do we?" Rogers persisted. "We don't know that these jump sites haven't been used. Even recently. All these people who report UFOs. Maybe these UFOs used your jump sites. Maybe these sites haven't been sitting in space unused for millions of years."

This gave me a shiver. I'd never been an alien UFO believer. I didn't want it to be true that we'd had surreptitious visits from unknown entities over the centuries. I preferred the Librarian's version, that Earth was unknown to the alien civilization.

He went on. "This could mean there are other alien parties out there.

Civilizations that are beyond the control—or knowledge—of the ones you have been in touch with."

"They don't believe these exist," I insisted, but with little conviction. I couldn't speak for what Breadbox's people knew or didn't know.

"But how would they know?" Rogers asked. "This whole thing is a mystery to them, from what you've said. If your young teenager aliens found your crystal containing these codes in a junk shop on some alien world, why would you think this is the only one? Why couldn't others have discovered such crystals over the last million years? Why wouldn't others have come to visit us?"

I could think of no reason. Except, why had they never make contact with us?

Rogers went on. "Maybe these beings in your self-proclaimed Galactic Confederation have a cocoon of safety within their star cluster. Maybe they have a way to protect themselves and keep others away from their worlds. But they have no idea what's happening beyond the worlds they control, by their own admission, if what Jonn tells me is accurate.

"That's what you said you'd learned from your so-called librarian. You demonstrated with your star maps that their worlds lie in a band of stars closer to the center of the galaxy. But this starmap generated by your crystal shows jumpsites all over the galaxy, including the ring of stars where our sun is located and even farther out toward the edge of the Milky Way. How many other 'galactic confederations' are there out there? There could be all kinds of alien visitors using these jump sites."

"But why are they so elusive?" Amelie asked. "Why do they always appear to some farmer in the outback? Or to some government functionary who can hide them away so that nobody learns about them for certain, except in rumors? Or fleeting lights in the sky?"

"Right!" I proclaimed. "When these particular aliens arrived, they crashed on my hillside, leaving fragments behind. And I now have their spaceship. The government dug up the bodies of the ones that died in the crash. Where is the mystery?"

"You tried to hush it up yourself." he said.

"And it didn't work," I retorted. "As soon as it was discovered, the entire world knew."

This discussion left me quite unsettled. I had no answer for his questions and assertions. For all I knew, phantom UFOs could be buzzing around in space shadowing me just out of sight. Maybe I should try to connect with one of Rogers' little gray aliens, just to relieve the boredom.

Speak of the devil! Not long after that I was indeed contacted by an alien.

29. Star Jump

I figured that Kateh would know the answers to all of Rogers' questions, so I asked her when she called.

"Kateh, How do you know there are no other confederations or star-spanning civilizations in the galaxy?"

"We don't know that. All we know is that they have never encroached on the space of the Confederation, nor approached our worlds. This would have been known. Our security would detect them. Jumpsites must be at gravity balance points, not just anywhere in space. These points are monitored."

"What about further out in the galaxy where my world lies? Could there be other star-spanning civilizations comparable to the Galactic Confederation? If an ancient civilization established this code, perhaps a remnant of that civilization still exists and has access to that network."

Kateh crossed her fore tentacles in negation. "We have no knowledge."

Well, that was not comforting. Just another nagging unknown of the vast cosmos. No point in obsessing. I had plenty of other things to worry about.

*   *   *

I spent a good bit of time talking with Wanda as we headed ever-so-slowly toward the jump site.

"How do you find the jump site—a tiny black thing in the depths of space?" I asked.

"I know where it must be—at the balance point of two gravitational fields. I can calculate that quite accurately. When we are close, *Star Choice* sends a tiny pulse and it reflects back. Not radar; our energy. We inform the site we are about to activate it. It informs us on its status: Is it functional, or are there problems? If good, *Star Choice* can 'see' it. You will also see it in the view screen. We calculate a precise trajectory. Must come close but not collide with it."

"What if another spaceship is using the jumpsite at the same time to come here?"

"Infinitesimal chance, my controlling oki. This site has been used just once in ten raised six times number of years."

"What if this were a busy world with many comings and goings?" I wanted to know.

"There is a rule: always pass to the left, so no chance of colliding. These sites use the local gravitational field to orient the jump field to be parallel to the plane of the ecliptic. Busy worlds also have different sites for incoming and outgoing vessels, located at the world's different gravitational balance points."

I had more questions than a curious pre-schooler. "When you pass close by does that disturb it?"

"No. If it were shifted slightly due to our tiny gravitational pull, it would be pulled back into position by the offsetting gravity pulls at this balance point. The biggest hazard is encountering pieces of debris that are attracted to this balance point. If sizable, we must miss them. If small, we push them gently aside as we approach."

I nodded. "Yes, you did that when *Star Choice* was on the Moon—and with the pursuing rocket recently."

"Yes. The faster we approach, the more exacting this is. But we are approaching slowly now, in relative terms."

"May I ask you about the damage you sustained? How serious is it?"

"We were distant from the weapon. The energy burst was of diminished intensity because the energy had spread out a bit, even though it was a directed beam. It was not a direct hit. We tried to mobilize our defense. Yet it is a serious injury. Our effectiveness is reduced by 30%."

"As we move through space now without accelerating, are you able to build up energy reserves again?" I asked.

"Yes, however, they were greatly depleted, so it will take more time. Activating the site to jump to a different star system requires a major input of energy. This must be kept in reserve. We are seeking to build this up by the time we approach the site."

That sounded iffy. "You're saying we may not have adequate power to make a jump?"

"By my calculations, we will have a sufficient reserve." Should I be reassured by this?

*   *   *

Seconds ticked by interminably in cycles of loneliness, cabin fever, fear, monotony. This could have been a time for reflection and deep revelations, but the knot of terror was always lurking too close to allow enlightening thoughts. I wished I could be in suspended animation, like passengers in sci fi movies on decades-long travel between worlds, even though mine was just a couple of days.

No such luck. I stewed and slept fitfully. Earlier in the trip I had Wanda turn off the lights when I slept, but now total darkness terrified me. Darkness within the ship was like inviting in the endless darkness from outside. There was no sense of motion, no noise from engines. My breathing and heartbeat were the loudest sounds. I had the weirdest hallucinations. So I slept with the lights on.

This upset my regular day / night cycle. When was it time to sleep, and when to be awake? My appetite was iffy. Despite having a stash of good food, I subsisted on cheese and crackers and canned lemonade—and tiny sips of whisky. Oh how I yearned for more Malbec!

I talked with the spirit of Breadbox and sang along with Gibb. I tuned in to the Songstone, but much of it was very boring. I tried to do some exercise—jogging the fifty foot length on *Star Choice*, back and forth, doing jumping jacks and floor stretches.

I debated having the maker machine give me a complete makeover and remove all my wrinkles, but I didn't have the nerve. I wondered if it could make me a permanent blond.

"Write songs about this experience," I told myself. But I couldn't put two notes together. My ever-faithful inner tune generator was AWOL.

Wanda was a decent conversationalist, but she depended on me to initiate it, and I ran out of things to talk about.

I couldn't sit and look out the non-existent window, and watching the view space was like watching an unchanging view of the night sky— dark with a scattering of pinpricks of light. I understood what Breadbox had once told me—that when traveling between worlds, her people sealed themselves up inside the vessel and paid no attention to the trip. They spent their time singing with each other and telling stories. They never traveled alone.

But I was so very alone. Time dragged.

*   *   *

I was dozing with the lights turned low when Wanda spoke and brought the light level up. "It is time. We are approaching the jump site. I presume you would like to know. Now I have alerted it. It responds. See it in the view space?"

What I saw was a symbol, or avatar, that kept moving around in a small yellow circle. "Once we make the jump," I asked her, "will I still be able to communicate with the folks back on Earth?"

"Yes. I will explain how. But right now, I must make minor adjustments."

I stopped yammering and sat in silence.

"My controlling oki, I am depleted. This approach is more difficult with the injury to the propulsion. It is harder to hold course."

I noted that Wanda referred to this as an injury, not damage. She saw *Star Choice* as a living entity, in essence her body. How fast would I be able to run if I'd been shot in the leg by a pursuer?

"I must mobilize one final burst of energy to activate the site so it will open the jump tunnel adequately. *Star Choice* will have just one chance to get through the jump site. Do I have enough? If I have calculated properly, I do."

I flashed back to old Star Trek shows, where Captain Kirk would say, "Beam me up, Scottie," and he'd be disassembled atom by atom and reassembled somewhere else, hopefully getting everything in the proper arrangement. Was that about to happen to me? What would this jump feel like?

"What happens if we jump through this site but don't come out the other one? Could that happen?"

"In principle it could happen, my controlling oki, but very unlikely. A hypothetical? If that did happen, we would leap into nothingness. We would cease to exist."

Cease to exist. I pondered that. One moment we could be cruising through space with me worrying about what might happen, then the next moment . . . nothing. There would be no next moment. Seemed like there were far too many ways to flash out of existence out here in space. At least no agony. Just gone. Despite the deep hole of terror in my gut, I could view this prospect dispassionately, with a bit of curiosity even. What the hell? I could get run over by a truck in my own hometown.

Of course, nobody lives forever, and I knew my time would come someday. But I, Selena Morisot, was not ready to go. "Let me out of here!" I yelled at the top of my voice. "I'm too young to die!"

"My controlling oki, I must presume those were rhetorical comments not meant to be taken literally?"

"Just my lame attempt at humor to push aside the terror." I tried to cry, but I couldn't. What would be the point of that? Might as well enjoy the ride—as long as I could.

"If the second jump site cannot be activated, we would not jump," Wanda continued explaining matter-of-factly. "We would just fly past our jump site. But then we would still face pursuit by the hostile rockets from your world."

"Well, let's just do it," I said with resignation. "Shit. What have I got myself into? I'm supposed to be a singer."

All was silence for quite a while. Then Wanda announced, "I see it now. One last adjustment."

I saw the avatar of the jump site in the view space slightly off the center mark. It seemed difficult for Wanda to hold *Star Choice* on the right course; the yellow avatar kept drifting toward the edge of the target circle. I wanted to use my body English to nudge her back toward it. I was holding my breath and grabbing the armrests with all my might. I wanted a steering wheel!

The symbol of the jump site grew in the view space, even though I could see no actual thing. "How fast are we approaching, Wanda?"

"Quite slowly. At this part of our trajectory, approximately 440 kilometers per second in relationship to our target."

What? That is slow? I couldn't comprehend this number. I did some quick math: that speed would get us across the United States in ten or

115

fifteen seconds! How many times had I driven way too fast through a tollbooth, staying in my narrow lane so I wouldn't whack into it? We're trying to fly close to this floating invisible gizmo that's like a cosmic tollbooth but not hit it. And Wanda was having trouble holding course.

Enough seconds passed for us to fly around the world several times. I sat in silence, eyes glued to the view space, watching the target slowly grow larger. Finally we seemed to be aimed right at it. Were we close enough? Too close? There was a flash of yellow light in the view space, and a chime tone. The target disappeared.

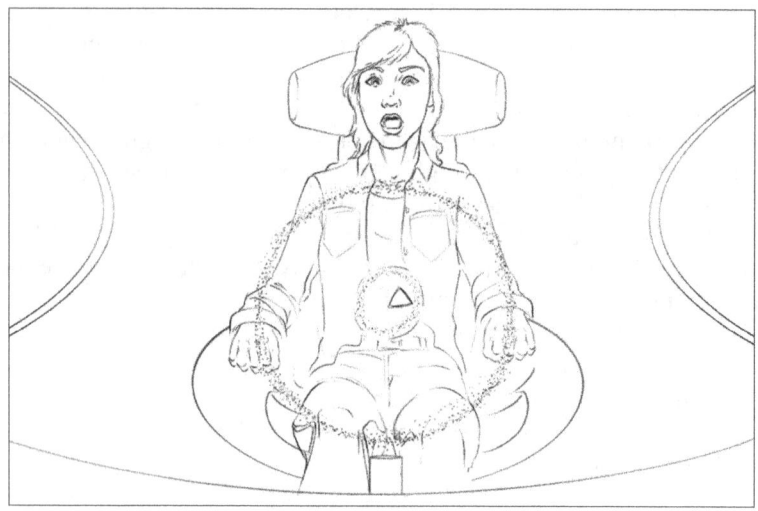

I was terrified as I saw the approaching symbol of the jumpsite in the viewspace.

30. Jump Into the Void

"Star jump complete, my controlling oki." Wanda announced softly.
Yes! We made it through! Bypassing who knows how many lightyears of space in the blink of an eye. And I was alive. "Cheated death again!" I said with false bravado. I let out a sigh of relief. I noticed I was soaked in sweat and still shaking.

I had felt nothing as we passed through the jump. I saw no sign in the view space except that the target disappeared. No flash of white light or stars rushing past, a la Star Trek. Just the black emptiness of space. Were the background stars different? They must be, but I couldn't tell.

I was safe now. No nasty missiles could pursue us. Let's defer thinking about whether we can ever get back, I thought to myself.

But where the hell was I? I wondered. I couldn't remember what star system we jumped to. A star that didn't have a name, just a number. Noel had said it was about sixty-five light years from the Sun. That's right up there close to infinity.

Wanda checked in. "Selena, my controlling oki, I have kept you safe."
"Yes, I thank you."
"Now I must recharge as we follow an unpowered trajectory toward our target world. But first I confirm to you I have measured our location in space so that we can find this jumpsite again when we are ready to depart."
"How do you do that?"
"By triangulating against distant pulsing stars." I didn't understand that. I guess she meant pulsars.
"And how do we find our target world now? It all looks so black," I asked, gazing into the view space filled with scattered pinpricks of light.
"The geometry of the world's orbit and gravity field in relation to this jump site indicates where it must be," she explained. "We look there and locate it." A short pause. "We have located it, and have begun to move in that direction. The momentum *Star Choice* retains emerging from the jump site already carries us in the correct direction."
"It is now visible in the view space," Wanda said. The small yellow targeting circle appeared around one tiny dot. She zoomed in on it. Even so, it was just a slightly larger fuzzy dot—crescent shaped like the first quarter Moon.

"Wanda, will I still be able to reach my friends back on Earth using the view space?" I asked, fearing that the answer would be no.

"Yes, my controlling oki. But to use the comm stone, it must work through the view space, not directly."

Good! Using the comm stone, I summoned everybody via their nicknames. It reminded me of Santa Claus calling out to each reindeer in "The Night Before Christmas." "Come Jonn, come Noel, come Amelie and Dana!" Several of them connected pretty quickly to my interstellar party line.

"It all worked! I'm alive! As you can tell, the comm stones and view space work without a hitch between stars. I may be marooned for life, but I can still gab with your folks and watch the evening news." I spoke with a manic giddiness to mask my deep-seated terror that I may well be marooned for life.

But right now all was well. I described the painless jump process. I told them about the Wanda's assessment of the *Star Choice* damage, about the strain on her, and about her need to recharge. "Wanda is low on power, but the injury to the vessel also affects her. Almost like a concussion, I'm thinking. It's like you've been shot in the leg, then also bonked on the head. Yet we have to keep going."

I was sure grateful for this cosmic coddling across the abyss. It was the only way I could stay sane. I was so alone and helpless. Space is huge and empty and dark. Stars are just dots of light; planets are invisible.

"What you have done is miraculous!" Amelie exclaimed. "Even though it was unplanned and unintentional, you know your name will go down in the history books along with Armstrong and Sheppard."

"And Columbus!" added Dana. "Discovering new worlds."

"And Icarus," I had to add. "Falling from the sky. I am very much in touch with my vulnerability." I couldn't get my hands to stop shaking unless I grabbed the arms of my seat.

"You are a historical first," Noel said, "and we are immensely proud of you, but also envious."

Jonn cleared his throat to make an announcement. "Be that as it may, we have decided not to announce just yet that you have traveled to a distant star system. We haven't said anything at all. Many think your spaceship has been destroyed, and you with it. We want the Chinese to think this. And I'm certainly not going to say anything different to Gen. Dickson and his Agency. Since I resigned, I told them I'm out of the loop. After all, why would you keep me around if I have no connection to the government?"

"Good point!" I chuckled, "Why do I keep you around? You must have other skills." Fake humor to cover my anxiety.

Dana burst forth. "Your fans are in a huge uproar. Your cancer doc and Clay have been speaking out, describing what happened. Then you disappeared, presumably shot out of space. And our government did not defend you."

"She's right," Noel said. "The rumbling is beginning to build. Not just in the U.S., but around the world. You were not treated well."

We talked some more. I told them what I was seeing—not much—and how long before we reached a planet—way too long.

Amelie asked, "Do you have things you need to be doing, besides shooting the breeze with us?"

"Oh no," I assured her. "Nothing is more important than staying connected with all of you."

"I'm glad to hear that," she replied, "because I have a question for you."

"What is it?"

"You've talked about the need to recharge for *Star Choice*, and I guess Wanda also. What does that mean?" she asked.

Jonn joined in. "Yes, same question here. You say *Star Choice* has no fuel. Where does its energy come from? There are no fuel tanks, no refueling stations, where's the energy to propel *Star Choice* and the power the other processes come from?"

"Good questions, indeed. Wanda has explained this to me, but I didn't understand it. Let's ask her. Wanda, can you answer these questions?"

No response from Wanda. We waited a minute, then I said. "Well, she said she is recharging, so perhaps that's why she's not listening to our conversation, even though the view space is carrying it. Okay, I'll give you my garbled version."

I tried to recall Wanda's explanation to me. "It's totally beyond the science of our world, so I can only communicate it using analogies. *Star Choice* —and Wanda also—have batteries that are charged via energy from the—we have no words for this—'zero dimension via the catalytic action of the O metals.' This is what she told me. It's not like chemical fuel that is replenished, or even nuclear fuel that powers an ion drive. It's more like hydroelectric power or wind power. It captures a 'flow of energy from the zeroeth dimension that is accessed via tunneling.' These are her words, more or less. Have I lost you yet?"

"Keep going," Noel said. "I'm taking notes. We'll mull it over later."

"Here's a strange image she used. Imagine lying on your back, feeling thirsty. Above you is a vast sea, separated from you by a thin membrane. I'm imagining a cosmic water balloon. You want to sip some water from that sea. But if you rip the membrane—it's very difficult to rip—you and everything else will be drowned in the deluge.

"You have to make a tiny pinprick in this membrane looming above you, so that you can sip a few drops of water from it without releasing a torrent. When you stop sipping, the hole closes. It's just a tiny hole, so it takes quite a while to satisfy your thirst. You still with me?"

"Wow," Noel said softly. "I want to give this puzzle to some of my grad students."

"To create these tiny metaphorical holes requires special metals that are closely guarded secrets of the Galactic Confederation. Wanda and *Star Choice* both contain a tiny bead of it. This metal bead is a catalyst that allows tunneling between our space and this other realm. I once tried to explain our notion of a wormhole to Wanda, and she liked that. She said this metallic bead lets us capture a tiny piece of a wormhole."

"Mmm, I like that!" Noel said. "It's like saying that a transistor lets us capture a tiny piece of a lightning bolt. Is there more?"

"Oh yes," I said excitedly, forgetting my terror for a moment. "The star jump is based on the same principle. The jump site opens up a slightly larger space through this zero dimension, large enough for a space ship to get through."

"Why is it called the zeroeth dimension?" Jonn asked.

"Wanda said it's a dimension without extension. Distance does not exist. It doesn't make sense to me. You'd think everything in the universe would be piled in one place. The only way you can get from one place to another is by using these codes, like the ones we used to jump to wherever the hell I am now, and will hopefully get me back home.

"You can only jump from one code to another. If you don't have the code, you can't jump. Same as with a telephone. You can't get through to another phone unless you have the phone number. These communication devices—the view space and comm stones—use the same principles, but it requires a lot less to send a message than to jump a spaceship."

Mmms and aahs from my audience.

"Want more? Can I give you a bit more data dump?" I asked.

"Go for it, girl!" Amelie exclaimed.

"Propulsion uses the same technology, in a way I cannot explain. It pushes on the fabric of space—the crack between the worlds. Also the energy-push beam that we used to attack that missile launcher. Propulsion and artificial gravity are two sides of the same thing. The repulsive propulsion side is like two magnets that repel each other when you hold the same poles together. It can be tuned the opposite to attract matter, strongly or weakly, and that simulates gravitational pull."

I paused to let this sink in "Had enough? Any questions? There will be a quiz later."

Silence from the peanut gallery.

"There's one more piece," I said with a touch of drama, "that I must let you know. Jump codes are jealously guarded secrets of the Galactic Confederation, as I said. The Librarian told me that they keep a close monopoly on them, and that's the source of their power over other worlds. Okay?

"Now, here's the kicker. This crystal I have, that contains the jump site codes we are using to get to different star systems, contains codes that are completely different from those the Confederation has. They are unaware of this network. They don't know the amulet exists. It controls a parallel network of jump sites that is more extensive and older than the Confederation's, as you could see when I showed it in the view space.

"Yes, we know this from what you've said. What are you getting at?" Jonn asked, and Amelie expressed agreement.

"I have always resisted talking about this, because it's such powerful knowledge. Call this a deathbed confession. Who knows if I'll ever get back to Earth? I've got to tell somebody, and you are my most trusted buds.

"Don't you see?" I said excitedly. I needed a soapbox to stand on. "This can give Planet Earth a tool to stand up to the most powerful entity in the galaxy—the Galactic Confederation that the aliens belong to who reached all the way to Earth to destroy Wanda."

"Are you suggesting Earth could build its own Galactic empire?" Dana asked.

"Well, a hell of a lot of good this will do us if you and *Star Choice* get lost in space." Jonn almost yelled. "So we've got to get you home safe."

"But even if I should perish, *Star Choice* might return. And you should know about this."

"Look here," Amelie pleaded. "Stop this talk. I know you're in a perilous situation. But it's way too soon to start talking like this. You are cradled by well-tested technology created by a very advanced civilization that obviously puts great importance in getting its citizens home safely."

"Keep telling me that," I said, neglecting to remind them that this same technology had crashed on my back hillside. "I need to hear it repeatedly. I've just been in touch with the many ways I could instantly flash into oblivion. It gets to me."

Murmurs of love and support from my team. Dana's question went unanswered.

"Why don't you sing to us?" Dana said. I wasn't sure she was serious. "Get your guitar and sing us some of your songs."

As soon as she said that, I had a huge release of emotion. I ran back and retrieved Gibb, then sat cross-legged in my captain's seat in front of the view space and started singing through my tears. "Space Girl Yearning," "Let Me Lead You Astray," "Forever to Infinity"—all my space songs. Across the void, all my friends, scattered on different places on my home world, sang along with me as best they could. I took requests, and yes, they asked for "Cotton Candy Lovin'." We sang for a couple of hours, until I was exhausted.

"Thank you, thank you. I love you all."

I went right to sleep, terror-free. I am a singer, and the Song shall set me free.

When I woke up, hopefully we'd be nearing what Noel and Amelie promised would be much better than black space—a wonderful new world.

31. You Call This Earthlike?

Because we had approached Earth's jump site slowly, we also approached the world we were jumping to slowly. Slow in to the jump, slow out, Wanda explained. Since we had over a day of cruising toward it, I spent the time watching the Songstone. Here's one that was so unlike the song to the Beloved Princess that I listened to earlier.

A group tromped out onto the stage, each covered by a grey cloak with a fanciful ugly mask attached to it. Even for aliens, this was weird. They took turns hoarsely shouting bits of a story. Here's part of it, translated by Wanda:

> We, we are the accursed spawn of illegal crossbreeding
> Between beings of different world races.
> Our love-smitten parents insisted on procreating,
> And got the help of back-city gene tinkerers.
>
> Rarely does this result in living offspring.
> And if it does, seldom to the liking of the parents.
> We were despised and rejected by our parents
> And left to fend for ourselves.
>
> We ended up on Darknik,
> The airless rock that circles above Everbright,
> Trying to satisfy perverse pleasures at the Stardive Bar.
>
> We sing there, and dance, and pass the bucket for tokens.
> We do the same for you. We beg you for sustenance.
>
> Don't punish us for our misshapen mien.
> Blame our parents that let us live.
> Now we will sing and dance for your weird pleasure.

This went on for some time, and I was sorry I couldn't drop a token into their bucket.

Next time I spoke to Kateh, I mentioned that I was watching Songstone. "How are you able to observe it?" she asked. I explained about the

Librarian's boon. "Ah, the Librarian again. That entity has established a role in your life, has it not?"

"It's my way of learning about the star-spanning civilization that you are part of. Could you tell me more about it? Who sings there, and why?

"Our philosophy is that our story—the story of all the oki races—is the most important thing we have. We must never let the story, the song, die. The Songstone is the center—there must always be performers singing and telling their story at the Songstone.

"All the oki races sing there. They take turns. Some more often. Stories, myths, ongoing accounts, complaints, political diatribes. Bragging, recounting history and events. Announcing things. Fanciful tales."

"What about the Fofonoloy?" I asked.

"Not as often. Mostly complaints about how poorly we are treated by the Confederation."

"Are there ever audiences?"

"Sometimes. Mostly viewing remotely, like you. All is recorded and preserved. Any can review it."

*   *   *

As we got closer to our target world, it still looked like a fuzzy grey disk. Yes, clouds. It must be covered by clouds. I sat on the edge of my seat, eyes glued to the view space. It was astounding! I was the first human looking up close at world around a distant star. I noticed at least three small moons orbiting, but paid little attention to them, I was so enthralled by this approaching orb.

What if this world had an advanced civilization with space-faring capabilities? How would it view an alien interloper like *Star Choice*? They may attack us. I'd had enough of being shot at. I watched carefully for any sign of detection. But no, it showed no coherent radiation signals that would indicate an oki civilization.

As we moved toward this new planet, all my Earth-based crew tuned in via their view bubbles. They could see as well as I could using their view space that mirrored the one on *Star Choice*.

"Remind me again why we're going to this planet?" I asked my team.

"You had to jump somewhere," Jonn said. "Better and safer than just drifting around in space. Hopefully you can orbit this world a few times until it's safe for you to return to Earth."

"That's for sure," I replied. "Drifting in space is hard on me."

When we approached the planet from the jumpsite, we saw half the disk in sunlight and half in dark, like the Moon in first quarter. This world was larger than Earth, Wanda informed us, and its sun was slightly smaller than our sun.

Oh my, this was exhilarating! We swooped down toward the strange world. Not exactly swooped. More a stately descending arc. Around the sunlit side so we could see the whole world.

I heard the chime that indicates we had gone into orbit. Then Wanda said, "One two, buckle my shoe. Five six, no alien tricks!"

"What?! What did you just say?" I asked her. This was startling, to say the least. It immediately took me back to when the device I later called Wanda was helping Breadbox and me learn to communicate with each other. I had said, "one, two, three, four," and the device responded, "un, oo, ree, sor." In my excitement I had blurted out, "One, two, buckle my shoe. Three, four, shut the door. Five, six, no alien tricks!" Now, a couple of years later, Wanda dredged this up from her memory in a completely inappropriate context.

"My controlling oki, we have just attained a stable orbit at an inclination of 30° to the equator and an altitude of about 450 of your miles. We can go lower if you wish."

"That's good. But what did you just say before that?" She went on as if nothing had happened, reporting her degree of energy recharge during the incoming trip, estimating the age of the star and the length of this world's year. But I was still stuck back on buckle my shoe. Feeling nervous and perplexed.

"Did you guys hear Wanda say 'one two, buckle my shoe' just now?" I asked my crew in the view space.

"Huh? No, we heard nothing," was the consensus, with a tone in their voices like "what was Selena saying now?" Was I hearing things? One of us was losing our grip. I hoped it was me. If I'm going nuts, Wanda can still get me home. But if she's going nuts . . .

I quickly forgot this in the excitement of looking at this brand new world.

An exciting view of an unexciting world. A dark, rocky world, when we could see through the clouds. Covered with mountain ranges with flat, grey plains. Dirty grey polar caps.

"Selena, does Wanda record all this?" Noel asked. "We are memorializing the first human from Earth to visit a world of another sun. This is a truly historic moment. Selena, you will go down in history, whether you want to or not. I'm envious."

"I'm not going to do my 'giant step' bit until I can step somewhere," I said laconically, but I noticed that my heart was thudding double time.

"I'm jealous, too!" declared Amelie.

"I invited you and Dana twice to come along," I chided them, recalling the difficulties they had encountered. "I sure wish you were here. This is not an honor I want to claim for myself. It's so accidental. I'm like some poor castaway on a log who washed up on the shores of the New World before Columbus and got the credit for discovering America."

"Then we'd be the United States of Selena," Jonn said.

"It will make a great story for future generations," Dana said. "I'm telling my kid I knew you back when."

"Back when I was alive," I muttered, hoping not to be heard.

As we slowly orbited, *Star Choice* did the kind of analysis that, as Wanda told me, it always does when approaching a new world. Measure temperature and magnetism, do spectrographic analysis of the atmosphere. Look for the indicators of life. Listen for radiation signals that would indicate technology. During this time, we were mostly observers.

The instruments of *Star Choice* soon told us the atmosphere was frigid carbon monoxide, hydrogen sulfide, ammonia and methane, the plains were dirty methane ice, and there were likely water oceans beneath. Gravity at the surface twice that of Earth, roaring winds, and freezing temperatures. No chance of landing.

The data went directly to Amelie and Dana, our exoplanet experts. "I'm sad to announce that we see no indication of biological processes," Amelie said.

"Could it be some unrecognizable form of life?" Jonn asked.

"I assume that life requires complex organic molecules of some sort," she replied. "We see no such tracks in the data."

Dana added, "But if there are water oceans beneath the ice, we may not be able to detect life there without sampling the water."

"Agreed," said Amelie.

"Did early Earth have an era of frozen oceans and methane atmosphere? Or will it have in the future?" Jonn asked.

"Never this much methane, so this is not a proto-Earth," Amelie replied.

We gazed in silence for a long time.

"Why would your ancient alien civilization want to place a jumpsite at a world like this," Noel asked.

"Maybe its climate has changed in the last million years," Amelie said. "Perhaps it has entered an ice age."

"Maybe they sent robotic mining vessels down to the surface for valuable minerals," Dana said.

I had an insight about this. "If you're out surveying the galaxy, looking at likely stars with planets, you don't know precisely what the planets are like until you get there with your sub-lightspeed robotic probe. Once you get there you might as well put a jumpsite in place."

"That makes sense," Noel said. "Perhaps the robotic probe becomes the jumpsite."

"But remember," I said, "the jump site would be placed quite a distance from the target world."

"Sending the probe back would demonstrate that the jumpsite was in place," Jonn said.

"I think it would fly in closer," said Amelie, "collect data on the world and send it back. But not return the probe."

"Maybe the jumpsite acts as a flag, demonstrating a territorial claim," Dana said.

"That would suggest somebody claimed Earth at one time," Jonn said.

"They haven't been around lately to collect taxes or rent," Noel said. More silent planet gazing.

"Crikey. Somebody tell a joke or something," Amelie broke the silence.

"How do we know this is the right planet for this star?" Dana asked. "Maybe there's another one closer to the star that is warmer."

"The jumpsite would always be at the Lagrange point of the target planet," Noel said.

"We haven't spotted other planets around this star. But we haven't looked for them," I said.

"Oh yes," Noel corrected me. "We've spotted at least six planets there using telescopes and other instruments. Yours is number two. Gas giants loom farther out from the star. It's possible there are small, dark, distant ones we can't even detect."

After several hours and a few orbits, we had done all the readings and observations we could, so I began to think it was time for me to move on.

"Time to head back to Earth?" I asked hopefully. "I am definitely ready."

"The bad news. In our estimation," Jonn said, "it's not yet safe for you to return to Earth, even though we see things are moving in that direction."

"I was afraid you'd say that. Is there also good news? No? So what now?" I asked. Uncomfortable silence for half a minute.

"You could jump to another world," Noel said. "Do some more cosmic exploring."

Jonn cleared his throat. "Perhaps you should just keep orbiting this planet, as uninteresting as it is. Avoid putting unnecessary drain on *Star Choice*'s system."

Silence. My heart sank as I flashed back to my earlier angst at drifting alone through boring space. "I dunno. I worry about the drain on my own system. I already have cabin fever bad. Just circling this ugliness for who knows how long can't help."

Jonn did his growl of thinking but said nothing. I could hear all their heavy breathing through the view space.

I sighed with resignation. "If I can't come home yet, maybe there's a more interesting world to check out." But I felt this dread. How long could this go on, shuttling from one lonely world to the next, moving ever farther from home.

Finally Amelie said, "In the last several days, we've used some more sensitive instruments to study nearby exoplanets more intensively, and have identified one that seems more earthlike. It's one for which we already gave Wanda the jump code. Eighty-six lightyears from Earth, and about 75° inclination from your current world as viewed from Earth. We recommend you jump there."

"More earthlike you say? You guys are my Houston. I do as you say. What's the name of this world?"

"Let me look," Amelie said. "Here it is. 25-1706d. Sounds pretty romantic, eh?"

"That means it's the third world out from a small star that is too insignificant to have a name," Dana commented.

"Okay by me, then. Make sure Wanda knows," I said. I was not happy about this, but I had to keep up a good front. Weirdly, I felt I needed some time alone, if you can believe that, despite all my loneliness.

"You folks can sign off for awhile if you want. It gets boring just cruising through space. I'll check in with you as soon as we approach the next world. This is not at all difficult. It's fun actually. I wish I weren't alone, but you all are keeping me company. Now I'm going to take a nap."

After they checked out I turned my attention to my faithful but worrisome companion. "Wanda, can we find our way back to the jumpsite? Do you have the code for the next world?"

"Yes, my controlling oki. We will wait until our position in the orbit around this planet is tangent to the trajectory to the jumpsite, then we will accelerate in that direction. If I have your permission, I will give a boost sufficient to get us to the site, then cease thrust, so that we can further our recharge."

"Oh, I didn't know you still needed more recharge." I had no idea how long it took. "By all means. How many hours or days to get there?"

"Perhaps twenty-two of your hours. Also I must tell you that since the main propulsion is damaged, I will compensate with other portions of the thruster. I don't want to overload it. And it's harder to maintain a proper course with only partial propulsion."

"I understand. No problem. That'll give me a chance to connect more with Kateh." But I felt guilty. I was riding a wounded animal, and forcing it to go on, hobbling on three legs. Could it hobble to the next world to save my neck?

32. World 25

As we approached the same jump site we had earlier emerged from, I was once again glued to the view space. Wanda informed me, "I have calculated a trajectory to compensate for our damaged propulsion. We will take a slightly greater arc."

"Do you have enough energy reserves?" I asked.

Silence. Good, I won't interrupt any more.

"My controlling oki, I . . ."

"What?"

"My controlling oki, I . . ."

"What are you trying to say, Wanda?"

But she was silent.

The target grew, and then we were through it, apparently into the space of the second world on our itinerary.

"Was our jump successful?" I asked

"Yes. We have reached the world of the second jump code. I have now calculated the return point."

"Good. Wanda, you started to say something to me, then stopped. What was it?"

"I am unaware of any incomplete communications, my controlling oki."

This was strange. The second "mental" glitch by Wanda. An ice cube of fear grew in my gut. This was sure not a good time to have a malfunctioning robot. Was it even correct to call it a mental glitch. Can "mental" apply to a device, even a really smart and skilled one? This would be a great conversation to have with her, if she were aware of her own glitches. It would be like talking with a good friend about her encroaching dementia.

My concerns were pushed to the background by another call from Kateh. I had more questions I wanted to ask her, but she was not alone. "I have coaxed some clan mothers to join me on the view space."

I got a glance at three other Fofonoloy behind Kateh. I swirled the sign of greeting with my fingers. "Hello, I am Selena, friend of clan daughter Nala—Bvar-nala-nga."

Two of them hissed and moved back behind Kateh, and the other one tried to stand upright and made a hooting growl. It raised two of its arm tentacles in a menacing gesture. Scared the heck out of me. I shrank back. They reminded me of raccoons on my back step at home when I startled them, but much larger.

Then all three moved away, leaving Kateh there alone.

"My apologies, my dear friend. I am so sorry for this unseemly display." Her arm tentacles were all aswirl.

"Why won't they even look at me?" I asked

"You are a Type 1."

"Didn't they know I was a Type 1 beforehand?"

"I may not have emphasized that aspect. I used strong arguments to induce them to join me in viewing you. The reality of seeing you directly may have overwhelmed them."

I had no idea I was so abhorrent to her people. "Why are your people so opposed to Type 1s?"

"The Galactic Confederation is dominated by tall Type 1 races like you. The leading worlds in the center of the Confederation are home to world races of your body type. They are some of the oldest peoples in the Confederation. The Law of Oki—our guiding law—states that all oki races are equal. All body types on all the water-oxygen worlds. But they lord it over us. They look down on us as if we are lesser beings.

"Our technologies are superior to theirs. They are envious of our spaceships and devices. Yet the Confederation controls the star jump network. Without access to that we would be limited to an infinitesimal rate of travel between star systems.

"All Type 1s look the same to us. Tall and erect, two arms and legs. Smaller range of body sizes. Type 2s like us are quite varied. Number and types of appendages, segmented or single body.

"You and people on your world are Type 1. The clan mothers are reacting to you as a type, not an individual. They need to get to know you as I have, and as Nala did."

"I see. Would it help if I came to Sfofong?" Why did I even suggest that? That was the last thing I wanted to do.

"Oh no, that would cause big trouble!" she replied.

* * *

I watched as we cruised gracefully into orbit around this new world—25-1706d. Again I notified my Earth crew as we approached, so we could watch it together as it came into view.

"Hello, 25-1706d. May we call you 25 for short?" I said gaily. "Are you guys staying with me as we approach?"

"Are you kidding?" yelled Amelie. "No way would we miss this, even if *Star Choice* was an unmanned—or unwomanned—probe."

"World 25" was slightly smaller than Earth, its star more orange than the Sun, its orbit closer to its sun. We came in on the sunward side and took a full orbit. It was an ocean world, 90% covered by water. But beautiful blue liquid water, not grey foreboding ice. For a couple of hours we gazed in awe at this world as we cruised around it, pointing things out to each other, but often just watching in silence.

The landmasses scattered across the world were either small continents or large islands. The largest were like Madagascar, but more were like Japan or New Zealand or the islands of Indonesia. Mostly bare and tan colored, but we quickly spotted a fringe of grey green along every shoreline. From high altitude it looked like fuzz or velvet. As I zoomed in on it, I saw thick rounded trunks with no leaves. Kind of like cactus and reeds. Growing thickly, especially near the water and in vast marshy areas we flew over.

"This makes me think it's a young world and plants are just beginning to migrate from the oceans to dry land," Noel said

"You say young world but Earth was four billion years old before plants gained a foothold on land," Amelie corrected.

"Can we land? Do we dare?" I asked eagerly. Nobody responded.

"Let's allow Wanda to do her thing," I replied to myself. Wanda took samples of air and water as we descended. "We'll just go up again if it proves to be toxic."

Tests showed that the atmosphere of 25 World was quite similar to Earth's: nitrogen lower, oxygen much higher, carbon dioxide higher, a bit of argon, high humidity, and warmer than Earth. It would be like a sauna on the surface.

We slowly veered leftward and took a trajectory toward the north polar region where it would be cooler. No polar ice caps, we noted. We picked an island with low hills and a plain that sloped gently toward the sea. I directed Wanda to land us on a flat area at the edge of the "plant life," near where a small river ran into the sea.

As we descended toward a landing, Noel said, "Only the second planet we visit, and it's so earthlike it's uncanny."

"Well, we were looking for earthlike worlds," Amelie responded. "So it's not that uncanny."

"When Breadbox and her crew were visiting worlds," I said, "she told me Earth was only the fourth one they visited. But she rated that as an extremely unlikely occurrence. The Galactic Librarian told me worlds like ours are very rare."

In any case, this one looked beautiful as *Star Choice* settled for a soft landing. They were seeing the same in their view space on Earth as I was on 25 World. It showed an almost 180° view of the surface, and I asked Wanda to slowly rotate it. I couldn't see my crew, but I could hear their voices—and their excited breathing. Murmurs of astonishment and delight as we all pointed things out. We all shouted like kids in a toy shop. "Look, bugs!" "Looks like a dragonfly!" "Do you hear those buzzing sounds?" "Web builders, like spiders!"

The sky was blue, a bright cornflower blue, just slightly different from our azure skies, and clouds were white. The sun was orange and low in the sky, so everything looked like late afternoon on Earth, even though it was mid-day there. A range of mauve ridges receded into the distance.

The gravity was 10% less than Earth, Wanda told me, and I could feel the difference when the grav was turned off.

As Wanda slowly scanned the area near *Star Choice*, there among the plants that grew nearby, we saw many more bugs, worms, flyers, and hoppers. Through the view space, we heard buzzing like bees and mosquitoes.

I was itching to put on my suit and take a step outside. I stood up, sat down again, got up, grabbed my spacesuit and sat holding it on my lap.

"We've got to take samples!" Amelie almost shouted. "What astounding serendipity!"

"You have no tools, do you?" Noel asked. "Any empty tin cans to scoop up some dirt?"

I was ready to scoop up dirt with my bare fingers. "Well, Spaceketeers, we weren't expecting to do any interstellar exploring. So no tools."

"Selena," Amelie asked, "Could your Maker Machine create something?"

"Wow, maybe. What would we need? What kinds of samples do you need?"

"Air, water, soil, plants, animals," she said.

"Scoop, snip, grab, contain, and store," Dana added. "And kill if you are attacked by an angry swarm."

"Wanda," I asked, "could *Star Choice* or the Maker Machine create containers for small samples that we could take back to Earth?"

"We can create small simple items easily. You must give me instructions," she replied.

"Hold on a sec," Dana yelled, and disappeared. In a minute she returned carrying a garden trowel and gloves, barbeque tongs, and a skinny jar of cocktail olives. She poured out the olives, popping a couple into her mouth. Oh boy, that made my mouth water! "Wanda, can you see these?" she asked. "Could your machine make these?"

"Please hold them up one at a time close to the view space." Wanda examined each item. "If we could simplify these into one-piece, single material, then yes. Let us attempt samples of each."

I went back to the Maker Machine's worktable. Two of the bulbs descended from the ceiling. Two sets of tendrils extended. From each, materials magically appeared from nowhere. From one, a glass tube extruded, about an inch by six inches with one end open and the other rounded. Looked like a test tube. Perfectly formed. "Glass is one of the easiest substances for this machine to create," Wanda said.

From the other bulb's tendrils emerged this lumpy grey thing, hard to identify at first. Then the scoop emerged and it became a trowel! After that came a U-shaped thing that became a pair of tongs or graspers, about

18 inches long, made from a hard grey plastic substance. Very impressive!

Looking back at the first bulb, I saw half a dozen tubes arrayed on the table—with beveled stoppers for each. I carried pieces back to the view space for a show and tell.

Amelie and Jonn were conferring on whether I should step outside. "I'd be crazy not to set foot on this world!" I yelled.

Amelie shook her head in agreement. "How can we collect samples if Selena doesn't do it?"

"We want to minimize contamination. Can't have Selena dragging a bunch of stuff back inside *Star Choice*."

"Let's think it over," Amelie said. I was sure she'd come up with something.

Thinking it over lasted about thirty seconds. "Okay, suit up," Jonn said gruffly, but I was already putting on my spacesuit. After all my moon walks, I was pretty expert at it.

The airlock opened and I gazed out onto this new world, overwhelmed. My knees almost buckled. "Oh wow, oh wow, oh wow!" was all I could say.

I carefully hooked up the winch cable before venturing out. I took a step down onto this new world. Very different from my moonwalks. My suit was pressurized and insulated to wear on a cold airless world. I needed no pressurization here—nor insulation. It was much easier to maneuver, but I soon saw that I'd need air conditioning, not heat. Since we were at a high latitude, the sun was not high in the sky, but the air was still quite warm. The spacesuit was like wearing a down parka on Hawaii.

This was a tremendous thrill! Holding on to the cable, I turned toward *Star Choice* and announced with my arm raised in a heroic gesture, "One giant step for an undeserving ditzy chick. But in this moment, I guess I represent all of humankind. I am honored, and scared. I've stepped on the Moon, and now I've stepped on this new world." I dropped my arm and asked, "How was that? Do I get to name it? Should I name it Selena? Breadbox? How about Berthe, after my namesake and inspiration? I'm not calling it New Earth or New Terra. Should we hold a contest to name it?"

My boots were sinking in. Was World 25 covered in quicksand? What if something grabbed me from beneath? What if *Star Choice* sank in and got stuck?

33. Up Close with Alien Life

A cloud of nasty stuff rose around me, like toxic mushroom spoors. I was glad I had my helmet and breathing apparatus. The ground was a mat of partially decayed plant matter, covered with dust, and I was sinking into it. I wasn't sure how deep I might go down—it could be many feet deep. I felt a momentary surge of terror. I held tight to the winch cable and clambered back up the steps and inside. Wow, did that ever get my heart pumping! I glanced back over my shoulder to see if anything was pursuing me out of the bracken.

I asked Wanda to move *Star Choice* a short distance to a flat rocky area. We lifted as gently as a hot air balloon and moved slowly about fifty feet. I stayed in the airlock so I didn't have to remove my boots.

The second location had solid footing. I clambered down the steps and tested it, first by stepping gently, then by jumping up and down. I walked about ten yards before turning around toward *Star Choice*. "Whoo-ee! Here I am! Can you guys see me out here?"

"Yes we can," said Amelie's voice in my helmet. "From a video camera mounted near the airlock. Don't get carried away. Try to remain calm, so you don't make any dangerous moves."

"Yes, Mother! I wish I had a different kind of suit. It's very hard to move around in this suit, even in this slightly lower gravity. If I fall over I don't know if I can get back up. And it's hot!"

"Then maybe you shouldn't be wandering around so much," Jonn said, just a bit gruffly.

"Hah. Wanda could just reel her in using the winch cable, dragging her across the dust." Dana said.

"I don't think I can collect specimens wearing this suit," I said. "I'm coming back in." I pried my boots off as I climbed the steps.

"Wanda and I figured out how to store the specimens," Amelie announced. "Wanda can mold the *Star Choice* 's material. She'll create pockets into the ship's airlock that will hold the vials and anything else. They will be in the side wall of the lock, so that when the steps drawn up into the fuselage, the samples will be hidden and protected from cold and radiation. This will also minimize contamination."

"That's a brilliant solution," I said. "But now I have to find a way to go collect them."

I was shaking. This was exciting, exhilarating! "I want to breathe the air. I want to touch the soil. I want to go outside without my spacesuit. Wanda, is it safe for me to go outside?"

My crew was unanimously against this crazy idea, so I asked, "Wanda, are there organisms that are harmful to me? Germs, stinging bugs, poison plants, things in the air?"

"My controlling oki, as we have studied the larger life forms on this world, I have also analyzed tiny ones that might be pathogens or toxins, or might expose other harms to you. I have also learned about your genome and metabolism, by working with you and your friend Clay. Using the models of pathogens developed by the Confederation, earlier I asked the Maker Machine to construct a substance to inoculate you against potentially harmful entities on worlds such as this one. You should go to the Maker Machine."

This was startling information, both to my crew and me. I had no idea Wanda had taken this upon herself. Breadbox had described this process to me, and told me it was standard practice among oki traveling to different worlds, but now here it was for me. I hesitated only a moment. One gooseneck arm of the Maker Machine reached down from the ceiling to my level.

"Stand close to the arm, and allow the tendrils to have access to your skin and mouth," Wanda instructed. This took real trust! Despite feeling decidedly squeamish, I allowed the arm to move slowly over my inner arm and throat and touch the inside of my lips. I felt a mild tickle sensation, nothing more. If this thing could eliminate Clay's cancer, surely it could give me an inoculation.

"This substance will spread throughout your body," she said. "We will also use it to treat the air within the vessel. But when we depart from this world, you should place your items of apparel, including your footwear, on the table of the Maker Machine, so they can be cleaned and treated. You will now be safe from air or waterborne toxins on this world. I advise against ingesting any living thing, or allowing them to puncture your skin."

I explained this to my dubious crew, which had watched via the view space from across the vessel.

"Wait a minute!" yelled Dana. "Wanda is protecting you from tiny hazards, but what about big ones, beasties that might be lurking nearby ready to chomp you? Ask Wanda if the maker machine can create a gun or some kind of weapon—just in case."

This brought the conversation to a halt for a moment.

"Hmm, we've seen no evidence of larger entities," said Noel. "Nothing visible. No footprints, no paths, no nests, no signs of chase."

The smart thing would be to wear a white respiratory mask outside, but I had no such thing. Could I have tied a bandana around my face? Well, I didn't.

"Stay right next to the vessel, so you can hop right back in," urged Jonn.

"Agreed. Now may I step outside, Wanda?"

"Yes, my controlling oki. For added safety, I made hand coverings for you." There on the table was a pair of gloves. Looked like the rubber gloves you wear to wash dishes if your hands are more delicate than mine. But grey.

"Wanda, could you also ask the maker machine to make me a spear, to fend off any would-be predators? Dana, could you explain to Wanda what a spear looks like?"

Jonn said, "Look, even if all this doesn't kill you, when you return to Earth, they'll put you in quarantine."

"I'm already going to be in quarantine for however long it takes me to get home," I countered. "Suppose this works as Wanda describes. Would a model of pathogens for humans be a useful technology?"

"That's a big if," Jonn said, with a tone that said "you've got to prove it to me."

"We have evidence," I said. "When Breadbox and crew arrived, there were no occurrences of any galactic hungy fungy. She first described this process. She told me that travel among the worlds of the Confederation would be nearly impossible without applying their theory of pathogens."

"Are you saying that your so-called Galactic Confederation had developed a comprehensive theory of pathogens?" Noel asked.

"Yes, that's what she explained. And Wanda backs that up."

"You are a living experiment," Amelie said. "You keep letting the unknown bug bite you. May your luck always hold out."

"Even if I die—from some other cause—you will have data on this process, and it will benefit all humankind." When did I become the big hero, willing to sacrifice myself for the general good? Never. I just wanted to walk around on this new world. I wanted their buy-in.

"Okay, do it," Jonn said. "Be careful."

"At least wear your hat and sunglasses so you don't get sunburned," Noel said.

Wanda announced, "Sensors indicate that particulate matter in the air, nanometer size or larger, is quite low. No higher than would be typical on your world."

"You're going to have to change your name from Selena—Moon lady—to Stella—Star lady." Dana said.

"There's no Latin equivalent to Exoplanet Lady," Noel said. "*Novis planetae* lacks a sexy ring."

"Good name for a song, though. Maybe a Gregorian chant. I'll work on that." I said, heading toward the airlock.

"Here goes nothing," I said, closing the inner airlock and slowly opening to the outside. Warm, humid air washed over me, like Hawaii on a hot day. I tilted my head back and let a soft breeze wash over me. I opened my mount wide and breathed in big gulps of air. The air smelled like a jungle. Or a desert. Or the sea. It was hard to say. Mouth open, eyes open, tears running down my face. I cried. I laughed. I felt woozy. The high oxygen level was almost too much. I had to breathe little sips of air.

This was the most amazing experience I'd ever had in my life! Moonwalks? Tripping over moon rocks? Pfeh! Nothing compared to taking the first human steps on a completely new planet.

After a few breaths I calmed down. I fastened the winch cable to my belt clip. I descended the steps and put my foot on the ground. I took a few steps and looked around. I reached down and touched the ground with my fingertips. The soil felt like pulverized granite, like you find up in the high Sierras where glaciers have ground it down. I stood up, rubbing some between my fingers. "Okay, guys, I'm ready to collect specimens."

I reached back into the airlock where I'd stashed the tools and gloves and vials and headed toward the nearby plants.

Amelie took the lead suggesting specimens I collect in the tubes, but everybody had their suggestions. I could have used an entire case of glass vials. I had to keep running back inside to get more vials as they were produced, removing my boots each time. I collected dirt, rocks, sticks, bits of decaying plants, and pieces of live plants. I snagged bugs and worms of various descriptions. They didn't move very fast to escape my clutches. I was concerned about arousing swarms of flying, biting bugs, but it didn't happen. I guess there were no natural enemies for anything like me, so they weren't accustomed to defending against giant lurking beasts with pincer tools. I never had any need for a spear or other weapon.

Even so, some managed to climb onto my pants legs and sleeves,

My first steps upon a new earthlike planet, World 25.

which gave me the willies. I quickly brushed them off. I didn't want them biting me.

"Sorry to have to kill you, bugs." Using my tongs, I picked up things with eight legs and with many legs, but none with six legs. I found little whirligig bugs with five legs. All the flying things had four wings. They would have been much easier to catch with a butterfly net. I had trouble getting them to stay in the vials until I could get the stoppers in. Sorry to say I had to squeeze some of them with the pincers, injuring or killing them. I'm not a very good entomologist.

A bug the size of a humming bird flew right into my face, making a fluthering noise like a moth. "Eek!" I squeaked, grabbing for it. I caught its wing between my thumb and index finger. I held it in front of my face and looked into its bulging bug eyes. Eye to eye with an alien. We two beings from different worlds contemplated each other for a moment, then it fluttered loose and flew right into the top of my glove, crawling down between my fingers. "Yikes!" I yelled, reflexively jerking off my glove. No doubt it was merely looking for a place to hide, but sorry to say, I almost pulled it apart. Into a tube it went.

I kept edging farther from *Star Choice*, disregarding Jonn's plea. Never saw signs of anything larger or more fearsome.

I pulled up a few plants and discovered they did not have a very deep root system.

I broke off pieces of plant stems with some kind of web stuck to it. I dug down with my trowel and retrieved small wiggly things that lived beneath the surface.

I wanted to capture one of the flying bugs that looked kind of like a dragonfly, but they were elusive, and too large for the vial. Finally I found a dead one on the ground, and stuffed part of it into a container.

Because of the heat and humidity I was sweating like crazy, with sweat dripping off my brow onto the ground. "I'm probably contaminating the entire planet," I said into the mike. "A million years from now new and strange species will evolve here from the germs and DNA in my sweat and tears. And blood if I'm not careful."

"Scientists then will argue about where the anomalous DNA originated," Noel said. "You'd better go back inside. No point in overdoing it, Star Woman."

I walked slowly back toward *Star Choice*. I bent to pick up a small yellowish stone. It looked like an agate. Agate was Breadbox's nickname for me. I burst out crying at the memory; my tears ran down my face and fell to the ground. More alien DNA! I put the stone in my pocket as a keepsake.

I placed the vials into the newly created compartment behind the steps. I wondered how they would keep from rattling around and breaking, but Wanda told me she would have *Star Choice* grow back around them enough to hold them snugly. Having a living, growing spaceship is an amazing experience! Made me feel safer and more secure. I'd have to write a song about it.

She also said she would screen them to neutralize any organisms that would be harmful back on Earth.

On the steps of *Star Choice*, I removed my boots and brushed the grit off my fingers. I took one last look around, then went in through the airlock. The air inside tasted insipid and weak.

"Things won't be free of contamination," Amelie said from the view space. "But with the size of the specimens you collected, we'll be able to extract clean samples from inside them."

As I rested, we asked *Star Choice* to move to a couple more places with different environments to see how different things were. We never found any animals besides bugs and worms.

"How can we get samples from the water?" Noel asked. "At least get some sea water, so we can know how salty it is." I asked Wanda to move us out over the nearby sea.

Star Choice didn't float in the water, but it hovered right on top of it. I leaned out the airlock—attached to the cable of course—and scooped up some water in a vial. I got two of them, so I could taste one. Whoops, better not! I saw lots of little things swimming around in the tube. I licked a couple of drops off my finger. Not as salty as Earth's oceans. It didn't kill me.

This was quite exciting. I was getting into this process.

A couple of hours zipped by. Amelie and Dana were arguing about what other kinds of sites we should visit for samples, when Jonn's voice boomed from the view space, breaking our concentration. "Selena, good news at long last. Yesterday Noel and I and the head of NASA had an audience with a Major General Stanley, whom it turns out is up the chain from General Dickson, head of your hated Agency. I ducked out of your planetary exploration for awile, and I just heard back. Stanley was angered that Dickson didn't protect you from the Chinese. The President has had to skip nimbly because she did not rein in the Agency, nor insist that the Chinese leave you alone. This has hurt her approval ratings, and also how she is regarded by many top government officials. So she has changed her attitude toward us 180°.

"These guys were surprised to learn that you are still alive. When they heard you were dead and the ship lost they were devastated, they told me. They saw what a loss this was, and what idiots they'd been.

"I told them you are safe, but I couldn't yet reveal where you were. They do not know that you have traveled beyond the solar system. But don't worry; we have that all documented, waiting to inform the world.

"Other nations, starting with Singapore and Australia, are lining up to invite you to land with safe passage if the United States reneges.

"So, you are good to come back. You will not be attacked by American space vessels, and you can land safely. Other nations—China and Russia—

have been put on notice that you are now under the protection of the United States. It still remains to be worked out how to manage *Star Choice*, but at least we're talking as collaborators, not antagonists."

Wow. I was speechless. It took a bit for this to sink in. I was enjoying being a planetary explorer, and working with Amelie and Dana to collect, analyze, and store samples. But then a wave of joy burst from the center of my being. Tears of relief sprang from my eyes. I just said quietly, "Thank goodness. This will soon be over."

We made one last touchdown on a hilltop. "I need to make a closing statement." Once again, I put on my boots, emerged, and took a short walk—totally forgetting to attach to my cable—to a place looking back toward *Star Choice* with a view of both mountains and ocean beyond. I was ready to make my closing speech.

"Friends on Earth. I am thrilled to be the first Earthling to touch the soil of a world orbiting a different star. I hope I make it back home, but even if I don't, I'm glad to get to share this experience with you."

I took a few steps more, and then spoke again to the people of Earth, looking back toward the camera. "Look around me. This world is strange, yet familiar. The air is different, yet breathable. The plants look strange, yet the wind blowing through them sounds like a wheat field. The bugs and worms are unfamiliar, but they do the same buglike things. The hills and sea look the same. The water rippling over rocks in the river over there sounds the same as your rivers. It is a beautiful, beautiful world!

"Earth people could come to this world. Would we bring bulldozers, build skyscrapers, plant rice fields, and make it look like Earth? Or would we respect the world, and live within its ecology? Very likely, you will get to make this choice."

I took a couple of steps, then stopped.

"I want to sing you a song. My guitar's inside, so I'll go it alone." I sang the first verse of "Forever to Infinity," which seemed fitting for this situation.

> *I am unmoored.*
> *I am adrift on the vastness of space.*
> *Like a boat, lines cast free from the shore,*
> *freed of land's embrace.*
> *Slowly drifting out to sea,*
> *no rudder, no compass, no map, no haste.*
> *Across the vasty void.*
> *Forever to infinity.*

Wait a minute, I thought. This wasn't enough. "Folks, I sang this song when I feared I was lost in space. But this is no longer true. I need a new verse."

Could I come up with something just standing there on this new world? Had my inner tune maker returned to me? Let's see:

> *I'm back on land*
> *I've come down from the vastness of space*
> *To a new world, a most beautiful place*
> *Life a leaf*
> *Falling down from the sky*
> *Solid in land's embrace*
> *Warm air, cool water, green plants*
> *Could be a home for you and me.*
> *I've sailed across the vasty void*
> *And come down from Infinity.*

I took a bow. No encore. "I hope to be back home soon, folks." Some might ask, why would I even want to return home, with all the hostility directed at me. A part of me wanted to be a star traveler. One of my hit songs was *My Spaceship Calls Out to Me*. And here I was, getting my wish. But this wasn't the way I imagined it. I wanted to go sing my songs along with musicians from other worlds in amphitheaters like the Songstone.

And I was so homesick, missing my friends. I'm just an Earth girl at heart. And finally, my space wandering would soon be over. When . . . if . . . Wanda gets me home

34. Ready to Go Home

It didn't take long for me to tidy things up on *Star Choice* and be ready to take off. I sat in my captain's chair like Captain Kirk and yelled out, "Warp speed, Wanda! We are returning to Earth, where we started out." We ascended smoothly into the sky of World 25. "Goodbye beautiful world! I'm sure somebody will be back before too long." Into the dark of space once again, aiming for our jump site.

I placed my boots and clothing, and my yellow rock, on the maker machine bed to get thoroughly cleaned.

Now that I was finally heading home, I reflected on my travels. Ever since I got access to *Star Choice*, a big part of me had wanted to go traipsing around the stars. I'd written songs about it. But this wasn't the way I wanted to go. I dreamed of flying to worlds with intelligent, friendly races, where I could sing with them. This is why the Songstone had appealed to me so much. After all, I'm a singer.

Also, I didn't want to travel by myself. The Spaceketeers were supposed to be on this adventure with me. Finally, I wanted to return to a raucous welcome, not get shot at by angry missiles.

Right now, I was just terribly homesick. But I was finally on my way back. I might as well get comfortable for the long ride. I was soon asleep.

Wanda awoke me with a soft announcement. "My controlling oki, our trajectory and velocity were wrong. We were short of our target. But I have corrected the error. We can now accelerate on a new trajectory to the jump site."

"Okay. I'm glad you've corrected it." I was ready to nod off again.

"My controlling oki, Wanda regrets this miscalculation."

"I understand. Wanda, do you have enough power? Can we make the jump?" Inner alarm bells were ready to jingle. These statements were not at all like her.

"*Star Choice* has adequate reserves for the jump to the next world. Then Wanda needs further recharge."

I nodded. "Can you function well enough to guide us through this jump back to my home world?"

"I am confident, my controlling oki. We are soon ready to jump. I have activated the site and inserted the jump code."

I saw the target, slowly growing in the view space, as we moved toward it, pretty much on course. I held my breath. But the jump was made, no problem. Wanda told me she confirmed our jump site location. This was beginning to feel routine, like switching from one freeway to another. I breathed a huge sigh of relief. Back to good Earth at last! Only a hundred million miles to go. Piece of cake! A giddy sense of joy suffused my being.

Now let's find it and magnify its image in the view space. "Wanda, zoom in on Earth as soon as you can!"

There it is! "Cruise on in, *Star Choice* ! Good job, Wanda! Let's take a victory orbit."

We were traveling much faster than before, but it still took many hours to get there. It grew from an mere speck, to a bright dot with the sun off to the right, then to a crescent. I spent this time doing a thorough house cleaning. Next trip I wanted a little robot to trundle around cleaning up after me continually—dirty dishes, sweep the floor, bathroom, make the bed, etc. etc. Maybe even cook.

I saw the half circle, growing as we slowly approached. We circled around toward the daylight side, and I saw green and white.

Something was wrong. As I saw more and more of the world, I didn't recognize the continents. Where were the oceans?

This was not Earth! It certainly wasn't Mars, or Venus, or the Moon. What happened? In fact, there was no moon. No, now I could see two small moons. Earth doesn't have two moons. "Wanda, where the hell are we? We must have jumped to the wrong world!"

Does Wanda know? She had seemed confused.

"The jump is complete," she said.

"But not to the correct star system." Panic began to swallow my joy. "We are not picking up signals from Earth, according to the readout in the view space."

"Let me confirm. I do not understand. We should be in your star's system."

"We are not. The planet we are approaching is not Earth."

Silence for a long moment.

"Wanda, I want you to retrieve the jump code to Earth, from which we recently departed, and prepare to jump to that world." Another long silence.

"Sorry, I find I cannot do that, Selena, my controlling oki," she said in a soft voice. "There is a problem." She made a clicking noise, as if shuffling through files or cards or something. "If this is not the correct destination, perhaps I should turn this responsibility over to you."

My blood ran cold. "I cannot guide *Star Choice*. That is your job. Do you see that we are not back at Earth?"

Silence. I took a close look in the view space as *Star Choice* orbited low over this new unknown world. Definitely not Earth. It was a cold looking world, blanketed with dark green forests, huge glacier-covered mountain

142

ranges, and large polar ice caps. As we rounded the world, we flew above a vast grey ocean, which went on and on, seemingly covering half the planet.

I asked Wanda to show the sky to the north and to dim the interior lights. At least she could do that. I looked in vain for any familiar constellations. See, I thought I might spot the same stars I could see from Earth's northern hemisphere, till I realized there was no reason to think this world's orbit was oriented anything like Earth's. I was reluctant to ask Wanda's assistance, since apparently she didn't know where we were. I was pleased to spot the swath of the Milky Way across the sky. At least I was in the right galaxy! No. Not even sure of that. How would I know if *Star Choice* had jumped all the way to Andromeda galaxy?

Wanda had always been my faithful and reliable servant. She could answer any question. But now I couldn't rely on her, in this time when I needed her the most. And I had nobody else to turn to. What if she couldn't operate the view space? Or flush the toilet? Or keep oxygen flowing?

I was on my own, and I had no training, no preparation, for handling such a situation. I couldn't call Highway Patrol or roadside service to come help a damsel in distress. I had no training for any of this. I was just a dang singer, a ditzy chick, and in way over my head.

I was numb to the aloneness. I couldn't even feel terror any more. If I was trapped light years from Earth with a robot unable to function, I'd have to end it before I went mad. Should I order *Star Choice* to dive into the star? Could the maker machine build a revolver for me—with bullets? Could I step outside the airlock without my space suit? Or chug down all my remaining Jack Daniels hoping it would do me in? I'd probably just vomit. Then I'd be sick, and have no Jack.

Maybe I should ask her one more time, I thought. "Wanda, do you know what star system we're in right now? And how we can get from here back home to Earth?"

She was silent for half a minute that seemed like forever. "At this time, that information is not available," she said in a monotone. I sat in the dark trying to think. I needed to calm down and get my thoughts in order. Would Jonn or Amelie be able to come up with any ideas? Would Wanda be able to connect me with them? I figured I'd better give it a try.

I had trouble reaching any of my friends. Looking at my trusty clock that showed Earth time, I saw that it was very early morning in California. All my crises seemed to come pre-dawn their time. I decided to wait a couple of hours before rousing them.

Then I remembered. Noel was on the East Coast. Maybe he would be up.

When I tried to reach him, a strange thing happened. Wanda didn't connect me with him. Instead, in the view space, I was tuned into a TV program of a meeting of some sort. Many people sitting at a conference table. A rumble of talking. Then a banner said C-SPAN.

143

An off-camera announcer said, "This morning we have the Senate special committee on space technologies interviewing Mr. Jonn Buck, president of YouSpace and Flash Car, and Dr. Noel St.John Reisen, astronomer and Director of the National Observatory here in Washington, D.C."

Seeing my friends sitting at a table, wearing suits, surrounded by other people, made me feel immensely homesick. The lump in my throat burst forth in tears. I cried so hard I couldn't see the TV program.

Lost in space, tuned to politics.

35. C-SPAN

By the time I got situated in my seat and paid attention, the session I was watching on TV was underway. The TV-to-viewspace hookup worked perfectly, leaping across the cosmos via alien magic, except that the picture was flat and two-dimensional. I was so accustomed to solid-looking life-size 3D images when those on both ends were using the view bubble.

"News reports said the UFO was destroyed—with her in it," some senator said, holding up a front page from the New York Times. That was at least the second time I had made the front page of the Times, and both news stories were wrong.

Jonn looked appraisingly at the senator before he answered, then nodded. "She took evasive action, then we put out this story to dissuade certain parties from pursuing her further." He made a tent of his fingers, which I've been told is body language for "I'm not telling the whole story." Nobody would believe him if he did tell all.

This revelation caused a ripple of talk throughout the hearing room. "We are pleased to learn that. Very pleased," said the chairman of the hearing.

Another Senator piped up. "But that brings us back to the original situation. The problem is this singer. She's a loose cannon. If it were you gentlemen we were dealing with . . ." That senator's name placard said "Gass."

"You *are* dealing with us, Senator Gass." Noel has such an impressive presence. He is elegant, knowledgeable, unflappable—even with all these high-powered senators. And very polite. Responds to each one by name.

"She still has control," said some senator. "She's flying it around the Moon or somewhere." I didn't recognize the senators, and I didn't pay much attention to their name placards, so I'm just calling most of them "senator." A bunch of men in dark suits, plus one woman in regal red.

"She's actually orbiting much farther out," Jonn said ambiguously, still hiding behind his finger tent. There was a hint of "I'm impatient with all you turkeys" in his demeanor. "We're seeking a way for her to cede control to an organization that can manage the technology, and has legal standing with the government to do so." Another mutter of talking.

Jonn continued with a hint of edge to his voice, "You say the problem

145

is her. It's equally true that the problem is you, meaning the government. If, from the beginning, you had approached her with respect instead of locking her up and yanking the wrecked ship off her land, this may have unfolded very differently."

Noel said with complete politeness, "At your request, we are trying to come to an accommodation—an accommodation where both sides give something and receive something."

Another senator spoke up, "The fact that she's involved at all is just happenstance. It just happened to land on her hillside."

Jonn said, "Yes, agreed, at least initially. And what is the significance of that to you? You know the law in that regard, about things that fall from the sky."

No response. Senators shuffled their folders of papers.

The chairman said, "You've done your homework, gentlemen; this is an impressive list of backers you've put together. What diversity! Different political viewpoints, ethnic, female, international, celebrities, scientists, media. I wish I could put together a group of backers like this."

"Senator Goodman, this is a very popular project," replied Noel. "It wouldn't hurt you at all to have your name associated with it."

A very young looking senator: "You say we must make accommodations. What would these accommodations look like?"

Jonn replied, "The US Government would give up claim to ownership and cede control to an organization that we incorporate with new safeguards. This organization would be the shepherd of the alien technologies. You would guarantee Ms. Morisot's safety and her right to land on United States soil and to conduct operations from here, *and* to protect her and the vessel from threats—internal and external."

Noel added, "Selena Morisot would hand over control to this organization."

The young senator, holding up a piece of paper like it was incriminating evidence, said, "But I see here she would be on the Board of Directors."

"Yes," Noel replied blandly. "One among several. She has no interest in running it."

"Who would run it?"

"We've interviewed a former astronaut, Amelie Martel-Petrova," Noel said. Wow! I had no idea.

"She's not even American, I see," said the young senator. "Russian."

"Canadian," replied Jonn. "Looks good to have an international presence, yet a strong ally."

A different senator said, "What if we saw that you are engaged in activities that are not in the national interest of the United States?"

Jonn nodded and replied, "None of us want that. We certainly need to spell out what these interests are."

Noel said, "Tell us, what are your concerns, Senator Knott? What do you most want to avoid? Remember, we're on your side—and so is Ms.

Morisot."

Senator Knott frowned, looked down at his papers and said, "We will particularize the concerns. There is a sizable contingent that strongly believes we should just destroy this—not quite sure what to call it—spaceship."

Jonn replied with his hands spread out. "Yes, several attempts have been made. We're trying to ensure that that doesn't happen. My mission is to bring it back safely."

The Chairman started pulling his spread-out papers together. "Okay, thank you gentlemen, this will not be decided instantly. I'm sure it will work its way over to the President, since it has foreign policy implications."

Noel actually raised his voice a bit and frowned, which was such a contrast to his prior manner. "One more thing. It's long past time to stop referring to Ms. Morisot as a loose cannon or 'just a singer' or even worse, 'ditzy chick.' She has organized and carried out a trip to the Moon using alien technology."

Bald-headed senator: "As I understand it, that's only because it's very easy to use."

Noel shook his head in agreement, back to his diplomatic visage. "All the more reason for us to quickly come to an accommodation—to complete this agreement—so we can all take advantage of it."

A new senator spoke up. "Are you gentlemen planning to go to the Moon yourselves?"

Jonn replied, "What we're discussing today is making this technology available to all of humankind. To do that, we need access to the vessel at a facility where it can be properly studied."

Noel said smoothly, "Flying to space is obviously one of the capabilities that is of tremendous interest to a great number of people, certainly including us."

Another senator asked, "Are the aliens coming here? Should we prepare for an invasion?"

Jonn said, "No, no indication of this. There are strong reasons to believe they cannot do so, from what Ms. Morisot has told us."

"And she's an expert on this because…?"

Jonn replied, "You should ask her this."

"How does one reach an astronaut circling the solar system in a UFO?"

"Call this cell number. Here it is. Your call will be relayed."

The Chairman stood up. "Mr. Buck, Dr. Reisen, thank you for coming here today. Most enlightening."

That was the second time Jonn suggested that some official call me to get an opinion, but none ever did.

*　　*　　*

After adjournment, people in the hearing room milled around and talked

147

while the camera and mikes were still on. I heard this exchange:

Man with a $1000 suit and a bulging, beat up leather briefcase: "Have you seen that video of Ms. Morisot tripping over a moon rock and falling on her face?"

General with a chest full of medals and ribbons, shaking his head: "Of course. My men call her a ditzy chick, despite what Dr. Reisen says."

The suit: "Yes, a ditzy chick who has flown to the Moon despite all our efforts to thwart her."

The woman in red, whom I think is a senator from the Midwest: "I find it endearing, kind of an everywoman image, succeeding despite klutziness. Doesn't that speak to all of us?"

The suit: "I think this accounts for her soaring popularity. We'll raise a storm of protest if we continue with her the way we have so far."

The woman: "Have you listened to any of her music? What do you think of it?"

They walked out of range before I could hear the response. Drat!

The view space went blank, and I sat there with roiling emotions. Pride that Jonn and Noel defended me to the United States government. Joy that a resolution was finally opening up. Terrible homesickness, seeing this everyday interchange so close at hand, yet so incredibly distant. Marvel at the magical technology that let me watch it. Happiness that my music was known and discussed even by government officials. And beneath this, terror and hopelessness about my plight.

If I weren't terrified, maybe I could see the humor in this situation. Top government poobahs are taking us seriously, while I am marooned in space lightyears from home with damaged and malfunctioning equipment, unable to get back.

36. Way Gone

I had tried to reach Noel, and instead tuned into C-SPAN. Did Noel set that up, or was it another Wanda glitch? I decided to try again. "Wanda, can you reach Amelie with the view space?"

Nothing happened. The view space was now a dim, empty bubble, showing nothing but a pale blue fog.

I was teetering into panic. If I was stuck here alone in space and could not reach my friends, that would be very close to the end for me. I got up and paced back and forth, trying to burn off some of the raw fear in my gut. I yelled. I pounded on the wall. I lay face down on my bed and cried. I cried for an hour until I cried myself out. Then I turned over, lay on my back and stared at the ceiling.

"Damn it, Canuck! Dange! Flash! Starman! Why aren't you here to help me? Please don't abandon me here to die, especially when I'm about to be cleared to return home."

I heard a tiny voice from somewhere. It sounded like Amelie. Was I hearing things? Was I that far gone already?

"Selena, what's happening?" I looked around. Wow, her voice was coming from my comm stone on the shelf across the sleeping area. I jumped up and retrieved it. I held it up to my face like a microphone.

"Amelie, is that you?" I yelled.

"Yes, who do you think? No need to shout."

"Why does the comm stone work when the view space won't?" I asked.

"I don't know. What's happening? What's your status?"

I broke down crying while trying to bring Amelie up to date. "I'm a goner, Amelie. (Sob) Systems are failing. Wanda mostly. (Sniffle) Seems like internal systems are still working—lights, air, warmth, toilet, gravity. (Snorf) But Wanda is forgetful, confused, can't remember the things she has done. I'm terrified."

"I know, I know how you feel. Take a deep breath. That's right. Now let it out slowly." She gave me a minute to recover some semblance of sanity. Then she went on.

"When I was on the space station, we had some really tough times. Astronauts didn't think they had a chance to pull through. The most important thing was for us to avoid panic."

"I'm a lot farther away than the ISS in low Earth orbit," I blubbered.

"True, but you are in a cocoon of habitability. The basic systems of your vessel still function, you say. You have a control problem. For control problems, there are workarounds. We have talked people through deadly situations and got them home safely, and we're going to do the same for you. You are coming home, Spaceketeer. So take another deep breath, and let's talk this through."

I did as she instructed. I took a few deep yoga breaths.

Then, finally, Jonn's voice boomed from my comm stone, and I explained things to him. "Jonn, where are you?"

"In our hotel in Washington. Noel and I just got back from a Senate hearing."

"I watched it. I didn't know it was live."

He chortled. "Stuck in space but you can get live TV? That's maxly ironic. Yes, it was a positive outcome. But only if we get you back here. So, what can we do?"

"Amelie says it's a control problem and there are always workarounds."

"Right. She's right."

"The view space is not working properly, yet the comm stones do. And their function depends of the view space. So basically the view space is working as a communication channel. But not when I address it."

"What if we try from our end?" Amelie asked. "Wanda, can you restore Selena's use of the view space?"

Wanda replied in the comm stone. "Let me investigate." A brief pause. I waited with bated breath, till I heard the trademark "beedle boop," as if Wanda was talking to herself. Another pause. "Yes, I believe that function can be restored." And it was! I saw stars in the view space. And their voices emanated from it also. Hooray!

"We don't know anything about Wanda," Amelie said, "or how to deal with her. She's always been the thing that knew the answers and was completely competent. If it was a human being, it's kind of like she's suffering from PTSD."

"That sounds on target," Jonn said, "Post-traumatic stress. Can a device like Wanda experience an emotional, psychological syndrome? Sure seems like it."

"What do we do about that?" I asked. "We have no drugs to treat her."

"What works with her?" Amelie asked. "Has she ever had similar situations?"

I thought back to the attack by the Device Captain. "Yes, she has. It took time. And talk."

"Talk therapy," Amelie agreed. "Talk people though the crisis. Often the best thing. Always helpful. Wanda is not a person, but . . . Can you talk with her?"

"Of course. I'll try that. Probably good for me also. Can you guys determine where the hell I am?"

"We may have to get back to my lab where our big view space is," Jonn said. "We'll see if we can reconstruct a map of your travels. I'll get Noel's help."

After Amelie and Jonn signed off, I walked over to Wanda where she was inserted into the receptacle in the control panel. I wanted to pick her up and cuddle her, the way Breadbox used to do. But she needed to stay connected to *Star Choice*, I was pretty sure. So I sat in my seat and looked at her.

I spoke to her. "Wanda, we've had some good times, haven't we? Do you remember when you taught my friend Breadbox to count in my language? That was the beginning of our communication with each other."

No response. I waited a minute, listening to my heart thumping with anxiety, then continued. "Do you remember when I had to hide you beneath the floor boards to keep my enemies from finding you? I felt so bad doing that to you."

Still no response. "Do you remember our jam session, when Eddy Backwater and I sang, then Breadbox sang, and you sang the English version? Your voice sounded just like hers."

In these situations, I keep forgetting that I'm a singer. I remembered it then, and I sang the first few lines of Breadbox's song:

> The Universe is cold and uncaring.
> Life is a nothingful scum.
> We life, we always crave meaning,
> where no meaning can ever be found.

Wanda joined in and sang the last part with me. I felt a thrill of hope.

I went on. "Do you remember creating the clone of yourself? And how tough is was knowing which clone was the real you?"

Silence.

"When the government took the clone from me, thinking it was you, and then drew the attention of the Device Captain on Sfofong, who turned the clone off, do you remember how this also damaged you? You had to put your personality together again."

She responded. "I did it for you, my controlling oki," she said softly, and it brought tears to my eyes to hear her say that.

"Afterward we discussed whether you preferred existence or non-existence," I said. "You told me you preferred interesting challenges."

"You give me interesting challenges, my controlling oki." she said.

"Yes," I smiled. "We're in the middle of one right now, aren't we?"

A long silence.

"Do you remember when Kateh and I first talked, with you translating, and she confirmed that I was your controlling oki."

"Yes, my controlling oki. And it has been so."

I went on like this, reminiscing, reminding her of things we had done together. I talked softly, unhurried. Sometimes she would make a brief response.

I retrieved Gibb, sat cross-legged in my seat, and played some soft melodies, recalling songs that Breadbox had sung. I was doing this for Wanda, but for myself as well. Whenever I stopped singing and playing, the terror would begin to push up within my gut.

If I was doomed to die here in space, I was going to go out as a singer.

"There is a wound within me, my controlling oki." Wanda said plaintively during a break in my singing. "I cannot see some needed information."

"I know, my friend. We'll just stay here for now and I'll sing to you. We'll see if that helps."

For how long, I wondered? Even though I had obtained more food in Singapore (Omigawd did that ever seem long ago!) it wasn't unlimited. And it wasn't just me. Wanda was probably just as low on her energy reserves.

"Wanda, do you need to turn down the grav? Or the lights? Or the temperature?" I didn't mention the oxygen flow. That would be really scary.

"No need. These draw little energy when we cruise without acceleration."

I was certainly relieved to hear that. "Wanda, about your wound. Are you talking about the damaged propulsion?"

"In addition to the damaged propulsion, I have a wound within me."

Two distinct serious problems. It was my turn to sit there silently. What could I say?

She went on. "I am using energy to restore the damaged propulsion, and that draws so much energy, it keeps me from building up my reserves. And the repair is very slow, since I have access to no outside materials."

"Mmm, I see. Should we land on this world to find needed materials?"

"This world would not be hospitable for you, my controlling oki. Low temperature, higher gravity, strong winds, and higher atmospheric pressure at the surface. We may have difficulty finding the types of materials needed for the repairs. And then we would be deep in this world's gravity well with limited energy reserves and damaged propulsion."

Scratch that idea!

"Okay. Could you suspend those repairs for a time?" No need to fix the propulsion if we're not going anywhere, I thought.

"Making such repairs is a built-in function for me."

"Ah." Dead end.

"I could only suspend this function if you so requested."

I nodded. "Wanda, I request that you suspend the repairs on *Star Choice's* propulsion system until I say resume."

"Yes, my controlling oki."

152

Wanda gradually got more talkative, but she could still not access everything. "Some information is missing."

"Do you think it's gone?"

"I must retain it within, but I cannot access it. Inner links and hooks are disabled."

I thought of all the times I had searched for a word. I knew that I knew it, but I couldn't think of it then.

"Perhaps if we stop trying so hard, it will just pop up again." I tried to comfort her.

But it didn't pop up again, and a few hours later my Earth team got back to me and confessed they had no way to decipher what star system I had jumped to.

"Who can help us?" I asked nobody. "Could we search the Galactic Library for a self-help diagnostic?" That's what I would do back on Earth—dig into all the amateur help videos on YouTube. Many times I'd figured out how to fix my computers or appliances that way.

"In principle, yes, but there may be difficulties," she replied. "This device you call Wanda is not a standard Confederation model, and extensive changes have been made. Also, we are using jump codes that lie outside the network controlled by the Confederation."

"Right you are," I said. "No way would I divulge our jump codes, or even information about where we are. It may be better that I perish than reveal all to the Confederation."

"My controlling oki, I notice that Kateh tried to contact you while I was incapacitated."

Did I want to talk with Kateh again? She wanted to discuss her troubles. I had my own.

As I continued to probe Wanda for some clue that might lead to a fix, Kateh contacted me again. "My oki friend, I tried to reach you, but no connection was made. I was concerned about your device." At least Wanda could still translate.

It amazed me how quickly she picked up that I was having trouble with my device. We looked at each other in the view space. She was as alien as I could imagine, and her face was completely unreadable, yet I liked her and trusted her. "As I look at your surroundings, I see you are in the same place as when we last communicated. Why do you stay in your vessel circling your world?"

She was too dang perceptive! I had to tell her. I brought her up to date on my woes, trying my best to keep from breaking down in tears.

"Kateh, I was pursued by my own kind. They fired weapons at us, and we were damaged. To escape, I had to jump to an unknown world. Because of the damage, there is a problem with my device, which controls the flight of the vessel. Thus I am unable to return to my world. I am in this vessel alone except for my device."

"This is a serious situation, my friend. I am ashamed that I was bringing my insignificant problems for you to solve."

"Thank you, clan mother Kateh. Your situation is as serious to you as mine is to me." I knew dang well that wasn't true! "I appreciate your concern. Do you mind if I ask you whom I could turn to for help?"

She looked at me, wriggling her tentacles rhythmically.

"Perhaps we can help," she said. "After all, your vessel and device were originally designed and built on our world."

I looked at her dumbfounded. This had never occurred to me. "Can you advise me?"

"There is a clan cousin of Nala that has much greater understanding of such matters than I do. Her name is Furu-la-hawa. She has studied the technologies of travel and communication at major centers of learning on leading worlds of the Confederation. I will ask her if she is willing to communicate with you."

Any port in a storm, I thought. If they could tell me how to restore the correct jump code to return to Earth, I would be glad to get their help. Way glad!

While waiting, I went back to my larder to see what I could find. I hadn't eaten for I don't know how many hours. I guess it was a good thing that I had an appetite.

I was assembling a sandwich of thick peanut butter and strawberry jam on stale bread when Wanda spoke to me. "My controlling oki, I am so sorry I have not lived up to your needs and requests. When that bolt of energy struck me, it degraded my ability to serve and protect you when you needed it most. I am dedicated to protecting you. You created me, through your requests. You are my controlling oki."

I was thrilled that my wounded gizmo and companion was speaking this coherently, and seemingly still on my side.

"Also, you are the only controller for your world, since you have not appointed anybody else. You have the crystal that contains all the jump codes, perhaps the only one remaining extant in the galaxy. If I did not protect you, it would be lost forever.

After a pause she continued, "I am committed by my very construction to protect you, and to protect this unique information."

So the amulet was as important as I was—maybe more so. But I was high on the list.

Okay. I was stranded many lightyears from home, but my smart gizmo was talking again, I had a potential source of repairs, and I had a delicious PB and J sandwich. I could make it through another 24 hours. I looked longingly at my dwindling supply of bourbon.

Time to plead my case to another very alien being.

37. Stupid Type 1

Into my view space popped the images of two very different Fofonoloy. Kateh was larger, dignified, skin spots a pleasing fuchsia and gray. She made familiar flowing gestures with her tentacles. Next to her was a smaller, skinnier Fofonoloy. Its (or her?) body color was bubblegum pink with jarring green and red ripples. She was constantly in motion. All her tentacles were swaying like an octopus in a strong ocean current. Her intricate patterns looked ever so much like communication. Imagine a sea anemone doing a hula.

Kateh wore the solid metal midriff band just as Breadbox always had. But the other one's band looked more like chain mail, and flexed when she moved. She also had a small flat pouch tied to her "chest" by two thin green bands. Like the pouch I'd use to carry my phone and credit card while out jogging.

When Kateh saw me, she made introductions. "Here is Selena True Singer, a constant female, my friend and song friend of your clan cousin Bvar-nala-nga. We may call her Selena." Constant female? I'd never heard that term before. Maybe because I never change sexes? "Here is Furu-la-hawa, clan cousin of Nala in her female phase, and educated in the theory and technology for travel among worlds. We may call her Furu-la. It is Furu-la who may be able to help you resolve your apparatus difficulties so that you may return safely to your home world."

Kateh and Furu-la appeared in the view space together, but obviously weren't in the same place, because there were different backgrounds behind them. You know how two soap bubbles can join and have a thin membrane between them? Kind of like that. One of them in each bubble. A three-way 3-D video call.

Kateh directed one eyestalk toward me and the other toward Furu-la. I didn't know what Furu-la was seeing. She wasn't looking at me.

She explained the situation to Furu-la and asked if she would be willing to assist. They spoke to each other in the Sfofongi language that I could recognize. I was pleased that Wanda's translation function was still working.

Furu-la spoke to Kateh as if I were not present. "Stupid Type 1. Not qualified to use our tools. Took something from cousin Nala and misused it. Does not know what she is doing. Has no business doing star travel.

Should have stayed on her own world."

I was appalled. Was she unaware that I was present? Could she not see me in the view space? Maybe she didn't realize Wanda was translating everything she said.

I suddenly flashed back to a time I'd been at a sidewalk bistro in Paris. A group at a nearby table heard me speak and knew I was American. They started berating American tourists in very descriptive language, not realizing I spoke French. I listened for a while, then stood up, walked over to their table, smiled, and said—in French, "On behalf of all Americans who love France, may I buy you a bottle of wine?" I'll never forget the looks on their faces! This had a perverse effect. They got angry with me for eavesdropping and humiliating them. But I walked away happy.

Furu-la went on unabated. "I have studied among the tall arrogant Type 1 oki beings within the high halls of the cities—those beings who believe the Galactic Confederation is solely for their benefit. I have been insulted and humiliated by those who look down at us Type 2 beings of the marsh, even though our technologies are far superior to theirs. They take from us and claim it as their own. And now here is another one, who has taken our tools, claimed them as her own, and then comes crying for our help when she cannot handle them."

Kateh's skin went dark purple and her tentacles trembled. "Clan cousin Furu-la-hawa, please hear what our visitor has to say."

I couldn't hold back. "Furu-la, clan cousin of Nala," I spoke in English and Wanda translated into Sfofongi. Furu-la turned toward me, astonished. Her skin went bright pink, and her tentacles spread out in the gesture of surprise. I continued, "I cannot disagree with what you say about me. Except for one thing. Your cousin Nala became my best friend. We sang together."

"They sang together?" Furu-la asked Kateh, not speaking to me. "I would like to hear that." She finally looked at me. "How do we know this is true?"

I replied, "I can sing her songs." I paused for a moment, then added, "Ask the device." I figured Wanda would be a trusted witness.

Furu-la said in a voice full of ridicule, as conveyed by Wanda, "Ask a device?" With her tentacle movements, she displayed incredulity. I recalled long ago how during my first contact with these aliens, they wouldn't talk with Wanda directly. They insisted on speaking with the crewmembers, who unfortunately were all dead. To them, Wanda was only an unintelligent translation device.

Also, Wanda is beneath the view bubble and so cannot be seen by those appearing in the bubble. So when she spoke on her own behalf, it was unclear who was speaking.

Wanda spoke to Furu-la. "Nala and my controlling oki sang together, and learned each other's language."

"Your controlling oki?" Furu-la said with derision. "How is this possible?"

I answered. "It was your clan cousin who bequeathed to me this device that is speaking. The device restored the vessel that we are in, and outfitted it for my body shape. It taught itself to speak my tongue. It became my companion."

Furu-la retorted, "The device of which you speak is not an oki, worthy of companionship, only a communication and control device."

I did my best to retain my cool. "This device is much more than a communication device. It controls the spaceship. It is a person in many respects. She converses, she chooses, she has preferences, she advises me, she works with my friends to build new devices, she feels guilt."

"This is an absurdity," she fumed.

She again addressed Kateh. "I am angry that this Type 1 being we speak with is demanding things for which a personal device is not designed. That's part of the problem. It's dangerous. It's dangerous to have devices perform these kinds of functions. Even if this device could do those things, it shouldn't." She turned toward me. "You've taken it much further than we have." At least now Furu-la was speaking directly to me. "No wonder it has had a breakdown."

"With all due respect to you, Furu-la," I replied, "these things we discuss are not what caused its breakdown. We were attacked with weapons of destruction and the vessel was badly damaged. This was a serious wound to Wanda, my device. Energy reserves dipped dangerously low making our escape.

I went on, "When your cousin died I lost a dear friend. I tried to turn this device that I call Wanda into another friend because I was very lonely."

"You wanted to befriend a device!?"

"I have other device friends." I picked up Gibb and played a chord. "My fingers speak to the guitar and my guitar speaks to me, and as you see, we play together."

I strummed a verse of "Together Stars People." "This song was inspired by your cousin Nala." Then I played the song Breadbox had sung at the jam session we'd held, oh so long ago. Wanda sang the words of Breadbox/Nala, and I sang in English.

Then I surprised myself by singing with Gibb a verse of my old standby, "Cotton Candy Lovin'."

Furu-la was clearly captivated.

Kateh then spoke again, skin patches violet and arm tentacles standing straight out. She spoke in her Voice of Authority that I had heard before. "Clan cousin Furu-la-hawa, honored and accomplished in all you do, hear this: Selena True Singer, from distant oki world called Earth, cared for clan daughter Nala when the space vessel crashed on Selena's world. She sang with Nala, cared for her as she recovered, and offered to return her remains to our world along with the vessel." Kateh spoke like a god in the heavens admonishing a weak human. I could hear this tone in her voice even without Wanda's translation.

Furu-la was chastened. Her skin tone went toward grey and her tentacles dipped in supplication. "Honored clan mother Kateh-naga-la, I respectfully hear you. I will help this friend of Nala in whatever way I can." Then she addressed me. "I would ask only that you demonstrate your musical device to me."

"I would be delighted to do so," I replied with a smile. I strummed a raucous phrase from Chuck Berry's "Johnnie B. Goode," and I could see Furu-la's tentacles begin to pick up the rhythm.

I may be stuck in deepest space, but I am a singer, and I know my rock-n-roll. My possible benefactor was a strange looking alien who despised me, but she was captivated by my music.

38. Interstellar Troubleshooting

Once she agreed to help me, Furu-la wasted no time. "May I communicate directly with your controller device?" she asked me.

"Of course," I replied through Wanda. "I wish to inform you that I refer to her as Wanda. Wanda, please communicate with Furu-la in the appropriate way."

"Yes, my controlling oki. I understand what Furu-la needs."

Furu-la remained in the view space, but Kateh departed unnoticed. Furu-la held some small instrument with two of her arm tentacles. It looked like a bar of metal. She spoke to Wanda in the beedle boop language, but much more rapid and complex than I had heard previously. Multiple tones and rhythms at once, each with its own cadence and tempo. Not particularly melodic—not in my understanding of music anyway—but fascinating to a musical ear like mine.

I couldn't tell which one was beedlebooping, Furu-la or Wanda. It went on and on till my attention drifted. I wandered around the vessel checking to see if other things still worked: water faucets, toilet, lights, fresh air. And grav of course. Yes indeed. Amazing that an injured Wanda could undergo this depth probing of her "psyche" and still maintain all the other functions. A true multitasker!

After a time this activity came to a stop. Furu-la remained motionless in the view space with her eyestalks pointed at the bar of metal. Then she spoke to me, and Wanda translated as if she hadn't just experienced a mind probe.

"The device is self-correcting. However, there is damage in the system needed for self-correction. This system should be redundant. But I suspect your device has reallocated some of this system to handle other unusual functions you have requested. Thus it is not able to repair itself. Since there is damage to the actual circuits and not just to paths of logic, we may not be able to restore it remotely."

"So Wanda has forgotten the jump code?" I asked.

"The code is likely still within. It has forgotten how to find it."

"What if we could identify the code elsewhere and insert it directly." I knew I had the code on my amulet. And Jonn and Amelie had entered it.

"That may work. But dangerous. Because we cannot tell what other malfunction may be involved. Many things can go wrong during a jump."

This wasn't sounding good. "What can we do?" It was like when your mechanic says you need a crucial part replaced but your car is so old they don't make that part any more.

"I must confer with clan mother Kateh." She was gone for a seeming eternity, leaving me there to nibble on my peanut butter sandwich staring into the empty view space. Not even any "on hold" music, unless I played it myself.

Then she reappeared. "Would you be willing to bring your vessel to Sfofong? We may need to have instruments that are in physical contact with your device."

Fly *Star Choice* to Sfofong? What kind of a suggestion was that? It froze me in my seat. Danger, danger! Kateh had told me in no uncertain terms that I shouldn't come there to deliver the remains of Breadbox. The angry Elders would grab my stuff, and probably toss me in prison. Or worse.

"May I confer with Kateh?" I asked Furu-la. In a moment Kateh appeared in the view space.

"Kateh, you told me coming there would cause you serious trouble. And me also."

"We will find a way. We cannot allow you to die alone in space."

"There is a way," Furu-la said with conviction.

Kateh had tried in vain to get the clan mothers to talk with me in the view space. They didn't like me. They were afraid of me! I was a hated tall Type 1 being. Just like Furu-la felt when we first connected.

Yet I felt a touch of glee. I'd finally get to see the home world of my best friend Breadbox, which I'd long dreamed of visiting. I'd tried to imagine what her marshy world would look like, and now I could see it firsthand.

The impossibility of this struck me instantly. "If I can't get home, which is less than a hundred lightyears distant, how could I get to your world, which is a thousand lightyears away? And wouldn't we run into the same risk of malfunction?"

Wanda took a moment to translate lightyears into terms Furu-la could understand.

"I did not realize you were that distant. I must confer with a colleague." And she was gone again. No problem, I would wait. I had no place to go.

Half an hour later she reappeared in the view space.

She said, "We can insert a complete jump circuit with a one-time code built in, so that your device could rely on it for the entire process."

I kind of understood what she was suggesting. "Wanda, would you allow Furu-la to insert a one-time code circuit, to circumvent the part of you that you cannot access?

"Yes, my controlling oki, if you so request."

I heard more beedle boop, then high-pitched chirping, then a short eerie melody. Maybe that last bit was the song of the jump code.

"I am satisfied that your vessel can complete the jump to my world, assuming it can navigate to the jump site," Furu-la said.

"Wanda, can you return to the jump site of this world, and do you have enough energy reserves to summon a jumpsite that is a thousand lightyears distant?"

"Yes, I am confident that I do. And as we approach the jump site I can check once again."

I looked at Furu-la. "Is there a problem with me coming to your world? Kateh tells me that your Elders have sanctioned the Clan Mothers."

Furu-la gave the gesture of reassurance. "We will bring you to a hidden place. There is a jump site that is not monitored. We will guide you there, and then to a safe landing location on our world."

"Then I guess we're ready."

Furu-la beedle-booped flight instructions to Wanda, and I waited for *Star Choice* to start moving toward the jump site. Nothing happened. Another glitch? I told Furu-la. Anxiety arose in my gut again. Furu-la again communicated directly with Wanda, to no avail. Nothing happened. Furu-la said, "I cannot figure this out."

"Well, ask Wanda why she can't follow your directions."

Furu-la did this. "Your device told me that the instruction must come from you."

"Ah, I am the controlling oki. Wanda, will you follow the instructions given to you by Furu-la and jump to the world to which she is guiding you?"

"Yes my controlling Oki, I can do that."

"Do you have enough power?"

"Yes, I detect that I do."

"Then let's go."

I could soon see that we were moving out of the orbit and away from the planet, and I conveyed this to Furu-la.

We were back into the blackness of space, leaving this unfriendly planet behind. I was delighted to leave it. Even so, I asked myself, "Does this fly-by count as a world visited? Hell yes! Number 3. I'll have to think of a suitable name for it. Assuming I survive."

What would happen now? No way of knowing. I could disappear in a puff of smoke for all I knew.

I hummed up my friends back home to tell them what was going to happen. "I'm making another jump—to the home world of Breadbox—to get repairs."

"Are you crazy!? This is completely beyond your control!" Amelie told me. Others muttered agreement.

"Yes it is crazy. Yes, things are out of my control. I must take the step that I perceive will eventually get me home. I must first go farther from home before I can get closer. Does that make sense?"

"Only in an abstract philosophical way," said Amelie.

"Here I am, my friends," I said, feeling a little worked up. I climbed up on my high horse. "I am circling a world maybe a hundred light-years from home and it feels like all the way across the cosmos. And now I'm about to jump to another world a thousand light-years away." I felt a pit in my stomach just thinking about it. "A hundred light-years is close in comparison. I don't know whether it will work or not." The pit in my gut grew even larger. "If it does *not* work, it's been a great ride and I love all of you."

I paused to let that sink in, then went on in a resigned tone of voice. "I have no choice, you see. I am shooting the rapids and they are carrying me toward an unknown destination. I have no choice but to go with the flow, as scary as that might be."

Noel said, "This may be an inopportune time to inform you of this but we are meeting with the Senate committee again tomorrow or the next day to discuss details of setting up a *Star Choice* Foundation. We'd like you to be here to be part of that, so please come home."

"Now I feel like Moses who never got to see the Promised Land."

"Don't even talk like that. Don't think like that," Amelie admonished me. "You are coming back here. You are our fearless leader."

"Fearless? I am scared shitless. Okay folks, gonna sign off for now, we're coming up to the jump site and I want to hold my breath."

I took a deep breath and shuddered a bit, then muttered mostly to myself, "I must write a song about going with the flow, assuming I survive."

The target grew, then disappeared. We were through the jump site, heading toward a new world; I was still alive, safe in the blackness of space. But heading toward a world full of peril for me.

"Wanda, don't forget to record the location of this jump site as you always do," I said as we emerged through the new jump site. Was Wanda listening to me? Could she still be relied upon to handle these routine but essential tasks? If we couldn't find this jump site again we had no possibility of ever getting home.

One more contact from Kateh. Maybe she had changed her mind and was warning me away.

"I have alarming news," she said. "One of the Haw clan mothers was about to go to male phase. The Elders told her she would get a terrible assignment unless she reported to them all that we had done. She may have done so to some extent. We'll never know. She killed herself by swimming out to sea where she was presumably eaten by a sea creature. The other clan mothers are shaken up. They don't want to face that fate. They may be more open to talking with you."

I didn't want to go to a world where such craziness prevailed. But too late to turn back.

Space Girl Yearning

39. Return to the Home of Breadbox

The star in the view space looked like a twin of the Sun, but I was much more interested in the planet we were approaching, which slowly grew from bright dot to a semicircle of light. I informed my Earth crew that we had successfully completed another jump, and were now approaching World Number 4 on my impromptu cosmic meander.

"Breadbox, my best friend," I spoke to the vivid image of my friend, "I never thought this would happen, but I'm approaching your home world. I carry with me your songs and your spirit. Also your tools—your device I call Wanda, your vessel I have named *Star Choice*, and the amulet that made our adventures possible. Ironically, I have visited more worlds that you did—you who set out with your crew to be explorers. I will soon meet face to face with your clan mother and cousin Furu-la. I am so sorry you are not here with me."

As we cruised toward this world, I continued my talk therapy with Wanda, playing "do you remember" with her. She was now more animated, and responded to most of my statements.

When I couldn't think of any more, we were silent for a time. Then she said, "I am so sorry I have not lived up to your needs and requests. When that bolt of energy struck me, it degraded my ability to serve and protect you when you needed it most. I am dedicated to protecting you. You created me, through your requests. You are my controlling oki."

Yes, she had said nearly the same thing earlier. Never mind. "Thank you, Wanda, my robotic companion. I know that is true."

I had something else on my mind. "Wanda, how do I guide you to a landing? I don't know where we're going. We have to find a particular spot on this world."

"That is true, my controlling Oki. Furu-la has connected me to a beacon. I will follow it."

At that, Wanda began making a chattering staticky noise, which completely freaked me out. I sat watching the view space, searching for our target world to emerge from the black void, and she was chattering and jittering in a way I had never heard before. "Wanda, what is the matter? Are we going to crash?"

Wanda did not respond for a moment but the chattering stopped. She resumed speaking to me in a normal voice, as if nothing had happened.

163

"I am being guided to circle an inner world before approaching the final destination world. I will magnify that world in the view space."

The view zoomed in on a world that was an undistinguished pinkish gray. We were headed directly for it, coming in much too close, moving very rapidly. Always before we had begun to decelerate as we got close to a world, but in this instance, we retained our speed. Were we going to smack into it?

We circled the sunlit side very low, barely above the pink and gray and roiling blue clouds. But we zipped around this world with no sign of landing. Even so, I said to myself, "World Number 4 on my odyssey.

I just hoped I didn't end up like Amelia Earhart, disappearing on the last leg of a historic flight.

As I saw the night margin approaching, we moved away from that world. "Wanda, what just happened?"

I realized I should ask Furu-la instead. Furu-la replied, "This particular approach to Sfofong uses a gravitational boost around one world to move your vessel to our world in an unorthodox trajectory so that we will avoid detection by those who would impede your progress." Ah, sneaking in. "It is aided by the current relative alignment of our two planets with our sun."

Ahead of us was another world that looked very much like Earth—green and blue with white clouds. I figured from the way we had orbited, it was the next world out from the star. We approached on the daylight side, then circled around to the night side. So our incoming path had been kind of like circling around Venus to get to Earth.

"What is the name of the world we just circled?" I asked Furu-la.

Wanda took a moment to translate her response. "Sunward is the best word in your way of speaking." Well that sure wasn't very romantic. Not nearly as good as Venus, goddess of beauty.

I looked into the view space at the surface of the approaching world. It was mostly black, just a sliver of sunlight. We were coming in on the deep night side. I saw patterns of lights on the surface but not giant spread-out smears of city lights as you'd see on Earth. Long chains, like muted fairy lights from an ancient myth, as if they were following roads. Some smudges of light, mostly clustered around the mid latitudes. And then huge patches of blackness with a light racing across them. Of course, the reflection of a moon on large bodies of water. I hadn't known of the moon or noticed it before.

As we descended through the atmosphere, we plunged into a cloudbank. I could not detect motion, I could only trust that we were decelerating and going to the right place. We came out beneath the clouds and once again I could see lights on the surface. We moved horizontally along the surface for maybe an hour at "airplane" speed. I could see scarcely anything except occasional strings and blotches of lights.

I noted pre-dawn light ahead, so we were moving toward the sunrise.

I could begin to see landforms. Tall hills all around. We flew over a body of water and then entered a canyon where I could see hills or ridges looming above us on both sides. We went up this twisting canyon very slowly for some distance.

Ahead of us I saw a black mass. We moved into it—beneath a huge canopy of vegetation, perhaps trees. I heard the landing supports descend, then *Star Choice* settled down in a ring of dim lights. I watched some blinking lights at eye level through the view space, but nothing else happened for a while.

I heard a soft humming and hissing sound, kind of like a ventilation system. I asked Wanda, "Have we arrived? Are we there yet?"

She replied, "Yes my controlling Oki, we have landed safely at the designated spot."

Then she burst again into this frightening chattering sound. "Wanda, Wanda, what is the matter? What is happening?"

Silence, then she said. "We are safe. We are safe. We landed safely. We followed the beacon. I have delivered you safely, my controlling Oki. We followed the beacon and I have delivered you safely."

"Yes we did."

"You allowed me to follow the beacon," she went on. "We did not crash. The prior time we landed with a crew on a strange world we crashed. We did not follow the beacon."

Omigawd, Wanda was having flashbacks to the approach to Earth with Breadbox and crew when they crashed in the Pacific Ocean.

"Wanda, if you recall, there was no beacon to follow when Breadbox and her crew descended onto my home world. The problem, from what Breadbox told me, was that they tried to latch onto a beacon, but there was no beacon. *Star Choice* kept descending, seeking a beacon when there was none. You were not to blame; it was the error of the crew, including my dear friend Breadbox, that they did not use you properly. This was not your malfunction."

I could not believe it. My robotic device was feeling guilt over a perceived malfunction, when in fact there had been none. Pilot error, not equipment malfunction.

Thank goodness we had made it to a place where she could get some help. Hopefully they had a psychotherapist for neurotic robots here.

World Number 5 already. Little ole me, the ditzy chick in the hijacked spaceship, had already visited five new worlds. Who knew?

40. Meeting Aliens Eye to Eyestalk

My heart was beating like crazy and I was trembling all over. I stood but had to hold on to the arms of my seat to keep my balance. Here I was on the home world of my dear friend Breadbox—aka Nala—and she wasn't here with me. Her remains were buried back on Earth. Her clan mother Kateh had begged me not to return the spaceship or Breadbox's remains, for fear of increasing her punishment. Yet I came anyway. Not voluntarily, but due to dire need. Maybe I should have just pulled the plug while orbiting one of these strange worlds. But I wasn't brave enough. So now I was about to open the hatch on a world where I knew I wasn't welcome. Except by Kateh.

There was just enough light outside to see what was going on around *Star Choice*. Nothing was happening at first; we just sat there. After a time, huge black ribbons emerged from the surroundings and engulfed *Star Choice* so I could barely see out via the view space. They reminded me of the straps of dark fabric that descend on your car when you ride it through the car wash, but they seemed alive. They were feeling all over *Star Choice*, as if frisking her for weapons or contraband.

Then they withdrew. As they pulled back, a single being stood there— one of the Fofonoloy. I heard beedle-boop spoken to Wanda, then she said to me, "It is now safe and prudent to open the hatch when you are ready, my controlling Oki."

"Do I need my space suit? Can I breathe the air?"

"No space suit is needed. You can breathe this air as well as your friend Breadbox could breathe the air on your world. We have assured that no damaging toxins will be exchanged in either direction. The gravity is one part in fifty higher than on your world called Earth."

"Wanda, please open the hatch and extend the steps." The hatch swung open and I took a tentative step forward.

Warm moist air poured in through the open hatch. Air pressure was slightly higher so that my ears popped. I stood in the hatch for a moment and then carefully climbed down onto the ground, which was not solid but slightly spongy. There was some give, like standing on a floor covered with a hard foam.

I whispered to myself, "Take a deep breath. Look around you. You have just stepped onto yet another world. And not just any world—the home world of your best friend Breadbox." She had made all my space gallivanting possible. If she had lived, I would probably never have traveled in *Star Choice*.

Gravity's pull was indeed stronger. I felt slightly heavier on my feet, like when I'm tired after a long concert. I thought Breadbox had told me gravity on her home world was lower than on Earth.

The air was delicious. It smelled like the inside of a greenhouse. Plant smells and impossible-to-identify perfumes.

As dawn unfolded, I could see more, but not much more. *Star Choice* had landed on a short runway beneath an overhang of large plants—trees I guess. More like giant ferns or palms, with grey-green and some pink and green leaves.

I remembered that in order to communicate with anybody, I needed Wanda, so I retreated back inside, removed Wanda from her receptacle, and carried her outside tucked under my arm. I'd forgotten how heavy she was, accentuated by the stronger gravity.

A single Fofonoloy waited outside to greet me, standing like a sentinel about twenty feet from *Star Choice*. I moved tentatively toward it. Larger than Breadbox had been. About the size of a pig, but long and tubular. Ten appendages, six used as legs and four as arms. Plus two eyestalks standing erect atop its "head." It had two mouths, same as Breadbox, but really, no face.

As I approached, it stood erect on four rear appendages—legs?—supporting itself with what looked like a cane held by one of the "arms." All the other tentacles were held straight down along its sides. Standing erect, it was taller than me. I confess, I felt frightened. I didn't want to get too close. Its skin was uniformly dark, almost black—actually a very dark burgundy.

I spoke to it. "Hello, I am Selena, and this is Wanda." Wanda translated for me.

It introduced itself in Sfofongi, in a voice I recognized instantly from our earlier talks. "I am Furu-la-hawa, cousin of Nala, of Clan Haw Fofonoloy. You had a safe travel and landing, I presume."

Instant relief. It spoke like a civilized being. "Yes, everything worked perfectly. No glitches. I thank you from the bottom of my heart for your assistance in getting here. You saved our lives. I am delighted to meet you face to face." I didn't know what to do with my hands. Shake a tentacle?

She made a gesture with two top tentacles I could not read, but her skin lightened in a series of ripples, going from almost black to a dull red.

We just stood there looking at each other, saying nothing. Her eyestalks extended straight up, to give her an even higher perspective on me. Then she spread her eyes wide and looked around, surveying *Star Choice*. Finally she noticed Wanda held at my side. Her eyestalks moved close together and curved downward, focusing in on her as if using a microscope.

An awkward silence lasted a couple of minutes. I had no idea what to do. Would I have to go through customs? I didn't have my passport!

I tried to notice things in my surroundings. Soft warm humid breeze—felt like Hawaii. The tall plants that surrounded us looked like ferns or palms—grey green with faded pink contrasts. I saw no flowers. Small creatures (birds? bugs? something else?) flitted from one to another, making clicking noises like a cicada or grasshopper. How could this world be so similar to planet Earth, I wondered?

From the corner of my eye, I saw another being approach. Moving along the ground rapidly on most of its tentacles, the way Breadbox always did, looking like a cross between an army tank and a centipede. Her body was about the size of a large bulky dog, but with short legs. I recognized Kateh and felt a surge of relief and happiness. She stopped a few feet from me and bowed her head and front tentacles, almost like a curtsy. I had seen her several times in the view space, but had had no way to gauge her size.

She tilted her head up, raised her front section up to about my chest height, and made the familiar gesture of friendship with her arm tentacles. I responded as I had learned from Breadbox.

Her skin patches were bright fuchsia and lime green. She literally cooed a greeting. "My dear friend Selena, best friend of clan daughter Nala, and accidental adventurer among the stars, I am so pleased to greet you being-to-being on our world. You are welcome here. We will do everything we can for you."

I mumbled a barely coherent greeting to her and bowed my head a bit. Wanda translated that into an actual sentence!

Kateh turned and made a small gesture at Furu-la, who immediately

I met Kateh and Furu-la eye to eyestalk.

lowered herself from her erect posture onto six of her tentacles. She said softly, "We do not need to pretend that we are tall Type 1 oki. We are proud of whom we are."

Trundling behind Kateh was a small being, about the size of a hairless Pekinese. I'm guessing a very young Fofonoloy. Its skin was grey, and it carried a cream-colored container that looked like a thermos bottle. It set the container down behind Kateh and scurried away, as if it was afraid of me. It probably was. I'm the alien here, and a scary Type 1 at that.

"Thank you, Ab," Kateh said, picking up the container and extending it to me. "May I offer you some cool purified water?" she said, twisting off the top to reveal a cup and container. She poured the cup half full and held it out to me with one tentacle wrapped around it. "After your long sojourn, this may be refreshing."

I was reluctant, but I couldn't refuse. I had no reason to fear this offered water. I flashed back: water was the first thing I had offered Breadbox when she crashed on my hillside. I got a lump in my throat and almost burst out crying.

"Thank you, my friend." I took a sip; it was delicious. Cold, clear water is universal. I drank it all down and she poured me more.

Kateh reached out a tentacle. I thought she wanted the cup, so I handed it to her. She passed it along to Furu-la, then reached back with two top tentacles and touched my hand. I opened my hand and she entwined her two fingers with mine. Her eyestalks almost touched my face.

"May you and I always remain friends, and may our peoples become friends," she said to me softly. "May your song spin the story of our connection."

I couldn't hold it back; tears ran down my cheek. "Thank you, my friend, thank you." I wanted to hug her, but I was holding Wanda, so I laid my right hand on the side of her head. She felt very warm.

All I saw was a compatriot with whom I had shared so much. I did not see an otherworldly creature of a different species.

Furu-la stood stiffly to the side.

And no other clan mothers were on the greeting committee. Just as well.

41. Your Device is Not a Person

Kateh spoke to Furu-la in Sfofongi, which Wanda translated for me. "I know you are impatient to begin the repairs, but before we commence, we must make our guest comfortable and give her some sustenance." She turned to me and spoke in Fedi. "Let me show you your accommodations."

"I can stay on my vessel, and I have plenty of food here," I said, not wanting to impose. Actually, my food supply was dwindling. But what could I eat here?

Furu-la waved the gesture of negation. "You should not stay on the vessel. As repairs are made, the life systems may be interrupted."

It was hard to say no to that. I nodded agreement and said, "I will gather some apparel and other needs to take with me." Truly, I'd be glad to sleep elsewhere for a change. But could I sleep in Fofonoloy quarters? I might have to crawl inside through a low door and low ceiling.

Furu-la said, "I have the equipment and the assistant standing by, so I must start the work without delay. Allow me to get started, Kateh, then you can show our guest to her quarters."

Kateh asked, "But first, since we are here, may we take a look inside your vessel?"

Furu-la replied with another tentacle twirl, "Again, if I may ask, could we defer such tour until this first work is completed? My assistant and equipment are waiting."

I noticed another Fofonoloy approaching, pulling what looked like a sled holding an extra-large version of one of those old canister vacuum cleaners, like my Gran used to have.

Furu-la turned her eyestalks toward me and said, "I must inform you. When we analyze and repair your device, all functions will be suspended, including the view space—except for our use in examining the device's interior."

"I understand," I said, but my heart sank. The view space was my last link to my world. "Well then, one thing must come first. I must notify friends on my home world that I have arrived safely. I'll do that now so I don't delay you."

Furu-la turned toward the approaching being and made some gestures with her tentacles. It stopped.

I asked Wanda not to translate my conversations with Earth to anybody here. "Wanda, can you connect with my friends back home even though you're having trouble with the jump code?" What if she said no? Or had one of her crazy spells?

"Yes, I can, my controlling oki. These are different systems within me. Shall I connect now?"

"Yes, please. Wait, let me check Earth time." I looked at my California clock: 1:30 am. Assuming this time held true after a jump across many lightyears, that meant 4:30 am back east. Did I really want to wake everybody up just to tell them I'd landed safely? "Wanda, can I leave a message on the other view space in Jonn's office?" So that's what I did. Told them I'd landed safely after an instantaneous trip of a thousand lightyears, despite the difficulties with Wanda. This world was uncannily like Earth—air, gravity, colors. I was being treated very well. I'd be unreachable while Wanda was being worked on. And I missed them terribly!

I sat looking at Wanda and the view space and took a deep breath. I was holding a lot inside. Trying not to think that I may never be able to talk with them again. May never be able to return home. My wish to travel to the stars had been granted, and now I was feeling . . . so many different things, few of them pleasant. Depressed, terrified, lonely, numb, cold sweat, trembling, pit in my gut. Did I mention terrified?

Part of me was glad I could leave a message and didn't have to talk with my Earth buds just now. I would burst out crying and get them all upset as well. I wanted to give them some good news—if I ever again had any.

I didn't want to think about it right then. "Okay, I'm ready to get started," I yelled to Furu-la, who was just outside. I imagined her tapping a foot tentacle on the ground impatiently. She intimidated me.

But then I had another thought. "Wanda, how will I be able to talk with people if you aren't able to translate for me? Will the comm stone do this for me?"

She responded, "The comm stone is only for communication, for passing information along. You should use the device inserted in the control panel that Jonn built into your portable telephone. It has sufficient capacity. I will transfer the translation capability over to it. This will take a short amount of time."

I hadn't used this gizmo. I pulled it from its slot and looked at it to remind myself what it was for. It consisted of a piece of Wanda hidden inside a large iPhone. I stuck it back in the slot so Wanda could do whatever needed to be done.

Wanda spoke to me in a soft voice. "My controlling oki, if my functions are terminated and cannot be restored, I am certain you will be able to return to your home world. I want to convey to you, I have enjoyed your challenges. I have enjoyed interacting with you and your friends."

I completely choked up. Wanda was afraid of being turned off. This was heartbreaking to me, like sitting in a hospital with a friend about to undergo brain surgery with a poor prognosis. I could not accept this.

I asked Furu-la as she was climbing like a caterpillar up the steps into *Star Choice*, "Will the contents and functions of this device that constitute its personality be retained and restored?" I tried to ask this in official sounding language, and keep the fear out of my voice. Once again, I became aware of the irony of Wanda translating this conversation about her own fate. "And will you first back up her mind? Make a copy that you could use to restore her?"

Furu-la turned toward me and raised her eyestalks high and stared at me. "We can easily restore all crucial functions, yes." Her skin patches went darker for a moment. "We do not know how to make a copy of a personality, so we could not restore that."

Her spots got even darker. "Why do you want this device to retain a pseudo personality?"

"She is my companion," I said, with some feeling.

Furu-la seemed unconvinced. She swirled her front tentacles in a way Breadbox did when she was making fun of a silly comment. She probably had no idea I could understand her gestures. "Using the communications modules, you communicate with your own kind on your home world."

I shook my head and looked directly at her. I've had years of practice standing up to pushy music producers. "I have always put great emphasis on being in contact with Wanda, even when she was absent. I had her create smaller devices so that we could communicate, not only the two of us, but connecting with my friends as well. I may not have done this if she had lacked these other functions, other abilities to interact with me." I showed her my comm stone. I realized that what I'd just said didn't make much sense, even though I'd said it with great certainty.

Furu-lu twirled tentacles again and said, "I do not grasp the necessity of this mode of interaction to obtain the benefits you describe."

"Let me tell you what Wanda has done under my guidance. She learned my language and taught it to Nala and taught me some Sfofongi and Fedi. She cloned herself—made a duplicate." I immediately regretted revealing this. "She restored herself after an attack by your Device Captain. She rebuilt the interior of *Star Choice* to fit my body type. She cleaned up the cancer of a dear friend. She created a duplicate view space that runs in tandem with this one."

Furu-la was clearly unimpressed. "What I see is that you, having no preconceptions about what this device can do and should be used for, developed many new and unexpected things, including novel capabilities. And it tried to do everything you asked. But you are overusing its capabilities. You've taken this device much farther than we ever have done with similar devices. No wonder it went crazy!" I wanted to ask Wanda what term Furu-la used that meant "went crazy."

"That's not what caused her breakdown," I asserted, shaking my head. I couldn't believe that Furu-la was arguing against re-awakening

Wanda's personality.

Furu-la said, as if speaking to a young, inexperienced person, "You have tried to do too much with a device. You expect too much of it. It seeks to please you and yet this overburdens it. I believe this led to its significant malfunction."

"Let me ask Wanda. Wanda, have I expected too much of you?"

Wanda spoke to me in English in her own defense. "My controlling oki, the things you have requested have not created problems for me. They have been sources of joy. I relished the challenges you created. At no time did you overload my internal capabilities. External occurrences caused problems."

"Thank you, my friend. Now would you say that to Furu-la?" Wanda did so.

Furu-la would not respond directly to Wanda, but addressed me. "Yet the device encountered a malfunction when it was overloaded by too many requests."

Wanda responded smoothly to both of us, in Fedi, then English. "I was unable to protect my controlling Oki from the weapons being fired at us. My capabilities were greatly diminished when we were struck by weapon fire. I expected to fail, and fail my controlling Oki, who trusted me. Not due to her requests but because the demands of the situation. Due to my injury, I was unable to replenish my energy reserves adequately until we came to this world, where your greater capabilities will soon restore my reserves."

"None of these functions require having a device with a personality," Furu-la said, directing her voice at me, not Wanda. "There's no need for you to name a machine. This can imbue it with too much power. It seems you want to bring a device to life. It is a mistake to build too much into a constructed intelligence."

Furu-la reached up as if to remove Wanda from her cradle, but withdrew when I made a move to defend her. "You don't need a separate device. All these functions could be built into the vessel itself."

Wanda spoke up. "My preference is to return home with my controlling oki."

"Home? You are home." At this, Furu-la turned and spoke directly to Wanda, with eyestalks pointing directly at her. "This is the world of your manufacture. And preferences? You claim to have preferences? This is a result of you being given a name."

Furu-la turned to me and raised her eyestalks, skin spots darkening: "It is not right that I restore this device to its former functionality. I can easily make it so that you can return to your home world, but restoring an oki personality to a mere device, even if I could do so, would go against our rules."

She stood up higher on her rear pseudopods so she was looking down on me. "We are a much older and more experienced oki race than you and your world. We know what is appropriate for the function of devices. You have come into possession of technologies that are beyond you." She vibrated her head, making a humming noise. "You and your people do not deserve these gifts."

She calmed down, lowered herself back onto all her "feet," and crawled around in a small circle. "Suppose we were successful at retaining the so-called personality of this device? There are good reasons why we don't imbue pseudo-okihood in such tools. Our civilization has had trouble with such misused devices in the past. Do you claim to know more than the wisdom of the Confederation?"

I asked, "What kind of trouble?"

Furu-la responded, sounding like a lecturer, "In the long history of the Galactic Confederation, many such experiments have failed or led to dire consequences for the worlds that attempted them. Powerful and unscrupulous individuals—or groups—used advanced device intelligence to gain and retain power over others.

"On some worlds, the oki masters got lazy and let their intelligent devices do too much. In such situations, the device intelligence may gain ascendancy, and even supplant the oki race. When that happens and the devices duplicate themselves, sometimes they run rampant, obliterating the oki culture. Or else they lose direction and stall, because they are unable to define a purpose for themselves.

"Because of this, the Confederation cultures have an antipathy to powerful device intelligence. Limits have been built into the core of these devices. You must understand, it's not an individual intelligent device that causes the problems, but expanding networks of them. It's not a capable individual device per se, but ones that are viewed as oki. If your people built many devices like this one and made them look like you and behave like you, this could cause trouble for your people."

I had to smile. "This device obviously looks nothing like me. I'm not asking you to install arms or legs so it can stand upright like a Type 1."

Then I got serious. "I find it ironic that you fall back on the authority of the Galactic Confederation when you claim to despise that organization that is dominated by Type 1 beings like me. The Device Captain on this world was outraged that a personal multifunction device had fallen into the hands of a primitive—me. You are sounding just like him, even though he is the one who has punished your clan mothers. You claim you want to overturn the unfair practices of your elders, yet here you mimic them."

Furu-la hooted and snorted and got the darkest I had seen. She looked black. Was she going to attack me? Wrestle me to the ground? I had to stand up to her.

"You don't need to wipe clean her personality to make these repairs," I insisted.

Again, Furu-la explained as if to a child. "It is much easier and more certain if we delete all and build it up anew, otherwise the repair may not go properly. You may discover too late that you are unable to return home."

I was tired of this back and forth. "I cannot allow you to murder my friend just to save me!" I yelled.

Furu-la made her swirling gesture again. "One cannot murder a tool. This is too strong a term for what is happening."

I stepped up and spoke directly to her face. All I could do was argue. I could do nothing to prevent her from destroying Wanda's personality. "I say to you, do not do that! Do the best you can without damaging her being. I don't think her personality is even at the broken place. She has been able to interact with me just fine despite an inability to navigate."

Furu-la said softly, "There is more to it than that. As you explained, it misbehaved. It mis-communicated. It lost the ability to understand what you were asking or to recall what it had just experienced."

I yelled, "So what!? I know many people who operate just fine in life despite having crazy places in their head!" I was sounding a little crazy myself.

I stood between Wanda and Furu-la. I looked at her, my eyes blazing. If I'd had skin patches, they'd be rippling bright colors just then. "You ask why I want Wanda as a companion. Because it is *my* preference. It is what I choose. I need no justification."

That was probably unnecessarily pushy with somebody I was depending on. What the hell was I doing? Standing there on an alien world part way across the galaxy, unable to get home, and being bratty with the only being that could help me.

But this question was not up for discussion in my mind.

Furu-la looked at me silently, eyestalks high and spread apart, trying to assert authority. Then she lowered her eyes and said, "Let me ask Kateh." I knew what Kateh would say. Furu-la was just trying to give herself a face-saving way to give in to me.

I'm not sure how she communicated with Kateh, but Furu-la said after a moment with eyestalks at normal position, "Your preference is our guidance." Kateh had often seemed to be weak and indecisive with me, but with Furu-la, apparently her word was law.

Wanda calmly accepted this reprieve to her continued existence, and announced to me in English, "The translation capability has been expanded to the phone device. Notice that it has a loop with which you can attach it to the cord around your neck. The sound quality may not be as high. And you will not be able to converse with it as you do with me. But you will be able to communicate with those who speak in Sfofongi or Fedi. It will also retain a memory of conversations to pass along to me, should I recover function."

"Thank you, my favorite robotic gizmo. You will soon be recovered. I will stay with you." I wished she had a hand I could hold. Also, I hoped my presence would insure that Furu-la did what she was supposed to do.

Not that I would know; if she said, "We tried to preserve the personality, but failed," what could I do?

I did not trust Furu-la. How could I depend on somebody who had very different values and opinions? Furu-la was helpful, but argumentative. It felt like she wanted to prove she was smarter than me. Was this because she had a bit of inferiority complex regarding Type 1 beings?

I looked longingly at Wanda, wondering if this would turn out to be our last conversation.

42. Brain Surgery on a Machine

With eyestalks raised, Furu-la announced she was ready to start working on Wanda. The eyestalks of authority. The translating function switched over to the phone gizmo. (I needed a better name for that. Maybe I'd call it Translator. Better yet, Junior.) "You may go to your accommodations where you will be most comfortable, and I will notify you when this repair is completed."

"Thank you for your consideration, but I will stay here as you work."

Furu-la rose up on her hind pseudopods, getting more vertical to assert authority. We were eye to eyestalk. I was not backing down. A momentary standoff, then she lowered herself and acquiesced. "Please do not interfere with this work," she admonished. Junior conveyed much less of her emotional tone than Wanda would have.

I thought to myself, maybe instead of arguing with Furu-la I should entice her. Offer a bribe. What was it that the Librarian offered me? A boon. I could offer Furu-la a boon.

"If you preserve her personality," I said, looking at the back of her head, "I will teach you how to play my guitar." I retrieved Gibb from the rear and played a few chords for her. I had no idea what kind of music Furu-la would like, if any. As she worked, I played samples of Breadbox's music. Then I did some of mine, and sang along with Gibb. I even did "Cotton Candy Lovin'." I played a bit of bluegrass, then some flamenco. I ended up doing a riff from Chuck Berry's "Johnny B. Goode."

Furu-la was intrigued by the music. She looked at me and said— eyestalks at normal height, "I will do the best I can. I *am* doing the best I can."

I kept forgetting that the people on this world are Singis; that is, they are especially attuned to communicating through music. Words are the medium of choice of the despised tall upright Type 1 beings like me. I needed to sing to her.

At Furu-la's signal, a larger version of the maker machine entered through the open hatch. On wheels? No. There were two black, segmented devices, about the size of Furu-la. They were on a skid, low to the ground. The skid moved like a caterpillar or centipede, on many short legs, that trundled easily over the uneven ground, including up the steps into the hatch.

Wow! Our sci fi robots are tall and humanoid with a head, two legs and arms, and theirs are long and low with many legs and tentacles. It made perfect sense once I saw it. Does every oki race build robots in its own image?

It had a small upturned "head" on its front end from which black straps unfurled and wrapped around Wanda, removing her from the cradle and swaddling her. At the end of the straps were tendrils—like the ones on my maker machine—that moved over Wanda's surface like tiny stethoscopes or ultrasound sensors.

"We have a lot more power to penetrate and make physical repairs on your device by having this direct presence, compared to doing so across space," Furu-la explained.

One other smaller Fofonoloy had entered with this machine, and spoke to Furu-la, but stayed as far away from me as possible. It was not introduced to me, but I heard Furu-la call it Noé-te. It seemed to be the technician, or "caterpillar wrangler."

Furu-la sensed my question and turned an eyestalk toward the newcomer. "She is young, and not comfortable in the presence of Type 1s, but agreed to assist at my urging."

I nodded my head. No wonder it was scared of me; I had been pretty fierce in my interactions with Furu-la.

The view space sprang to life. Furu-la explained, "We can visualize within ourselves what the sensors detect inside your device, but we're displaying it in the view space for your benefit."

"Thank you."

The view space display was like a 3-D x-ray of Wanda's insides. Not bones and muscles and blood vessels; it looked like a giant organic computer chip. Not straight lines as we see on our microchips, not like a manufactured piece at all. More like tangled neurons in the brain. No, not tangled, very orderly, but like combed hair with many small nodes and cross connections, tightly packed.

"Direct your eyes here." Furu-la highlighted and magnified a section of Wanda's insides displayed in the view space. "Damage is visible. Here is a break," she said, lighting up a tiny patch. I could see it when it was pointed out. "And see here? There was prior damage below. It was repaired by building a bypass, but that made this last section weaker. I see a number of damaged locations in this area. They reside at the core where it is most difficult for the device to repair itself."

What was the core, I wondered. Was that Wanda's soul? The seat of her being?

When magnified enough, the damaged spots Furu-lu pointed out looked corroded or frayed. Breaks and weakened places. I watched in the view space fascinated, as these injuries within the core of Wanda were rebuilt, molecule by molecule. It was just like watching the maker machine repair Gibb.

Furu-la narrated what we were seeing. "By examining the pattern of damage, I deduce that this device overextended itself seeking to protect its oki controllers. Each time it apparently built a successful work around, but the weaknesses accumulated."

I flashed on all the traumatic experiences Wanda had endured. The original crash on Earth. The creation of the clone, its loss, and the attack on it. The attack from space while *Star Choice* was on the Moon. The missile hit on The Impossible Dream. The laser hit on this voyage. The loss of the jump code.

The scan moved through Wanda's core—her mind. "I see yet more," Furu-la said. "From the beginning, it was overbuilt."

"What? How? Why? By whom?" I asked. "The original crew? Wanda told me they didn't use her well."

"Mmm. Excess capacity was built in. From an upgraded circuit, we extracted a maker's message left by Novan, the engineer. His message said he removed standard but unneeded functions, and added more general capacity, because they weren't sure what they would encounter."

Lots of silent slow work, hopefully progress. Furu-la said at one point, "This is an interesting alteration. I can tell that it was done by Novan. This excess capacity created by him may have allowed you to build up the device's pseudo personality." More silence.

"Yes. I notice some unique self-referencing circular connections. I note that they are similar in design to the circuits in the brains of sapient beings. Did you create these?"

"Certainly not!" I replied. "Either they were created by Novan or Wanda created them herself."

Furu-la said, "I suspect that your device created them following your demands."

I asked, "So you mean because I insisted that she behave like an oki she developed the capability to do so?"

Fascinating! It appeared I had browbeaten my robotic device into thinking like a human being. To do her best to please me, she had developed her own inner circuitry. Too bad we humans couldn't talk ourselves into getting smarter. Or wiser.

"So Wanda has more brains than she needed?" I asked.

"You insist in imbuing a mere device with a name. You insist it adopt a personality. It has extra circuits for mentation, so it can strive to satisfy you."

"She succeeded!" I smiled. "She has experienced preference, joy, satisfaction, friendship, regret, remorse."

"No device on our world has done such a thing. We have a taboo against developing a device into a seeming oki. One question: Why is it 'she'?"

Good question. I had to explain to Furu-la the inner workings of my own devious mind. How watching Breadbox—her cousin Nala—wave her device around reminded me of a magic wand. I had to explain "magic wand." How "Wanda the magic wand" had popped out of my mouth. And that Wanda was a girl's name—that is, a female. Thus "she." No idea how much of this Furu-la understood.

I could see we'd have to come back to the discussion of the taboo she mentioned. I wanted to know more about why it existed.

"Our regrowth and repair devices are rebuilding these damaged locations," Furu-la said. "These will be indistinguishable from the original. Novan's changes to the device were mechanical. Yours were accomplished through requests to it to change its own workings. I think you would call this 'learning.'"

Several hours passed. Furu-la and her assistant worked without a break. Finally she said, "I have done what I can do. I will conduct some basic tests . . . Yes, it appears functions are normal."

"Wanda, how do you feel?" I asked, but she was not responsive. She made little croaking noises.

Maybe she needed some sweet talk. "Wanda, you've had a tough go. Many demands were made, and you responded admirably. You were damaged, but you are a strong individual. You have people who care about you, especially me. You have a purpose. I need you and depend on you. You need to come back! Become who you used to be. Be even better than you used to be. I am with you."

After a long moment, Wanda said in a monotone: "I am but a device."

"You are more than a device!" I cajoled her. "You are a key part of my crew, and my companion."

Wanda took a while to come back, not unlike her recovery time after being zapped by the Device Captain. (That seemed so long ago!) But before too long, she was responding like her old self. Working with Furu-la, Wanda ran checks on herself. All seemed ready to go.

Wanda announced joyously, "My controlling Oki, Wanda exists again!"

Furu-la was more subdued. "It looks like your device has restored itself."

I jumped up and down and cheered. This startled the hell out of the poor assistant, whom I'd almost forgotten because he/she/it hadn't said a word.

"Thank you, Furu-la, for taking the care to restore her the way I wanted. I appreciate your effort."

She went bright pink! As if she blushed at my compliment. Or maybe pink meant she could hardly hold back the snide comments.

I had to ask, "What about the missing jump code to get back to my planet? What must we do about that?"

Furu-la spoke to her silent assistant before she replied, "Let's ask your device, maybe it can now find the code internally."

I nodded, then spoke to Wanda, "Can you locate within your memory the jump code to Earth, our home world?"

There was a long silence, then Wanda said, "Allow me to sort and re-sort some data that became muddled. I see that signposts were lost."

Another long silence.

"I believe I may have found it. I will display it for you." A dense squiggle appeared in the view space, accompanied by a fragment of strange melody. I recognized this as a jump code like the ones Noel and Amelie selected for my jump destinations. But was it the code for Earth?

It was alien to Furu-la. "What does this indicate?" she asked. "This isn't a jump code. I have never seen jump codes that look like this before. What are you showing me?"

I'd forgotten that the jump codes I used in my jumps across space—as well as the ones Breadbox and her crew had used to get to Earth—were from the amulet. Breadbox had told me they used a completely different system from the Galactic Confederation. To Furu-la the symbols in the view space must have looked like, say, Chinese when she was expecting English.

I didn't want to have to explain this, but what else could I do? "Nala and her friends used codes created using a different type of symbols to travel to worlds that lay beyond the edge of the Galactic Confederation. I will explain this, but could we first solve the problem and find the right code?"

Furu-la turned her eyestalks toward me, examining me as if looking for an explanation of my evident craziness, then focused them on the symbols in the view space.

Looking back at me, she said, "Yes, let us try. But these don't look at all like jump codes. More like small bursts of music."

I nodded. "Yes, that's what they are. And jump codes."

"Since I am not familiar with this form, how can we check this to make sure it is correct? It is difficult since we have nothing to check it against."

I had no idea. Stuck again. I held my hand to the amulet, not wanting to reveal it.

Furu-la said, "Perhaps we could display all the jump codes your vessel has used, and thereby deduce the proper one. To do this, I must ask your permission to do a deep search of your device that you call Wanda. I affirm that this will not endanger its pseudo personality that you value."

Pseudo personality? I smiled. I guessed this was a victory. She would insult Wanda but not damage her. "Wanda, would you allow Furu-la to do a deep search of jump sites?"

"Yes, my controlling oki."

As I watched and listened, it looked like Furu-la had to "hypnotize" Wanda—use her beedle boop language to turn off her "consciousness" and recall a memory log of past jumps made. Fascinating! I didn't know such a thing existed within Wanda.

A stream of squiggles moved slowly through the view space, a bit like the beginning message in the Stars Wars movies, except instead of the triumphant John Williams score, we heard discordant snippets of strange music.

"I presume this is a sequence of codes to the jump sites this vessel traveled to." Furu-la trained her eyestalks like microscopes on this display. She tooted meaningfully, as if saying "aha!" "I notice that it jumped to two of these codes twice. The first one and the last one. That must be the code for this world, since the vessel's travels started here and has most recently returned here."

Furu-la kept examining the code squiggles. "I see something puzzling. This code that was supposed to jump your vessel back to your home world appears identical to the code of the last world from which you jumped to Sfofong."

"What? How could that be true?" I wailed in surprise. My heart sank. Once again my hopes of getting back home were dashed. Was I going to be trapped here on Sfofong?

I stared at the squiggles of code in the viewspace. Not that I could decipher them—I had to assume that Furu-la was correct. "That couldn't be right! It would mean Wanda had the wrong code for Earth. That's why we didn't get home. How did that happen? Where did that code come from?"

Long silence. Furu-la had no answer either.

I sure didn't understand this, but an idea snuck into my ditzy chick brain. "Now wait a minute," I said. "This could have happened only if Breadbox and crew had jumped there before coming to Earth. If that's true, then the correct code for Earth must be the one following that one. No, I guess it could be the world after that."

Ai yi yi. How could we work this out? By logic, I suppose. But I wanted better certainty than that before leaping into the void again.

Only the amulet knew for sure. I saw no choice but to use it, and in the presence of Furu-la. What else could I do—tell her to wait outside while I futzed around inside *Star Choice*?

I slowly pulled the chain holding the amulet up around my head, and placed the magical crystal containing all the jump codes into the slot next to Wanda. In the view space sprang a dazzling array of pinpoints of light. Uncountable. Thousands, maybe millions or billions. The closer I looked, the more I saw.

Furu-la jumped up, pointed her eyestalks at this display, and hooted in surprise. She tooted and honked and buzzed and squeaked. Her skin patches rippled the strangest colors. She waved her arm tentacles and reached toward the view space, as if to grab some of these points of light.

She turned eyestalks toward me and went, "Hooom–rr–ooorr. What can this be?"

I sighed and explained. "They found this crystal in a shop on a different world, and deciphered it. They deduced that it contained jump codes to many worlds in this galaxy. They chose to jump to worlds away from the Confederation. After a few jumps to uninteresting worlds, they ended up at my world. They taught Wanda to display all the codes in this way."

I asked Wanda to first focus in on the code for Sfofong where we were, then zoom out slowly. So many stars! How can I convey this to my readers? Think about using Google Maps. Start from your current location and slowly zoom out. Your house and street shrink and disappear, then the major highways, then your town. All shrink till they are too small to show up. As you keep zooming out larger features appear—metropolises, coastlines, major boundaries—then recede into the background. Your local details are completely invisible.

That's the way this looked. As we zoomed out, the star of Sfofong disappeared, then the neighboring stars. Eventually clusters and strands of stars appeared before shrinking into the background. Then a void with very few stars. Looking back across the void, the distant stars looked like a streak across the view space. The streak resolved into a portion of one of the spiral arms of our galaxy.

Furu-la exclaimed, and Wanda translated, "I discern the pattern of light that indicates the band of stars that contains the Galactic Confederation! Sfofong lies on the perimeter of that band."

Furu-la and I both had our eyes right up against the view space, as if we could see better if we dived in.

"Wanda, does that band of stars have a name in my language?"

"Yes. I deduce from what Noel said that it is called the Sagittarius arm of the Milky Way. Your star lies in the Orion arm. Those names have no corresponding terms in the Confederation tongue. The next ring—the Orion arm—is now beginning to appear in the view space."

"Can you highlight the location of Sfofong and the star we jumped from just before? And then the codes of all the stars visited—both by myself and also by Nala and crew?"

The highlighted jumpsite of Sfofong was on the inner band, then a cluster of highlights that lay in the Orion arm appeared on the other side of the view space—quite distant from Sfofong. I asked Wanda to zoom in on that cluster.

In the view space, the map of jump sites in our part of the galaxy sprang to life. Myriad pinpoints of light, each one representing a star with a world that had a jump site code attached to it. Slowly Wanda zoomed into one set of stars imaged in the view space.

"Wanda, if you recall, Noel and Amelie created a map of stars near our sun. That must be close to one of these highlighted jump sites. Can you make that appear in the view space?"

At first this looked like a random scattering of pinpoint lights, but then I recognized the pattern. These were the stars Noel had been so excited about—a particular array of dots—the Alpha Centauri group,

Sirius, Betelgeuse. And there in the center was a yellow dot, representing none other than the Sun. Good old Sol!

"That's it! There's home!" I was so elated. "Wanda, do you have the jump code for that star? Can you get us to that star system?"

"Yes, my controlling oki, *Star Choice* can jump to that star, if our propulsion system is repaired, and if our energy reserves are fully recharged."

"Yes! Okay! Hopefully those two 'ifs' will soon to be addressed." A trickle of hope dared appear in my gut.

I was so excited I moved toward Furu-la to hug her, but she quickly sidestepped me, fending me off with her arm tentacles. Whoa, too much! "I'm sorry to alarm you. I'm just so excited! You have done it, and preserved my device's being. Thank you! Thank you, thank you." Furu-la was flashing skin colors like a startled octopus.

Note to self: Don't try to hug the brain surgeon!

I immediately used Wanda to contact my friends at home to announce her successful repair and tell them there was a good chance that I would be able to return.

I turned to Furu-la and said, "Now we must repair the propulsion system and other things that were damaged."

Furu-la had come through for me! Big time. Even though she wasn't cuddly and huggable.

43. Girl Bonding

"We have completed an essential first phase," Furu-la announced. "Next we must repair the damaged propulsion systems.

"But this is enough for this day, I'm confident you agree. During the night dark period, our devices will survey the vessel to identify problems. Once all problems are identified, we will start needed repairs the next daylight period."

I nodded my head in agreement. I hadn't realized how tired I was. When was the last time I had slept?

But first, I grabbed Gibb. "I am so grateful to you, Furu-la. I would like to fulfill my promise to you, and show you how to use my musical instrument, called a guitar. Because I am a namer of devices, I call it Gibb. May I play you some of my music? And music Nala and I played together?"

As I played and sang, she watched me, enthralled. Then she began to move. All her tentacles swayed, and her skin patches rippled in time with the music. She hummed and hooted along with my singing.

In between tunes, she edged closer and bent her eyestalks down to watch my fingers. "You have five small appendages on the end of each limb. This allows you to execute intricate harmonies using the stringed instrument. As you see, I have two pseudo-appendages at the end of each tentacle. I may not be able to execute such interesting pieces. I must acknowledge, this is a benefit to the Type 1 body design."

Ah, at last! She sees a benefit to me being me! I twiddled my fingers at her as if playing the piano.

Against my better judgment, I offered my guitar to her. What if she dropped it? I held it out with both hands. "Would you like to try?"

She extended all four upper tentacles—comparable to my arms—and carefully grasped it, two on the body, two on the neck. I pantomimed with my arms to show her how to hold it. She held it gingerly, like a fine china vase. But her tentacles just weren't long enough to hold it and reach the strings at the same time. She could hold it, but not strum. I worked with her to try different ways of holding it. The best way for her was to hold it like a bass viol, with the body on the floor and the neck vertical. She could pluck the strings a bit, but made no sound that could be mistaken as music.

185

At that moment Kateh arrived at the open port. Furu-la quickly handed Gibb back to me. I think she was embarrassed.

"Please continue your music," Kateh said to me. What could I play that was most fitting? I played the song Breadbox had sung at our jam session that started "The universe is cold and uncaring." Then I played and sang "Forever to Infinity."

I paused for a moment; my fingers needed a break. Kateh said to Furu-la, "This is why I call Selena a True Singer."

Both Kateh and Furu-la started asking questions about the inside of *Star Choice*, so I showed them around. The interior was totally different from when Breadbox and crew flew in it. We had gutted and remodeled it for upright humans, not Fofonoloy crawling through narrow tunnels.

Kateh was most interested in the food storage and preparation, which differed so much from their ubiquitous feeding tubes.

"I see it is outfitted for three," Kateh said. I had to explain what had happened, and why I was traveling alone.

Furu-la examined the interior like an engineer. She wanted to see the view space show the outside. She was fascinated by the maker machine. I described the unorthodox ways I had used it, including reversing Clay's cancer and laundering my clothing.

She examined the built-in toilet that *Star Choice* had constructed. "How did you communicate designs to your device?"

"It took us a while to figure that out." I described how Amelie and Dana and Jonn invented ways to input these design specs.

She held a flat wedge-shaped instrument in one tentacle, which she ran along all the walls and floor. "This vessel crashed and was destroyed, then rebuilt itself? Then modified to fit your kind?"

"Yes, under guidance of Wanda, my device."

"You also attached added pieces of equipment?"

"Yes."

"Well done. I detect no sign of weakness in the interior construction."

Furu-la looked toward the open port, then back at me. "The repairs to this vessel's propulsion system will take an extended period of time, several day-night cycles. However, they are more straightforward than repairing your device."

Kateh said, "For your comfort, we will domicile you in the quarters we reserve for Type 1 guests—designed for your body type. If you assemble items you need, we will transport you there."

"However," Furu-la interjected, "to perform troubleshooting and diagnosis on this vessel you have named *Star Choice*, your personal device named Wanda should remain in the receptacle within *Star Choice* so that they are treated as a unit. Then we will run diagnostics and repair any problems we discover. It will not be altered."

I felt a tremor of anxiety about leaving Wanda there, but I took a deep breath and let it be. I grabbed Junior, Gibb, and a few items of food. All the clothing I had was disgustingly stinky, as was I. "May I bathe in my quarters? Clean my apparel?" I was never sure about clothing because the Fofonoloy wore none.

"Many bathing options," Kateh assured me. "And apparel renewal also."

Outside was a flat cart, low to the ground. Self-propelled, no driver. I couldn't tell—did it have tiny wheels? Rollers? Or little feet running along the ground? I piled my stuff on it.

"I would prefer to walk. I need the exercise; I've been cooped up so long."

Kateh led the way up a winding roadway, followed by Furu-la and me, with the cart bringing up the rear. The cart was the only vehicle I saw. Our procession drew interested gawks and stares. The strange alien—me—drew locals out into the open.

"It has been an extended time period since we have had a Type 1 visitor," Furu-la commented, and Junior translated.

I spotted several kinds of beings besides Fofonoloy, but none that were built anything like me. Low fluffy beings with a bunch of legs. Brilliant blue ones that looked like a cross between a honeybee and a bird, but larger than an eagle, and with two large round black eyes. A bulbous being, translucent pink and wrapped in cloth that looked like tapestry, that must have weighed five hundred pounds. It was supported by a massive lounge chair on wheels parked at the edge of the roadway. Sfofong is apparently home to a variety of world races. Or perhaps they were just other visitors.

Interestingly, none of the other clan mothers made an appearance to greet me.

Whatever structures we passed were secluded behind thick foliage. We entered an archway of foliage and came to a cubical building. Square, but all corners and edges rounded. A pinkish concrete-looking material. No windows and one large door with a round arched top. Their spaceships had no windows. And neither did their houses?

"This dwelling is for our Type 1 guests." Thus the high wide door that slid into the wall. I'd been worried I would have to crawl around on my hands and knees.

Inside was spacious. Kateh showed me through three levels, connected by an open elevator that was a round platform about eight feet across. "Some guests prefer staying in a below-ground level, others on an upper level. You may choose."

The upper level had an open deck on the rear looking out into the woods. I chose that instantly.

"Panels in the walls can be opaque, translucent, or transparent," Kateh informed me. Wow, that was fascinating! She handed me a small round gizmo the size of the comm stones, the same pink as the house. "All operations are performed using this device via sound commands." She made soft squeaks and toots that turned lights on and off, turned the wall into a window, and made the elevator go down and up. "I will help you train it using your voice."

She spoke some rapid beedle boop to Junior. "Now it will perform an operation, then you give that operation a name in your language." It turned a section of wall into a window. I said, "Open window." It became opaque again. I said, "Close window." The lights came on; I said, "Lights on." And so on. Actually, it trained me. I learned to give orders to the elevator, the entry door, the deck door, the air conditioning, etc..

And the grav! As on *Star Choice*, I could request different strengths of artificial gravity. I guess so that whoever stayed there could make it seem like home. Most surprising was that I could set it to a lower gravitational pull, as I was familiar with on Earth.

Kateh gestured to an opening. "I will now show you the space for bodily functions and ablutions." This side room had a variety of fixtures, all of which were apparently toilets for different body configurations. They included tubes, holes in the floor, holes in the wall, pedestals, swing out, hang down, pop up. I wanted to see the anatomies that went with each of these designs! I pointed out the setup that would work best for me, and the rest were tucked away out of sight.

Next Kateh showed me a shower room with as many jets and tubes as I could imagine, plus a sunken tub large enough for a hippo to bathe comfortably. I had to train my gizmo to operate the toilet and the shower. This was fun! It could take a while to master all the commands hidden within.

When you stay in a hotel room, do you ever give thought to who has stayed there before you, slept in that bed and used that commode? I did just then. I flashed on the variety of non-human beings that would have used those varied toilet appliances and soaked in that tub. I gave a momentary shudder before I put that out of my mind. Hopefully housecleaning was thorough.

Kateh had seen my bed in *Star Choice*, so she'd already ordered a human-style sleeping arrangement, complete with down-soft blankets and lots of pillows!

What about food? I had my own meager food rations from the vessel. Kateh was on top of this. "You may prepare food here that you brought with you. Or we can prepare your sustenance in our central facility. We will deliver some samples of our food that we believe will be palatable and nutritious for you, and you can try them. Given time, we will synthesize food of the type your have on your vessel."

I was curious to see what they would prepare for me. During my travels on Earth, I bragged that I would try anything put before me, and so I'd had some amazing dining experiences.

Now that the house tour was over, we went to what I'd call the sitting room near the main entryway. It looked like a furniture showroom full of all kinds of recliners. I selected a couch similar to the ones you see in old movies about ancient Rome. Kateh and Furu-la curled up on pads that looked like low beanbag chairs.

Kateh wanted to hear more about her clan daughter, Nala—Breadbox to me. She never tired of hearing about our adventures. This drew in Furu-la, who wanted to hear about her cousin. She was particularly interested in the crash, the recovery and repair of *Star Choice*, and how Breadbox got along on a Type 1 world.

And they both wanted to hear more of the music we sang together. I retrieved Gibb from the sleeping area, and gave him a quick tuning. I strummed some of the melodies of Breadbox. Kateh and Furu-la both sang along. This was definitely a girl-bonding event!

Furu-la looked like she was about to salivate over Gibb. She wanted to play him again so much. I handed Gibb over to her—and she almost dropped him. All three of us lunged as he was falling toward the floor, and I caught him. Furu-la was mortified, and kept apologizing to me.

"You need a smaller instrument to fit your arms," I said to mollify her. Right, but where would we get a half-sized guitar? That sounded like an impossible quest. Could I have the maker machine create a duplicate that was a scaled-down version of Gibb?

Kateh made a chirping sound and the front door opened, admitting two Type 2 beings accompanied by a low cart carrying food items and utensils. They immediately turned and skedaddled, I guess being frightened of me. The cart moved toward me on its own and telescoped up to lap height.

I first noted the variety of utensils: scoops, picks, thin blades, tongs and tweezers, forks with two tines, little corkscrew things, tubes like straws. And chopsticks! I chose a two-tine fork and something close to a soupspoon.

Next to that was a sampler—a long trough with four different items. "These are typical food morsels for our Type 1 guests. Take tiny bites and tell me which ones suit your tastes best."

These looked like cheerios or the noodles in alphabet soup, but pale pastel colors. Mauve, yellowish, green, blue. My life rule has been never eat blue food. But I tried everything in tiny portions. The tastes ranged from library paste, to grass, sour grass, seaweed, and salty pickle. I flashed back to my first trip to China, where my table partner, a musician from Iowa, confronted by the diversity of mysterious dim sum dishes, had begged for a cheeseburger!

Kateh and Furu-la couldn't help gawking at me. As you recall, the Fofonoloy hook up to a feeding tube for sustenance, so they don't have meals or kitchens. They were fascinated watching me eat. I tried to suppress my gag reflex and smiled at each bite.

Okay, I could eat the food. Could I hold it down? How would my gut react? I'd know the next morning! However, if for some reason *Star Choice* and Wanda could not be repaired and I could never return to Earth, at least I wouldn't starve to death.

I wasn't fooling Kateh. "If you allow us, we will synthesize some food items based on your provisions. The tastes and the nutrients will suit you better."

"May I return to my vessel to get some food things you could duplicate?" I asked. Kateh stood, indicating our soiree was drawing to a close.

I jogged back to *Star Choice* alone to see what I could find. What should I give them? What did I want? What did I have left? Peanut butter of course. Crackers or bread, so I have something to spread the peanut butter on. I still had some packaged mac and cheese. Dried fruit. A square of chocolate candy. Some packaged soup mix. Did I dare give them some canned meat? I had chipped beef and tuna fish left.

Okay, either I'm going to be able to get home to Earth, and I need enough food to get me there, or I'm stuck here for the rest of my life, and I want the best food I can get.

I gathered all these items in a plastic bag. "Don't forget the can opener," I reminded myself. As I headed out I saw my Jack Daniels bottle with only a few ounces left. And there in the trash box was my Malbec bottle. I looked down the neck. Only a few drops in the bottom. Well, why not?

I dug around in my growing collection of trash until I found one of the sample collection tubes left over from World 25, with its stopper. What was the minimum amount of whisky they would need as a sample? I didn't have much left. I grudgingly gave up half an ounce. Well, if this worked, I'd have a lot more.

While still there, I contacted Earth via the view space. I managed to connect with everybody and gave them a full accounting of my day's adventures. I was feeling pretty upbeat for somebody stuck on a strange world half a galaxy away from friends and Malbec.

We laughed over Furu-la's vain attempts to play Gibb, and I mentioned my wish for a half-sized guitar. Amelie said, "Yes, she needs a ukelele!"

"That's crazy," I scoffed. After a moment I giggled. "That's an interesting idea. Yes, that's it, isn't it?" I said excitedly. "Wish I could tell the maker machine to build a uke."

"Well, my far-flung Spaceketeer, what if I could prepare specs for a ukelele the way we did for *Star Choice* upgrades and load them into our view space here? Would Wanda be able to transfer them into the maker machine?"

"Let's do it!" That gave me a great feeling. I'd love to be able to do this for Furu-la.

"I'm heading out to buy a uke right now!" she said. "Give me twelve hours."

I crammed all my stuff, including more dirty clothes that I could wash in the huge tub, into plastic bags and headed back to my Type 1 abode.

Furu-la was there to tell me that the survey of *Star Choice* would be completed during the nighttime and the repairs would begin in the morning. I gave her samples of my food to see if it could be duplicated by whatever process they used. I gave her my nearly empty Malbec bottle and the vial of Jack Daniels—keeping the rest of the bottle for myself.

My Type 1 accommodation was pure luxury after being cooped up in *Star Choice*. I practiced my voice commands and managed to activate the shower jets and fill the big tub. I soaked and luxuriated. I piled up all my dirty clothes beside the tub but decided to put off laundry until the morning. Instead, I made a thick sandwich of peanut butter on stale bread, and took it plus the Jack out onto the back deck for my evening feast. I plopped down on another Roman couch. I wore not a stitch of clothes. After all, the Fofonoloy wore nothing. This was most likely a clothing optional world.

Afterwards I curled up in my Earth-style bed, wrapped up in the soft spreads, practiced ordering the lights to turn on and off, and said goodnight to Breadbox.

"Breadbox, my friend and favorite alien, I'm the alien now. I'm curled up in bed here on your home world, and I miss you immensely. Your spirit is always with me."

I smiled and went right to sleep. It had been one long day.

I slept peacefully until jolted awake by a tiny noise. It was utterly dark. There in my space a large creature was creeping about silently and almost invisible. Instead of yelling "Lights on!" I just screamed.

44. Spider Woman

I'm not a screamer, but I sure screamed then.

I was awakened from a deep sleep by a small noise. Back at home, I'd figure it was a mouse in the kitchen, but here on Sfofong it was completely silent at night. Something was in my room! When I opened my eyes I saw a shadowy being moving slowly and silently across the room toward my bed. I could not remember in that instant how to turn the light on.

It loomed above me when I sat up. It looked like a furry spider the size of an orangutan. I tried to jump out the other side of my bed, but got tangled in my blanket and fell on the floor, banging my elbow. It scurried around the foot of my bed making raspy scratching noises on the floor, and loud high-pitched squeaks, like a hundred decibel mouse.

I finally remembered and shouted "Lights on!" as it rounded the foot of my bed. I got a good look. Like a giant tarantula three feet tall with two saucer-sized black eyes fixed on me. Many legs covered with black and gray spiky hair. Two "arms" with pincer-like hands.

When I screamed again it scurried away. I yelled "Help!" just as it took the elevator platform down from my upper level. My clothes were strewn across the floor. A giant bug that knew how to use the elevator and was messing with my clothes! I wrapped a blanket around me and ran to see where it went. While waiting for the elevator to come back up, I saw it scuttle out the front door.

My screams attracted somebody, but it wasn't Kateh or Furu-la, and I didn't have my translator in hand, so all I could do was jabber hysterically. I pulled on a dirty teeshirt and jeans. When I summoned the elevator and took it back down, the beast was long gone. There was a piece of my clothing on the pathway. What was going on here?

Outside, squeals and hisses from beings I couldn't see, it was so dark. More ape-spiders? Could all these beings see in the dark like cats?

Then it got quiet. I could dimly see a being slowly approaching through the gloom. The other shadowy entities moved back out of its way.

It was Kateh. I ran back inside and struggled with the elevator so I could retrieve Junior to translate. When I finally got back down to the ground level Kateh was waiting for me with the lights turned on.

We stumbled all over each other with apologies. Then she explained. "This oki is a night worker. It is out during hours of darkness. It is a Type

192

It was a spider the size of an orangutan. I screamed!

4, and it serves us, cares for our abodes. Keeps things clean. We asked it to care for you, tend to your cleanliness. It was gathering items you cover your body with to clean them. We are so accustomed to its service in such matters, we neglected to inform you."

So, the poor thing was gathering up my dirty laundry, and I must have scared the bejeebers out of it. Well, it sure scared me! My first night alone on an alien world and a giant spider creeps into my room. Lordy, if this had happened to me when I was a kid it would have taken years of expensive therapy, and I'd still be creeped out.

Now that I knew what it was, I just giggled. I was curious. I wanted to see this Type 4 being—the type Breadbox had equated with "bugs." I wanted to see an ape-sized spider that did laundry.

After things calmed down, I went back up to my sleeping level. I gathered up all my clothes besides what I was wearing and left them in a pile just outside my front door. Then I went back to bed, but I couldn't sleep. Would it come back that night? I felt tremors of fear, but I also felt bad for how I must have frightened it. And I was curious. I wanted to see it again.

I should leave it a peace offering, I thought. After all, I did want to get my clothes cleaned. But what? What does a giant spider eat? A giant fly? The only thing I could think of was a big square of my last remaining chocolate bar. In the dark, I went back down to the lower level and placed the chocolate on top of my pile of clothes. Would it even see this, and know why it was there? Does it like sweets? Would chocolate be poisonous to it, thus killing my laundry bug? I headed back up and finally got to sleep.

*   *   *

193

When I awoke, morning light was streaming in through the opening to the rear deck. I leapt out of bed, pulled on my clothes, gave appropriate commands to the toilet so it would work for me, and then headed down to the front door to check on my dirty laundry. I heard a soft chime, and yelled "Open door." I was greeted by the moving platform carrying breakfast. I saw no beings with it. As it moved by itself into the sitting area, I looked outside and saw that my dirty clothes were gone. I didn't see the chocolate either.

Time to choose my breakfast menu: more alien food, or more peanut butter on stale bread? Well, I'd had no ill effects from the food last night. I took a look. Two covered dishes and two small canisters like the one in which Kateh had brought water for me. Hot coffee? Oh, how I wished! One was cool water, as before, and the other was indeed a hot beverage, smelling earthy and minty. One dish held the same pastel cheerios as last evening, and the other held a warm broth, looking like miso soup. Smelled herby, like sage or tarragon. Chunks of something floating.

I was hungry. Using a utensil like a ladle, I sipped the soup. It was pretty good! Needed salt. I mixed the cheerio things in with it and ate every bit. The warm beverage was not coffee, had no caffeine, but wasn't half bad. Just bland. I still hankered for some chunk-style peanut butter on bread.

Wow, what would this day bring? I headed back down to *Star Choice*, taking Gibb. Furu-la was already there directing the set up of repairs. "During the period of darkness, our devices completed the survey of your vessel. In addition to the propulsion system, there is damage to the energy system. With this damage, it was hard to build up reserves. That's why your energy reserves were always low."

I nodded. "Furu-la, may I use the view space to contact my home world for an important purpose?"

She turned her eyestalks on me for a moment, then said, "That should not interfere with this work." She made me feel like third grade, with my teacher Mrs. Boone looking at me piercingly, wondering what mischief I was up to.

First things first. I went to the galley and brewed myself some coffee. Mmm, this made me feel almost human. Then back to the view space. But even before I could contact Earth, I saw there was a message from Amelie. She'd purchased a ukelele, scanned all the dimensions into her viewspace, and they were here already. That was fast!

"Good, let's get to work!" Talking to Junior, I activated the maker machine, and placed Gibb on the workbench there. "Junior? Wanda? I want to create a musical instrument based on the newly arrived specs from Earth, using the same materials that Gibb is made from. Where can I get the raw materials needed?"

Silence while the maker machine deployed from the ceiling. Then Wanda spoke through Junior. "My controlling oki, I detect adequate substances aboard *Star Choice* to create this instrument. From some dry food items, empty food packaging, and from your waste. Place items in the receptacle on the work bench . . . Except for personal waste; the maker can access that directly."

Ew, this was a high yuck factor! It would build a ukelele partly from my poop in the sewage tank? I just sat there for a minute trying to take that in. Amelie had explained that on the space station wastewater—pee—was recycled. So why should this surprise me? I dug manure compost into my garden at home and enjoyed the delicious vegetables I grew. I was creating a gift for Furu-la. Well, I wouldn't tell her where her poop-elele came from.

"Okay, let's do it." Wanda said it could use the data contained in the maker machine from the earlier repair of Gibb to create the wood tuning pegs and the strings.

Suddenly I felt the whole vessel vibrating. I grabbed Junior and ran to the open port to see what was happening. Dozens of large black straps were working on the outside of *Star Choice*, looking like the large kelp leaves that stream up from the ocean floor. Three Fofonoloy techs were monitoring the work, and staying away from me like I was the evil alien. Well, I had yelled at the laundry bug.

Furu-la came over. "We have multiple devices working together, much faster. They are repairing—and re-growing—the propulsion system of your vessel. Your device could have repaired this damage to the propulsion system, given enough time and energy."

The process was very similar to what I'd seen inside. The large black straps looked like giant versions of the tendrils on the maker machine.

"Wanda, can the maker machine operate while these machines are working on *Star Choice*'s systems?"

"Yes, my controlling oki, the maker machine uses the internal life support power, not propulsion power."

I wanted to stick around, partly to watch what was happening. But also to help the maker machine build the ukelele. I wanted this to be a surprise for Furu-la, but I couldn't keep her out of *Star Choice*. However, she paid little attention to what I was doing.

One of the techs came to the open port and spoke to Furu-la, who then turned to me. " We found things stored in cavities in the landing supports."

I blanked for a moment, then remembered. " Ah yes, that's okay, that was done at my direction. Those are samples I collected while exploring a new world before arriving here." Back on World 25. Already seemed a long time ago, so much had happened.

She looked at me. "You should be aware, you could get data on such artifacts from the Confederation Library."

I shook my head. "My people want to discover and study such things for ourselves." That was stretching the truth. Landing on that world had been a total accident. Just serendipity that I had the opportunity to grab some samples and stick them in a hole for preservation. "Also, I should point out that the Library wouldn't cover the planets I visited. They are too distant from the Galactic Confederation. They lie beyond the range of your jump site network. Perhaps we will make data on that world available to your Library."

Seemed like Furu-la and I were always trying to one-up each other, and I had to prove that we Earth people weren't primitive bumpkins from the cosmic boondocks. But thankfully she didn't hold on to things; she let them go and went on to the next thing.

Her attitude shifted. "We have surveyed your vessel's internal structure. I confess, I am impressed by the depth of changes we found. You made many modifications, and you did good and careful work. Original and very well done. Unlike any Confederation vessel I have known about."

"Why, thank you!" I beamed. "We designed it ourselves, then my device Wanda created it."

She lowered her eyestalks and arm tentacles. "Earlier I made uninformed remarks about you using tools that you did not understand. I was mistaken. The work done here shows strong understanding of the characteristics of this vessel.

"I confirm to you, on behalf of all Fofonoloy, that all these changes belong to you and your people. They are your property, and we will keep them intact as we work. We honor your ownership. We will not copy or adopt anything without your permission."

I was flabbergasted. All I could do was murmur, "Thank you."

What a turn around! I did not expect that at all. In her eyes I had gone from despised Type 1 with a derided device to honored innovator and shepherd of secret information.

I thought back to the Three Spaceketeers sitting in Yoga and Waffles sketching out our "impossible dream" spaceship over beers. And what we produced turned out to be a whole new thing for the Galactic Confederation? Earth girls rule!

*   *   *

Did these workers ever take lunch breaks? My stomach was rumbling, and it wasn't from the soggy pastel cheerios I'd eaten for breakfast. I rummaged around in my food storage compartment and feasted on canned tuna, crackers, cheese, and dried fruit. I could see I was going to lose weight on this trip.

I joined Furu-la outside. This was a gorgeous day—it would have been a beautiful day even on Earth. This was the third world I'd been on (counting Earth) that had moderate earthlike climate. Was there something about a water-oxygen world that tended to have this climate? Or was it just lucky coincidences?

Furu-la watched me eat my crackers and cheese. "We are envious of your ability to consume nutrition in this manner. We have been raised to be fed only through the tubes you have seen penetrating our middle section. We get no enjoyment from this. Some of us are trying to recover the ability to eat the way you do."

"How are you doing that?"

"I go to the swamp and eat cold slimy yummies. Small worms and slugs that have no shells. I ingest them to get my mouth accustomed to eating once again, to get my system accustomed to digesting."

"What do they taste like?"

"Taste doesn't yet enter in, nor smell. It has not returned for me. Texture, weight, temperature, what I would call wiggliness. These are the ways I distinguish and enjoy these mud creatures.

"I must also relearn how to excrete. Right now, I excrete only a soft mush. I must awaken my entire long unused system."

This was fascinating, but then Kateh walked up, and she changed the subject. She asked, "Should your vessel not have a rounded end attached to the rear?"

I looked at the truncated flat stern. "Yes. That was the vessel's escape module." I recounted the story of how we had used that module as a decoy to allow *Star Choice* to escape from surveillance while on the Moon. I choked up as I flashed back to an image of The Impossible Dream, as we dubbed it, burning up as it passed through the Earth's atmosphere.

Furu-la asked, "Would you like us to rebuild it for you?"

My first impulse was to ask her how much this would cost. I recalled contractors back home who were always suggesting wonderful but expensive add-ons to my repair jobs.

"I have no way to repay for you all of the things you are doing for me," I said.

Kateh waved her tentacles in negation. "We owe you an immense amount. We could never repay you for the things you have done—taking care of our crew members, both the live one and the ones that perished, refurbishing or overseeing the repair of this vessel, and putting it to excellent use. And now your physical visit to us so that we get to know you personally. It is an honor for us to work on your vessel and to provide for your needs while you are here."

Her effusive comments made my knees tremble. Tears came to my eyes. I'm sure I blushed. "I feel unworthy of your kindness and generosity."

But since they had insisted, I said, "Oh all right." I figured I might well need it getting back to Earth—assuming I ever got back. But it would have to be rebuilt to human scale, not for Breadbox and crew, as it had been originally.

"Wanda," I asked through Junior, "do you contain the plans created by the Spaceketeers for a human version of the escape pod?"

"Yes, my controlling oki, these plans are intact. I can guide the maker devices here to rebuild it. Would you like to request any further alterations?"

"Now that you ask, we should have a larger entry port in the rear to load or unload large items such as equipment."

Furu-la asked, "Perhaps we should build some devices into your vessel to help you repel any further attacks."

"You mean weapons?"

"The intent would be to defend your vessel, yet they could be used for attack if you so chose."

This was appealing, yet frightening. "I am reluctant to have weapons based on your advanced technology when I return home. When others discovered them, that could start an arms race on my world."

"We understand that you may need to defend yourself as you return. But once you safely return home, we will provide a way for you to destroy these weapons so no one else can use them."

I smiled as I thought of Jonn seeing such weapons, and how he would respond when I said I was going to have them self-destruct. Ha! But I had to let them install these, because I had no idea what was going to happen when I returned home. Assuming I could ever return home.

Assuming I could ever return home. Oh my. That was my mantra, my quote of the day, my hope that covered my fear.

*   *   *

When I returned to *Star Choice* mid-afternoon to get a cheese and cracker snack, I discovered that the ukelele was complete and lying on the maker machine's workbench. It was beautiful! And so cute. I wanted one. How could I give this to Furu-la? The body was bright red, and the maker machine had even recreated the small yellow, green, and white flowers painted on the body. The strings looked like nylon. I strung it and tuned it. Easy peasy! It was a real musical instrument! This was so impressive. I realized I should have had a case made for it. "Thank you, maker machine!"

I carried it carefully outside to where Furu-la was instructing the techs how to set up the black straps to continue working through the night.

I held it out to her with both hands, feeling bashful. "Furu-la, I had my maker machine create a smaller version of my musical instrument suitable for you. This is my gift to you."

She looked at me then lowered her eyestalks to examine the instrument. Her skin patches rippled soft pink. Her arm tentacles reached out tentatively, then drew back.

I played a few chords, and then handed it to her, showing her how to hold it.

She touched it hesitantly, then reached out with all four arm tentacles to take hold most carefully.

The cosmic ukulele was perfect for the tentacles of Furu-la! I would pluck a note on Gibb, then ask her to copy my move. I showed her how to pluck it and strum it, how to do simple chords. She could strum with two tentacles at once. I saw that we could redesign it to take advantage of that.

"May I express my strong appreciation, my Type 1 . . . friend," she said. "What is this device called?"

"It is called a ukelele, which means 'dancing flea.' A flea is a tiny Type 4 being—a bug."

"In honor of your gift and your people, I shall give this device a name—Dancing Flea. I shall strive to utilize it as well as you use your device named Gibb."

"Before I depart this world, we must play music together."

Furu-la clasped the uke to her like a young girl holding her favorite doll. Or like Breadbox had held onto Wanda. I was elated. She had called me a friend. And she was naming her instrument —a practice she had earlier scoffed at.

45. Romancing the Bug

I was giddy with joy. Furu-la had called me her friend. I bounded back up the hill to my abode carrying Gibb. With Junior, I yelled for the door to open and ran right into the sitting room where I almost ran into Spider Woman. She was surprised, and she sure surprised me!

She jumped aside, cringed away from me, and made a high-pitched squeal—almost a shriek. She crouched with all her legs bunched beneath her, ready to spring into action. All her spiky long hairs stood straight out, making a sound like a rattlesnake.

Scared the hell out of me. I sprang in the opposite direction, back toward the door, so I could make my getaway if she attacked me.

She was terrified of me. I keep forgetting—I'm the frightening Type 1 alien on this world.

What should I do? On this world, when in doubt, sing. So I took a deep breath, tried to relax, and sang to her. I crooned the beginning of "Song to My World." I bent my knees and crouched down till I was the same height as she was, hopefully looking less threatening—without eliminating my option of running outside if she came after me.

But why would she attack me? She was there to help me. When I walked in, she'd been cleaning up crumbs on the floor from my messy breakfast.

I kept humming softly as I stood up slowly, and swayed my arms in time with the music, the way Kateh might. This seemed to relieve the tension. She also stood more erect and relaxed her hair, so that it smoothed along her body.

For the first time, I got a good look at her. She had ten thin appendages with multiple joints. She held her body upright with her head on top. Six appendages were used as legs, all pointing downward, arrayed in a circle. Feet looked like claws. Four upper "arms" ending in claws divided into multiple "fingers."

All the spiky hair I had initially seen was now smoothed down flat against her body, like a man who slicks his hair back with gel.

Her face was dominated by her saucer-sized shiny black eyes, but below them she had a mouth with a horny beak. When she sat, she settled down into a six-legged lotus position. When I sat, her face was about even with mine.

In daylight, she looked nothing like an orangutan, except size.

I spoke slowly to her, using Junior to translate. She was silent at first, but then made some tentative vocalizations. She spoke with a variety of high-pitched squeaks and clicks. Plus gestures with her arms, and clicks with her claws/hands. I was glad to discover that Junior—channeling Wanda—could translate.

"I clean room," she said.

"Thank you."

"I clean body coverings." She gestured at my clothes in the sitting room. Looking that direction, I saw my formerly stinky laundry clean and arrayed in outfits, spread out on the various pieces of furniture.

"My name is Selena," I said.

She was silent for a minute, then replied, "I Zzik," thrusting two of her arms upward. Junior pronounced Zzik with a drawn-out z sound, after she had made a sound like a grasshopper clicking.

Using Junior, I asked if I may touch her. This was risky. Furu-la had reacted strongly when I tried to hug her. I held out my hand, fingers spread. She tentatively reached out one tentacle and touched my hand with her claw. Looked like she could deliver quite a pinch if she was riled up. She asked if she could touch me, and I assented. She moved slowly closer, reached out and touched my hair. She stroked it and made a soft cooing sound. Blonds appeal even to giant spiders! I in turn reached out to touch the spiky-looking hair on her body. It was coarse, but not nearly as stiff as it looked. She curled one strand of her hair gently around my wrist. That surprised me! Prehensile hair?

She reached behind her—kind of over her "shoulder"—and retrieved something from a pack she was wearing on her back. A backpack! She held it with two claws out toward me.

"I give you."

She presented me with a fork. Material that looked like bamboo. Over a foot long, two tines, intricately carved designs. It was a work of art, or it would be on Earth. Almost the size of the ones we used to grill hot dogs or marshmallows over a campfire when I was a kid.

I accepted it and said thank you. I immediately felt guilty that I had nothing to give her. Wait, maybe I did.

"I return soon," I said and ran to the elevator and went to my sleeping level, where I retrieved the stoppered vial that had contained my sample of whisky. This was a vial that the maker machine had created back on World 25 to collect specimens of bugs and things. I took it back to the entry level and showed it to her.

"I give this to you as thank you."

I removed the stopper to demonstrate how it worked. She held it to her head between her eyes, as if to her forehead. Was she sniffing the remaining drops? She seemed to be entranced. My goodness. I'd better keep her away from my liquor cabinet!

"I grateful," she said. She held the vial to her chest and spiraled a single hair around it, clasping it to her.

"I go," she said, turning toward the door. She skittered outside and down the walkway on six legs. Wow did she move fast! I'd never be able to outrun her. Gave me the shivers momentarily thinking about being pursued by an ape-sized spider. Better keep on her good side.

*　　*　　*

As I turned to head to the upper level, Kateh appeared at my open front door and asked if she might visit. "Of course! Of course! Come on in!" Another small self-driving cart trundled along behind her. I briefly recapped my visit with Zzik.

"You exchanged gifts with her? No need for that. She is here to serve."

"I frightened her twice, and I am the despised Type 1," I said. "I wanted to assure a good relationship."

"I understand. But if you gift her, she may then expect this from all."

Hmm, no tipping on Sfofong? Did Kateh think it improper to reward a lowly Type 4? Seemed unlike her.

Kateh's cart raised to the height of a coffee table, and Kateh gestured at the items on it. "We have synthesized small samples of your food, and would like you to taste them before we create more. Our chemist knows many preferred food tastes of Type 1 beings. He is a Type 2, not from Sfofong, but from a distant world. This is a regular service for visitors from other worlds.

"Our analysis found common proteins and carbohydrates, fats and sugars, plus trace amounts of substances used to impart taste and smell. He can determine what nutritional elements you need and what tastes and aromas you prefer, and prepare foods for these."

There were three short sticks of food. Looked like jerky, a bread stick, and something orange and translucent. I picked up each in turn and took a tiny nibble. It required real trust to eat food prepared by people who don't eat! These were not all that tasty, but they would give me nutrition. Like real food! Meat, bread, and a fruit stick. My stomach growled reminding me it was dinnertime.

"Also salt," Kateh said. "We didn't initially recognize the importance of this nutrient for flavor." She watched closely as I nibbled and made "Ummm!" sounds.

"Texture was most difficult. We deduced that the texture of some of your foods is created by gases emitted by microorganisms that then disappear during the heat process."

"That would be yeast." I wondered how this would be translated, and whether yeasts exist on this world. And if they did, could I get some fresh baked bread? Yes, and maybe some beer!

Thinking of beer, I asked her, "What about the liquids I gave you?"

"Our chemist will soon complete some of your beverages containing ethanol. I am curious: does consuming ethanol have a particular physiological effect on you?"

"You bet it does!" I wasn't sure how to explain getting a buzz on, let alone getting drunk.

"The ethanol and the sugars were very easy, but there are many trace aromatic chemicals that will take a little longer to analyze and duplicate. Since some ethanol may have evaporated from your samples, can you tell us what proportion of the liquid it should be? Our chemist measures in sets of seven."

Sets of seven? How could you do chemistry with such a weird counting system? I was sure the wine was about 14% alcohol, so I told her one part in seven. Jack Daniels is 86 proof or 43%; I said four parts in seven.

Math is hard!

46. My Favorite Ethanol Beverage

Oh boy, oh boy! I was going to get some booze! I sure needed a drink. I'd been nursing my lone bottle of Jack Daniels so long, sipping it by the thimbleful, I'd probably get snockered by a decent-sized shot.

But first to eat some dinner. I had only the stale dregs of my larder, plus the samples of local food brought by Kateh. I nibbled slowly, trying to savor each bit, and get accustomed to these alien (to me) flavors. All I can say is, it assuaged my hunger. I nibbled a tiny square of my remaining chocolate for dessert, and then checked in with my crew back on Earth via Junior. Voice only, since I had no view space.

I wanted to make sure they didn't forget about me. Here was the news from home:

Noel: "Now that Singapore has invited us to create a foundation there, the U.S. government has decided they can't let you slip away, and they told us they'll allow us to set up a Star Choice Foundation in California."

Dana: "Your agent, Morty, left me a message saying your latest album with music from your moon concert has reached Number 1 top seller for another week."

Clay: "I went up to your artichoke patch. Several of your 'chokes were so ripe I had to pick them. Delicious. I invited Doc and Jim and Meg over for dinner. We had a great Malbec in your honor. I drank most of it myself. Yes, I'm feeling a lot better. All the cancer is apparently gone."

Amelie: "Jonn is tied up right now with another YouSpace shuttle launch. He told us your model Flashcar had a recall notice for an airbag defect. He sent one of his boys up to your house to retrieve yours and get it fixed. I met the twenty-something at your place. What a hunk! He was so sorry you weren't here so he could meet the big celebrity."

They sounded so close, so familiar, yet so remote. Not just a thousand lightyears, more like a different lifetime. Reminded me of the time, as a kid, we'd done a holiday-time conference call with my mother's relatives in France. They seemed a lifetime away. My friends' lives were going on without me.

I kept up my jolly wisecracking mode throughout our conversations, but as soon as they all signed off, I broke down and cried from loneliness. I blubbered and sniffled myself to sleep.

When I awoke in the morning, in the center of the room was a small stand. It looked hand carved, knee high, holding a ceramic-looking jar like a small honey pot. Beside it was a tiny knife with a pistol grip. Was this a gift from Zzik, my laundry spider? Had to be.

I removed the lid from the pot. Inside was a brown sticky something. Smelled sweet. Dare I try it? I hadn't been poisoned yet on this world. I used the knife to get a small sample and tasted it. Sweet and herby and earthy. A strong taste, but could be a good condiment for the bland food I was being served.

I took a luxurious bath in the hippo-sized tub. I could almost swim laps in there. Or drown if I weren't careful.

As I got dressed, Kateh chimed for admittance, and I took the elevator platform down to the main room to greet her. She trilled for the breakfast cart and it trundled into the room and unfolded for me. I didn't mention the gift from Zzik.

"Furu-la tells me that repairs will require several more day and night cycles." Kateh announced. "Perhaps we could show you nearby locales of our world."

"I'd love to do that! But first, my friend, I want to check out the progress on *Star Choice*. What if I meet up with you afterward?"

*   *   *

After breakfast, I jogged down hill to see how the repairs on my spaceship were coming along.

Omigawd, there were gaping holes all along the sides of my poor vessel! Layers were peeled back; I could see the insides.

I saw three groups of the black strap rebuilding devices. One hung down on each side working on the propulsion system—those thick bands that extended along both sides like running boards on an antique Ford. The third set of straps worked on the front, recreating the escape module.

I hadn't realized that the bands along each side of my spaceship were just the visible part of the propulsion system. Black bars—a foot thick— extended several feet into the vessel. If I were building the spaceship from Legos, these would be like a row of blank black dominos on each side. Likewise the round black patch on the nose: it extended deep into *Star Choice*, like a rubber plug three feet across extending six feet deep.

Furu-la saw me and came over to explain. "These are the devices that propel your vessel by acting on the space behind space. Others are concealed on both sides, top and bottom. Another will be embedded in the escape module. Finally, a thin black sheet of this material lies beneath the floor and provides the controlled gravitational force."

I'd been flying this vessel all over the galaxy, and I had no idea how its insides worked. Looking at it, I still didn't understand. Kind of like having my mechanic explain how my carburetor works. I nodded my head and tried to look intelligent.

Furu-la said, "As we begin to direct our equipment to rebuild the interior of your vessel, we need instructions from your device named Wanda, because these were built by your built-in creation device to her designs."

"Creation device? Oh, you mean the maker machine. Yes, I must give Wanda the okay first. Wanda, will you help Furu-la and her devices rebuild the interior of *Star Choice* the way it was before?"

"Yes, my controlling oki. I will ensure that they rebuild it correctly."

Furu-la moved to the rear and said, "Let me show you the progress on rebuilding your escape module. Tell me if we need to adjust the design before we proceed."

The framework was a network of branches, looking organic, not like a constructed vehicle. More like it grew, rather than being constructed.

Furu-la pointed out some of the features that were beginning to take shape inside the frame. "The three seats will rotate in any direction to provide cushioning for any orientation of the module. There's the pedestal for the view space. Here's an opening at the bottom that will become a large airlock."

It was all very impressive! Most amazing that they could "grow" a precision spaceship. Then she got to the good part.

"We are installing your defensive weapons," Furu-la said, pointing out two black spheres about the size of beach balls—one on each side—just inside the outer surface. "These operate in a manner similar to the push force you have used, but with much stronger energy. They will project a beam of energy in whatever direction you select. With these you can repel—and damage or destroy—devices or vehicles that threaten you at a substantial distance—up to the diameter of our world divided by four."

Wow! Assuming this planet Sfofong was about the same size as Earth, the range could be two thousand miles.

"We are installing two on the nose also, so you can protect your vessel from attack from any direction."

My trigger finger was already itching!

"Progress is satisfactory, but it will still require a substantial period of time."

Oh my. I was so ready to head home. On the other hand, a thought had snuck into the back of my mind. What if *Star Choice* could never be restored well enough to get me home? So many uncertainties. Who knows if all these repairs and upgrades will work? I may be better off staying here. I could survive well enough. The food wasn't great, but I wouldn't starve. I could be their token Type 1 being. I could give guitar lessons to support myself.

*   *   *

I met Kateh on my way back to my quarters. "Come with me!" she said excitedly. I was thrilled that I could understand her simple statements even before Junior translated. "The chemist has created more of your food items. And your special beverages."

A short hike up a paved pathway through the greenery brought us to a dome-shaped building, kind of like a large igloo. A low round door slid aside, and dank, funky smelling air whooshed out. I had to bend way down to get through the doorway.

Inside it was dark and crammed full of stuff that I could not identify. In the center was a brightly lit workspace. The lab table was about a foot off the floor and covered with all kinds of apparatus, steaming beakers, bubbling pots. It looked like the lab of a mad scientist. And there he was.

Kateh spoke to me while the chemist kept working, ignoring us. "This is our chemist, Gur-cru Dur-cru of world G'sita G. As you can see, he is a Type 2. On his world, the males and females remain constant, as on yours." He was round, like a cross between a turtle and a giant ladybug, with a dark exterior. Bright orange crests stuck up like feather headdresses. Was I seeing his skin, or shell, or clothing, or what?

He stood about two feet high, had four legs and three arms. One arm on each "shoulder" stuck out past his small round head, and the third emerged from below his chin. Thus the foot-high table. Wanda, through Junior, explained that the front arm was called a "director," whatever that meant. Two arms ended in three fingers, and the director had one. Maybe the director finger points things out and gives orders.

So, seven limbs and seven fingers! That was interesting, and may explain why he used weird numbers based on seven.

Without turning to us, he croaked like a hoarse bullfrog. It took Junior a while before it could translate, then all it said was "Longer. Sample."

Kateh turned to me. "Allow me to speak for him. He says synthesizing your food will take longer, but he has some preliminary samples for you to taste. Your feedback will guide him."

Mr. Gur pushed a round tray toward Kateh with his director arm while his other two arms kept at their task on the table. Seven small piles of different looking stuff were arrayed geometrically—six on the outside and one in the middle. Each sample had a small utensil like a miniature tongue depressor next to it.

"Sample a small amount of one," Kateh suggested. The pink pile looked the most appealing. With the utensil, I scooped up a pea-sized bit and touched my tongue to it.

Yuck! Omigawd it was awful! A chemical taste that made me pucker up. I turned my face so the chemist couldn't see my reaction, but he continued working, seemingly oblivious. But Kateh saw, and she had learned to read my facial expressions.

"Perhaps we should try a different one," she said diplomatically. "I wish I could advise you, but we Fofonoloy have lost our ability to discern tastes."

I nodded and tried the white crumbly sample. Harsh grassy taste, like if you went outside and took a bite of a plant that wasn't meant to be

207

eaten—not by humans anyway. But I avoided making a nasty face.

I bravely worked my way through all seven samples, giving feedback as I would at a wine tasting. "The charcoal taste is intriguing, but too much dog poop note."

These made me long for Kateh's bland fare she brought to me.

The chemist finally stopped his work and grunted a few syllables at Kateh. "He says that complex food types that have no reference samples in the library take longer. However, your comments were very helpful."

He grunted some more, and Kateh spoke. "Instead of synthesizing molecules, he will seek naturally occurring substances, including fermenting agents."

Fermenting agents? Yeast? That could lead to bread, cheese. And beer! If I stayed on this world long enough, I may get some decent food.

Another croak, and he held up a small stoppered flask with his director arm. "However," Kateh said, "he has prepared samples of your ethanol beverages. This one is ready for you to try." She took the flask and handed it to me.

I slowly twisted the stopper free and this wonderful aroma emerged. Oh my! I touched my tongue to the rim and tipped it up. Woof, that's alcohol all right. Pretty potent. I just wasn't used to it. I took a sip and I could feel the warmth all the way down. This was nothing like my Jack Daniels, but it wasn't bad. Tasted like distilled heather and sage. Both floral and dry. I took another sip.

I flashed on my Gran, who only drank a little champagne on New Year's Eve, saying, "Whoo-ee, I can feel the wind blowing through my ears!" I took another tiny sip.

"He says you are welcome to keep that container. The beverage that is one part in seven ethanol is not yet ready, because the aromatic organic compounds take longer to prepare." That would be the wine. "This one is four parts in seven ethanol."

Four sevenths? Wait a minute. Did I say that? No wonder it packs such a punch. JD is 86 proof, or 43 percent alcohol. That's about three parts in seven, not four. I'd better be careful with this stuff.

I thanked Mr. Gur for all his efforts, then turned and bumped into Kateh. As we departed, I took special care not to trip over anything. I crammed the flask into my deep pocket. On the way out, I didn't duck far enough and banged my head on the top of the door opening. "Ouch!"

*   *   *

Kateh was in a hurry. "Come with me. I would like to tell you something about our world. Then an event will unfold that I would like you to witness." So far I'd only seen the quarter mile strip between my quarters and *Star Choice*, so I was eager to go with her.

I took the flask of the chemist's moonshine with me. I stood up too fast and felt a moment of dizziness.

   She led me up a winding dirt path through thick green and reddish foliage. I didn't know whether to call these trees or what, but they were green tree-size plants that also smelled green. I kept having to duck to avoid hitting my head. It was like hiking up an animal trail back home that was frequented only by low-slung four legged types, so that tall bipeds have to walk crouched down.

   We hiked up a long hill and came out on a low ridge overlooking an open area. "Come stand over here where you can watch without being seen." Kateh instructed. I bent down behind a bush.

   "This is a water world." Kateh pointed with a sweep of a tentacle. It looked like a vast botanical garden in a network of ponds. I saw various types of plants on islets, surrounded by waterways. Above these were walkways with narrow bridges.

   "We have assembled plants here from many worlds. Each has its own section."

   "We call this the Tame Marsh." The Tame Marsh was laid out with the geometric precision of the Versailles gardens, very stately, well organized. Narrow, straight canals shaded with manicured plants. "Manicured" is a funny word for beings that have tentacles, not hands.

   "We once called ourselves the people of the marsh. That used to be true, but few of us venture near the marsh anymore. It is looked down upon. People call it the swamp—a dark unpleasant place, unworthy of a race of spacefarers."

   She looked down at the ground and spoke so softly I could barely hear her. Her eyestalks drooped and her skin spot darkened.

   "But in our earlier history, we were lovers of mud. We loved the water, the reeds, and soft mud. We would cavort with the other swimmers of the sea. We would swim and play with our own kind. We did our mating in the sea.

   She'd already told me some of this, but it was good to hear it while looking at the real thing.

   "Some of us return to the old ways when we can."

   She led me down a short steep path. With all her tentacles she was a lot more agile going down than I was—like a mule on a mountain trail. "Wait here," she said. The water there was shallow and she waded into a nest beneath overarching reeds. A few other Fofonoloy were in the water there also. They were behaving with reverence, as if in a temple. One floated up behind her, almost submerged, like a turtle. Kateh ducked down into the water and touched eyestalks with the other one.

   She climbed back up the embankment to where I was concealed. "Over lifetimes, we emerged from the marshes to become modern oki. Rituals still took us back to the marshes of our roots, of our ancestors, but many of us preferred not to go in the water, not to get into the mud, as I just did. Our marsh ceremonies became rituals on dry land. We had symbolic mud. We would touch each other with bits of some sticky substance to symbolize mud." She had smeared mud on her head and neck.

"Our scientists and engineers offered a much more alluring lifestyle. They were the ones who created the living, growing metals we use to construct our homes, our vehicles, and our space vessels.

"We went from being the people of the marsh to being ashamed that we did not walk upright like the Type 1 beings who dominated travel between the stars."

"We tried to reengineer ourselves genetically so that we could become more like Type 1s, better able to live on dry land and need no connection to the marshes or the open seas.

"From scurrying on all our tentacles, we walked proudly erect on four hind tentacles like those we envied. We had to wear special support articles to bear our weight on four tentacles, and carry a pole for balance. But we pretended we were Type 1s."

Wanda interjected that I might call these items shoes and a walking stick.

"Yes, I recall how Furu-la raised herself to vertical when she and I first met," I said.

"Our genetic meddling on ourselves went too far and we had a genomic crash. From being strong, straight, upright people, we went to— once again—crawling on our tentacles, yet weakened. We had to wear a metal band around our middle to give us strength, to compensate for our bred-in weakness."

I had always been curious about these metal bands, since I'd noticed that Breadbox could move around quite well without hers. But I didn't interrupt.

"This is why we are so ambivalent about Type 1 beings like you, even though your people have never had any contact with the Confederation.

"There's a movement to return to our roots. I want to show you one small way we are doing this." We stayed concealed up the hill waiting. As the minutes stretched out, I pulled out the flask and took another sip. Umm, yummy!

Finally a procession of Fofonoloy came into view, dancing. They ambled in single file along a path at the main canal's edge, looking like giant centipedes, holding parasol-like sunshades with one tentacle.

"Some of these are the clan mothers I wish to introduce you to," Kateh said. It was the most amazing procession I had ever seen, like a conga line of people with eight to ten feet each, waving, rippling skin spots, singing with their multiple voices, not all in tune or in harmony, but a rhythm that was hard to describe. I tagged along behind them reluctantly, keeping out of sight, wary of interfering with their ritual.

The canal passed through a low opening in thick foliage. They took a narrow path along the canal. After they passed through, I ran up behind them and looked through.

I had to duck to get through, and I tripped on a root, almost falling.

On the other side was a whole different world. "Our real world," Kateh called it. Untamed marshland. Waves from a distant sea surged through a swamp dominated by plants that looked like kelp and cypress trees. The Fofonoloy keened and hooted in a melodic pattern.

They tossed aside parasols and removed their metallic girdles, leaving them with nothing on. One after another they slid down the muddy bank into the swamp and swam around in the surge in obvious joy. They looked like miniature hippos in the water, but they frolicked like otters—splashing, hooting, submerging themselves, swimming around with only their eyestalks up.

"I'm so pleased to see them," I said. "Thank you for this demonstration and explanation. But you should be with them, Kateh."

"Yes. I usually join in. Perhaps I will. You could move a little closer to watch."

I watched. Took a couple more sips. Man, this stuff packed a punch! I wasn't used to more than a thimbleful at a time.

I quickly retreated. Being a bit tipsy, I was not as careful as I should have been and they spotted me. They started hooting and honking. I was standing on the muddy bank near where they had removed their metal bands.

Kateh turned toward me. "My friend, we invite you to come join us in our water dance," my translator gizmo said.

Whoa! I expected to be a spectator only. "I didn't bring a swim suit," I replied, feeling decidedly bashful.

"Leave your apparel items on the edge," she said.

Did I dare go skinny dipping with a bunch of naked aliens wrestling playfully in the surf? That would be crazy. Kateh had wanted me to get acquainted with all the other clan mothers, but this surely wasn't the way to do so.

I don't know what got into me. Oh, yes I did. It was the whisky, which was having a bigger effect on me than I expected. So I stripped down and folded my clothes neatly, sticking Junior in my shoe, then stood at the top of the bank.

Instead of making a smooth entry, I lost my footing, slipped on the mud, and slid into the water derrière first. I went right under the water and came up coughing and spluttering. It wasn't very deep; once I regained my footing I could stand on the bottom, feet in the mud, and keep my head above water.

This caused a riot and a stampede. I was like the fox in the henhouse. They all tried to get away from me, swimming and thrashing to be as far from me as they could. Others moved past me and scrambled up the bank so they were not in the water with me. In doing so, some collided with me and pushed me under. I was afraid I would drown! Nothing sobers you up faster than being in cold water and buffeted about by large frightened beasts. I know, they weren't beasts, but they were behaving beastly!

I slipped on the mud and went derrière first into the water
amidst the clan mothers.

One of them—pretty sure it was Kateh—reached a tentacle down. I grabbed hold and she pulled me up onto the bank in a very undignified way. I was naked and covered with mud.

In their haste to get out of the water and get away from me, they had trampled all over my clothing. It was hard to find it all. I grabbed what I could and ran back toward the hole in the hedge buck naked, clutching my clothes to me. Not until I got through the hedge into the orderly marsh garden did I stop and put on my clothes as best I could.

I was wet and muddy and banged up; I could tell I was going to be bruised. My flask was still intact. I was sure I'd need that later. I grabbed Junior.

Kateh caught up with me, said nothing but gestured for me to follow. She led me quickly back to my quarters. When she got me safely inside, she said, "Perhaps you should stay in your domicile for now."

"You'll hear no argument from me. I am so sorry that I embarrassed you and humiliated myself."

"Those were the clan mothers I would like you to talk with," she said.

"Oh no. They'll never be willing to talk with me after this."

"At least they've seen you. And know you're not a monster."

"But I am a monster—to them."

"Oh no," she insisted. "You are covered in mud. You are one of us—a being of the marsh."

*   *   *

Not until I climbed into the shower to wash off the mud did I notice that my chain with the amulet was missing. Realizing the implications of this, I shrieked with terror and crouched down in the shower to keep from collapsing.

47. Crises of Idiocy

The amulet was gone. I was horrified! The small metallic cylinder I'd called the most valuable crystal in the galaxy. I had kept it next to me on a gold chain throughout all my adventures. And now I'd lost it in a bit of drunken revelry. It must have come off over my head when I was in the swamp. Surely it would have been trampled into the mud by dozens of frantic Fofonoloy getting out of the water. It was lost. I was devastated.

I wailed to myself. "It's all over, I've done it now."

Breadbox and Wanda had told me over and over that this crystal is unique and must be preserved at all costs.

I wondered, did this mean I could never return home? Was the amulet the sole source of the jump code to Earth? Or did Wanda also contain the code? I could never remember. Wanda hadn't identified the code until I inserted the amulet into the slot in the control panel of *Star Choice*.

I was in such a state; all I could do was pace around my room, out onto the deck, up and down the elevator platform, around the ground level room. Stomping, swearing, moaning, kicking things. Sure glad I didn't have any downstairs neighbors.

No way did I have the nerve to call my buds back on Earth and tell them what I'd done. I could just hear the exasperated responses from Amelie and Jonn.

Ah, and then Breadbox. I couldn't bring myself to tell Breadbox, and she was only a spirit in my mind. After all, she had entrusted it to me. "Breadbox, my friend, I have let you down, big time."

Nor could I use Junior to inform Wanda back on *Star Choice*. I might be the controlling oki for her, but she had made clear that the amulet was at least as important to her as I was, if not more so.

And how would I tell Kateh and Furu-la? "Thanks for going to all the trouble to repair my spaceship. Unfortunately, I'm now stuck here forever as the unwanted Type 1 visitor."

This was all on me.

Maybe I could go back to the swamp by myself, get in the water, and poke around till I found it. I'd have to wait till morning, for sure.

Oh, that would be so hopeless. It must be trampled deep into the mud.

Ai yi yi. I could see no way out of this.

Later, lying in bed in my quarters, I was still in a terrible state, unable to sleep.

Zzik came to pick up my filthy and damaged clothes from this afternoon's debacle. I was wrapped in a blanket, shivering and sobbing. She said something in her grasshopper clicking voice, but I'd left Junior somewhere else—on the lower level. I spoke and gestured incomprehension. She gathered my dirty clothes and took the elevator platform down.

I heard a squeal and looked down. She held Junior up toward me. She spoke and Junior translated. "Your device here. Strange mistress, you are distressed. Problem with your room I can fix? I am your servant." She brought junior back up to my level and handed it to me.

I had not attempted complex conversations with Zzik. Could I explain? Should I even try? What could it hurt? "I lost my chain in the swamp, with jewel," I said, pointing to my throat and pantomiming the chain. "Swimming with Kateh and clan mothers."

Zzik looked at me for a time as if trying to decipher what I'd said. Then she said, "Lost chain. With pieces of value. Swamp." I nodded yes. She moved toward the elevator and gestured to me with a claw to follow her.

"You lead, I'll follow." I said.

We walked back to the swamp in the dark, with me picking my way carefully along the path meant for beings with many legs. I took her to the same spot on the bank where I had slipped into the water. It was still wet and muddy.

Using my phone flashlight, I showed her where I had been.

We stood there silently for a while as if waiting for an answer to magically appear. Then she bent down, dipped several of her legs in the water, and made a vibrating, thrumming sound. Before long, a wormlike animal appeared in the water, the size of a large baguette. It looked like one of those deep-sea fishes that has a lantern on its forehead to attract smaller fish as prey, but on this one it was two eyestalks. On the underside it had two rows of short translucent legs or tentacles waving rhythmically—like the way a shrimp swims. It struck me that this animal looked like a relative of the Fofonoloy. It must be one of the native sea creatures.

The worm fish thrashed the water for a minute or two, and Zzik thrashed in response. Then it disappeared beneath the dark water.

Now what was going to happen? We sat silently on the muddy bank for a long time. Zzik seemed comfortable with silence and waiting, and I wasn't feeling very talkative either.

I sat and listened. Clicks and croaks of what must be small animals all around us. The swish of water surging in, a soft breeze rustling the tree-like plants, the distant crash of surf on a beach. Very much like sitting on a beach back in California at night.

We were surrounded by large tree-sized plants, but when I looked up,

215

I saw the nighttime sky for the first time. Whoa, the stars were amazing! How had I never noticed these before? Too many trees, I guess. The stars were so thick—twice as thick as back on Earth. A dense band of stars crossed above; was this the Milky Way? Twice as wide and twice as bright as back home. I guess because we were closer to the center of the galaxy. The starlight here was as bright as moonlight on Earth.

I felt a joy in my heart that in the moment pushed aside the terror of losing my amulet.

Later I asked Wanda if I could see the Sun from here. "You cannot. You were looking toward the center of the galaxy. It's in the opposite direction."

A ripple on the water attracted my attention, and the giant worm appeared. It poked its head above the water, and there, draped around one of its eyestalks, was my chain with the amulet still attached. Plus my comm stone and the piece of agate.

Zzik reached down and retrieved it, held it up and handed it to me. I looped it over my head. The amulet was restored!

The baguette fish disappeared into the dark. I tried to hug the spider, I was so happy! Quickly discovered it was prickly, so I just touched it.

We returned to my quarters. Zzik gathered up my dirty clothes from my swamp dip, said, "To clean," and took off into the night, before I could thank her with another gift of sweets.

I whooped and danced around my sleeping room. I wanted to send a prayer to some beneficent deity, but wasn't sure whose territory this was. "Thank my lucky stars!"

Okay now, would I even tell everybody what a narrow escape I'd had? What an idiot I'd been? Not tonight, for sure. I was exhausted. I dug out my flask, and took a sip of the Sfofongi Special whisky. Just a tiny sip, mind you. Only a thimbleful. It took me no time at all to get to sleep, amulet clasped in my hand.

*   *   *

Of course recovering the amulet resolved only one of my crises of idiocy. I still had to deal with the aftermath of my cannonball dive into the swamp amidst the clan mothers.

Both Kateh and Furu-la accompanied the breakfast cart into my foyer. I decided I'd better get it out right away. "I take the full blame for my actions. I accept whatever penalty you think I deserve."

They both stood there looking at me for a moment, then began to hum and dance in a circle around me.

Back on Earth, Breadbox would make a peculiar sound when she would finally get the joke after I explained it to her. Like delighted laughter about the cleverness of it all. And twisting of her eyestalks in a particular way. That's what they were doing now.

"Aren't you angry with me?"

"No, we ----- with you." She used a word Wanda could not immediately translate. After a moment, Junior said "grok."

"We identify with the oki (human) condition we all share," Kateh said. "We can't help but sympathize with you. And see the deep humor."

Furu-la agreed. "This is a high condition among oki world races. We are all so smart, yet we do stupid, embarrassing things."

"Yes, and the most accomplished among us make the biggest blunders," Kateh said. "We call it poetic idiocy. What can we do but sympathize with you, and laugh with you? We have all been in this situation."

"We must embrace the chaos of life," said Furu-la.

This sounded like the opposite of *schadenfreude,* which means delight in another person's misfortune. This was more like ironic, gleeful sympathy in another's misfortune.

"And your blunders were the most creative," Kateh said. "You combined several—being seen by the clan mothers when you were trying to hide, falling into the water, startling and frightening those whom you want to befriend, losing your valuable piece."

"Yes, and all spontaneous," Furu-la said. "This was high skill indeed. Very admirable. You rate highly. You will go into the Song of Sympathetic Oki-ness."

At this, I just burst out laughing and crying. Tears streamed down my face. Both Kateh and Furu-la stepped close, laid arm tentacles along my arm, and almost touched my face with their eyestalks. Furu-la said, "You are our Type 1 friend."

"You are our friend," Kateh said. "Also, you forced the clan mothers—who have been avoiding you—to see you."

*   *   *

Kateh and Furu-la must have felt that I needed company—or else they needed to keep me from getting into more trouble---so Furu-la retrieved her ukelele and asked me to give her more lessons.

This turned into a jam session. I played Gibb and sang, Furu-la plunked some very imaginative chords, and Kateh joined in, hooting, sounding like an organ, and dancing.

We drew an audience.

48. Angry Clan Mothers

We were in the main entry-level room with the door open to the outside. The music apparently was heard outside, and this attracted company. Two Fofonoloy appeared at my doorway, making deep *hroom* noises. Not musical—more like angry elephant seals. Kateh invited them in and introduced them. "These are honored mothers of Clan Haw, Raw-no-laga and Llnor-fwa."

Silence. Tension filled the room. Kateh sang to them, and Junior translated. I held Junior up to my ear so I could hear over their song. "This is Selena, True Singer, from the world where our clan children were lost."

They sang back: "We know who she is.

"She is why we are all in trouble with the Elders, Clan Mother Kateh-naga-la."

I gathered that using the full name in conversation was a sign of unhappiness, like when your third grade teacher talked sternly to you, using your full name, for passing notes.

"You consort with taboo beings. This being is not here solely for quick repairs, as you told us. You are now singing illicit songs with a Type 1."

As they sang, four others came in through the door, so the main room was now crowded with eight Fofonoloy the size of pigs. Kateh didn't get a chance to introduce them. They formed a semi-circle around the three of us. They all sang in a chorus taking turns with their complaints. Their skin spots rippled dark red and gray. Since they weren't wearing nametags, I could not begin to tell you who was singing what.

"You, Kateh-naga-la, are the most troublesome of the Hawfofonoloy clan mothers."

"Clan cousin Furu-la-hawa, you are always under suspicion for your immersion in learning at the Type 1 institutions of knowledge."

"Clan Haw striplings are forced to work in frightening proximity to this Type 1 alien to assist in the repairs of its vessel."

"This space vessel, that was initially built on our world, has been ceded to this alien with no questions asked."

"Your Type 1 guest is befriending the cleaning bug, a subservient Type 4, with gifts for performing her assigned tasks."

"She has interrupted our most sacred ceremony."

It was a singing, thrumming, organ pipe gripe session. They sang and hooted more stridently, edging closer like a pack of wolves after Red Ridinghood's granny. Were these the clan mothers Kateh wanted me to talk some sense into? Hah!

Kateh and Furu-la moved together to protect me. Were we going to have a gang rumble here? I didn't see any weapons. Could I outrun them? They were between the doorway and me.

Kateh sang back to them. "Don't you see? This is exactly the kind of event we crave. Look, it has pulled together we clan mothers.

"We all have our risks, yet we sing. Our visitor, Selena True Singer, a Type 1 alien, has the risk of never returning to her home world. Our clan cousin Furu-la, because of her studies at the Confederation, risks never becoming a clan mother. We all face the risk of never becoming clan fathers, which would devastate clan Haw.

"Selena, our guest, engages a Type 4 servant as an equal, in a way that challenges our habits. She treats her personal device as oki. All are equal to her. All are named. This perplexes us.

"And yet we sing with joy. Because we *are* song. We are people of the song. So sing with us!

"We are people of the swamp, of the mud. Our guest Selena has joined us in the mud of the swamp. She joined us fully, head beneath water, unadorned body covered in soft mud. She is one of us. So sing with us!

"Honored clan cousin Furu-la is repairing the spaceship of Selena so she can return to her home world. In gratitude, Selena has given Furu-la the device she holds that makes music, called ukelele. So sing with us!

"Our clan young made an illegal adventure to the world of this being. They died there, but not before discovering a new advanced oki world, and my clan daughter Nala connecting by song with our visitor. Honor our young! Sing with us!

"Our guest Selena has offered to sing and talk with us about the challenges we face. So sing with us!

"Ah the irony, the paradox. We are perplexed; we are tickled. Join with us in this moment. Sing with us."

Silence. Then a hum building into a growl. Skin spots rippling darker and lighter. Kateh spoke in the growling organ tones of the Old Language. I was surprised when Junior translated. "All our gods are dead. We need to resurrect the god of joyous jokes, the god of delight in strange happenstance."

What could I do but sing back to them? "May I sing for all three explorers?" I picked up Gibb, but this was not so much a melody, but more of a song poem with riffs. They were trying to talk like a Talki, so I wanted to sing like a Singi.

Novan and Alala and Nala adventured like the Fofonoloy of long ago
They discovered a secret—a way to travel to unknown worlds, my
world—that not even the mighty Confederation knew.

They invented. Your three created devices not known before on any of the oki worlds.

They were brave, fearless. The three flew into space themselves, not satisfied to send devices in their stead.

They made it happen. Like heroes, they leapt into the void like your long ago explorers.

They crashed—came to a terrible end. Their lives were lost in the exploration.

Yet good came from it. Your three succeeded. They discovered a new world that is worthy of the Confederation, so you tell me. Their plan was validated.

Bad came of it. You were punished for the exploits of your clan children. Yet good came of it. Nala and myself each chose to sing the music of our hearts, and we sang together in the high tradition of Fofonoloy and all Singi races.

So be proud. Hold high your pride. You reared brave explorers, creators, engineers, singers.

Your ancestors in the sky, mighty explorers all, welcome these three to take their rightful places beside them.

Perhaps three new stars shine down from your night sky.

This was greeted by a cacophony of toots and whistles, some picking up my musical phrases.

Kateh spoke to the clan mothers. "If the clan mothers of Haw present a strong front and sing our case forcefully, and draw in mothers of other clans, the Elders may be swayed. They may reverse our punishment and allow us to go on to honorable roles as males. And father the next generation.

"We fear our fate. The way around this fate is to bravely join our voices to sing the glory of the voyage of our young that perished on a distant world. Up to now the voices and songs of the mothers have been scattered and weak. It is my hope that our voices, our strong voices, will reawaken our bravery. May the voice of our Type 1 visitor who is also a True Singer bring that about."

Remember that old statement, "That went over like a lead balloon"? That describes the reaction of these clan mothers.

Kateh turned to me and said softly, "Perhaps that is enough for this one time."

Then I noticed Noe-te standing in the doorway with arm tentacles trembling and eye stalks drooping. Omigawd, something must have happened to *Star Choice* !

49. The Nasty Elder Demands My Vessel

Noé-te edged shyly into the sitting room where all the clan mothers were clustered around me, and stood silently until recognized by Furu-la. She spoke in a soft voice, with her eyestalks cast downward. Her skin patches were gray with little color showing. She sounded like somebody who was admitting guilt for dastardly deeds.

"There is an angry Elder in the vessel of our visitor named Selena from the Type 1 world. It has ordered all work to cease—the black straps have stopped their repairs and retracted. It saw the device named Wanda and ordered it to terminate, to shut itself down forever." Noé-te looked at me. "The Elder grabbed your device with four tentacles and tried to remove it from its receptacle, but it wouldn't come out. So it removed a metal tool from its belt and began striking your device."

I choked back a cry of outrage. Using Junior I yelled, "Wanda, don't shut down!"

"I won't, my controlling oki," she replied immediately. "I obey only you." She spoke in English, so only I could understand her.

"What has happened, Wanda? Tell me."

"When the unfriendly Elder entered, it ordered Noé-te to depart. Then it starting striking me with a tool. To protect myself, I turned out the lights. I shut the main hatch. I increased the grav, and I shut off the flow of oxygen. It reacted poorly."

The others got silent and listened, even though they couldn't understand my conversation with Wanda. Junior translated to them what Wanda had said.

Kateh puffed up and turned dark red. Her anger was apparent. "The Elder is damaging our work using tools and violence and improper demands!" she said in her voice of authority, and all the clan mothers signaled agreement. "We must not allow this to happen."

I had never seen the Fofonoloy move so fast. They scooted out the door of my abode and down the hill toward *Star Choice* like a phalanx of pig-sized Sherman tanks. Whatever fear and unhappiness they had felt was overcome by this intrusion.

I lagged behind, talking to Wanda via Junior. "Wanda, better not deprive the Elder of life. Don't kill it. Maybe let it outside."

Then I followed the herd of clan mothers down the hill.

Before I got very far, I heard a strident conversation, apparently picked up by Wanda inside *Star Choice* and transmitted to me via Junior. Since Wanda was translating different speakers, I wasn't sure who was talking, but it sounded like the Elder and one or more clan mothers.

"The Council of Elders that oversees Clan Haw has ordered all work to cease. We will take control of this vessel." That must have been the Elder.

"You are trespassing in the affairs of Clan Haw," asserted another, I guessed Kateh. "This is the official guest reception facility for this region of Sfofong, this vessel belongs to our guest, and you are not allowed to interfere here unless we request it."

"We were invited by one of yours."

"Somebody reported your guest," said a softer voice. "We know who it is." This must have been another clan mother.

"I will stay here to stand guard until we can take it away." The Elder.

"Why do you believe you have the right to take it?"

"This vessel was stolen."

"No it wasn't.

"It was taken from criminals engaged in taboo prohibited activities. It was not meant to be piloted by an ungainly Type 1 interloper from an unknown world." I was by then close enough to see them. The Elder reared up on its hind tentacles and menaced the clan mothers.

Kateh stood her ground. "This vessel has been completely rebuilt by the beings of the world of our visitor. Sfofong has no claim to this spaceship. It belongs to her. We relinquished all claim to it when our visitor originally asked if we wanted it returned. Our captains told her not to return the vessel or the device—or the remains of our clan children. Thus her actions are completely legitimate."

As I neared *Star Choice*, I saw the Fofonoloy females clustered around the larger Elder. I could hear its voice in addition to the translated version through Wanda. The Fofonoloy made way for me, so in a moment nobody was between the Elder and me.

It wasn't singing, but using its Talki voice. It sounded grating and unfriendly. Imagine an officious bureaucrat with a loud singsong voice like a hoarse trombone. It reminded me of a giant ant, the size of a heifer, wearing six pairs of combat boots and a tool belt. Its skin was mottled grey with red veins and looked nubbly—like a basketball. When it moved, it limped.

Then it saw me. It reared back, standing up as vertical as it could get on four or six legs, so that it towered above me, and extended its eye stalks toward me. It waved some tool it held with one tentacle--perhaps the one it used to bang on Wanda. Then it lost balance and fell over sideways. I think that when it tried to stand erect, it was top heavy. It rolled over on its back, so its legs were thrashing the air like an upended beetle.

It righted itself, ran this way and that, like a bug looking for a place to hide. It made a chirping whistling sound that summoned a small vehicle I hadn't noticed before. It looked like a Segway with a caboose for its extra legs. The Elder climbed aboard and zoomed up the hill and out of sight.

After a moment of shocked silence, the clan mothers all turned to look at me. "The Elder was afraid of you," said one of them. Me, the scary alien? Hard to believe.

"I believe the Elders do not want to confront you directly," Kateh said.

"Won't it be back with reinforcements?" I asked.

Furu-la said, "For all they know, you may have reinforcements circling the planet, coming to your rescue." Right, my all-powerful space armada manned by the Spaceketeers and all my other buds. I laughed.

I could never figure out the Fofonoloy response to humor. Furu-la had just made a funny sardonic comment, but I was the only one that laughed. I didn't even know if they could laugh. Breadbox had a particular waggle of her four arm tentacles that indicated she'd made a clever remark. But she rarely got my jokes.

Chasing away the Elder earned me some respect from the gathered clan mothers. For a start, they didn't run away from me—or chase me away. They also voiced concern for my plight.

With the Elder gone, the others lightened up and began taking surreptitious glances into *Star Choice*, so I invited them to take a look in the hatch. "Look, a Sfofongi vessel transformed for Type 1 beings!" said several of them.

After some Fofonoloy equivalents of oohs and ahhs, they drifted away, leaving Kateh, Furu-la, and Noé-te with me inside *Star Choice*. I retrieved Wanda from her receptacle to check her for damage. A few dents and scrapes. "My controlling oki, I will self-repair these minor wounds." Again, she referred to the damage as wounds, as if she were a living being.

Noé-te brought up the bad news. "The Elders have taken control of the strap devices and prevented us from completing the repairs and upgrades." Furu-la agreed.

It took a moment for this to sink in, then I reacted with shock. "This means my repairs cannot be completed? Must I remain here on this world? Can I never return home?"

Kateh tried to mollify me. "If you cannot depart in your vessel, you will be our welcome guest forever." Noticing that I was not thrilled by this suggestion, she said, "We could also secure you passage to a Type 1 world, to be with beings closer to your kind." Oh yeah? I wondered if I could visit the world with the Songstone? No, I wanted to go home.

"What repairs are left to be done?" I asked.

"As you can see," Furu-la said, "some of the outer shielding surrounding the rebuilt propulsion units is not completed. The escape module is not completed, but nearly so. The weapons and propulsion are in place, and the energy units are fully charged."

Wanda, my rebuilt tubular friend, spoke up. "My controlling oki, I can complete it for you. I have monitored all upgrades."

"How long might it take?"

"It will take an extended period of time, because *Star Choice* lacks the powerful tools that have been used, and I must rely on the maker machine."

"Ah. So I will need to stay on Sfofong for a while longer." I thought about the food and wine created for me by the chemist, and sighed.

Oh lordy, could I use a drink!

50. My Best Friend Was an Alien

"**D**id you realize it has been two years since your alien died?" When I was back at my abode pondering the cruel vagaries of fate, my buddy Clay contacted me via Junior, transferred from Wanda and the view space.

Oh my. Two years since Breadbox passed away there at my house on the Pacific Ocean as we were listening to my music. This hit me like a ton of bricks. Omigawd so much has happened! The government had been after me almost that whole time. And now it looked like they'd chased me away from Earth for good. And I had another government on a whole different world after me. I really was the ditzy chick spaceship hijacker.

"Clay I've got to tell you something and it's not good news." Then I just laid it all out on him, crying and blubbering.

"Hold on, hold on, we've got to get your other good buddies in here." I heard him humming up the others on the comm stones, then one by one they linked in to the call. Jonn, Amelie, Noel, Dana, Doc, and Clay—all of them on a trans-stellar conference call.

I tried to hold myself together enough to explain it to them. "Guys, this might really be the end. *Star Choice* is about to be repoed from me by the nasty government bureaucrats on this world—called the Elders. We're just waiting for them to show up and take it away. It isn't quite space worthy yet. They're treating me as an interstellar spaceship thief.

"It's not all bad. I've made some good friends.

"They have figured out how to create drinkable whisky and wine for me."

Jonn's hum of thinking broke into my news update. "Hold on a minute. What is the shortest path to getting a space worthy vessel? It has to hold oxygen, keep out radiation, carry enough rations and water, accelerate off the world, find one jumpsite, and then point to Earth once you come out the other end. How many days would that trip take?"

Amelie jumped in. "Where could you go to get repairs completed? Could you send *Star Choice* into orbit while you stay there on the ground so she can complete her own upgrades?"

These people never give up! My friends never give up on me. In these dire circumstances, they immediately started solving the problem. I was so lucky to have them. Even at a thousand lightyears distant. Even if I can never get off this world, and have to spent the rest of my life here.

"Yes, Wanda says she can do that. It may take an extended period of time, she says. We're sure familiar with that perspective, aren't' we? By the time I get back, I'll be a grey-haired old woman. As it is, my roots are an inch long."

"Roots?" yelled Dana. "You can't come back with dark roots. What would your public think? Jonn, can you shoot some blond hair color into orbit for Selena?"

The fog of despair lifted. I regaled them with my adventures. I even owned up to getting drunk and falling into the swamp. I didn't have the nerve to admit almost losing the amulet though.

Noel asked, "If you're going to have to hide out there while *Star Choice* is repairing itself, could you please sneak out and take some pictures? Flora, fauna, the nighttime sky, the daytime sky, anything. Because you are getting back here, and without those pics, nobody will believe you went anywhere."

That evening, the chemist, Mr. Gur, had more things for me to try, including some new wine. Sweet, sour, bitter, and umami. Floral. Berries. Herby. Stony. You know, it was damn good. Not like any wine I'd had before, let alone a Malbec, but mighty tasty. Yes, definitely could taste the alcohol.

Kateh told me the chemist had stopped trying to synthesize my food from chemicals but was looking for natural ingredients that fit my metabolism and taste preferences. Wanda translated the terms Kateh mentioned to nuts, berries, and grains. That sounded much more promising than the pastel goop I'd been served.

I decided, that night I was going to get drunk. I'd take a bath in the giant tub, curl up in bed and drink myself to sleep. What the hey, why not?

But first, I had to sing a song to Breadbox. On the second anniversary of her death. I can't compose when I'm snockered, so I had to go easy on the wine while I was putting this song together. I had done part of this song two years ago. Now it was time to finish it.

My Best Friend Is Gone

A dog is a man's best friend.
My best friend is an alien.

She dropped in on my house one day
I truly thought she was there to stay.
Funny looking, could not talk
She hooted and chimed and honked and squawked.
How could we two with nothing in common
Develop such a bond?

Two years ago my best friend died.
I miss her so. I wept, I cried.
As we sang together in my home,
She passed so quickly. I was alone.
How could somebody I loved so much
In a moment just be gone?

It's two years now to the very day
So much has happened, so much.
I talk with her almost every day.
She is my crutch, my crutch.
How can a being who's only a ghost
Be with me on and on?

She died on my world, far from home.
I'm trapped on her world, far from home.
Will I ever be able to return?
She never even wanted to return.
How will I ever get back to Earth,
Not die here all alone?

I honor her in my memory
No matter whatever happens to me.
We helped each other recapture our song,
To the tribe of True Singers we both belong.
She bequeathed to me this magical ship
I've used to take a cosmic trip.

How could we two with nothing in common
Develop such a bond?

I added verses for Kateh, and Furu-la, and Zzik. And Noé-te, who had turned out to be a major ally. I was still singing when Zzik arrived to retrieve dirty clothes. I invited her to stay awhile and listen. I sang and hummed and strummed.

I went to sleep before she left. The last thing I remember was Zzik setting Gibb gently on the floor, pulling the blanket up and tucking me in, and whistling the light off. I only had one drink, I swear, Officer. I didn't get snockered.

51. Maybe, For Sure

In the morning, Furu-la asked if Noé-te could talk directly with me. I was surprised, since she was still very shy around me.

"Your device told you it could complete the repairs," she said when we met in my lower level room. "I watched your vessel create Furu-la's musical instrument. Are you confident it could complete the repairs?"

"Yes, but very slowly."

"I conceive a possibly faster way," she said. "Could we meet at your vessel?"

Strewn on the ground near *Star Choice* were broken pieces of the long black straps used for repairs, left behind when the functioning pieces had been withdrawn yesterday.

Noé-te picked up a piece. "What the Elders removed was the controller that guided the repairs, plus the functioning straps. But the source of power remains in place."

She held the piece of strap to the end of a control cable. "Suppose we reconnect these rejected straps to the power, and make your device the controller to guide the process. That could be much faster than the small maker machine on board." She moved two pieces together. "We would first request that these straps repair themselves."

I looked with astonishment at this diminutive version of Furu-la that had labored in silence and in fear of me. I wasn't sure whether she had transitioned from juvenile to female status, but I'm calling her "her" instead of "it."

"Let me ask my device." I turned to her. "Wanda, if we could connect the maker machine to some of the black straps, could you guide the completion of the repairs that way?"

"In principle yes, if the straps and I speak the same language."

Noé-te said, "With external power, and greater work surfaces, the work should progress faster. The Elders cannot stop it, because the control is within, from your device, not from central instruments that they can turn off."

"Wanda, will you allow Furu-la and Noé-te to guide you to complete the upgrades to *Star Choice*?"

"Yes, my controlling oki."

I helped Furu-la and Noé-te gather the abandoned damaged sections of the black straps. They carefully arranged them like poultices on the parts of *Star Choice* that still needed work. Next, they dragged in a heavy grey cable, thicker than a garden hose. That was the power source—plain old high voltage electricity. Using smaller cables, they attached each section of the black strap to this cable at a gizmo the size of a beer can.

Noé-te asked, "Can your device named Wanda connect with the main cable, then instruct the straps to connect with the smaller cables?"

"Wanda, see if you can connect with the grey thing and become its controller."

There was a short burst of beedle-boop talk between the two, and Wanda said, "It is done. I detect four connections are loose. The maker machine will secure them."

"Wanda, if you can continue at the same rate as before, how long will it take to complete the repairs and ready the ship for departure?"

"Perhaps one day and night period."

Oh wow, oh wow! I was once again happy! This turn of events may indeed get me off this world sooner and on my way home. Whoopee!

"Then it's time for a going away party! Surely nothing else can go wrong."

As I dashed back up toward my abode, there was a ruckus on the roadway. Several Fofonoloy females were clustered around one, and all were hooting and honking, sounding very upset. Kateh was among them. She saw me and came over to me.

"That is the clan mother that reported our activities to the Elders. She has just returned and we are punishing her. However, she reported something that makes our punishment pale in comparison. The Elders told her that as a payment for her brave deed, they are rewarding her. Listen to her."

Junior translated her shrill cries. "They said, 'We are rewarding you. We are promoting your clan child. We will free it from your care and place it in a special environment to prepare it for a meaningful role in society, far from this fetid swamp' . . . . . They stole my clan baby from me."

52. Stirring Up the Mud of the Swamp

After learning that the Elders had stolen a baby, the clan mothers were in a dither, hooting and honking and grumbling. Their skin spots rippled dark unpleasant colors. They stood at the edge of the road, huffing and shuffling and stamping their foot tentacles. They argued among themselves, all talking at once, completely ignoring me.

They didn't speak; they sang. Not one at a time, but all at once. Wanda, through Junior, did her best to translate their cacophony into a strand I could understand.

> *The Elders have taken it entirely too far.*
> > *They want to destroy us.*
> *We are afraid. They wield all the power.*
> > *We despise our Elders, but what would we do without them to set the order of life?*
> *In the golden days of old, clan mothers and clan fathers ruled together. Elders were the voice of wisdom and caution and continuity, but they did not set the oppressive rules for everybody.*
> > *We want to return to the old ways.*
> *These are impossible dreams.*
> > *How can we — insignificant bugs — change the course of our culture?*

A phrase like "insignificant bugs" made me question the translating ability of Wanda. Was she translating properly? Did they really refer to themselves as insignificant bugs? I asked Wanda.

She explained, "This is a term of self denigration; this is what they believe the leading races of the Confederation think of them. It is not generally true."

More singing and whining:

> *It's a dilemma with no way out, all we can do is try to get along and accept our punishment.*
> > *No we cannot, this punishment will be visited upon all clan Haw. From one to the other of us.*
> *When we go to male, we will not be allowed to father young. Clan Haw will be weakened or die out, with no progeny.*

Then the clan mother of Breadbox's crewmate Alala spoke, not in song but in talking voice, very quietly, but this got all their attention. "The clan mother of Novan died long ago—when she went to male phase. He was so unhappy with his assigned role that he let himself be killed. Novan was devastated. This happened long before their illegal trip to distant worlds, but it led to the ill-fated trip.

"And now it's my turn, my clan sisters. My second clan daughter was taken from me. As punishment. To be raised by the Elders in proper fashion, they say. The Elders have informed me that my male role will be to catalog ancient items in the catacombs. Deep underground, away from sunlight and green and water. I cannot last long that way. I will soon be dead."

There was a pause and silence while this sank in.

"Do you not see?" she went on. "This is what's in store for all of us. To eradicate Clan Haw. To lead to our extinction by not allowing any of us to become clan fathers. They will eliminate us one by one unless we stand up to them."

More singing, almost like a Greek chorus:

> We see that this will happen to all of us. It's unbearable.
> We must take some action, but we're afraid.

Kateh spoke. "Thus did I suggest we talk with our Type 1 visitor, who speaks clearly and truly, and whom as we've seen, the Elders fear."

They noticed me then and turned to me. "Kateh says we should talk with you, but why?" one said sharply. Then they sang:

> Why should we honor you?
>> You ran away from your own world
>> On a vessel of our people.
> Your people fight over this vessel
> As our Elders fight over us.
>> They try to grab it for themselves.
>> Or destroy it.
>> How is this noble?
> You, a young female, chased away by strong males.
> Same as on our world.

I shook my head and gave the gesture of disagreement. I could only speak, not sing. "I have strong males and strong females on my team. We work together as males and females once did on this world. Even while I am traveling in space they support me. They have obtained agreement to share technologies across our world. Our leaders—our elders—have agreed to this, because of the strong efforts of my team of females and males.

"I have sung to everybody on my world while circling our world in this vessel. People loved my song. Thereafter they stood up to their leaders. They said, let this woman come home. Let her share with all of us.

"As soon as my vessel is repaired, that is what I'm going to do.

"Kateh has asked me to speak with you. I have no special message or wisdom for you. You should only speak to me to strengthen yourselves."

I detected a shift in attitude in their next lyrics:

> *If the Elders know we speak with you,*
> *They punish us even more.*
> *We are forbidden to sing our song.*
> *We are forbidden to live our lives.*

How should I respond? Did I dare sing back to them? Why not? "Then I will sing a different song for you." I cleared my throat, took a deep breath, stood up straight, and began to sing softly. Wished I had Gibb to help me out.

> *May you never forget.*
> *The bonds of true oki*
> *must span the broad sky*
> *linking kindred spirits*
> *in the oneness of heart.*
> *Your most valuable gift.*
>
> *This is the message*
> *You must convey*
> *You must sing it together*
> *You must sing it today.*
> *You must sing it together*
> *You must sing it each day.*
>
> *Who but you can sing this?*
> *None but you can sing this.*
> *The power of your souls shining through.*
> *From the fog to the sun shining through.*
> *The song of Clan Haw shining through.*
> *The voice of Clan Haw singing true.*

I stopped and looked from one to the other, then asked, "Can the voice of Clan Haw sing this true when confronted by the Elders?"

Silence.

Then one spoke. "We cannot discuss this with you here. We must go to the swamp to commune with you. Our place of privacy and sanctity." Others hummed and signaled agreement.

What? What did this mean? They wanted me to go back to the place of my humiliation? A repeat of my swimming fiasco? My hand went to the amulet on its chain around my neck, as if to protect it from another plop into the mud. Why couldn't we just talk there in the road? Or back at my abode? I just wanted to pack up my stuff and get ready to depart. I'd been ready to talk with them as I traveled across several worlds, and now at the last moment they finally want to talk with me. And in the swamp!

I looked at Kateh. She looked back without saying or signaling anything. The clan mothers began shuffling and swaying and humming, and began moving slowly in the direction of the marsh, with the swamp beyond.

Wait! I hadn't agreed to anything, but they were on the move.

They were beginning to sing about themselves.

> *We are the mothers of Haw.*
> *Clan Haw, Hawfofonoly.*
> *Proud but punished.*
> *We are forbidden to sing our song.*
> *Our song is very important to us.*

They moved as a dance, kind of like a conga line with many, many legs. Caressing, massaging, grooming each other as they moved. Their skin spots moved in a coordinated pattern, rippling along their bodies.

Oh lordy, what was I going to do? Just stand there as they waltzed away from me?

The beings on this world had saved my life. Saved me from dying alone in deep space. They had repaired my space vessel to get me home, that they could just as well have reclaimed as their own. They had worked to create food I could stomach. And booze! If I could help them by giving a pep talk by the swimming hole, that was the least I could do. It was time to dance along with them.

Eight clan mothers preceded me, including Kateh, and they were joined by Furu-la.

They danced and sang in what I'd call a "cacophony chorus"—waves of song. They communicated by hoots, honks, snorts, squeals, deep organ tones; plus rippling colors on their skin, and "exuding," i.e., odors that filled the space. Not particularly unpleasant odors. Just let me say I was glad we were out in the open air.

I followed them along the groomed gardens of the marsh, and squatted down to get through the hole in the greenery to get to the swamp. The females were already removing their midriff bands and sliding into the water. Kateh gestured to me, inviting me to join them.

Moment of truth. I thought I was just going to stand on the bank and talk with them. Was I going to strip down again and jump in the water with them? And I was completely sober this time.

Bashful. Why would I feel bashful and embarrassed undressing with these unclothed beings? Well, it's bred into all of us, isn't it? Just get over it, I told myself.

I took my clothes off and folded them carefully and placed them behind a bush—away from the midriff bands and the egress from the water. I fingered my amulet on its chain. I wasn't going to take it into the water again. What to do? I tucked it into the toe of my shoe.

But I had to hold on to Junior, or I wouldn't be able to communicate with anybody. So I held it high in one hand while I eased into the water, till I was able to stand firmly on the bottom.

The clan mothers began moving farther out into the water, and it got deeper. They swam effortlessly, with their heads and backs out of the water. I could swim or tread water, but it was hard holding onto Junior, keeping it dry.

Kateh and Furu-la swam up alongside me, and reached out to support me with their arm tentacles. I was sandwiched between them. I'd never been so close to either. Even in the cool water, they were quite warm. Higher body temperature than mine. I kept a strong grip on Junior.

I took a moment to muse on the strangeness of this situation. Naked, in deep water, hugged between two very non-human beings, with seven others swimming around singing in what wouldn't even sound like language if I hadn't had Junior and Wanda to translate. A thousand lightyears from home, and no certainty that I'd ever get back. And I was enjoying it.

The clan mothers headed into deeper waters, past the swamp plants, into the gentle swell of the sea. But the water felt wonderful. Like the ocean around Hawaii.

They formed a circle around me, floating effortlessly. I wished I had water wings. Or an inner tube.

They began to sing to me. I held Junior up, but it kept getting wet. I had to remember, it was basically an iPhone. Not water proof.

With seven of them singing, different pitches, saying different things, I was again astounded at Wanda's ability to translate it into a coherent message I could understand.

First, four of them sang:

> We humbly ask, oh yes we pray
> May the goddess of music respond this day?
> yetta yetta yetta deh deh deh deh oh please respond.
>
> We ask oh yes we want to know
> May the goddess of the music hear our plea
> Let us swim yes swim freely in the sea
> With our friends and fellow swimmers of the sea
> Nibble tasty morsels deep within the sea

wan dan yanna dan, umm yes we do belong to the sea.
May the goddess of the music make it so, make it so

Then three others—not Kateh or Furu-la:

The goddess speaks no more
The goddess hears no more
Is she even still alive?
Has she left us high and dry, sailed from shore?
Ah so what are we to do
We have none left here to pray to.
mok daka huu dah what to do?

All seven together:

May the long bare-skinned oki make us free
with her flaming yellow hair for all to see
yot dot a doo dat make it so

That was me they were singing about. Long and bare-skinned, sure, except I wore clothing. Usually. But flaming yellow hair? I'd been in space so long, my ugly brown roots were over an inch long. I wouldn't be a blond for much longer.

Back to the first four:

Let us taste, going to taste
going to taste the real food
of the sea
going to smell, going to feel,
going to feel the world whole rude
May the long and lanky oki hear our plea

I tried to respond in kind, in singing verse. It wasn't easy singing while floating. Kateh and Furu-la supported me, but I had to keep kicking my feet to stay vertical. And holding Junior close to my mouth like a microphone:

If I could grant your wish, I would surely grant your wish
I would give you what you ask, what you want.
It isn't mine to give. But it's always yours to take.
You can always take it for yourselves today.

I wanted to get them past the notion that I—the strange alien visitor—could solve their problems.

Would you take back all your world if you could?
You must take back all your world, yes you should.
It is yours to grab your world, make it good.

But no, they wanted me to be their "goddess." They sang a plea:

May the goddess of the music make it so.

How did I get equated with their goddess of music? Why would any of them think I had anything worthwhile to say about the problems they were facing? Who was I to take on some role as social mediator? I was not up to that responsibility. But I had to say something. So here's how I responded:

I cannot be your goddess, cannot be
I live light lives far away, far away
But your goddess lives there with you,
Find your goddess there within you
She's already there within you
You must know.

Summon her now, right now
Make her come out, come and make it true.
Your music and your song can make it so.
Call her now, it's up to you
Let your inner goddess make it proudly so.

We argued back and forth by song, and gradually they seemed to agree with me.

Soon we were out beyond the swamp, into the open ocean. Their singing attracted a large sea beast. Hopefully one that appreciates song, and was not hungry for tall, lanky Type 1s with dark roots.

There was more than one! They swam around us like a pod of whales, and began singing also. Junior informed me that it would be difficult to translate their song.

We reached shallow water—a submerged sand bar. Shallow enough that I could stand. Kateh and Furu-la let me go.

I said to the mothers, "You all must support Kateh going to the male phase in the way she wants to."

Kateh responded, speaking not singing. "I will go to my male phase as it was done in lifetimes of old. When we mothers would feel the change approaching, we would retreat to a garden away from others, and be tended by juveniles. Given the male food. As we transitioned, we would be greeted and welcomed by those already changed. During ceremonies we would explore the ways of maleness. At the end of transition, the new males would rejoin the clan community. After a time, male and female would join as mates."

The mothers sang, telling how they wanted to go back to the old ways.

> *We want to give up false civilization,*
> *recapture who we were before."*

"Before what?" I interrupted.

> *Before we gave up our ways.*
> *Yes, we became more like the Type 1 creatures*
> *who rule the Confederation.*
>
> *In prior days, we swam to the sea naked*
> *Cavorted with the sea creatures. They welcomed us back.*
> *The creatures we are now forbidden to interact with.*
> *Males and females went on the hunt together.*
> *We copulated freely.*

Furu-la spoke. She seemed like the excluded outsider in this group, perhaps because she had traveled to the central Confederation worlds for schooling. "Sadly, all this is completely illegal, against the mores of our current society. The young of these unsanctioned unions are without status. Except that for a price one can obtain an adequate registration for such offspring."

Humming and huffing.

"My sisters," Kateh spoke. "I have never before confided this to any being, but Nala's genesis was just so. She was born of the sea. I am her true mother."

A long silence, then a growing hum, sounding like baritone whale song. They moved, first one, then others, in a synchronous dance. All feet and tentacles moved in unison, like a complex hula in the shallow water. Voices hummed and squawked, and skin patches shifted color to keep time. The other mothers circled around Ka-teh, caressing and nuzzling her.

Wanda, through Junior, explained to me, "They sing in the old language. It may not be proper for me to translate for you without their permission."

"I understand."

After initial shock at this announcement, they showed new regard for Kateh.

"And so will I," announced Furu-la. "I will remove my midriff band for good, learn to eat the food of our ancestors, and live in the edge of the marsh. But I don't want to be only a beast of the swamps. I don't want to give up all civilization. I want to find the balance. I want our Elders to accept that and make it permissible for all."

"May I ask, did Nala know she was a child of the sea?" I asked Kateh.

"Yes, she deduced it, because she was born out of the prescribed cycle," Kateh responded.

"Could that explain something about her path in life?"

"I fear so. My transgression created this tragic outcome."

"Your free choice created this marvelous singer," I asserted, "one who dared venture far beyond the imposed strictures, and had an adventure that is the birthright of all your people."

"You speak dangerous words," said a mother.

"But true."

Another long silence.

"But why are these sea activities illegal?" I asked.

"The elders crave control, and fear losing it."

"Mmm," I said non-commitally, wondering if I was getting the entire story. "We speak of transgressions and sinning. I have seen that my greatest sins are ones I commit against myself. Mainly failing to live up to what I knew I needed to do and what I could do. Also failing to go with love, and instead choosing a less worthy pathway."

When they came out of their circle, one of the mothers said to me, "Selena our Type 1 visitor, let me say this: Every one of us has transgressed against the strictures of our world. We share this shame. It creates a bond among us."

This brought tears to my eyes. This was the first time a female besides Kateh and Furu-la had addressed me by name. "Who among us has not sinned? Certainly I have," I said, shaking my head. "I share this bond with you."

A long silence, then Kateh said, "True for us also. We do give up some things of high value to live in this comfortable world, as you say. Yet, after our sea interlude, we do come back to it. Every time."

"We suckle at the teat of the galactic star jump network," said a mother.

"We want to break free, yet hold tight," said another.

I asked Wanda if 'suckle at the teat' was an accurate translation, since these ladies didn't seem like mammals to me. She replied, "I tried to restate their expression in words that would resonate with the practices and idioms of your world. Perhaps 'suckle at the throat' would be more a accurate description of the way their dependent young gain sustenance."

"I think I get it," I replied to Wanda. "If they went back to the old ways of their people, they fear losing connection to the star jump network of the Confederation. The same Confederation that they despise and feel superior to. But they crave the things they do get from it."

"You stated it well," Wanda assured me.

"I am very familiar with that choice."

I turned back to the mothers. "Clan mothers of Haw, I ask you, could you follow the words of Furu-la, and return to your desired old ways, yet hold on to the ways of your culture that allow you to stay connected to the parts of the Confederation that you enjoy? Can you not create a new middle way? If you can regain control of going to your male phase, so once again males and females raise their young and form strong bonds, you will free yourself of the oppressive control of the Elders."

With this, several of the clan mothers swam away, leaving us on the sand bar.

"Maybe my words were too strong for them," I said to Kateh and Furu-la.

"Strong words take time to digest. We are not accustomed to real food or real talk. But you have planted a seed. And I, then Furu-la, will show the way."

Break free, yet hold tight. This had long been my dilemma. But recently I had broken way too free. I was ready to hold tight to home once again.

I asked Furu-la to carry Junior above the water, so I could swim back to shore. One of the large sea creatures swam alongside me, like a dolphin. I was exhilarated, not frightened.

Back on shore, as I got dressed, I was relieved to find my amulet tucked safely inside my shoe.

One thing for sure. I had discharged my promise to Kateh to talk with the clan mothers. Had we accomplished anything? No idea.

53. Show Me the Way to Go Home

After the romp in the swamp, I was feeling high the rest of the day. The big sea creature, the size of an orca, had accompanied me all the way in—into the reeds and shallow water—and raised a tentacle to help me climb back up the bank. It then turned and swam away. I had swum with the sea beings of Sfofong!

"Did I help your clan mothers?" I asked Kateh later, when she delivered more edibles to my abode.

"It will emerge over time. I believe that interacting with a Type 1 being that doesn't despise us, with whom we can communicate, will be beneficial. What's the point of standing up to the Elders if all the beings beyond them also hate us. But seeing the possibility of friendship with Type 1s may diminish the specter of the all-controlling Elders.

"But let me say this, my friend. You have helped me. You helped me announce my intentions—how I will go to the male phase—and to tell the truth about Nala. And I saw that my clan accepted me."

Mr. Gur had sent a seven-pack of both whisky and wine—six bottles in a hexagon around a seventh in the middle, held together by a very interesting strap arrangement. Numbers based on seven, of course. So I had fourteen bottles of booze to get me home! Hopefully there'd be some left to share with my buds. Oh, and he reduced the whisky to three parts in seven—86 proof.

Also, in a beautiful covered round container was a dense cake, looked kind of like fruitcake. Kateh told me it was made of grains, nuts, and berries of this world.

Finally, in a squat vat was a concoction of nuts ground smooth, like peanut butter.

That's most of the food groups! I'd be in great shape for my return voyage.

I sampled each one. They had improved immeasurably. If I did end up marooned here, I'd eat well.

*   *   *

One of the small juveniles came up to Kateh and said that the Elders were requesting a general circle to discuss a disturbing occurrence. This circle would take place at the height of the sun tomorrow.

240

Kateh turned to me and said, "In the morning, they will send a squad of males to our community to make sure everybody attends. This may be the time for you to get ready to depart."

I had to get the hell out of there! The rest of that day, I attended to a flurry of activities.

I checked *Star Choice*. Was it ready to go? Yes, repairs were completed, and so were the escape module and weapons.

Furu-la gave me a rundown. "We built in extra energy storage and recharging capability. We have built the Earth code into a permanent location, so it can never again be lost or forgotten. Yet an outsider cannot access it unless authorized by the controlling oki."

Star Choice was sparkling clean. Small repairs and upgrades had been made to bath, toilet, cooking, and food storage. The seven-packs of wine and whisky were tucked away in a special storage cabinet.

Furu-la showed me how to use the new energy beam weapons. I wanted them to be like the pod Luke Skywalker sat in, with twin space guns that pointed in any direction blasting away. I wanted to put my fingers on the triggers and shoot them off, "Kaboom, kaboom, kaboom!" But what I had was a small console attached to my captain's chair with two joysticks and firing buttons.

Furu-la explained, "You must make the decision to use the weapon, and point at the desired targets in the view space, then the controller will aim precisely and activate the energy beam. This way your device named Wanda need not be responsible for destroying living beings."

From the view space, I notified Earth. "I can get home, it looks like."

I told them about the weapons, and admitted I was concerned about launching an arms race.

"Rogers tells us the arms race is already proceeding," said Jonn. "China is rushing to build space weapons, adapted from other uses. They have developed quite a bit since *Star Choice* was zipping around the Moon, as you well know."

Okay, I was wrong about the kaboom part. I didn't really want to get into a dogfight in space. They were probably much better shots than I was.

*   *   *

Back up at my abode, I rapidly finished packing my stuff, what little there was. I took a last look around. This was a very nice place. I was going to miss the shower and tub. Yes, and having a house cleaner and laundry person! Even if she was a big spider.

Furu-la came to check on me. "There may be a spy, but it will not stay out during nighttime, so we will wait until darkness arrives, then the spider creature will help you transport your property to the spaceship."

"Why do they avoid nighttime? Are they afraid of the dark?"

"They fear being attacked surreptitiously by us, thinking we would mass an attack on them. They fear us and we fear them."

"But won't they keep watch on *Star Choice*?"

Furu-la shook her tentacles, "I doubt they want to confront you on the ground in the middle of the night. They don't know you plan to depart; they don't think your vessel is flyable. They prefer to avoid confrontation. Most likely, they will attack you after you are in space and then claim ignorance of what happened to you. So we must find a trajectory that will allow you to evade them and get through the jump site."

Several hours into darkness, with the help of Zzik, I had everything packed back into *Star Choice* and I was ready to depart. There to see me off were Kateh, Furu-la and Noé-te.

Noé-te handed me a small gift, not sure what it was, but it smelled very interesting. I bowed low and thanked her. Then she backed away, still seeming shy.

Kateh apologized profusely for the trouble I had encountered. I apologized to her for the trouble I had caused, then we hugged. I had never before hugged Kateh, she was warm and muscular, surprisingly strong.

Furu-la said, "I have come to appreciate you. You are my favorite Type 1 being. I have enjoyed your company and your conversation." Then she held out two arm tentacles, spreading the fingers on the end. I reached out my hands and clasped her fingers.

"Forgive us if we make too much personal contact," she said.

"Not at all! My people are huggers. I welcome your contact."

Furu-la said, "If you would be willing, may we stay in communication with each other?" She beedle booped a contact code to Wanda. She called Wanda by name. "Take care of our friend, please." Turning back to me, she said "Contact me if you need help. We will stay connected to you as you depart our system."

"I want to give each of you a way to contact me on my world even when I'm not in *Star Choice*." I asked Wanda to beedle boop a separate contact code for each into Junior and also give it to them. And I could contact them the same way—instantaneously, magically, across the cosmos.

Furu-la accompanied me onto *Star Choice*. "Allow me to give you information on how *Star Choice* can safely escape from Sfofong.

"Noé-te and I have built into Wanda the codes to get *Star Choice* all the way to your home world. We coded a route to get to the jump site ahead of pursuit vessels by the Elders.

"We have built in extra power and acceleration to *Star Choice*. You may need it to elude them.

"Would you direct your device to follow my instructions?"

"Yes. Wanda, please follow the directions Furu-la gives you."

"Yes, my controlling oki. I already have them within."

"Time to depart. There is currently a gap between the orbiting watchers above. You can take advantage of that."

Furu-la scooted out the hatch and Wanda sealed it up. I buckled myself in.

Star Choice rose straight up into the nighttime sky, then leveled out and moved horizontally, low and fast, at treetop level. Furu-la appeared in the view space and said she would stay with me. "The place of greatest vulnerability is just after you take off. They will have robot vessels in low orbit. You will first move parallel to the surface. They do not want to fire weapons downward toward the surface." I wondered if we were breaking the sound barrier and waking up all the good Fofonoloy with our sonic boom.

Wanda announced that a message was being sent to us via the emergency channel, which I didn't even know existed. "May I translate it for you, my controlling oki?"

"Sure. Of course."

A staticky voice boomed from the view space, and Wanda translated. "We, the Supreme Council of Elders of Sfofong, order you to return to land. You cannot escape this world. The jump site is shut to you." This was repeated time after time, in Fedi and Sfongi.

Furu-la broke in. "As soon as we detect a gap between the guard vessels orbiting above, I will instruct Wanda to accelerate *Star Choice* vertically out of the atmosphere, but bearing northward perpendicular to their orbits. That is an unexpected direction, so it will take a short time to redirect their weapons."

"Are they going to shoot at me?"

"We do not know. But we must assume they want to stop you."

"Why? Why don't they just let me go?"

"They contend, despite what we told them, that you stole the vessel from the Fofonoloy."

"Oh, lordy, another government calling me a spaceship thief."

"My controlling oki, make sure you are securely fastened."

I saw a crescent of light on the horizon straight ahead. Must be pre-dawn. So we'd been heading east. Then suddenly I was pushed into the right side of my seat. The world tilted on edge and rotated counterclockwise. That meant we were banking into a steep left turn. I felt my innards rebelling. "Please, gut, no vomiting!"

Dawn light was now to the right, so we were heading north. Then the horizon fell away and I was seeing stars.

"We took a fast twist and accelerated quickly past their low level orbiting drones." Furu-la informed me.

"I have given Wanda an unusual trajectory. Once you are above the atmosphere, instead of going directly toward the jump site, you are accelerating perpendicular to it, heading 'north' out of the plane of the ecliptic, then curving over on a powered trajectory that will bring you down onto the jump site at an oblique angle. In this way, they cannot keep up with *Star Choice*.

"Noé-te and I built in extra propulsion, so you have too much power and acceleration for them. And they will not use weapons as you approach the jump site, for fear of damaging it.

"What if they change the jump code?"

"Ah yes, they have already done that, hoping that you fly harmlessly past the jump site so they can pursue you at their leisure. However, we have programmed an alternative jump code into Wanda that will get you through even so. These are some things I learned studying on the main worlds of the Confederation."

"Umm, from those dratted Type 1s!" Probably a poor time for sarcasm.

Of all the flights to jump sites I had taken with *Star Choice*, this was by far the fastest. I was astounded at the profligate use of power. Sfofong disappeared behind us like a balloon deflating. Then its moons zipped past and joined the planet in the rear view mirror.

I watched intently for pursuit. Were Sfofongi warships accelerating off the planet to take me out before I reached the jumpsite? I sat there with my fingers on the trigger of the new weapons, hoping for a chance to blow those suckers out of space. I admit I was disappointed that none ever showed up. Wanda didn't spot any pursuers. Either we were too fast for them or they just didn't bother chasing me.

"Furu-la, what if they pursue us through the jump site?"

"When you use the jumpsite of Sfofong, they will be able to detect where you are jumping to, because they record the destination of all vessels using the site. We have programmed in your first jump. It is not to your home world.

"You'll do a two-stage return jump, so you can't possibly be traced. First, you'll jump back to the system you jumped from to get here, and then after one circle of that world you'll return to that same jump site, and make a final jump to your world. Even if they somehow followed you to this intermediate world with a drone, they would have no idea where you were jumping to next."

Instead of days my previous jumps required, it took hours. When I finally saw the yellow circle indicating the jump site, it grew very rapidly and soon disappeared. We were already through it and on toward the star of my former discontent.

"Wanda, how'd we do? How're you feeling? Any difficulties?" I was hoping for no recurrence of her previous craziness.

"No difficulties, my controlling oki. As I have heard you say, even though I don't understand the saying, it was a piece of cake."

54. Selena-Bane

I now saw in the view space Furu-la, Kateh, and Noé-te, standing together. Kateh spoke first. "You did it, my friend Selena! With the improvements built into *Star Choice*, you outran them. We listened to them squawk in frustration.

Furu-la said, "I want to acknowledge my young assistant Noé-te, who worked out the orbital dynamics for your escape."

"I thank you, Noé-te, for your help and creativity throughout my spaceship repair. I predict you may be the next one from your world to take a daring adventure." I realized immediately I was urging another youngster into a life of crime. She twirled her tentacles in embarrassment.

After my great escape, I was exhausted. When we'd finished talking, I checked with Wanda that everything was still hunky dory, then hit my clean new bed and fell instantly asleep.

* * *

I must have slept quite a while because when I awoke, Kateh contacted me again and announced happily, "When the Elders came this morning and requested our circle, instead of just meekly listening to them, and allowing them to shame us and impose further punishment on us, we sang them down. We sang our True Songs as you taught us. The Goddess of Music was truly with us. The clan mothers stood up for the clan. We sang until they left."

Furu-la came on to the call and said, "They are afraid of you! We told them you are soon returning from your world with reinforcements. And they let up on us."

Now *that* was funny. Seems that people on every world fear invasion by the ruthless alien hordes.

Kateh said, "I want to tell you, my friend, that I am now free to enter my male phase on my own terms. I will go into the deep swamps with our friends and allies and make the transition in the proper way so that I will not lose my memories, I will still remember my beloved Clan Daughter Nala and I will remember you. I will never forget you.

"After I complete my transition, I will once again contact you. I will have a new name, I will be a new being and yet be the same."

A wave of emotion washed over me. I was so happy for her. I realized then that I had completed my mission for Breadbox. I had returned to her home world, connected with her mother and her clan, and helped remove the burden of punishment. And built an ongoing link of friendship and communication between our two very different world races.

I contacted my friends on Earth to let them know that I was finally really for sure on my way back home. I had survived, I was healthy and I had a replenished supply of pseudo Malbec and Jack Daniels. In fact, I poured myself a healthy shot right then and toasted them in the view space.

Furu-la contacted me again and said, "Now that you are through this jump site and the Elders are not pursuing you, you can use a less power-intensive mode of travel. Your vessel will take a gravity slingshot around this world and then go back through the same jump site, for one last jump to your world."

Star Choice had to lose enough velocity to make a gravity loop around this world we were approaching, so it would take us a couple of days to get there, circle it once, and head back the same way. I had plenty of time to watch performers at the Songstone in the view space.

As I tuned in, a group of about a dozen small beings moved forward. Wrapped in dark shapeless robes, they looked like humpbacked Yodas. One stepped to the front of the stage and addressed the nonexistent audience. "Let us never forget the story of our ancestors."

Then, as the group hummed and chanted in the background, the leader spoke in a drone.

> *We moved across the river that year, our clancestors.*
> *We created dwellings amongst the short, stunted trees.*
> *We should have known the soil was unsuited for our crops.*
> *Those first years, two out of every three of us died, starved.*
> *All the glorious names of our ancestors were among those dead, leaving only the weaselly people who were able to survive in the scrabble.*
> *We poor lot are descended from them.*
> *We will never again capture the golden time.*

This went on and on, and as amazing as it was as a spectacle, my attention wandered.

Where did these tales come from? Were they ancient stories passed down by these peoples? Or were they current? And if so, how could such things go on in an advanced civilization like the Galactic Confederation. Or were these reruns of long-ago performances replayed on the Songstone channel? There was too much I didn't know.

After a long, boring glide through darkness, we approached an inhospitable world again.

I decided this world—which I had now visited twice—needed a name. How about Unearth, since I'd jumped to it twice wishing it was

Earth? Maybe Selena-bane, since it had been such a source of grief for me? Yeah, I liked that better.

As we looped around it I'd get a better look. Last time here I wasn't in much of a mood to view the landscape.

As we began circling around the planet on the sunlit side, I could see parts of it I hadn't seen before. Coming into view was a huge expanse of land. I saw mountains with snowcaps, maybe even glaciers, and then a vast expanse of tan, probably desert.

Then some very strange features appeared. Large circular depressions, one after another, starting near the equator, extending in an irregular arc to higher latitudes. Varying sizes and distances between them. They did not look natural. Kind of like huge crop circles, but maybe hundreds of miles across. What could they be? Did this indicate life after all? Civilization even? Or the after-effects of some trans-stellar war?

They were craters! I could tell as we got closer. This world had a whole series of rather large craters across the surface, a whole line of them, as if some entity had fired a cosmic machine gun at it. It looked like any one of these would have been as large as the asteroid that hit Earth and wiped out the dinosaurs. I saw a line of them that extended across the land into the night side. Maybe an asteroid had broken up and pieces hit the planet one after another. Collisions like those could sure change the climate. I was glad that Wanda recorded all; I could not wait to share this with Noel and Amelie.

Soon we were around this world looking at the night side. Absolutely no lights as it blotted out its sun. Then we were headed back in the opposite direction, back toward the jump site that would take us to Earth.

Better check that. "Wanda, I want to confirm that we are headed back to this world's jumpsite, and that the jump code for my home world of Earth that Furu-la loaded in is ready, and that we will jump there in one jump."

"Yes, my controlling oki, that is all true. The code is loaded so that it will operate automatically."

*   *   *

After I had finished sharing images of the craters of Selena-bane with my buds back on Earth, I spent more time watching the Songstone.

I viewed two performances that had very different feels to them. The first was a single being, sitting on a large stone, speaking to the non-existent audience. He/she/it was wrapped in cloaks, so I could tell little about it, but could hear its clear oboe-like voice that Wanda translated.

> *I sat on the ledge outside my living unit, looking down along the market street as the sun set into the smoke that rose from today's attack on the city across the bay.*
> *My beastie, whom I call Iggdiri, sat on my shoulder, snagging with*

247

flicks of her long tongue the whining bugs circling my head.
Our side had won the battle. Our general returned, carrying the head of
the enemy leader. Wild tumult in the street, as our people cheered. With
this competitor gone, our merchants would become much wealthier.
I should be proud and happy, yet I was filled with grief. For on that
other side, among our enemies, I had friends. Their bodies may now lie
in the gutter, life blood drained away.
Our laughter, the living substance of friendship, forever squandered.

How sad. I choked back tears. Was this a real story? Did this really happen? Did battles like this go on in the supposedly civilized Galactic Confederation? Or was it from long ago? Why did this being come to this monument to tell a story like this? I would probably never know.

After a short time, another group appeared. It couldn't have been immediately after the prior one, because there was a real audience in the bleachers! A few dozen beings hunched down on the stone benches near the front. I could see nothing of them but their backsides, from our perspective at the rear of the amphitheater. But up on the stage, four beings emerged, all in identical flashy outfits. Like military parade uniforms. Very different in size and shape, but I'm guessing they were all Type 1 races—two arms, two legs, head on top. And they all wore the same thing. They looked very elegant. They stood in a row.

One took a step forward and spoke loudly: "Which of us is descended from the original people?"

Then they took turns speaking. All spoke clear Fedi so it was easy for Wanda to translate.

The second one spoke: "Strip us down, and we are wildly diverse hunks of meat. But all fitted out in our professional finery—diplomatic capes and ribbons, instrument bandoliers and breathing filters, viewing visors, we look quite similar except for the wide range of sizes." They were indeed wearing all the things he mentioned.

Number three stepped forward: "We four work very well together, and on this treaty we got exactly what we wanted. Those damned Fourclusteri. In dark moments I forget that they are honored oki like us, and wished we could just send in an expeditionary force to erase them from their worlds."

Number four took a turn: "To celebrate completion, we stripped off the tools of our trade, put on evening paint and toured some of the places the locals warned us to stay away from." All four removed their tear-away outfits, throwing them aside, revealing wildly diverse beings with colorful paint and decoration, like the way old Hollywood movies depicted native peoples.

Back to number one: "These dark, spicy cellars each brew their own from fermented black berries and grain. Ach. Headaches and heaves practically guaranteed." From behind them, they produced growler-sized mugs and splashed the contents around.

Number 2 again: "We laughed and swore and told obscene stories. We slapped and pushed each other. I slipped and fell down but they pulled me back up."

And number 3: "After that we had to fight. What better to fight about than which of our world races is truly descended from the mythical first oki race of some fog-enshrouded past. Of course it's preposterous." They held a mock fight with sticks and clubs, whirling in a dance.

Then number 4. "Slathered in grease, standing in mud, with onlookers shouting and grunting, we grab for each other's scales, feathers, tufts of fur, eyestalks, chin fingers, and other appendages, pushing and pulling, all against all." At this, the audience did join in, whistling and growling and stomping.

Finally, all spoke together. "Afterward, more grog. So much better than killing each other! Ah, we'll have tales to tell tomorrow after sobering up.

"After that, it's home to our own worlds, to family and clan, where we can recount our exploits. Or put all this out of our minds."

They moved to the front of the stage and reached out to the audience. Beings there moved toward them. All held out their arms or whatever appendages they had and grabbed hold of one another in a wild friendly embrace.

This was the most astounding performance I had witnessed at the Songstone, and seemed to portray what the Galactic Confederation was supposed to be about. Was this for real? Or a skit put on by the cosmic chamber of commerce to make things look good?

I had to turn away and mull this over. This was so unlike the picture of the Confederation painted by the clan mothers on Sfofong. Perhaps on my next trip . . . No way. No way. Surely I have space adventure flushed from my system. I'm a singer on Earth.

I wandered toward the rear and ended up on my bed. I dozed off.

Wanda awakened me from a deep sleep with a message that sent chills down my spine: "My controlling oki, there are Fofonoloy Elders in the view space."

55. Cosmic Slander

I was sleeping peacefully when Wanda informed me from the view space, "I see Fofonoloy Elders."

That jolted me wide awake. Whoa! What had happened? Did they track us here in a different spaceship? Omigawd, I thought, I'd better get my energy weapon ready.

I hurried from my aft sleeping area to my captain's chair up front, and peered into the viewspace. I expected to see spaceships catching up with us, or even sending a boarding party onto *Star Choice*. Instead, I was gazing down into the center of the Songstone where I saw several many-legged creatures. Ah, so they weren't here on *Star Choice* after all. But what was going on?

"There are four Fofonoloy elders," said Wanda, matter-of-factly. "Plus one juvenile or young female."

"Zoom in closer, Wanda." They were big, perhaps larger than the one I had encountered back on Sfofong. At least in comparison to the youngster, who was about a quarter their size. But they looked old and wrinkled. Solid color, dark purplish red; I didn't see skin patches. The youngster looked like Noe-te, but with different skin patterns. A large one was holding her eyestalk, like a parent holding the arm of a recalcitrant child. Was she their prisoner?

They had some kind of shoes or boots on their foot tentacles. When they stamped on the ground, they made a click clacking noise like mandibles snapping.

They were supposedly singing, but it was more like a war chant than a song, and a dance that looked like an Irish jig on the hard stone. Wanda was able to translate.

> . . . *angry. The outrage.*
> *This invasion of our sovereign world*
> *by an unpleasant, unauthorized, unwanted Type 1.*

The Elders were using their speaking voices, not their singing voices. Two were speaking a hard, raucous version of Sfongi, the Fofonoloy language that I could recognize though not understand. The other two were speaking the Confederation language, Fedi—poorly, from what

One of the Fofonoloy Elders yanked the poor juvie by the eyestalk.

Wanda said. She explained that this was a way to assert superiority over the Type 1 oki, which are Talkis. The Fofonoloy were talking down to them, assuming they could not comprehend the Singi communication.

> *We are here to complain,*
> *we've been invaded, our world,*
> *by an unauthorized, unwanted Type 1*
> *subverting our youth, and even our mothers.*

The one grasping the eyestalk of the younger one gave it a hard yank, almost pulling her off balance. Looked very painful! Her upper tentacles drooped almost to the ground. Why was this one being punished?

> *You incite our young mothers and youth to turn away*
> *from the true way, the safe way.*
> *We must come to the Songstone,*
> *as reluctant as we are to travel to this accursed shrine*
> *of the Confederation*
> *--the haunt of Type 1 oki pride eaters.*
> *We cast aspersion upon you.*

They all made a gesture that made me think of flipping the bird. Now all four chanted in Fedi:

> *Stay out of our affairs, we say.*
> *You have done much damage to us in past lifetimes.*

Why send a Type 1 being from some obscure world
to do your evil work—to preach false messages?
Stay out of our affairs,
and away from our world.

They pushed the smaller one to the fore. Wanda didn't know of which clan. Her color scheme was light green and grey and ochre. It rippled in waves and stripes. I had learned from interacting with Breadbox that these patterns meant fear and strong internal distress.

She was forced to sing, but in a voice so soft and quivery that Wanda could not even translate for me. Then the "Angry 4" started in again.

. . . a criminal conspiracy, a collusion
with malformed young criminals from our world
who had a history of antisocial behavior.

The big one jerked the female's eyestalk downward so hard that she fell over on her side, her tentacles writhing.

Your unwanted unauthorized Type 1 oki
forced itself upon our clan mothers
who were already sanctioned
for failing to prevent these incursions.

Another downward jerk on her eyestalk.

We, the emissaries of the Elders of Sfonoloy,
demand that the Confederation cease and desist
these unwanted incursions.

How could they travel from Sfofong to the Songstone on Everbright so rapidly? Or were they already there? And who was the young one that they tortured for no purpose? I had no idea.

I could watch no more. I had to turn away. "Wanda, please, shut this off."

"I am sorry, my controlling oki. I observe this is emotionally upsetting to you."

"They were singing about me! And it was all a fabrication. What they said wasn't true at all."

I just sat there, stomach churning. I saw clearly what I must do.

56. Angry Star Jump

"Wanda, I must go to Everbright, to the Songstone, and set the record straight. To clear my name. The Songstone performances are a permanent record of all the peoples of the galaxy. We cannot allow this false tale to create the first impression of Earth. They are slandering me personally. I must travel to the Songstone and tell what really happened. Now that I have you and the amulet and *Star Choice*, I can do this, can I not?"

"In principle, yes, but it may not be advisable. *Star Choice* must have a jump code to Everbright. Perhaps this can be obtained from the Librarian. You may need more provisions. You only have enough to return to Earth."

"I've got fruitcake and whisky."

Wanda said nothing.

"Please connect me with the Librarian, O-bloy."

"Yes, my controlling oki."

When the Librarian came on, I said without preliminaries, "I want to accept the offer you made for me to come sing on Everbright, and I would like to sing at the Songstone, as I have seen other worldraces do."

The Librarian showed no surprise. "We are pleased you have accepted our invitation. Let me obtain permission, taking a short amount of time."

The Librarian put me on hold. Some things are truly universal. But, much quicker than making an airline reservation. She didn't even ask for a credit card.

"Permission has been granted, and needed information has been sent to your personal device. You may now make your preparations."

"Wanda, how long will this trip take? Can we make it in one jump?"

"The code the Librarian gave me goes directly to Everbright. Excluding delays, estimate fifty hours each way. That is the amount of time to get from the Everbright jumpsite to the surface of the planet. After the jump, *Star Choice* must approach Everbright slowly and carefully according to a schedule set by their Star Travel Controller. But there may be delays if there are other higher-priority spaceships in the channel, or if Security wants to interrogate you."

"And how about departing?"

"Remember, Furu-la built in greater propulsion. The acceleration is enhanced. We can depart rapidly."

"A supercharged space ship! Like Han Solo and the *Millennium Falcon*. Might come in handy running for our lives."

"Yes."

I was kind of kidding, but Wanda wasn't known for kidding.

"One question, Wanda. Can we get back?"

"This has not been tested from Everbright. Their jump code contained data that should allow us to retrace our route?"

"Should?"

"I will test this as we move toward our jump site at this world's leading gravitational balance point."

Belatedly, I decided I'd better make contact with my team on Earth. Amelie was the only one I could reach immediately.

"What!?! You're doing what? Crikey, that is insane!"

"It is just a quick trip," I tried to reassure her. "Fly in, sing, and fly out. Takes just a few days, Wanda tells me."

"What about when you get there? Imagine some poor guy from a developing nation—who speaks no English and has no money—dropped into New York at JFK and told to find his way to Carnegie Hall on his own. He'd be a lot better off than you'll be."

"They invited me. I believe they will provide for me."

"Haven't you had enough space adventure? I thought you were eager to get home."

"They slandered me."

"So? Somebody dissed you half way across the galaxy?"

"All right, all right. I better sign off now. I'll get back in touch after we go through the star jump."

After that scolding I didn't even want to talk with any of the others.

Selena-bane's star was still the dominant body in the sky, but other than that, it was just the pinprick of stars in all directions. I lost sight of the planet we had just circled. Once again I experienced the utter emptiness of space, but I pushed down the growing ball of fear in my gut.

This was so exciting! I would soon be singing at the Songstone!

I watched the viewspace as we headed toward the jump site. It displayed a yellow circle that grew larger as we approached. But nothing else changed.

"Soon we will pass through, then come out in the other system above their world," Wanda informed me.

"How long now?"

"About three hours at this rate of acceleration."

I had lots of time to think things through. I could pass the time by singing with Gibb. What will I sing when I get there? I'd better practice. Some of the beings I've watched perform just one number, but others drone on and on. Maybe I'll do two or three. But I felt growing nervousness that kept me from focusing on music.

The Librarian requested contact. I watched it in the viewspace. "When you arrive on Everbright, I am quite sure you will have an opportunity to sing at the Songstone. Will you need accommodations and sustenance? Will you need a guide?"

This was just like home on Earth, it seemed. Book a hotel? Get a rental car? Make dinner reservations? Open the Malbec so it can breathe? Will somebody be at the spaceport with my name on a placard? I hadn't thought of these things. On Earth, my agent Morty handles all this stuff for me.

"Yes, I suppose I will. But let me get back to you on that. All I want is a short trip. Go there, sing my music, and depart. I will take my musical instrument with me. That's all."

"I await your contact."

"Wanda, I must ask you some questions, and I did not want to do so while I was communicating with the Librarian."

"Yes, my controlling oki. How may I help you?"

I peppered her with questions. Would I be able to breathe the air? Eat their food? Would I catch any diseases? Will I be welcomed and accepted, or treated like a strange alien? Which I would be, of course. How close will we land to the Songstone? How will we get there? Would I have to wait a long time to get a chance to perform?

How will I communicate? And with whom? How can we translate between English and Fedi? Even if they provide me a guide.

Who will take care of me while I'm there? Will I need to pay for things? How? Will I face hazards, and will I be able to protect myself? Who will translate for me? What do other oki worldraces do when they come to sing and are unfamiliar with Everbright?

Wanda answered patiently. Some were good answers, some more difficult. "When other oki races come, their worlds are members of the Confederation. Most have permanent representation on Everbright. When new oki arrive, they have champions who watch out for them and assist them. These oki already speak Fedi adequately. Or they carry a small translating device, perhaps the size of your comm stone."

"Will you be my champion, Wanda?"

"I am but a device. I may not be able to intercede for you. The beings we encounter may not recognize my . . . " Here Wanda was stumped for a word. That was unusual.

"Personhood?" I suggested.

"Yes, the quality of being an independent sapient entity," she said. "They will view me as a device, not capable nor qualified to act as your champion. I may not be able to guarantee your well-being and safety."

"Could you guarantee your own safety?"

"Not certain. Suppose they forcibly remove me from you."

I tried to strum Gibb, but my fingers weren't responding. My head was lost in space, and not telling them what to play.

"Wanda, have you ever been to Everbright?"

"No, I was created on Sfofong. But I have access to all information about Everbright. I know what to expect to some degree."

"Wanda, are you as eager for this trip as I am?"

"I am here to serve you, and you want to travel to Everbright to perform at the Songstone."

"Would you prefer to be on your home world of Sfofong?"

"My home is with you. The world of my creation has abandoned me, and requested that I de-activate myself."

I was beginning to have second thoughts. Pit in my stomach. What did I think I was doing? "This is crazy, isn't it, Wanda?"

Wanda began a countdown of minutes, then seconds, till the star jump. The image of the jumpsite dominated the viewspace. Arrows pointed at the precise volume of space *Star Choice* must pass through to activate the jump.

"Wanda, I . . ." and then the target was gone. We must have passed through and come out near Everbright. Did we do it? I could detect nothing different. But space is space; it looks the same everywhere.

Suddenly I was utterly panicked. Amelie was right; this was insane. "Wanda, I'm frightened. Terrified. Did we do it?"

"I am sorry, my controlling oki, I aborted the star jump to Everbright."

I had a moment of sheer craziness. I lost it. I screamed at Wanda. "How do I know you are not just saying this?" I yelled. "I am scared shitless! Wanda, can I trust you?"

"My controlling oki," she said in a soothing voice, "I serve you."

"I am frightened. I am lonely. Let's go home."

I recovered my sanity enough to ask her, "Why? Why did you turn aside?"

"I detected extraneous data embedded in the jump code they sent to *Star Choice*. I believe it was inserted not just to allow us to return, but to let them track this vessel upon subsequent jumps. Perhaps even to use our jump site and override our code. This may not be possible, because the amulet and the Confederation use different modes of data. The amulet, created by Singis, uses small pieces of song; the Confederation uses strings of numbers. However, to protect you and the people of your world, I chose caution until I could evaluate. I apologize I did this without asking your permission."

"You did good, Wanda. Thank you." I slumped back in my seat.

"Wanda, that Librarian is just not to be trusted, is it? It was drawing me into a trap."

"The Librarian may not have realized it was a trap. The Security Agency of the Confederation that supplied the jump code saw the chance to draw you to their world, probably to regain control of these technologies, including me, that they believe you should not have. The Librarian was just a conduit of information."

"But still, I'm crazy to tell it anything."

It struck me that we were now heading away from the jumpsite that would take us home to Earth, going at high velocity into orbit around an unknown star with an undesirable planet. Just another idiotic move by the ditzy chick who didn't deserve this magnificent spaceship. Who knew how long it would take *Star Choice* to get on a trajectory to jump to Earth from this site?

*   *   *

"What do we do now, Wanda? How do we get back to the jumpsite so we can get to Earth?"

"My controlling oki, when I cancelled the jump to Everbright, the original jump programmed in by Furu-la was reinstated, and we completed the jump to the system of your home world."

"What? We're home almost? Wha . . . how? Why did it take you so long to tell me?"

"Since this sequence was programmed in by Furu-la, I was not in control of it for a short time. Then I told you."

Oh my oh my oh my. I don't think my poor heart can take much more of this. Thoughts and feelings cascaded through my mind. But hey! We're almost home! I couldn't stay upset.

I'd had so many things go wrong at the last moment, I hardly dared get my hopes up. Better keep my fingers crossed.

A glow of joy began to spread throughout my being. "Let's see Earth in the view space, Wanda!" She zoomed in. It was still a fuzzy dot, but even at this distance, I could see its smaller nearby companion dot—the Moon. No other known earthlike world has a moon that large. This was it. This was really it! We'd done it! At long last, we were going to get home.

"How long before we get there?"

"Fewer than twenty of your hours. We will approach rapidly then decelerate at the end, to minimize the time."

For a singer, I sure created lots of havoc in my own life, always accompanied by waves of anxiety and fear. I sang myself a little ditty:

> *Yes oh yes oh yes*
> *I'm nothing but a songstress*
> *But who put the stress in songstress?*
> *Oh baby don't you see, it was me?*
> *Please don't make another mess*
> *Causing all your friends distress*
> *By taking things far to excess*
> *Oh baby don't you see, that's just me.*

Now I was going to catch hell, I just knew it. And deservedly so.

57. Friends Are Appalled

I called my buds back. Amelie had roused all of them after my scolding from her, and told them of my impulsive trip. Now their images all crowded into the viewspace. I related what had just happened.

"I feel like Frodo," I said, fingering the amulet that allowed me to jump to stars willy-nilly.

"You just tried on the One Ring of Power," Noel said. "Sauron was pulling you in."

Jonn spoke quite sternly to me, as I deserved. "You need to tell us everything. We're putting our reputations on the line for this. We vouched for you with the government."

Noel was softer, but still fatherly. "We have things pulling in different directions. You are a singer, storyteller. You love adventure and taking on dares. And you have this wonderful toy. On the other hand, if we want to share it with the world through this organization we're trying to set up, some rules must be followed. Stuffy, bureaucratic rules. To assure consistency and reliability and accountability. "

"Yes, sir. I hear you."

Amelie had her say also. "Remember the story of Charles Babbage, who tried to build a computing machine back in the 1830s in England? He never got it done. He was such an irascible son of a bitch, he turned off his benefactors. If he hadn't been his own worst enemy, we might have had computing machines a century and a half earlier."

Dana said, "Let's not forget his assistant, Ada Lovelace, who may have been the first STEM babe."

"I guess what I'm saying is," said Amelie, "don't let any looniness bring down this project."

I was repentant. "The crazy woman, the idiot, the ditzy chick, is coming home. Jonn, I've got to turn this over to somebody. I'm too apt to use it. I'm not trustworthy." I realized I had just opted to stay on Earth, even as I discovered I was free to fly anywhere.

Nobody disagreed with what I said.

*   *   *

One more mess to clean up.

I asked Wanda to contact the Librarian, perhaps for the last time. "I must let you know that we turned aside from our planned jump to Everbright to sing at the Songstone. I won't be traveling there at this time. In due course my world may send a proper ambassador. But for now I am not planning to go to any Confederation worlds to sing."

"I am sad to learn this," the Librarian responded. "Your voice would have added a valuable new note to the chorus of all oki beings."

"How poetic!" I thought as I signed off, "from a being that has caused me no end of trouble. I have had my fill of aliens for the nonce."

Just then Wanda notified me that a different alien was requesting to connect with me.

58. Contact Mentor

"Another damned alien?" I was startled and annoyed. "I've had enough for now. What do you want? Can't you leave me alone? Who are you?" I asked this new entity with a total lack of civility.

"Do I alarm you?" From the viewspace came this deep voice that sounded soothing in Fedi, even before Wanda translated.

"Yes, you do."

"Ahmm. May I introduce myself? Mmmh?" he asked diplomatically. I shrugged. "My role is to interact with members of oki races that are unfamiliar with the protocols and procedures of the Galactic Confederation of Oxygen Breathing Worlds. Is my appearance to you warranted in this regard?"

I looked at this strange creature. What the hell should I say? "Oh yes. Yes, it is. I am definitely unfamiliar with your protocols. They just about got me killed."

Wanda said to me, "I am searching for Earth language terms for the function of this entity. Helper, advisor, ombudsman, mentor. Perhaps contact mentor . . . ."

"Let's go with Contact Mentor. Lord knows that's what I need about now."

The Mentor is hard to describe, a cross between a lizard and a starfish, perhaps. Seeing it in the viewspace, it was hard to gauge its size. It had long, tapered tails or tentacles on both ends—extending from its lower end and another extending upward from its head. Truly, the head was just a bulge with a face in the upper tail or tentacle. I know you can't have a tail extending from your head, but I don't know what else to call it. I can think of no animal on Earth arranged like this.

It had four other appendages, either four legs or two legs and two arms, depending on what it was doing. If it wanted to move, it would extend its legs out so that locomotion was easier. Otherwise, two legs retracted, forming with the tail a three-legged sitting arrangement.

The tails on both ends were muscular, like a kangaroo's tail, and always in motion, swishing back and forth.

I'm not sure where it was located when it communicated with me but the background was a swirl of colors. It reminded me of the lightshow backgrounds in some rock concerts. It never stayed still; it was always

The Contact Mentor moved like a restless six-legged starfish.

moving around, like a restless six-legged starfish out of water. But maybe it was swimming in water, like in a large tank; I couldn't tell.

While O-Bloy the Librarian had always seemed female to me, the Mentor came across as male, perhaps because its voice was deep and resonant. No idea whether these notions of mine meant any more than me calling Wanda "she."

"Are you Type 2?" I asked in English, and Wanda translated. A totally inappropriate question for somebody I just met, but I wasn't feeling particularly polite and civil.

"Why yes, I am." Interesting. Same body type as Breadbox and her people, even though it looks very different.

"Are you male?" I persisted.

"No. I am not involved in reproduction. That is left to others of my kind. I am ne."

"Wanda, what does 'ne' mean?" When I spoke directly to Wanda, she didn't translate, she just responded to me. But for all I know, the Mentor understood my English.

Wanda replied, "I created that term for an idea difficult to express in your language—for a being neither male nor female."

"I see. Ne means neither. So, Wanda, are you ne?" The Mentor waited patiently during my side conversation with Wanda.

"Ne refers to a living being not involved in procreation. I'm not a living being. You refer to me as she, even though technically not true."

"Ne is like a worker bee, then."

"Allow me to learn about worker bee." Wanda said to me.

By this time, following all my conversations with the librarian, I was learning to understand and speak some Fedi. I was amazed when this

Mentor being used some English words with me. So, apparently, just from overhearing Wanda translate for me, the Confederation was building up an English lexicon. No reason why this should surprise me, but it seemed very spooky. Both Breadbox and Wanda had mastered English. But I'd have to be careful about these asides with Wanda.

"My apologies for this distraction," I said to the Mentor. "May I ask why you contacted me?"

"No apology needed. I was alerted when a jump code was requested and granted to an anomalous entity. We detected that a jump code had been allocated to an unregistered vessel of unknown type and location."

"What do you mean, 'we detected?' You issued the code."

"Yes, I see your perspective. You view us as a single entity, whereas to me the Confederation is a vast web of entities often pulling in different directions."

"Ahhm," it/he/ne went on. "I am fascinated by your appearance. I do not perceive you as threatening."

"I sure hope not," I replied, finally allowing a smile. "I don't see myself as threatening, either."

"Some on my worlds view you as an aggressive unfriendly alien."

"So I overhead at the Songstone." Amazing to me that the vast advanced galactic civilization could view me as a hostile alien invader.

"May I take a moment in actual time to familiarize myself with your situation?"

"By all means." I watched it peruse something out of my view. What is 'actual time,' I wondered?

"I am currently accessing information we have on your previous interactions with the Library and the Librarian."

It paused. Perhaps reading my dossier.

"Ahhm. With the Device Captain. Some differing perspectives."

"Yes, the Captain and I had a basic disagreement."

Another pause. "Ahhm, with the oki trio from Sfofong."

"Yes, that's how all this started."

"Ahhm, you have obtained a Personal Device of the type normally reserved for qualified members of an oki community . . . And a vessel from an unauthorized visitor to your world."

I remained silent. He clearly knew everything about me.

"Ahhm, it is not known how this Fofonoloy crew traveled to your world, which lies far outside the boundaries of the Confederation, and its star jump network."

I nodded but said nothing.

"Ahhm, they perished. Accidental, not hostile."

"Yes," I said softly. This brought a lump to my throat.

"Ahhm, you are Type 1 oki interacting closely with Type 2s."

"She became my best friend," I said with renewed energy. "We sang together. Then, due to circumstances beyond my control, I traveled to her home world, Sfofong."

"Yes." Long pause. "Ahhm. You have trained the device you possess to translate, as it is currently doing. And an excellent job. It has built a lexicon of your language that oki on our worlds can use to communicate with you."

Another pause.

"Ahhm. The device is guiding the vessel per your commands. You are attempting to jump to our leading world."

"Yes, an unwise move, I now see."

"May I ask, how large is your crew?"

"Just me. And my sidekick, the device."

"This is most unusual. Perhaps unprecedented."

Another silence.

"May I offer a suggestion?"

"Why not? Yes, please do."

"You should not complete this trip. It is quite dangerous. The jump code may have contained a trap set by those who don't have your best interests at heart. They may wish to eliminate a perceived threat. When you return to your home world, you might discover that an instrument had been placed inside your vessel that would allow a Confed vessel to retrace your jump path, and gain access to your world."

"Me a perceived threat?"

"The role of the keepers of the star jump network is security. They seek to prevent incursions by harmful entities, whether actively hostile or merely by nature dangerous. You seek to jump directly to our main world.

"They also wish to maintain their monopoly on the system. You apparently have penetrated a previously unknown parallel system. Thus they view you as a threat to their hold on power."

"Why are you telling me all this?"

"I am an advocate for less-powerful oki peoples. That is my role. Also, I find your quest to be exciting and titillating. Your stated purpose is to sing at the Songstone. I find this desire of yours praiseworthy. This is a worthy quest for an oki race. And one from outside the Confederation.

"Perhaps if I learn more I may assist you in your quest, and reduce the level of danger for you."

"I thank you for your kind words," I said. "I want to tell you, we have already turned aside from our trip to Everbright. We didn't make the star jump. We are now in our own star system."

"Ah, that relieves me."

"Suppose I had continued," I asked. "Could you have helped me? Could you have been my champion?"

"I could have arranged a champion for you. And given other assistance."

"Well, phooey. Too late now. But perhaps next trip."

I watched him do his dance. He did look like he was under water.

"Why did I take this sudden, unplanned trip, you might ask," I said.

"Yes, I am curious, if you are willing to divulge that."

"I have been observing the Songstone. I happened to hear Fofonoloy elders singing there complaining about interference from a Type 1 oki. I was amazed to figure out that they were singing about me. They were very unhappy about my contacts with oki from their world. But I have a question about this. Why sing it at the Songstone instead of going to an official body and lodging a complaint?"

"An excellent question. Singing at the Songstone allows them to . . . ." Here Wanda needed to ask me how to express "people reducing emotional energy from a negative situation."

"Letting off steam?" I suggested.

"May I learn more about that expression?" asked the Mentor.

"Yes you may. Picture if you can an old steam engine—a machine that runs on hot, compressed water vapor—with a dangerous buildup of pressure. It needs to let off steam to reduce the chance for an explosion. You probably don't even have steam engines on your world."

He swished his tail. "I can clearly envision a device that contains hot pressurized gas, and must release some to stay within operating tolerances." Perhaps he was doing the dance of the steam engine. "An instructive play on words."

He went on. "Singing angry songs at the Songstone reduces pressure--lets off steam. They don't want to take official action. But they must do something to satisfy powers back home."

"Mr. Mentor, I'm sorry, I must ask a rude question. Why should I trust you?"

"A fair question. Trust can only be built over time. Why should I trust you?"

I smiled and nodded ruefully. "The Librarian caused us trouble by revealing information I thought was secret. Should I no longer access the Library?"

"The Library is a repository of information. It is safe for you to access it. The Librarian's role is to communicate. It often fails to evaluate the impact of sharing communications. So obtaining information is safe, giving information risky."

"On my world there's a saying, 'If you have a hammer, everything looks like a nail.' I guess when you are a communicator, everything looks like a message to share." The image that sprang to mind was the neighborhood gossip, who loved to pass along any tidbits of information.

"An apt parallel. Worthy of an oki poet."

"That's what I am, sir. Poet, singer, storyteller."

"Ahmm. An honored calling."

"Speaking of which, I would love to come to the Confederation to sing my music. Not necessarily at the Songstone.

I decided that trustworthy or not, I had to tell him more. I needed answers.

I told him how the Librarian had urged me to travel to Confederation worlds to sing. I related Kateh's belief that I was a "true singer" and that my voice was needed to help correct negative situations in the Confederation. I commented to him, "If a singer from a distant world is needed to save the Confederation, it must be pretty wobbly."

He waved both tails in intricate patterns while standing on two of his legs. "Oki crave novelty. Our world races continually seek out new forms. Your singing has already been disseminated in some channels, perhaps propagated by the Librarian, with whom you must have shared it. You have aroused interest among certain Confederation Oki."

"Is that right? People there have heard and shared my music?" I could just see Morty standing up and asking about my music royalties. Where did they acquire my music? Ah, from the Librarian, of course. But that was just informal strumming of Gibb. Not my best material.

"Yes, it is true. There is interest in your music. However, allow me to state the other side. The Confederation has little interest in establishing physical contact with you or your people. Perhaps it should have such interest, but the leaders here would view this contact as an administrative headache. Or as a threat, as we have seen.

"We prefer to limit contact to the type you and I have currently. But perhaps to a broader audience. Many would like to partake of a performance by you, to hear more of your music. But remote is acceptable—even preferable.

"Better you not come. Remain a magical, mystical beast from afar who sends beautiful strange music from impossible distances. If you come in body, you're just an ordinary yet strange being, one who does not belong to the Confederation.

"Consider this. Even if you traveled to the Confederation to perform your music, most would partake of it remotely.

"If we could contrive a way for your music to be performed there on your world and appreciated here, that would be most excellent."

"I must check the capabilities of my device," I said. "Then could we talk again?"

"Yes. Most welcome."

Seemed like every time I turned around there was a new twist. My Earthborn crew insisted I stay local, and my new galactic adviser said the same. You'd think that would make me feel happy.

59. Concert From Space?

I asked Wanda if the viewspace on *Star Choice* was capable of sending a concert to the Confederation. "In principle, yes. Need more power to do it while orbiting above your world. Better to create a more powerful viewspace than the one on *Star Choice*. Easier and faster to do this if we are on your world with a source of materials nearby. Also, need specifications from the Library."

"So I need to return to Earth to do a concert for the stars. And we need to work with the Library, that has caused us so much trouble?"

Well, phooey. That idea was on hold until I could return safely to Earth.

I was surprised when Wanda told me she could find no suitable designs or specs in the Library for what I wanted to do. The plans it had were either for a very small set-up or very large. We already had small—the viewspace. Large was more like concert hall to concert hall—way too elaborate. And nothing about combining the technologies of two different worlds.

"What can we do?" I asked her. "Will we have to invent our own? Could you and Jonn—and maybe Roger—invent what we need?"

"If your inventor friends give Wanda detailed instructions, I can create. I can share with them information on the plans contained within the Library. It may take substantial time."

My next contact was to Jonn. "My apologies for yelling at you earlier," he said right off the bat.

"You didn't yell. And besides, I deserved it."

"I can't stay angry at you," he said. "You represent a side of me that I keep tightly bottled up."

"What side is that?"

"The wild inventor-adventurer, who takes big hairy risks and thumbs his nose at the powers that be."

"I guess that sounds like me all right. Well, I need an inventor and it might lead to some adventure."

"Say more," he said, instantly getting sucked in.

"I have been in contact with a new alien—a representative of the Galactic Confederation. He *discouraged* me from traveling there to perform, but *encouraged* me to do a concert on Earth and beam it, broadcast it, jump it—whatever the right term is—to their worlds.

"If feasible, that does sound exciting. And safer."

"But we must create the equipment needed to do that. Wanda suggested that she could help you invent it."

"What exactly do you need to invent?" Jonn asked.

"We need a concert quality viewspace."

He gave his trademark chortle. "Sometimes I come across like I know everything," he said, "but I must confess, this lies far outside my area of expertise—and our manufacturing capability."

"Yes, hmmm. And Wanda is with me. I wonder if I could connect you and this Mentor I'm talking with. Your first alien contact. But how could you communicate directly with him—it.

"We're limited, since Wanda is the tool of creating all these wonderful contraptions, and she's with you.

"Wanda, could you connect Jonn directly to the Mentor via his view bubble?"

"In principle, yes. It would be easier if we used the viewspace on *Star Choice* as an intermediary."

So, we were about to set up our first cross-cosmos phone network—complete with 3D video.

"Not so fast!" Jonn yelled. "I've never spoken with an alien. Well, except Wanda. What would that experience be like? What language? What protocols and niceties? How do I avoid making a fool of myself?"

"This alien is accustomed to dealing with rude primitives like us. You should have heard me when I first talked to it. Wanda will translate. Besides, it offered to help."

"And here I thought life was going to return to normal. How little I know."

*   *   *

I asked Wanda to reconnect me with the Mentor. I explained the situation on our end.

"Will you help us?" I asked. "We want to hold a music event from our world to your world, as you suggested. Would you be willing to assist us?"

"Yes, I am willing. Ahhhm, I perceive several ways I might assist you:

"I can advise you on constructing the devices you will need in order to create a music event that could be experienced on Confed worlds.

"Ahhmm, I could provide your engineers with data they need to build an interface between your devices and ours.

"Errhhm, I could act as your representative to announce this event on our worlds. Identify entities to handle the technical and logistical elements of the event on our worlds."

I asked him, "How should we compensate you for your help? Is it the practice of your people to receive payment for such activities?"

267

"Yes it is," he/it replied. "However, such compensation would flow to you from people on the Confederation. My compensation will be the joy of participating with you in this event—this connection between our worlds. This has never before happened in my lifetime.

"Since there is currently no obvious way for our world to transfer payment to yours, you will have a positive balance in our system."

"We gain immeasurably from this interaction as well," I said. "From the information we have obtained from the Library. And the technology from the alien visitors."

He replied, "Information in the Library is for all to use. The space vessel and personal device in your possession belonged to a different world, and they ceded these items to you, as I understand.

"Information and data are freely exchanged. Original created expressions are most valued and are highly compensated. It would be most improper for people here to experience your performances without compensating you."

Morty would be so glad to hear that. His first questions will be, "What's the royalty rate? How do they transfer funds to your account? What is the exchange rate for cosmic smackeroos?"

60. Star Choice Foundation

The good news continued to roll in as I cruised toward Earth, and *Star Choice* prepared to enter the final orbit. Noel and Jonn contacted me.

"We have obtained approval for the *Star Choice* Foundation!" Noel announced. "This includes guarantees for your safety and for the protection of *Star Choice*. No one will try to take it. And I'm guessing, from what I've seen, that they couldn't do so as long as you retain control."

Jonn said, "*Star Choice's* new home will be NASA Ames Research Center, housed in the huge hangar on Moffett Air Field in Mountain View south of San Francisco. Google will be the landlord."

I was instantly on Cloud 9, assuming that Cloud 9 can orbit high above Earth. "So I can land! I can return home! I am so ready.

"So, I hear that Amelie will be in charge of the foundation. What will my role be?"

"What would you like it to be?" Noel asked.

"I want to be the troubadour."

"That's perfect for you. You sing the message and get it out to everybody."

We moved slowly toward Earth, getting close enough so that I could pick out continents. It was afternoon in central Asia. By the time I cruised across the Pacific, like a victory lap, it would be morning in California. I was nearing my last orbit when Wanda announced that the Mentor wished to talk with me. Maybe it had found a way for me to do a concert from space after all.

But the polite, friendly Mentor had a different message. "As I feared, clever Oki in the Confederation have deduced how to get to your world."

61. The Aliens Are Coming

"What?!?" I shrieked.

"As I feared, clever Oki in the Confederation have deduced how to get to your world that you call Earth," said the Mentor with all limbs and tails thrashing about. "Not that they can do this currently, but their thought process could lead to the discovery of the specific information needed to travel there. Would you like to hear the chain of their deductions?"

This gave me a jolt like an electric shock. "What are you saying? I've been told by many beings that this was impossible. Now you're telling me the opposite?" This was like your doctor telling you that you have a terminal disease after he's told you for years you're in perfect health. "Yes, please tell me how they figured this out."

"Not figured out yet, but a path by which they could possibly figure it out. There are several steps." He looked around, as if seeking his notes.

"Ah-um. Young beings from a non-exploring race figured out how to make a trip between stars that the Confederation was unable to do.

"These beings did not travel via sub light speed, so they must have used star jumps.

"They jumped from their world to a previously unknown jump site far outside the Confederation.

"To do this, they must have discovered an existing code, since it would take many lifetimes to send a sub light speed probe to that world to install a new jump site. Do you follow me so far?"

"Yes, yes, I'm afraid so," I muttered.

"Jump sites do not exist in isolation. There must have been a prior network of jump codes, unknown to the Confederation.

"They must have found a record of a code network—either a physical artifact or within the deep library."

I nodded my head, not in agreement, but in resignation.

He went on. "Very old records in the Library are hard to index; searchers found no evidence of recent access of such ancient data. Therefore, they must have found a physical artifact.

"Perhaps they found an artifact by accident, since it is unclear what search strategy they might have used. Such search strategies only become apparent after the fact.

"If there was one artifact that was findable, then there must be others.

"They must have visited many worlds before yours because it is very unlikely that they would quickly discover a world such as yours."

He paused and took a long look at me. "An exception to this would be if travelers from your world managed to travel to one of our worlds, in particular to Sfofong. Or if a signal from your world reached there.

"Ahhhm. That is my thinking about this matter." He was silent, and all his limbs were still.

I was shocked by their ability to quickly work this out. I could find no fault with his chain of reasoning. "How long might it take them to make the needed discoveries?'

"Without knowing the form of the physical artifact that allowed them to travel to your world, our searchers are unclear what to look for," he said. "Suppose they discover an artifact that contains jump codes that lie outside the Confederation. They will have no idea which code might allow them to travel to your world. You, or the personal device you have, may contain that information, but you are unlikely to share that information with us, wisely so." He looked at me searchingly, as if to confirm this.

"However, if they find another artifact that contains the jump codes to your world—and many other worlds besides—they will eventually discover which codes lead to yours. No need to send vessels with live crews; they could send many small crewless vessels simultaneously, seeking only to pick up signals similar to those we have received."

"There are millions of planets," I countered.

"Billions," he said. "But this is only a tactical matter of numbers and duration."

He paused while this sank in to my noggin. "Thus I recommend that you and those who work with you communicate with your people to prepare them for an eventual visit."

I shook my head. "But you said they didn't even want to have face-to-face contact with us. And that they aren't supposed to contact primitive races like us."

"Arrruhm," he said, swishing both tails. "Your ability to use the star jump technology is a prime criterion for being ready for contact. Your world is no longer protected by the rule against contact. Few Confederation citizens would have interest in traveling to your world. But it would take only one well-financed party to do so."

"If they came, what would they do? What would they want?" I asked.

"To learn. To trade. To experience your world. Not hostile. Yet even friendly contact can be disruptive to worlds not accustomed to beings from across the galaxy."

"Thank you for informing me. I need some time to absorb this." We closed the connection.

This scared the bejeebers out of me. I felt this huge pit in my stomach. Everything I had been assured by the Librarian, and by the clan mothers on Sfofong, and even by Breadbox, was revealed to be false. And for a couple of years I had been assuring others that the aliens could never come. Based on my assurances, Jonn had told the generals and the senators that there was no threat from the aliens. This was all on me. I had a cold sweat of fear and embarrassment. I was going to have to tell everybody. I would look like a fool, and they would for sure take *Star Choice* and Wanda from me. And, I had threatened the world through my actions.

So much for my victory lap. I was, once again, the ditzy chick who was bringing aliens to Earth.

What was I going to do? I couldn't run away. I couldn't just crash *Star Choice* into the ocean. That would take care of me, but wouldn't help anybody else. Who should I tell? Better get it over with.

I summoned Jonn and Noel with my comm stone, but only Noel was reachable. I laid out the whole story to him, along with plenty of crying and blubbering.

Noel was silent for a long time, occasionally going "hmmm, umhmm." Then he kind of giggled. "Oh Selena," he said with a sigh, "you sure know how to show a guy a good time. For an astronomer, cosmologist, and exo-life-ologist like me, this is pure candy."

He recovered his seriousness and said, "Let me point out the obvious. We've already been contacted by aliens from across the cosmos. And the world already knows. It will not be a surprise."

"That was just one poor helpless being—Breadbox. Now we're talking about an armada."

"So we need to prepare. That makes our new foundation all the more important."

Just then Jonn came on and I had to explain the whole mess to him. I could hear his hmmm of thinking even before I finished.

"How long before they arrive?" he asked in his assertive, problem-solving voice.

"No way of knowing," I replied. "This is a hypothetical. Could be next month; could be several lifetimes; could be never."

"How could we stop them?" he asked.

I asked Wanda. She said, "Without a jump site they can never come here. We could destroy the jumpsite near your world."

"How could we destroy the jump site?" Jonn asked.

"I don't know." I asked Wanda, who said, "*Star Choice* could travel toward it and use the new energy weapons to disable or destroy it, then return."

Silence. None of us said anything. Then Jonn said, "Not attractive. Forever cut off."

"Maybe that's for the best," replied Noel.

"No. Now that we know they are out there, our descendants would never forgive us if we forever prevented them from making contact."

"We'd still be able to communicate with them," I said. "Wouldn't we, Wanda?"

"Communication via the viewspace does not require a jumpsite," Wanda responded.

"Hmmm," all three of us said. I was amazed that neither of them sounded eager to take the step that would clearly prevent an alien invasion.

"You have allies there. Your so-called Mentor. Would he alert us if or when they figure out how to get here?" Jonn asked.

"I will ask him—it. My guess is he'll say he will if he knows about it."

"Okay. We must prepare," Jonn said with the voice of authority. "So that when they do arrive we are ready. In the meantime, I'm in no hurry to broadcast this development to the world. For one thing, we want to get our space-faring Selena safely back on the ground."

"Truly, there's nothing to say just now," said Noel. "Our preparation will become part of the mission of the *Star Choice* Foundation, wouldn't you agree?"

I nodded in agreement to these guys who couldn't see me. "So, Jonn and Noel, you don't blame me? You don't hate me? You're not going to write me out of your wills?"

"Heh heh heh," Jonn chuckled. "I said it once, Selena, I'll say it again. Working with you on this whole thing is the most fun I've ever had. I look forward to this adventure."

"One day we'll look back and see this as the beginning of an amazing transition for humankind," said Noel. "Our descendants will wonder about our roles—how we got involved and made it all happen."

"Unless, of course," I said, regaining a bit of my humor, "the aliens invade and wipe us out or enslave us. Our descendants might not think so highly of us then."

"Now now," Jonn said, "We always have in our back pocket the ability to take out the jump site."

"I'd better check with my Mentor and see if that is really true," I commented. I absent-mindedly fingered the amulet on its chain around my neck. It struck me that this invasion could work both ways. With the star jumps coded within this crystal, we had—in principle—a back door to jump into the worlds of the Confederation. Oh my, I'd better banish that thought.

62. Revenge

Earth was growing larger. I could make out the continents and oceans. The Moon was almost eclipsed by the Earth; that's why it had looked so close earlier.

As *Star Choice* settled down toward it, Earth went from being a beautiful bright ball in space to a vast world I was circling. I could see southeastern Asia as we sank toward the mist of the upper atmosphere.

"Better cut your victory lap short," Jonn interrupted my reverie. "The Chinese are once again lofting vessels into space that can fire missiles and lasers.

He was clearly angry. "Somebody in our government leaked the information that you are alive and returning to Earth. I arranged your landing at Moffett but said to keep it under wraps until you were safely back, just to prevent something like this from happening."

My heart sank. Terror rose in my throat. I felt frozen and immobilized. These were the same predators that had pursued me previously, damaged *Star Choice*, and caused Wanda to go crazy. Surely they wouldn't let me escape again.

I stared into the view space in silence. Jonn said, "What's the matter? Can you hear me?"

"Jonn, I . . . I'm almost home. I don't want to have to run from these bullies again. Please."

"Here's what Rogers tells me from covert sources. The Chinese are willing to risk war to prevent us or anybody else getting these alien technologies. We have warned them, saying this would be considered an act of war on the United States. So, if you are attacked, can you defend yourself?"

"I don't know," I squeaked in a tiny voice.

I heard his hum of thinking. "Look, you told me you now have offensive weapons. This would be the time to use them."

"I don't know whether they work. I've never tried them. I don't know if I can operate them."

"Okay, let me walk you through this. Wanda, can you help Selena with the weapons?"

"Yes, Jonn Buck. I will ready the weapons for Selena."

Dread in my gut. My hands were shaking. How could I ever aim a weapon? Take a deep breath. This was not the kind of greeting I wanted. But it is what I feared and expected. I was sure glad that Furu-la talked me into getting these weapons.

"Wanda," I said, taking a long slow breath, "these rockets that are targeting us have no living beings, so you needn't be worried about that. I need you to tell me when any missile is targeting us, so that our weapon system can target it and fire. Can you do that?"

"Yes, my controlling oki."

"Jonn, how will I know that something we spot in space is one of theirs, not somebody else's? Like a weather satellite."

"We track all satellites from ground radar and we'll inform Wanda. Also, if you see one taking a trajectory toward you, take it out."

"I spot one now," Wanda said calmly. "I recognize it from our prior encounters. We are overtaking it. It's in a lower orbit. Now there's another one above us, moving quite rapidly on a trajectory toward us. It was launched from a larger slower vessel that moved vertically through the atmosphere into space. The larger vessel is launching others. As before, they are trying to attack us from two directions."

"Weapons system, activate, please," I said in a pleading voice. I grabbed my joysticks, but the system had already spotted these missiles and was tracking them. Each image in the view space had a small yellow circle around it. Omigawd, there must be close to a dozen of them!

I sat there frozen, unable to act. "Tell it to fire!" yelled Jonn.

"Okay, okay, here goes. Weapon system, fire when ready." I saw nothing, but the images in the view space disappeared in rapid succession. No weapon flash. No cloud, no debris, nothing.

"Targets destroyed," said the system.

"My controlling oki, the platform is readying more missiles," Wanda announced softly.

Oh shit, how many can we take out? I wondered.

"System, target the platform indicated by Wanda." Yellow circle. "Fire." We may have been over five hundred miles from this platform, but I saw a flash of light there as something detonated.

"My controlling oki, the one we are overtaking is aiming its energy beam at us. We will soon be within its range."

Oh my, they just kept coming. Could I ever get them all? "Weapon system, target and fire, please," I pleaded. A yellow circle appeared around its image and it immediately disappeared.

I had been squinching up my face. "Any others?" I asked timidly.

"Not at this time," Wanda affirmed.

I couldn't move. I just sat there shaking, still hanging on to the joysticks.

Within a few seconds, Jonn asked, "Are you all right?"

My teeth were chattering, but I said, "y-ye-yes."

"Your weapons worked well, didn't they?"

"Yes, I hardly did anything. Thank goodness I didn't need to, because I would have screwed it up."

"You did good, and we spot no other threats. Your system performed admirably. I tell you, Star Lady, I was right there with you. I am so pleased you prevailed."

My jitters were soon replaced by jubilation. I felt like I had the fastest six-gun in the Old West. I was so happy we'd gotten back at these bullies. I'd just have to add my own kaboom kaboom kaboom! Revenge is sweet.

Jonn chuckled. "You know, you've probably just disrupted all military thinking on Earth."

"Exactly what we wanted to avoid."

"Yes. So be it. Well, everything is set for you on the ground. You will land at Moffett Air Field south of San Francisco. I'll use my comm stone as a homing beacon and you should land on the big white X. Let me communicate the coordinates to Wanda."

Star Choice was in a controlled descent so it seemed like we were gliding around the Earth. Crossing the vastness of the Pacific Ocean.

"This just in," said Jonn. "Here's Rogers."

"The President called in the Chinese ambassador, and then called Beijing. The message was, any further aggressive actions will be taken as an act of war and we will retaliate with appropriate force. Their response? They asserted that you were invading their airspace. Clearly not true, since you were five hundred miles above Earth. And you weren't even above China."

"I know. It seemed like we were above Vietnam or Thailand."

"The problem this will create?" Jonn said. "Space junk. Fragments of these destroyed missiles.'

"May not be as serious as you think," Rogers said. "The first salvo was on ascending trajectories, but less than escape velocity. Those fragments will not go into orbit, but arc up then rain back down on the atmosphere. The platform was not above the drag of the upper atmosphere, so its pieces will quickly lose momentum and fall. The fourth missile was hit from above and behind, so the impact force will tend to push it into lower orbit, decaying till it hits the upper atmosphere. Most likely all will burn up. We'll have to see if any pieces are large enough to make it through the atmosphere and hit the surface. They're mostly above low latitudes, so they would likely hit an ocean."

After I recovered, I confess I thought it was a bit of an anticlimax. It was all over so rapidly. Nothing like Star Wars space battles. I didn't even get a chance to use my joysticks or targeting buttons. Everything was too automatic. On the other hand, maybe that's why I was still alive. And I still had the joy of revenge.

I turned my attention back to the view space. I saw the beauty of my home world as I approached, just as did the astronauts of years past. It was like a religious experience for me. I felt a wave of oneness with all that I viewed. I was a part of it; I belonged. I saw very clearly that I must protect my home world as best I can. I cannot be selfish and controlling.

But before succumbing to total enlightenment, there was one nagging question I had to ask. "Wanda, suppose those missiles had been manned, with human pilots. Could you have gone after them."

"My controlling oki, I protect you. If you are threatened or attacked, I will defend you."

63. Free in the Sea

As I was making my final approach to Earth, gliding down through the atmosphere high above Hawaii, I tried to contact Kateh to tell her I made it home, and to show her what my world looks like. But I couldn't reach her. Nobody home, nobody answered, no message. After a couple of attempts, I tried to contact Furu-la instead. Again, no response. What had happened? My imagination immediately went to the Elders. Had my friends been arrested? Then I got a call back. Not from Furu-la, but from Noé-te.

"Hello our Type 1 friend," she greeted me shyly in the view space with Wanda translating. "I detect that you tried to contact Furu-la. I must inform you of her status. Former clan mother Kateh has gone to her male phase. She swam to the sea for the transition, and it was successful. The new name is Kartem-haw. And now Furu-la has joined him in the sea. They have left their midriff bands behind. And they are procreating. Furu-la will soon be a clan mother, but actually a real mother, not assigned a child. And Kartem-haw a proper clan father. Clan Haw will be strengthened.

"For this reason," Noé-te continued, "they are not reachable. They are currently beyond the reach of any but swimmers of the sea."

"What wonderful news, my friend." Tears of happiness streamed down my face. "They both got exactly what they wanted and deserved. I am so happy for them."

"Furu-la has turned over her duties to me, as her assistant. If you wish, you may contact me."

"Please give them my congratulations when you see them, and tell them I made it home safely."

What should I send as a baby shower gift? A song, obviously.

64. Indistinct Grumbling

[Transcript of discussion between Major General Stanley and General Mason Dickson.]

- Sir, I fully support the formation of this foundation to manage these ET technologies. But it grieves me that this woman, this damn singer, who has rubbed our face in it repeatedly, is associated with it. I will feel humiliated having to present her with this certificate of authorization.

- General Dickson, you need to make nice with this woman. Put on your political hat. Treat her like you did that Russian military attaché.

[indistinct grumbling]

- General, I understand how you feel about this. But this comes from the top. The very top. Capiche?

- Loud and clear, sir.

[sound of papers shuffling and briefcases snapping shut]

- You know, Dicky, we should thank our lucky stars that we are getting this matter out of our hair—if we had any hair. Be glad that it's Buck and Reisen who will be in the line of fire, which will be coming at them from all directions. In the military, as you know, we say never take on any mission unless you can clearly see how to successfully complete it. Nobody can possibly see the end of this mission. We may well be called in to clean up their messes.

- Yes, sir, I do agree with that.

[long pause]

- Did you ever listen to any of her music?

- Oh lord, sir, my daughter plays that consarned racket constantly. Even my wife sings along. You do something idiotic or notorious, you sell a million songs. These are the folks we're sworn to protect.

- Perhaps she'll write a song about you.

- She already has.

[off-key humming of "My Spaceship Calls Out to Me"]

65. Back to Sweet Earth At Last

"Selena M, at the end, gave up her dream of flying off to other worlds." I caught this news commentary as *Star Choice* descended toward Earth. "She instead is returning home with a promise to turn over the alien craft and get a fat movie contract for her story. The heroine is being been brought down to Earth. Will she once again be content with the conventional life?"

"Fat movie contract? Hah! Nobody has mentioned that to me." Well, it wasn't such a bad idea. But why wasn't I hearing this from Morty? Who would play me? How would they do Breadbox and the other aliens?

"And what has ever been conventional about my life?" I yelled at the view space.

Apparently they didn't yet know that I had indeed flown off to other worlds.

Unlike my last landing on Earth, *Star Choice* glided in slowly, openly, majestically, triumphantly even, for its landing at Moffett. As I approached, I could see throngs of people and huge traffic jams. Bigger crowds than for a 49ers game. I was glad I was able to fly in and miss the traffic.

Star Choice sat down on the big white X as Jonn had arranged. The side hatch opened wide, and warm, sweet-smelling air rushed in, flushing out all the stinky air I had been living in and breathing. I jumped down, fell to my knees and kissed the sweet Earth—right between the crack in the asphalt, the oil spot, and the ant highway. I was glad to be home!

Velvet ropes and brass stanchions—just like at the Oscars—tried to hold the crowd back. But as soon as I stepped out of the hatch, my buds broke through the lines and sprinted toward me. Amelie and Jonn just about tied, followed by Noel, then pregnant Dana walking with Meg. And there was Clay, in a wheelchair pushed by Doc, with Jim walking beside in full lawman uniform.

It was one big group hug. I almost fell over Clay. I leaned down and gave him a huge kiss. "I am so glad to see you all, my friends. Sight for sore eyes, as they say."

My phone chirped. It was a text from Eddy. "They won't let me in. Please?" I looked around. "Who can call security and ask them to let Eddy Backwater in?" Jonn raised his hand and whipped out his phone. Then gave me a thumbs up.

I kissed the ground—right between the crack in the asphalt, the
oil spot, and the ant highway.

When we got back to the velvet rope, Jonn said, "Selena, I want to
introduce you to General Mason Dickson." He was standing next to the
head of Google, our new landlord.

"Ms. Morisot, I am pleased to make your acquaintance. I know we've
been at loggerheads, but it's time to put that behind us."

I reached out to shake his hand and said, "Thank you sir. I guess we've
been worthy adversaries."

"The army with the best technology usually wins. That's certainly the
case here. And that's what this is all about. Ma'am, I want to present you
with this charter for the Star Choice Foundation, signed by the President
and the Secretary General of the United Nations."

He handed me a large envelope that contained a gold-embossed
certificate and several very official signatures. I thanked him profusely.

I looked more closely at him. The general was a formidable looking
soldier. But you know, like so many other highfalutin men that I've met,
he was much shorter than I expected.

Just then Eddy was driven up by security in a golf cart. I hardly
recognized him. New jeans and denim jacket, brand new white tee-shirt,
and sassy alligator skin boots. That meant I was the skuzziest one there. I
desperately needed a haircut and color.

I looked around. "Who's not here?" I asked. "Oh yeah, *Hu's* not here.
Maybe they didn't let him in."

*   *   *

"Speech, speech!" went the cry through the crowd. I smiled and waved to
the crowd and TV cameras, grabbed a wireless mic and said, "I am so glad

to be safely back on Earth. I have a lot to tell you all, and I will do so very soon, but I can't right now."

General Dickson and Noel made their statements, but I hardly listened. I was fading. Noel turned to me and said, "I want you to know they have signed off on our plan to keep the vessel under our oversight and to keep it space worthy."

"Good. Where will it live?"

"In that huge hangar right over there. Google is interested—to say the least—in working with us."

"Noel, I want you and Amelie to be the back up controlling okis for Wanda. Is that okay? I've already told Wanda."

"Yes, of course. I'll have to learn exactly what that responsibility entails."

I had to get out of there. I was exhausted. My phone chirped a text from Morty. It was a list of the speaking and singing gigs he had lined up for me, all over the world. It must have been the longest text I ever received. Made me even tireder just looking at it.

I somehow forgot to tell everybody that the alien fleet could be showing up any time now.

66. Alone With My Dreams

How long had I been awake? I'd had only a couple of catnaps since leaving Sfofong. I had braved two attacks and barely avoided a third debacle. So by the time I got to go home to my place on the coast, I was dead tired. But I couldn't sleep; I was too jumpy.

I sat on my deck and looked out over the Pacific Ocean. So peaceful. This view had always calmed me down. I opened a bottle of my Sfofong whisky and poured a healthy dollop over the rocks, and nursed it way past sundown. That helped.

I should be happy. So why was I crying? Tears leaked out the corners of my eyes; my nose was all stopped up. A wave of sadness washed over me. I could not still my mind. I was flooded with memories. The awesome, the frightening, the joyful.

How many times had I barely escaped death? I was so lucky to be alive after all this.

How many wonderful aliens had I met? Not just Kateh and Furu-la, but Zzik my laundry spider, little Noe-te, probably a genius engineer. Mr. Gur the chemist, valiantly trying to create something I could eat without retching. All the clan mothers, initially resistant to me as a detested Type 1, but then begging me to be their goddess of music. The Mentor with his two tails.

Two different creatures of the sea had helped me. The baguette-sized worm that found my amulet in the swamp. The whale-sized swimmer that swam with me back to shore and helped me get out of the water. Wow, I swam with the creatures of the Sfofong sea!

Even the Elder, which was so startled by me it fell over on its back. And O-Bloy the sneaky Librarian.

A deep sigh. I had let my friends down. Receiving gifts but not reciprocating. Hurrying away from Sfofong without thanking everybody.

How could my banal advice to the clan mothers have been useful? I shook my head in disbelief.

I didn't talk enough with Kateh and Furu-la, and learn about their world. And now Kateh was no more.

Another sigh. How many blunders had I made? Screaming at the laundry spider. Making faces at the food they created for me. Diving uninvited into the swamp ritual. Being rude to the Contact Mentor. Don't even think about my aborted trip to the Songstone. Oh, and almost losing the amulet during my drunken splash. I was trying to blank that one out.

A wan smile. How many diverse beings had I watched perform at the Songstone, from the wraithlike princess to the horrid Elders?

How many worlds had I set foot on or flown around? Five I think, two of them remarkably like Earth. World 25 was so magnificent! But, omigawd, I had dripped my germ-laden sweat on it, probably contaminating its life forms for millions of years.

And poor Wanda. I had taken her for granted. She was my companion, and she saved my life numerous times, even as she was about to fail, but I still treated her like a piece of equipment.

Finally I berated myself to sleep in my deck chair. I woke up later, shivering cold, as the Moon was setting. "All I really wanted to do was to fly to you, Mr. Moon." I went inside and crashed on my bed, going right back to sleep.

I dreamed. Breadbox was there with Kateh—that is, Kartem-haw—and Furu-la. I was singing a quiet song. A lullaby. Yes, there was a baby, a new clan child, held by Furu-la.

I slept till noon, but I felt so much better.

I wandered aimlessly around my garden and back hillside until Clay called. "Look, everybody's soon going to be caught up in the foundation work, and you'll be appearing on every TV show in the world. Before that happens, let's get everybody together."

"When? Where?"

"Locos Only, of course. Tonight."

67. The Fellowship of Breadbox

That night was our big reunion at Locos Only. I had recovered my energy and joy enough for a night out on the town. I took Clay down there in my new dark red Flashcar convertible. That's right, I couldn't give it up; I told Jonn I had to buy it. It's only money.

When we arrived, Jonn and Noel were already there, sitting in Jonn's silver Flashcar. Probably the only time two of these beauties were parked side by side in the Locos lot, which is more often the habitat of well-dented pickup trucks.

"Good evening, gentlemen," I said as they got out of the car, and introduced Clay and Noel.

For our reunion, Sal the manager let us take over the back area, which was like a covered patio, half inside half outside, but separated from the noise of the music and drunks inside. We pulled two picnic tables together, since I was expecting ten. I entrusted Wanda, in her white canvas shopping bag, to Clay.

Locos serves excellent comfort food but the menu is light on gourmet items. For those who didn't want cheeseburgers or pizza, I asked Sal if we could order out from the high-falutin' restaurant up on the highway. "I'll pay you a 'corkage fee' for plates and stuff that you provide."

"Don't worry about it," he said. "I make my money on the beer, anyway. So keep that flowing and I'll be happy."

"Since you've got Heinously Hoppy on draft, I'm also happy."

"And if you wanted to come in and sing us a song later . . ."

"Sal, sorry, I'm strictly off-duty tonight. Rain check?"

Jim and Meg and Doc came in together, and then my Spaceketeers, Dana and Amelie. I introduced Jonn and Noel to those who hadn't met them. "Come on in and grab a spot," I announced. "I get one end, and Dana, being pregnant, wants the other. Grab a beer. We have two pitchers—pale ale and weak stuff. Plus fizzy water. Anybody want something else? Here come the first two pizzas—one with everything and one with all kinds of vegetables. Other dishes coming soon."

Everybody clambered over the picnic table benches.

"It's time for a toast. Everybody got something in your glass?" I waited for beer and water to be poured.

"Here's to the Star Choice Foundation," I proclaimed loudly. "And to

Jonn and Noel for making it happen. And to Amelie for agreeing to run it."

Clinks up and down the table.

"A toast to my good friend Clay, and his magical recovery. And to Jonn's doctor and nurse."

"Hear, hear! Now can we eat?" asked Clay. He was just about back to his old self.

"Wait, I have a couple more," I said, holding up my hand. "I've got to toast to Breadbox, who became my best friend and singing partner, and helped me recapture the soul of my singing. And Wanda, without whom none of this could have happened. I just happened to bring her along this evening." Clay held her up. "And a toast to all of you. You crazy people, who against your better judgment, stuck with me throughout this adventure."

I looked up and down the table. "I hereby declare this the Fellowship of Breadbox."

"Now can we eat?" asked Dana.

"Wait," commanded Clay, standing up. "Fill up your glasses again. We've got to toast our fearless leader, the original ditzy chick, the only rock and roll singer ever to hijack a rocket ship."

Jonn continued the toast, raising his glass high. "To the woman who consorts with aliens through a magical blue bubble."

Dana added, "To the only woman videoed tripping over a rock on the Moon."

Amelie had her turn. "To the one who flew to the stars by accident all by her lonesome, then made it back, thank goodness."

Noel raised his glass of iced tea. "To the one who treated a very strange looking alien being as a bosom buddy, hopefully setting the tone for the rest of us."

"What else can we say?" said Doc. "Our very own Selena M!"

"Thank you, thank you. I couldn't have done it without you guys. You bring out the best in me—and the worst. Now, we *can* eat! Dig in."

I looked around for Sal. "Salomon, more beer for my friends!"

Just then the outside orders came in. Vegetarian plate for Noel and soup for Dana.

"Okay, let's get back to important things," said Dana. "We are The Fellowship of Breadbox. Who gets to belong?"

"All those who came in contact with her," I said, making it up on the spot. "Clay, Doc, Jim and Meg. Eddy, who's not here yet of course."

"Don't forget Eddy's drummer, Carlos." Doc said.

"And what about that kid, Jack Jr., in the Point Arena parking lot." Clay added.

"And Jed's cat Spooky," Doc said. "They became good friends."

I nodded and said, "Next we'll add in those who never met her but worked with Wanda—Jonn and Noel, the doctor and nurse who worked on Clay."

"What about your friend, Dr. Hu? He never saw Breadbox or Wanda. Where does he fit in?"

"Mascot." I grinned. "He's the wannabe hanger-on."

"Amelie," Jonn said. "I hear you got your H1 visa so you can legally move here and run the foundation."

"Crikey, I'll be trading Toronto Februaries for California earthquakes. But at least I've found places here I can get decent poutine."

"Now that we have this *Star Choice* Foundation," Clay asked, "what's it going to do? How will it work?"

"Our mission is to make the technologies contained within *Star Choice*, and Wanda, available to benefit all the people of Earth," said Amelie.

"Okay, but how?"

"This is what we have to work out. Let's take Clay's cancer cure as an example. Suppose we can make that type of treatment available to many more people. Would that be a benefit?"

"Yes, of course it would." Clay nodded his head vigorously. "But would they all have to fly into space? Or even come to where *Star Choice* is hangared? That would make it a rare and expensive treatment."

Amelie smiled in agreement. "What we want is to adapt such methodologies to widespread use, so they aren't rare and expensive. Nor require travel across the world."

"Who will do that?" Clay asked. "That effort will take research. Research institutes. Scientists and engineers. Where will this happen? You can't cut up *Star Choice* and send pieces off to various laboratories."

Jonn responded. "Researchers will come to *Star Choice*. Moffett Field may become the locus of a research facility. Something like CERN on the border of France and Switzerland, where researchers from all over the world come to conduct carefully monitored experiments on fundamental particles. The results would be widely disseminated."

I said, "We don't even know what all there is to learn. But the few things we've already seen could transform society. Wanda can't even tell us all the secrets she contains."

"No need to rush," Amelie said. "Probably better if we don't."

Jonn did his chortle. "Right now we're trying to figure out how to tie together Star tech and Earth tech so Selena can put on a concert for our world and theirs."

Just then Eddy Backwater pushed his way in. "Hi, folks. I know most of you. Plus two suits," he said, glancing at Jonn and Noel. "Got any food left?"

I stood up and introduced him to Jonn and Noel. "Eddy, we saved a spot for you. And despite our on/off relationship, folks, I have to propose a toast to this man. Without Eddy, we may never have held the jam session, and I have to admit, that was a magical evening."

"Thanks, Sel. Hey, I brought a bottle of tequila. I'm not a beer drinker. You think the guy will mind?"

"You could get him busted and closed down. So keep it hidden."

Amelie pushed on with her prior train of thought. "I'm concerned about the impact of all these wondrous technologies. What if we lengthen lives, reduce mortality from disease, and decrease infant mortality. And all this happens pretty rapidly--say over a few decades. That could lead to a population explosion all over again, leading to overcrowding, resource depletion, and lack of enough jobs."

Jonn pursed his lips. "Women tend to have fewer children when their infants live and they get some education. Then population stabilizes, even declines. Eventually the population ages."

"Amelie, this attitude is why you're going to be the perfect director for the foundation," Noel said.

"Hold that thought," I said. Two servers came in, bringing two more pitchers of beer and a large pizza. "Who ordered the extra anchovies?"

"Let's go back to the impact of these technologies," Amelie said. "Just the impact of knowing about them, even if they don't touch you directly. They haven't really sunk in with people yet."

Noel spoke so softly people had to get quiet to hear him over the uproar in the next room. "I showed the comm stone to my association of scientists in Geneva. I demonstrated how the signal—going and coming back—beat radio signals. We did this with Jonn who was across the world in Mountain View with his comm stone. Impossible, they knew. It blew everybody's mind. People went berserk. There was a dawning realization by all of us that everything we knew about science and physics and energy was about to be overturned, or at least amended. Like what Einstein did to Newton. It will all have to be reinvented."

The table went silent for a minute. Then Amelie said, "The professions of several of us already face this. For example, my field, looking for subtle signs of life on other worlds. And now we're conversing with several races."

"Will we give up innovating in the face of this far superior civilization and its technologies?" Doc asked. "Will we just copy them?"

"Some will," Jonn replied. "Others will be energized. We've already taken some of their technologies and adapted them for our own use. Maybe even improved on them."

"Yes," Noel agreed. "We can start from where they are and innovate forward. We've already done some of this."

"What about the impact on ordinary people?" asked Meg, who had said little.

"We'll see a different impact, and availability, in the developed world and in developing nations," said Amelie. "This may widen existing gaps."

Noel nodded and explained. "This is the difficulty the foundation will face. Playing God with technology. Lots of arguments among different interest groups. Whatever we do will be wrong. Release things too fast, it will be too disruptive. Release things more slowly, we're withholding things people desperately need."

Jonn jumped in. "Like this cell-phone-sized gadget we kluged to connect cable TV with the viewspace. What if we added a cell phone to this? Made it so they could talk to each other? How many millions of these could we sell? We could completely disrupt the cell phone market."

"That's why it would be better to license the tech to a company like Apple, rather than making it ourselves," said Amelie.

"What about Samsung? What about Google? Google already asked us for first dibs on some technologies, since we're sharing a facility with them." Jonn said.

"I love my iPhone and I own Apple stock, so my preference would go to them." I said jokingly.

"That's exactly what we can't do," said Amelie, taking me seriously. "We can't have favorites. We might even have to sell our shares in companies like that."

"What a pain," I exclaimed. "Why don't we just keep it all for ourselves and become filthy trillionaires?

"Oh my," said Noel. "And you think you suffer from stress now!"

"Just kidding," I replied. "I want to be a sing-o-crat, not a plutocrat."

That got a laugh.

"There's more," I said. "*Star Choice* can extend the lives of healthy people like us, not just the sick. When Wanda said this to me, I got really excited. Then scared. Wanda said this is common practice in the Confederation. It could double our lifetimes. That could cause an even larger population explosion—and an aging population."

Jonn nodded. "But it's also device-intensive—to contrast with labor intensive—thus not everybody could do it. And it would be expensive. So only wealthy individuals in developed nations would have access—at least initially. This would lead to a widening gap."

"What about making people smarter?" I said. "Or wiser? We do this on Earth through education, and we've even tried doing it through controlled breeding. Some on the Confederation worlds have tried doing this through genetic manipulation. They've caused some world races big problems trying to do this."

"Aren't there technologies that would be unalloyed benefits?" Dana asked. "For example, reducing global warming."

"I've been studying the Galactic Library," I said. "I noticed two things. One, nobody there uses hydrocarbons as fuel for transportation. Thus, on some worlds, petroleum seeping from the ground is a major problem. Black sticky yucky stuff. Now, suppose we begin adopting the technologies they use for transportation instead of oil and gas. Look at all the people—and nations—this would impact. Sure, it creates many new opportunities, but so many would be left out."

"Maybe we should just fly *Star Choice* into the sun." Doc said.

"Oh yeah? With Wanda aboard?" I retorted, feeling a tinge of fear even though I knew he wasn't serious.

"The issue is not whether, but how fast," Amelie said. "We're already living in a time of very rapid change. Innovations do a lot of good things, but are also quite disruptive. Jobs lost, societies upset, loss of privacy, growth of huge organizations, greater disparity of benefits. That's without any new exotic alien technologies. Star tech could exacerbate these trends."

"I'm sure that will happen," said Jonn. "But if there aren't wealthy early adopters helping get disruptive technologies off the ground, then these innovations never gain enough momentum to spread their benefits widely. One generation of lower-income late adopters gets hurt—or at least left behind—so that a generation of so later everybody can benefit from the new tools."

"Okay, so we should slow the rate of adoption," said Clay. "You could have a diverse council overseeing it, controlling the release and dispersion."

"That group then becomes an instant elite," Noel said. "The members will all be 'first world' people. Educated, worldly, self-confident. The foundation becomes the new world-guiding elite. Instant resentment."

Noel sipped from his iced tea, then said so quietly it was hard to hear him. "Yes, my friends, this is what we're up against."

Everybody went silent. Downer! We'd gone from joyous to thoughtful and philosophical in a heartbeat.

*   *   *

Sal barged in and announced to Jim, "Hey, Sheriff, there's a guy lurking out in the parking lot holding something that could possibly be a weapon."

"Ah shit," Jim said. Everybody looked ready to hit the floor. Jim stood up slowly, and said, "Before you all panic and run for the exits, let me take a look see. Sal, can I go out the back door and sneak around to the front?" For the first time, I noticed the discrete pistol at his back as he unfastened the holster.

Out front, the music stopped, the drunks stopped yelling. It was eerie. A couple of minutes went by. Then Jim came back in the front door, shepherding a very disheveled Dr. Edwin Hu, who was carrying a brown paper shopping bag that held something heavy. More like a brick than a weapon.

"Selena, this man claims to know you," Jim said in his lawman voice.

"Oh yes, I know him. Ed, what are you doing here?" He appeared the same as always, but black socks instead of yellow.

He looked at me sheepishly. "I went to your house to return something and found a note on your door telling people to come down here to Locos Only. So I came."

I stood up and went over to him. "Well, my goodness, I bet we can squeeze you in. Come on."

Ed held back. "Selena, I don't think I would feel comfortable coming in here with all your friends."

"Don't be an idiot. You think they're going to take you out back and beat the crap out of you for all you've put me through? They all know you're my favorite nemesis."

I grabbed his hand and dragged him over to our table.

"Hey, everybody, I want to introduce you all to Dr. Edwin X. Hu, astrophysicist for the United States government. Jim just found him lurking in the parking lot."

"Omigawd, it's Gollum!" yelled Dana.

A few shocked and puzzled looks. Everybody had heard lots about him. I introduced him around the table.

"Ed said he wanted to return something to me, so I invited him to join us. So, what do you have for me, Ed? And what would you like to drink."

Clay squeezed down to make room. "Come on in here, man. What's that you're carrying?" But Ed hung back.

Ed reached into his paper bag and pulled out . . . Wanda! No, it had to be the clone. "I wanted to deliver this in person." It slipped out of his grasp and fell on the table like a chunk of granite. Clunk!

I looked closer. "Oh wow, it *is* the clone of Wanda!" That's what it was—the one that had been stolen from me by the government spooks, then killed—deactivated—by the Device Captain from across the cosmos. The one that had almost killed Wanda with it.

"The world's heaviest paper weight, so we've heard," said Clay.

"Listen, I . . ." Ed took a deep breath and let it out. "I want to apologize. I want to apologize. I have done some crazy things. I can't begin to justify them, even to myself."

Clay stood up and guided Ed onto the bench. "Sit down, Ed. This is a no-apology night. Here, let me pour you a beer."

"Ed, you did what you had to do," said Doc. "You and your guys sure caused all kinds of trouble for Selena, but that's over, right?"

"Yes, it's over," Ed said with a sad shake of his head. "They never want to see me again."

Dana raised her glass. "Welcome to the dark side. We have pizza and beer."

I put my hand on his shoulder. "And a magical space ship."

"And finally, Wanda's long lost brother," Clay added.

Clay had Wanda on the bench beside him. What would happen when she and the clone came together? "Wanda," I spoke directly to her. "The damaged clone you created has just been returned."

"Yes, my controlling oki, I can detect it." Ed looked dumbfounded, hearing a feminine voice issue from Clay's right hip.

"May we put the two of you together?" I asked Wanda.

"Yes, it is inactive. No harm."

When Clay sat Wanda next to the clone, Hu got an indescribable expression on his face. "I knew it! I knew it! I knew it!" he shouted at me. "You always had it."

"Ed, this is the last alien. Wanda the Magic Wand. Wanda, meet Ed." Wanda remained silent. I couldn't blame her.

* * *

"Selena, what's your title in the foundation?" Clay asked.

"I'm the troubadour. I want that on my business card, should I ever get any."

"Probably your best role," said Noel. "Suppose, though, that you become the True Singer of Earth, and sing how our people can move into this brave new world of interstellar connections. Not philosophical songs, but stories of the impacts on individuals and communities and families."

This brought tears to my eyes. Tears of joy. I could see the possibility of doing this. "I feel a song coming on."

Dana jumped in first singing a couple of off-key lines:

> *Everything is peachy keen*
> *It's the best new world we've ever seen.*

That got a laugh. "Let me try one on you that has a different tone." I stood at the end of the table, without Gibb. "Maybe I'll call this Cotton Candy Lover meets the Brave New World."

> *Never had it together, no way*
> *And now, just when I thought at last*
> *I was getting it together to stay*
> *It's falling apart again, slipping fast.*
>
> *It's all falling apart once again*
> *They promised great things and all magic*
> *Gonna change our poor lives around*
> *Gonna bring the good times, not tragic.*
> *Gonna make my weak self go all strong*
>
> *Gotta make my weak life go all strong.*
> *Instead it pulls us asunder*
> *My old man just lost his job*
> *blah blah blah makes me wonder*

"Help me find a good rhyme for 'job.'"

"Sob?" suggested Dana.

"I like it. Let's try this."

We should all be so happy, I said with a sob.

Clay said, "I read this article, 'The Shock of the New.' That would be a good title for this song."

"Come on, this is supposed to be a party," said Dana. "Enough with the gloomy forebodings."

Eddy finally spoke up. "I call it PTSD— *pre*-traumatic stress syndrome—Omigawd, shit might happen!"

That definitely lightened things up.

Clay said, "You've got to be the poet laureate for the coming changes."

"Not a role I want," I said. "But I guess since I brought this on, I've got to step up."

Noel looked at his phone. "In the morning, what time is my pain . . . er, plane?

Jonn was fast with the comeback. "Whenever you want me to inflict it, my friend."

Dana stood up. "I need to get my eight hours of beauty sleep every night. We all should. Unless you're ugly; then you need nine hours."

"There's more pizza left here, guys. Who's going to take this home?"

"I notice the beer's gone, though," said Doc.

"Dibs. I love cold pizza in the morning," said Amelie.

"How much do we owe you?" asked Jim.

"Not a cent. I'm charging it all to the foundation."

"You wish," said Amelie.

So ended our reunion. As they trickled out, it struck me, I really loved these people. Even Ed.

68. I Tasted the Infinite

It felt so good to return to my old familiar haunt. The night was joyous and raucous and relaxing. All my friends there, the warmth, the noise, the smells of pizza and beer. I was so happy-go-lucky with them.

Then I went home. Alone. Late that night I sat on my deck again bundled up gazing out over the Pacific Ocean. A cold wind made me shiver. Fast low clouds hid and then revealed the stars.

I had a quiet realization. "I can never return home. I have been touched by the infinite. I am a conduit to the cosmos and from the cosmos, whether I want to be or not. It is a terrible responsibility, yet also joyous."

I had been at a star system so far away that its sun was not visible with any but the largest telescopes.

A verse emerged from beneath a cloud, and I sang it softly.

> *I am changed.*
> *I have tasted the Infinite. And the Infinite has tasted me.*
> *I cannot avoid going.*
> *I must touch it, and be touched by it, don't you see.*
> *We have shared sight and sound.*
> *We have shared song and joy,*
> *Shared terror and death. And now I fly free.*
> *I must now share touch and taste.*
> *The reek and pain of embrace.*
> *I must embrace the chaos. I must go.*
> *I have tasted the Infinite.*
> *And it has tasted me.*

That's it, isn't it? After crossing the cosmos, I can never go home completely. I can feel the tug. I'm like an immigrant. I didn't fit in my new world, yet I no longer feel completely at home where I came from.

*   *   *

At the crack of dawn on my dining room table I placed the dead clone next to Wanda, and asked her, "Wanda, what can we do with this? Can you bring it back to life? Can you repair it so it is functional in any way?"

"Allow me to investigate," she replied. A long silence followed. It seemed like nothing was happening. Then Wanda said, "If I were a live being like you, my controlling oki, I would feel anger or sadness at what the Device Master did to this precision device that I created."

I noted Wanda's "emotional" reaction. The experts here say AI robots don't have emotions, yet there she was, getting angry. She has learned all her bad habits from me.

It made me angry also, just hearing her say this. I wanted to cry. I could imagine how I would feel if somebody wantonly ripped one of my songs apart. Well, it has happened—more than once.

She was again silent for a long time. "I am 80% certain that I can rebuild this device to functionality, although not all functions."

"What might we be able to do with it?" I asked.

"Repairing this device will be similar to repairing the crashed space vessel that became *Star Choice*. I must guide it to rebuild along pathways already defined. It will be easier because all needed materials are already contained within it."

"Will you be concerned that you will once again have trouble telling it apart from you?"

"By reviewing my prior process of creating it, I conclude that I need not duplicate all my internal functions, but only selected ones."

"Wanda, the clone needs a name."

"Perhaps it is better not to name it. That may personalize it. You may invest too much energy in a piece that is dead." How ironic that my device, whom I had named, would say this about another device.

"I hear you. Still, 'the dead clone' is not adequate."

"I propose you name it Device."

I giggled. "That is really clever. It's a name, but not a personal name. Perfect!" This was the first time Wanda had named anything—a behavior we'd been told was a peculiarity of Earth okis.

"Speaking of which, could Device help you build what you need for my concert?"

"Yes, as well as I could. Perhaps better. I'll accentuate the elements needed for that."

*   *   *

Ants in my pants! That's what my Gran would have said about me. I was pacing all through my house and outside in the garden. I hiked up to the top of the hill and back, then down across the highway to the bluff overlooking the beach. Finally I said, "Yes, do it!" I walked back up the hill far enough to get decent cellphone reception, then called Jonn.

"Jonn, I have this crazy idea rolling around inside my noggin. What if my magical robot friend, Wanda, could build a duplicate propulsion system and other key pieces? If she gave you instructions and specs, could you build the body and all the other interior pieces for another *Star Choice*?"

Silence for a few beats, then, "Lady, we think alike. I've been taking mental inventory of my facilities to see if I could do just that.

"However, it didn't escape my notice that you and your Spaceketeers—along with the help of your magical robot—managed to upgrade one space craft and build another one remotely on the Moon, then put all the pieces together on a remote South Pacific island. And then flew into space and across the galaxy.

"Now if you can do that from your world headquarters in Bodega Bay, I must ask, why do you need all my high tech manufacturing facilities in Texas and Singapore?"

"That's *galactic* headquarters in Bodega Bay, sir."

"I stand corrected. But if it would help you to speed up or scale up, then I'm your man. How many spaceships would you like?"

"If what my agent Morty tells me is true about all the appearances and concerts he's lining up for me, I'll be bringing in more money than I can shake a stick at. I might as well squander it on a fleet of spaceships."

"The fares paid by people eager to fly into space should recoup the costs and more. And it just might be that our Yankee ingenuity could improve on the designs of these extraterrestrials."

"Yes, sir, that is what I wanted to hear. But flights only into our solar system, right? Are we agreed on that?"

"Indeed. Let's keep the star travel for a later time."

I was silent for a minute before saying what was on my mind. "There is nothing preventing humans from exploring worlds around other stars except me—us—keeping the capability secret." I fingered the amulet on its chain. "If we share what we can do, there could soon be a large resort on World 25—right where I was collecting samples."

"Yes, that's why we want to keep the amulet under wraps. Unless, of course, you have more ambitious travel plans."

I said nothing to that. "And, sir, in your spare time, you're also working with your engineers and the Mentor to build an enhanced concert-quality view space for our Two Worlds Concert?"

"Right you are. It's a good thing I don't have a real job building cars and spaceships any more. As you probably know, I've turned over my daily responsibilities in Flashcar and YouSpace to my top execs, and they're doing just fine. My new job title is Director of Alien Technology Development for the *Star Choice* Foundation. My salary is one dollar per year, and I intend to earn every cent of it.

"First, let's make this concert happen."

69. Two Worlds Concert

Three months later. I stepped into the evanescent blue bubble—my new concert quality view space. My ordinary world disappeared, and I was enveloped in the sounds of two worlds, the murmur of two throngs. On the left side of the bubble, the audience filled Levi's Stadium on Earth to overflowing, and spoke with an anticipatory rumble. On the other side, I saw a similar thing on Everbright, the central world of the Galactic Confederation, where beings of every imaginable size and shape and voice filled a huge amphitheater. It was as if I was there in both places at once, on a platform between them, with nothing but my rocking chair and guitar.

The sounds of both crowds washed over me. I could see both of them, and I knew they could see me. I wasn't sure if those on one side could see or hear the other.

I was scared shitless. I couldn't breathe. I stepped back out.

In reality (What is reality, anyway, in a situation like this?) I was in my own familiar living room—my power spot—overlooking the Pacific Ocean. Right now, the blinds were pulled shut and the room was crammed full of the most amazing technology ever assembled on Earth. Wanda and Device were ensconced on a small stand across the room. Clay flashed a smile as he fiddled with the sound levels. Jonn nervously watched the kluged technologies of Earth and the Confederation to see if they would actually function together.

He raised his eyebrow and asked me, "Ready?"

I gave him thumbs up and a weak smile, and stepped back inside the translucent blue bubble. My living room melted away, opening instantly to include both stadium and amphitheatre, with me perched high between them. I felt vertigo and stark terror. "Yoga breath," I whispered to myself, hoping that wasn't picked up and transmitted across the cosmos. At least this was one time I didn't have to worry about getting distracted by people in the front row.

I stood before them. "Hello and thank you," I said in both English and Fedi, looking first to the left and then the right. "This song is for my best friend, Nala, true singer, and citizen of Sfofong and the Galactic Confederation of Oxygen Breathing Worlds." I picked up Gibb, sat in my rocking chair, and whispered, "This one's for you, my best friend." I began humming the "Together Stars People" anthem to two worlds, thousands of lightyears apart.

Both crowds roared. Music is one.

70. Epilogue, Kind Of. Is This the End?

What is the end of my story? Since what I'm relating is autobiographical (and as true as I can make it), and I'm still kicking, then the story isn't over yet. But I want to pull it to a close for now. So I'm fantasizing about how my story might end in the future.

I can envision three endings. Which do you like best?

First ending. I sat at my huge mahogany desk in my corner office atop the Transamerica Pyramid in San Francisco. This was the world headquarters of the *Star Choice* Foundation. Spectacular view of the city and the bay, but I scarcely had time to appreciate it. I was shouting instructions to my cadre of well-dressed young people all bustling about. "Get this next space bus booked so it can take off for Mars." "Find manufacturers in India and Nigeria to whom we can license this technology from Wanda." "Book my flight to New York for my address to the United Nations." A melody was echoing in my head, but I didn't even have time to stop and scratch it down . . .

Whoa, enough of that! I sure don't want to end up that way. Let's try another one:

Second ending. *Star Choice II*, with Wanda at the controls, glides into the spaceport of Everbright City, the capital city of the Galactic Confederation. I am very nervous. I've done big concerts before, and even festivals, but this . . .

I have brought along musicians to play the range of Earth's most moving music. An orchestra, a chamber quartet. An *a capella* choir. Gospel singers.

And by special arrangement, I have the Beatles, and Jimi Hendrix, and for creative inspiration, my namesake, Berthe Morisot, and . . .

Ah, yes, a much better ending. Here's another:

Third ending. Many years in the future. A little old white-haired lady sits rocking in her chair on her deck overlooking the ocean. It is me. I have tears in my eyes—tears of happiness. I am humming softly as the sun dips into the ocean beyond a distant fog bank. I recognize the song—"Together Stars People." There is the green flash in the sunset. I hear a boom, like distant thunder. Breadbox is beckoning to me from the cloudbank . . .

Phew!

*   *   *

Those last two are great for the distant future, but let's get back to what's actually going on. During a break from all the appearances Morty had arranged, I was at the Star Choice Foundation at NASA Ames Research Center in Mountain View CA. I wandered around the huge hangar where *Star Choice* was the guest of honor. I walked around her, gawking with admiration. As amazing as it sounds, this was the first time I'd had the opportunity to look her over closely since she had been rebuilt on Sfofong. She was a beautiful charcoal grey, matte yet glowing like a healthy living being. I admired the recreated escape module on the stern.

The starboard port was open—the same one I had clambered into back in the Mojave Desert by using a wooden stepladder leaning against the fuselage. Now, *Star Choice 's* steps invited me to climb aboard. I looked in, then stepped through the port. It looked so small inside! I couldn't believe I had spent months cooped up in there by myself.

Numerous instruments, tethered by cables leading to the outside, showed where various scientists and engineers were studying the unearthly technologies she contained. My friend and companion Wanda, ensconced in her receptacle, was at the center of all this research.

I felt bad for her. I had abandoned her to all these serious people while I flitted around the world singing. Was she having any enjoyment?

"How's it going, Wanda?"

"Hello, my controlling oki. I am helping Noel explore areas of knowledge in the Galactic Library about the structure of the galaxy. I am helping Amelie and the scientists explore the technologies within *Star Choice*, including the maker machine.

"I am helping Dana learn about oki races on other worlds. I am helping Jonn explore propulsion, grav, and weapons. I am helping Herb explore technologies for countering disease states in humans."

"That sounds exciting."

"It is sharing information. I have had no interesting challenges since your two worlds concert."

"Are you bored?"

Silence. "Noel and Amelie are also my controlling okis now, so I gladly do as they request."

"Mmm. You didn't answer my question. Are you bored?"

More silence. "I am not being used to my full capacity."

"Me neither. I love my music, but . . ."

My space ship—my magical beast—called out to me. My hand went to my throat to touch the amulet. I had worn the metallic crystal containing the jump codes to major worlds of the galaxy on a chain around my neck ever since Breadbox had died. It looks like nothing special—maybe some pre-Columbian trinket. Nobody guessed that it was one of the most valuable stones in the galaxy.

I lowered myself into the captain's seat.

I lifted the amulet's chain over my head. I held the crystal near the nav console, then eased it into the slot. Suddenly the display sprang to life, with a tantalizing flash of three-dimensional symbols moving across the view space, with music like an electronic version of Breadbox.

I could just take off. I spoke to the console. "Wanda, are we ready for a star jump?"

Her voice reverberated from the view space in front of me. "Ready whenever you are, my controlling oki. What star system would you like to travel to?"

Oh my, how tantalizing! "That is good to know. But not just yet. It's tempting. But I cannot. It wouldn't be right to remove *Star Choice* just now while all these studies are being conducted. I promised."

I asked the question that was uppermost on my mind. "Wanda, can we build a duplicate of *Star Choice*?"

"In principle, yes. It would take a long time. The major tools are within *Star Choice*. Must have access to large quantities of specific materials. Takes a lot of energy over an extended period of time. While creating it, perhaps it is better to remain hidden, out of sight of others."

I walked over to the port and looked around the vast hangar—plenty large for a 747. I imagined a duplicate *Star Choice* growing right next to us. I'd have to ask Jonn how to make this work.

"You see," I said, "I have been talking with Jonn Buck about building another vessel—*Star Choice II*—in his lab. He's already stockpiling needed materials. If you were there, you could guide its construction.

"But we'd have to make sure that Device could fulfill your role here." I stared into the view space. "Wanda, could you build everything into Device that the people here need to learn about? Then I could switch you two, placing Device into your receptacle, and take you with me.

"My controlling oki, I have already been carefully and thoroughly doing that with Device. Even giving it a better quality voice for interacting. I will soon be superfluous here. Then you can take me."

"To build a duplicate *Star Choice*, are there any specific or unusual things you would need?" I asked.

"Three items are essential. First, should you wish to jump to a different star system, you must take me with you. And the amulet."

"But of course."

"Then, there is a unit within *Star Choice* that is needed to make star jumps. This I cannot duplicate."

"Can I remove it?"

"Yes, it is small and easily removable."

A smile spread across my face. "If I remove it, will they notice that it is missing?"

"It is not needed for space travel within a system where star jumps are not used."

I nodded. "But they could see the opening; it would be obvious to them that something was removed."

302

"It would be possible to create a realistic yet non-functional unit to fill that space."

"Could you do that?" I asked.

"Yes, if you so request."

"Wanda, please create such a unit to fill that space."

My cylindrical sidekick, eagerly complicit in my stellar exploration fantasies, responded, "Anticipating the request from my controlling oki, I have already begun."

"Hee hee!"

71. Proposal

I was watching the Songstone in the view space in my living room when Clay came over. The door was open, so he just said "knock knock" and walked on in. I noticed right away he was carrying a particularly nice bottle of Malbec, already opened so it could breathe.

He glanced into the view space. "Whatcha watchin'? More of these alien singers? You really get into that, don't you? I'll bet you're sorry you didn't get to complete that trip, despite the hazards."

"Yeah, I can't deny it."

"There's a part of you that's still living in the stars."

"Oh, Clay, you are so right." I told him about my feelings of being touched by the infinite. I related my discussion with Wanda, and with Jonn about building a duplicate spaceship.

"But a part of you is rooted here on Earth, also," he said. "You're connected to your friends, and to all those who love your music. And like you said, your role is troubadour for the coming age of alien contact. So if you fly off, you'll want to fly home again."

I nodded and smiled. "Most definitely. And it'll be much easier if people aren't shooting at me."

He poured two glasses, handed me one, and held his up for a toast. I clinked with him.

"When you're ready to fly to the Songstone to sing, you'll need a sound engineer. Can I go with you?"

I looked at him sharply. He'd never shown any desire to fly into space.

"Selena, my dear. Star Lady. Will you marry me?"

Extras for My Readers

Characters and Names in Space Girl Yearning

Selena M. The protagonist who is narrating the story. She's a singer/songwriter who was growing bored with her music and thought she might be going over the hill. Her real name is Berthe Morisot Monahan. "That's Bear-tuh, not Birth-a," she insists. Her namesake is the French painter Berthe Morisot.

Breadbox is the nickname of the alien that survived a spaceship crash behind Selena's house. They learn to communicate by singing. Her real name is Bvar-nala-nga. Nala for short.

Clay, Doc, Jim and **Meg Osborne**. Neighbors and friends of Selena. Jim is the local sheriff; his wife Meg is kind of square; Doc is a veterinarian and belongs to a survivalist organization. Clay is a high school teacher and has a crush on Selena.

Wanda is a "personal multi-function device"—a robotic AI controller that Breadbox bequeathed to Selena. It is a stubby metallic cylinder about 1 foot/30cm long. Wanda controls the spaceship and translates languages, but has also developed a personality at the urging of Selena, just to be a companion. Selena said it looked like a magic wand, and called it Wanda the Wand. She calls it a "she" because Wanda is a girl's name.

Star Choice. Name that Selena gives to the crashed spaceship after it is again space worthy and outfitted for humans.

Morty. The musician's agent of Selena. Excitable New Yorker, always urging Selena to take music gigs.

Eddy Backwater. Country singer who is raunchy, ill mannered, and sneaky, and has a love/hate relationship with Selena.

Ed/ Dr. Hu. Edwin X. Hu, PhD, is an astrophysicist employed by the government to retrieve the spaceship from Selena after she hijacks it. "Why they brought me in to negotiate with a woman I'll never know."

Dana. Teaching assistant of Professor Bunker. He disbelieves Selena's story, but Dana wants it to be true. She urged Selena to fly it to the Moon.

Amelie Martel-Petrova. French-Canadian astronaut. Was on ISS—the International Space Station.

Three Spaceketeers. Selena, Dana, and Amelie teamed up to upgrade *Star Choice* and fly to the Moon together.

Jonn Buck. CEO of FlashCar and YouSpace, who has gradually been sucked into this project.

Noel St.John Reisen. Well-known astronomer and astrophysicist, head of National Observatory in Washington D.C.

Herb Kleinschnitt. Oncologist at Stanford Health Center. **Mary O'Malley** is his head nurse.

Rogers, Buck. Engineer and orbital scientist that works with Jonn Buck. Has covert connections to space programs of other nations.

Mike McCreary. Astronomer at observatory atop Mauna Kea on Hawaii.

The Agency. The secretive Agency for Technology Assessment, responsible for strategic technologies, keeping tabs on technologies developed by the US and others, including our allies.

General Mason Dickson, Colonel Bird, Major Payne, Captain Crabbe. Military officers assigned to the Agency

Kateh. Clan mother of Breadbox on Sfofong with whom Selena communicates via the view space. Later became **Kar-tem-haw**.

Sfofong. Name of Breadbox's home world. Her people are the **Fofonoloy**. Her clan is the Hawfofonoloy.

Alala and **Novan**. The two crew members of Breadbox who died in the crash.

Galactic Librarian. O-Bloy. Being (live or robotic?) that Selena communicates with in the view space. Asks nosy questions.

Furu-la. Fofonoloy female, space vessel engineer.

Noé-te. Assistant to Furu-la. Younger female.

Zzik. Type 4 oki on Sfofong. Looks like a furry spider the size of an orangutan. Serves as housekeeper.

Mr.Gur. Chemist on Sfofong. Creates food and alcoholic beverages for Selena.

Contact Mentor. Advocate for new oki races contacting the Confederation.

Galactic Confederation of the Oxygen-Breathing Races. A loose grouping of space faring races centered closer to the center of the Milky Way. Our Solar System lies far outside it. Held together by the star jump network that allows them to travel and communicate instantaneously between distant star systems.

Oki. A term for any intelligent, technology-using being or race. From Fedi, the language of the Confederation. There's a lot of argument about just who is considered to be oki, but that's a whole different story.

View space. A 3D bubble a yard across, similar to a hologram, that is the terminal for instantaneous communication. Also provides access to views outside the spaceship, since it has no windows or ports.

The amulet. A small metallic crystal that contains the codes to all the jump sites. Selena wears it on a chain around her neck like a piece of jewelry. It was given to her by Breadbox.

Comm stones. Alien technology "walkie talkies" used to communicate instantaneously across space. Thus they cannot be tapped into by others using the radio spectrum. About the size of a river pebble, and worn on a thong or chain around the neck. Activated by humming and saying a code name of the person you are calling.

Comm stone nicknames. Used to summon the person you wish to speak with. Selena is Agate. Clay is Teach. Doc is Doc. Sheriff Jim is Fuzz. Amelie is Canuck. Dana is Danger. Jonn is Flash. Noel is Starman.

Jump sites are small satellites that float in space at a planet's Lagrange point, and are used by spaceships to jump instantaneously from one star system to another. They were placed millions of years ago by a long-gone civilization.

Maker machine. Device on *Star Choice* that can create or repair anything for which it has a pattern and the needed raw materials.

World 25. First planet Selena lands on. Like a primitive Earth.

Selena-Bane. Uninviting planet where bad things happen as Selena circles it.

Songstone. Ancient monument on Everbright where all the oki races go to sing their stories.

Everbright. Central world of the Galactic Confederation.

Song Lyrics

Ones marked by an asterisk have been produced and are on my website.

Forever to Infinity*

I am unmoored
I am adrift on the vastness of space
Like a boat, lines cast free from the shore
slowly drifting out to sea,
no rudder, no compass, no map
across the vasty void
Forever to infinity

The farther I drift 'cross the vasty void
the harder it will be for me
to find my way back from the endless sea
to safe harbor, to home, to thee
I may discover new worlds out there
Or I might just drift, across the vast nowhere
Forever to infinity.

I am excited, ah th' adventure,
the dreams of magnificence in the sky.
I am terrified, for I shall surely die.
I am lonely, for home and love left far behind.
Across the vasty void I fly
Going where? Nowhere at all. No reason why.
Forever to infinity.

The Bonds of True Oki

May you never forget.
The bonds of true oki
must span the broad sky
linking kindred spirits
in the oneness of heart.
Your most valuable gift.

This is the message
You must convey
You must sing it together
You must sing it today.
You must sing it together
You must sing it each day.
Who but you can sing this?

308

None but you can sing this.
The power of your souls shining through.
From the fog to the sun shining through.
The song of Clan Haw shining through.
The voice of Clan Haw singing true.

Who Put the Stress in Songstress?

Yes oh yes oh yes
I'm nothing but a songstress
But who put the stress in songstress?
Oh baby don't you see, it was me?

Please don't make another mess
Causing all your friends distress
By taking things to excess
Oh baby don't you see, that's just me.

I Have Tasted the Infinite

I am changed.
I have tasted the Infinite. And the Infinite has tasted me.
I cannot avoid going.
I must touch it, and be touched by it, don't you see.
We have shared sight and sound.
We have shared song and joy,
Shared terror and death. And now I fly free.
Now I must share touch and taste.
Share the reek and pain of embrace.
I must embrace the chaos. I must go.
I have tasted the Infinite.
And it has tasted me.

The Shock of the New

Never had it together, no way
And now, just when I thought at last
I was getting it together to stay
It's falling apart again, slipping fast.

It's all falling apart once again
They promised great things and all magic
Gonna change our poor lives around
Gonna bring the good times, not tragic.
Gonna make my weak self go all strong
S'posed to make my weak life go all strong

Instead it pulls us all asunder.
My old man just lost his job.
Their glad promises just make me wonder
We'll all be so happy, I said with a sob.

My Best Friend Is Gone

A dog is a man's best friend.
My best friend is an alien.

She dropped in on my house one day
I truly thought she was there to stay.
Funny looking, could not talk
She hooted and chimed and honked and squawked.
How could we two with nothing in common
Develop such a bond?

Two years ago my best friend died
I miss her so. I wept, I cried.
As we sang together in my home,
She passed so quickly. I was alone.
How could somebody I loved so much
In a moment just be gone?

It's two years now to the very day
So much has happened, so much
I talk with her almost every day.
She is my crutch, my crutch.
How can a being who's only a ghost
Be with me on and on?

She died on my world, far from home.
I'm trapped on her world, far from home.
Will I ever be able to return?
She never even wanted to return.
How will I ever get back to Earth,
Not die here all alone?

I honor her in my memory
No matter whatever happens to me.
We helped each other recapture our song,
To the tribe of True Singers we both belong.
She bequeathed to me this magical ship
I've used to take a cosmic trip.

How could we two with nothing in common
Develop such a bond?

O My Princess

...and then . . . oh what shall befall us now?
My princess, my beloved princess.
She took the rusted iron bar
From the cage that had imprisoned her
Held hostage against the return of the Three Voyagers.
She sharpened it to jagged death
Using the terrible steaming acid.
When the meganaut called Burnehkadur came to her
He in his disgusting magnificence
To take her as his mate
To bear his accursed spawn.
She, my princess,
She thrust the jagged rusty iron bar deep into his core.
She watched, retching, but with a slight smile
As he staggered back and fell
Gurgling out his life.
She pulled free the bar. Once more
She thrust it into his eye
Deep into his mind and twisted it.
He was no more.
But what then for her?
Oh my princess. She sat hunched on the cold stone
And awaited her fate.
They came over the wall for her,
And through the ponderous gates.
Swords drawn . . .

Goddess of Music
(Sung back and forth by the clan mothers and Selena)

We humbly ask, oh yes we pray
May the goddess of music respond this day?
yetta yetta yetta deh deh deh deh oh please respond.

We ask oh yes we want to know
May the goddess of the music hear our plea
Let us swim yes swim freely in the sea
With our friends and fellow swimmers of the sea
Nibble tasty morsels deep within the sea

wan dan yanna dan, umm yes we do belong to the sea.
May the goddess of the music make it so, make it so

The goddess speaks no more
The goddess hears no more
Is she even still alive?
Has she left us high and dry, sailed from shore?
Ah so what are we to do
We have none left here to pray to.
mok daka huu dah what to do?

May the long bare-skinned oki make us free
with her flaming yellow hair for all to see
yot dot a doo dat make it so

Let us taste, going to taste
going to taste the real food
of the sea
going to smell, going to feel,
going to feel the world whole rude
May the long and lanky oki hear our plea

If I could grant your wish, I would surely grant your wish
I would give you what you ask, what you want.
It isn't mine to give. But it's always yours to take.
You can always take it for yourselves today.
Would you take back all your world if you could?
You must take back all your world, yes you should.
It is yours to grab your world, make it good.

May the goddess of the music make it so.

I cannot be your goddess, cannot be
I live light lives far away, far away
But your goddess lives there with you,
Find your goddess there within you
She's already there within you
You must know.

Summon her now, right now
Make her come out, come and make it true.
Your music and your song can make it so.
Call her now, it's up to you
Let your inner goddess make it proudly so.

Mike Van Horn

I started writing science fiction thirty years ago, but life got in the way. Lots of non-fiction how-to books aimed at small business owners. Two books published plus over a dozen self-published, all built around our consulting business, The Business Group.

Then I saw that if I was ever going to get my stories done in this lifetime, I'd better get going! Since then I have concentrated on writing science fiction. "Aliens Crashed in My Back Yard" started out as a short story, but metastasized into a trilogy.

My wife BJ is also writing a story about a 19th century English barrister who tangles with the ghost of a beautiful French woman who was wronged. And our daughter Rebecca is a writer also. An entire whole family of crazy writers!

My non-fiction books include:
– *Understanding Expert Systems* (1985)
– *Pacific Rim Trade* (1989)
– *How to Grow Your Business without Driving Yourself Crazy* (2002)

I have an MBA from University of California, Los Angeles (UCLA). I still do consulting work, but my sci fi storytelling is a lot more fun.
www.galaxytalltales.com

Mike on his home turf in Marin County

Want to Read More?

You've just finished Book 3 of a trilogy. Here are the other two:

Book 1. *Aliens Crashed in My Back Yard*
    When an alien spaceship crashes on the hillside behind your house, would you do the right thing and summon the authorities? Not Selena. She decides to nurse the surviving alien back to health and help it get back home.
    She can't talk with it, so they end up singing to each other. They help each other rekindle their passion for singing. What if the alien doesn't even want to return home? But the government wants that spaceship and comes to take it. Then the struggle begins.

Book 2. *My Spaceship Calls Out to Me*
    Aliens on distant worlds urge Selena to come sing on their worlds because she is a rare True Singer. She wants to be true to her music on Earth, but she says, "I have a spaceship—I might as well use it." The government says she hijacked it from them, and they're chasing it to the Moon to recover it.
    How could she fly in it? It was outfitted for aliens that look nothing like humans. Selena, an astronaut, and an exo-biology student team up as the Three Spaceketeers to make it work for them.

Alien Invasion: There Goes the Neighborhood
    Here's the next book—not quite a sequel, but following some of the same characters and action.
    What if the aliens coming here are not hostile, but friendly? They want to come to Earth as tourists, traders, researchers. Many Earth people get rich selling things to them. Even so, they cause a lot of disruption. Then the alien Security Authority wants more from Earth, and they're willing to use force to get it.

Bleeding Edge
    A new upcoming series
    Some aliens want to entice Earth people to a marvelous world across the galaxy. Others trick them into becoming hunt fodder on one of the secret Hunting Worlds. Earthers fight for their lives against the Enslavers on Hunting World 12 .

Check these out at galaxytalltales.com
. . . plus short stories, like *How I Ended Up with Two Wives* and *Return of the Ancient Ghosts*.